If I Never

Gary William Murning

Legend Press
Independent Book Publisher

Legend Press Ltd, 3rd Floor, Unicorn House,
221-222 Shoreditch High Street, London E1 6PJ
info@legend-paperbooks.co.uk
www.legendpress.co.uk

British Library Cataloguing in Publication Data available.

ISBN 978-1-9065581-4-7

Set in Times
Printed by JF Print Ltd., Sparkford.

Cover designed by Gudrun Jobst
www.yotedesign.com
Front cover image supplied by Getty Images

Legend Press

Independent Book Publisher

For Bill and Sandra, my parents, who taught me – among many things – the value of hard work and perseverance. With love.

Acknowledgements

Between the time when the first words are written and the day when the finished novel is finally published, it is touched by many people – people without whom it might never have reached publication. It's impossible to thank all of them, but I would, at least, like to try to thank a few.

Two friends and fellow writers who I have known for many years. Jane Adams and Jean Currie. For your friendship, guidance and support – thank you.

Also, my journey as a writer has brought me into contact with many wonderful people all over the world (thanks to the internet.) I would therefore like to thank all my blogging friends, my friends on Facebook and, especially, my friends on Twitter who over recent months have been supportive, enthusiastic and extremely generous with their time and suggestions. Thank you, each and every one.

I'd like to also thank a few people who managed to restore my faith in the publishing industry. Emma Howard (formerly of Legend Press), who saw the potential in the first novel I sent her. Tom Chalmers, publisher extraordinaire and really nice guy. It's fair to say that had you both not succeeded in understanding what I was trying to achieve with my writing, I may well have finally hung up my writing hat and found something more 'sensible' to do. To you both – and to the rest of the Legend team – thank you. It is an opportunity I truly appreciate. Here's the future.

Finally, it would never do for me to overlook the one person without whom this whole process would be pointless. You. The reader. Thank you.

Gary William Murning
21st of June 2009
www.garymurning.com

Chapter One

It had never been a joke that I'd found especially amusing, and George Ruiz was more than well aware of this. Squinting at me through the oddly static cigarette smoke, he waited for my response—seemingly counting off the seconds it took for me to raise the coffee cup to my lips and take a sip. When one was not forthcoming, however, he merely nodded thoughtfully, taking it all in his stride, and leant over the table, winking playfully.

"I said," he said. "'My dog's got no nose.'"

"I heard you the first time."

"And that's it? You're not going to play the game?"

We'd been sitting in his mother's grotty kitchen for the past hour, talking about everything from the state of local politics to the way the rain ran through the dirt on the kitchen window. It had been riveting stuff, and had I had anywhere else to go on such a grey, shitty winter's afternoon, I would have. As it was, I'd decided that this was at least better than sitting in my flat listening to Ray LaMontagne and picking my toenails. Even with the dog joke.

I looked about the kitchen at the pots piled up in the sink, the greasy newspapers stacked by the kitchen door and the three in-need-of-emptying litter trays at the side of the sink—and thought that maybe there were advantages to my condition after all. I was sure that had I shared George's olfactory ability, I'd have been well on my way to lung cancer, too.

"So you're just going to keep right on ignoring me?" he said.

"I'm having a bad day."

He sniffed with disgust and lit a fresh cigarette off the butt of the last. "You're always having a bad day. Your life is one long run of bad days, mate. If you want my opinion—"

I didn't, but that had never stopped him before.

"—what you really need to do is get a fucking grip. Not being offensive, you understand, just telling it like it is."

One of his mother's cats—Gemini, I think she called it, though for the life of me I didn't know why—had oozed around the door from the hallway. George got to his feet, sticking the cigarette in the corner of his mouth and picking up the moggy by the scruff of the neck. Opening the back door, he threw it out into the rain and returned to his chair at the table.

"Bloody things get right on my nipple ends," he explained. "If it was up to me, I'd drown the bloody lot of them. Or just hit 'em with a good, hefty brick."

"You could always set your dog on them."

"I haven't got..."

George wasn't the nicest man on the planet, which was understandable, really, since he had never been the nicest boy on the planet, either. He was a bully and a lout—the kind of person I'd always striven to avoid, even as, all those years ago in the school playground, I'd found myself perversely attracted to the prospect of being his friend. He was more than happy to ridicule another's failings, publicly mocking the dragging-footed gait of cripples and cruelly toasting port-wine stain birthmarks with a nice glass of the house red. But when the joke was on him, when the tables were turned and he found himself caught out, George was unexpectedly generous. His smile would light up the room with its nicotine glow and he would positively chortle at the absurdity of it all. It didn't do to push it, however—as I'd learnt on more than one occasion.

"Bastard," he chuckled. "Nice one, Price. You got me for a second, there." He slapped me on the upper arm; a little over one year and one adventure later, it's still tingling. "Don't let it happen again."

As the afternoon dragged on, George became increasingly morose. We sat in that kitchen, the light fading completely, the windows misting up (*on the outside*, George insisted, the room was that cold), and what little conversation there'd been had totally dried up. I wanted to leave, but all I had waiting for me were four channels on a cracked fourteen-inch television and two working bars on a five-bar gas fire. That and five tins of beans and one bottle of Stella. Not the most promising of Saturday nights, then.

"I've been invited to a party," George told me, without looking up from the tabletop. He said 'party' as though it were fatal blood disorder. I could understand that.

George shrugged and sat up a little straighter in his chair. His lank, greasy hair fell across his face and, perhaps for the first time, I noticed he was greying at the temples. It wasn't the startling shade of grey that would make him look distinguished in middle age, either. Rather, it looked as though he'd rubbed cigarette ash into his scalp and I knew it could only ever contribute to his unhealthy air of disassociation.

"A family gathering," he told me, begrudgingly. "Stale sandwiches and dentures. You know."

I nodded. I'd been to a few of those in my time. Yet another bond to tie dear, despicable George and I together.

"I take it you're not going, then?"

"I have to." He smiled. Or sneered. "Call it familial obligation."

"There might be some money in it for you, you mean."

"Pots of the fucking stuff." His eyes were sparkling with malevolent glee—the prospect of such unrivalled riches almost more than his little heart could bear. He told me of his ailing Aunt Martha, a spinster of this parish and drowning in financial success. As he told it, her investments were famous in family lore. She saw opportunity where others saw 'inevitable' financial ruin, and had never been afraid to pounce—accumulating the kind of wealth no one in their family had ever dreamed of.

"And me," George Ruiz said, winking at me, "I've always been her favourite, Price. She thinks the sun shines out of my shit-hole."

"Which it does."

"Naturally."

A sound came from upstairs. A dull thud that no doubt meant his mother was finally getting up. We both looked at the ceiling, George still puffing on his ciggy as if his life depended on it.

"She doesn't want me to go," he told me. "Thinks I'm spoiling her chances—which, I have to admit, I am." He looked at me and shrugged, a sadness behind his eyes that I didn't think I'd seen before... or, at the very least, one that I had seen and somehow managed to block out. "It's all academic, anyway," he continued. "I'm probably not going to go."

This was a fairly typical tactic of George's; as he saw it, his self-contradictory statements kept the enemy guessing. And in his confused little world, everyone was the enemy. Even me, it would seem.

"And miss out on a sausage on a stick and the promise of untold riches? Are you a fool, George Ruiz?"

He smirked and defiantly stubbed out his cigarette on the tabletop, a few inches away from the overflowing ashtray. "Maybe I am. Wouldn't put up with the likes of you if I wasn't, now, would I?"

The sound of movement upstairs was growing louder and more urgent. I heard a grunt of frustration and a barely muffled curse, before something fell to the floor with a muted thud. George said, "She always drops it when she's getting it down off the top of the wardrobe. Especially if she's been on the piss the night before. I've told her, keep it by the bed, where it's handy, but..." Again he shrugged. "You know what they're like. Can't tell them a bloody thing."

I shook my head and smiled sympathetically—wondering just how bad it was for him, living at home with Carla Ruiz, her prosthetic limb and all her cats. Whenever I met her, she was always polite, if a little crapulent, with the air of one who felt as though she should have been born into more elegant times. Her cigarettes were always smoked through an ivory holder and she often enunciated with a mathematical precision that was never quite convincing. Occasionally, as she passed him on the way to the drinks cabinet, she would ruffle her son's hair affectionately, but George's reaction would always tell me far more than the act itself. Pulling away and cringing, it would have been obvious to anyone observing that he detested her with a passion. What they may not have noticed, however, was the tension in his neck and shoulders; the tightness around his jaw and lips that informed me, the more educated observer, that George Ruiz was afraid of his mother... or, perhaps, afraid of what she could inadvertently do to him.

"I think you should go," I said, a little sadistically. "You can't let yourself miss out on an opportunity like this, Georgie. It's too... you know, *monumental*. Money like that... it could change your life forever."

It was the most I had said all afternoon. He eyed me suspiciously as I tried not to let the guilt show, imagining Carla beating him over the head with her false leg when she found out that he was intent on stealing her sister's money out from under her nose. For a moment, I thought he was onto me. If I could see his vulnerability through the angry, violent façade, it was no doubt true that he could also read me like a book. In the playground— the memories of which still haunted me some twenty years later— he had always worked me like a well-trained puppy, knowing just what to say and how to say it. He'd called me to heel and used my fear of exclusion (from our gang of two, rather than school itself) to make me do things I wouldn't ordinarily do. Today, however, he seemed oblivious to just what was going on inside my head. Or, if he wasn't, he certainly hid it well.

He rubbed his face and sat back in his chair, rolling his head from side to side to relieve the tension in his neck. "Don't think I could stick it," he finally admitted. "*Familial obligation* or not, I hardly know any of them and..." He twitched his eyebrows at the ceiling. "Well, she'd be looking daggers at me all night. More than a boy could bear." Lowering his eyes to meet mine, suddenly smiling, the realisation that I had yet again been played came too late.

"Unless..." he said.

***

It was still raining heavily when I left, but it was nevertheless a huge relief to be out of the Ruiz household. I had escaped, it was true, before Carla had managed to hobble her way downstairs for her 5pm breakfast of cigarettes and Malibu, but I had not successfully avoided the snare that had followed George's planned 'unless'. Better men than I had been trapped by his machinations, this I knew—but as I pulled up my jacket collar against the wind, the welcome rain beating down on my balding head, I couldn't help feeling that it would have been better if I had spent the afternoon alone in my flat after all.

Cursing my bad luck and rank stupidity, I stopped at the kerb, preparing to cross. A piece of cardboard floated by in the gutter, as limp and lifeless as I felt, and as I looked up from watching it slip down into the drain, I caught someone scrutinising me from the other side of the road.

She stood within the shadow and shelter of an old familiar oak—holding a cat that, although I couldn't have been certain, I thought might have been Gemini beneath her chin, stroking it mesmerically and staring at me unashamedly. Wearing a long, unfashionable raincoat and green Wellingtons, her drenched auburn hair plastered to her head, neck and face, she was anything but attractive... and, yet, I couldn't stop looking at her.

She looked at me.

I looked at her.

And the rain continued to fall.

I raised a hand uncertainly, wondering if I should cross the road and talk to her—ask, perhaps, if she was lost or if there was anything I could do to help—but my hand got no higher than my waist before she turned and started walking down the road, away from me, in the direction of the abattoir. Hunched against the onslaught of rain, she looked somehow older from behind. I estimated that she was possibly only in her late twenties and, yet, as she walked quickly away with the cat still tucked under her chin, she looked much older... forty and prematurely frail, I thought, weighted down by innumerable burdens.

As I started to walk after her—not quite knowing why, or what I was going to say once I caught up with her—a car pulled into the kerb behind me and beeped its horn. Turning, I saw the familiar Renault Clio and groaned, torn between running after the old young woman and returning to the car. The cat-cuddling woman promised something—I didn't know what, but it had to be preferable to the bad news the car and its owner would inevitably be delivering. And, yet, it would look odd if I didn't do what I knew I must. To chase after a stranger was one thing—but to do it while my father was sitting in his car waiting for me to get in was another.

I thought of George's phrase *familial obligation* and opened the passenger door.

"Now don't say a word," Dad said. The dry, warm interior was welcoming—reminiscent of the family days out we'd suffered through my childhood, when it had *always* rained. I very briefly wondered if I could get Dad to follow the strange girl with the cat, but as he continued talking, I realised just how impossible that was. My fate had been sealed the minute I got into the car, as surely as if I had been a little boy accepting a lift from a stranger. I really should have known better.

"This is how it's going to be," Dad said, pulling back out into the road. He put the windscreen wipers on their fastest setting as the rain came down more heavily and I had to look away. "I've stuck my neck out for you, here. No question. But I don't mind because that's what fathers do for their offspring." Only Dad could make me feel like a malfunctioning mattress. A rare talent. "I had a word with Tony Fraser. You remember him, right? Used to fix fridges for McArgills? Anyway, he works for the parks and gardens people, now –"

"Fixing fridges?"

"Eh? What?—No. Not fixing fridges. Jesus, Price, get a bloody grip. What on earth would he be doing fixing fridges for the parks and garden people? No, what he—"

"Do they still call them that? Parks and garden people, I mean."

Dad stopped at the traffic lights on Waterhouse Road. He took a long, deep breath while I looked out of my side window. Twisting his hands on the steering wheel, the vinyl squeaking against his sweaty palms, I imagined him counting to ten under his breath—and took far too much satisfaction from the thought.

"I did say, didn't I?" He spoke with a forced calm that had once terrified me. Now it just made me smile. "When you got in the car—I told you, right?"

"What did you tell me, Dad?"

"I told you not to say a word, did I not?" I nodded, not saying a word. "So don't. Ok? Just sit there quietly like a good lad and listen to what I have to say."

I pointed out that the traffic lights were on green and he muttered something I didn't quite catch as he put the car into gear and drove on. I expected him to immediately pick up where he had left off, but instead he sat quietly for a few minutes, concentrating on the road and sucking on a Werther's Original that he got out of the glove compartment (without even offering me one.) Thinking that this might go on all evening, I used the conversational lull to look for the mystery woman, even though I knew that we must have overtaken her a good way back. We passed closing corner shops and disused cinemas, school grounds and multi-storey car parks. Five more minutes of silence and the rain started to ease up. I listened to Dad crunch the last of his sweet, feeling suddenly quite old and pathetic—sleepy from the warmth of the car's impressive heater.

"So, like I was saying," he finally continued, "I was having a word with him and I happened to mention that you were looking for a job."

'Looking' was probably stretching it a bit, but now didn't seem a good time to point that out.

"He always liked you, you know," Dad said. "He told me that. Said that he saw something in you. He didn't say what, and I didn't ask, but to cut a long story short, they're looking for... they're looking for an assistant gardener at the Italian Gardens at Redburn and... well, the job's yours if you want it."

I didn't want it, of course. The last thing I wanted to be was a *gardener*, assistant or otherwise. Unqualified for the job in every respect, I could already see just how much of a disaster it could well be. It wasn't so much that I wouldn't be up to the job; the truth was, I could pretty much turn my hand to anything. But my heart needed to be in it. Were I to do a job as well as it had to be done, it required a certain degree of motivation and commitment on my part.

"An assistant gardener," I said, trying to figure out the best way of breaking the news to him.

"Could be quite an opportunity," he told me, indicating a left. I didn't know where we were going, but I had a funny feeling. "There's the chance of promotion and, well, who wouldn't want to work in such beautiful surroundings?"

Redburn was a peculiar leftover from Victorian times. Perched on the edge of a cliff, the townspeople and their foreboding architecture traded on their meagre heritage, keeping the funicular railway running and suckering the tourists in once a year with the fabled and originally titled 'Victorian Week'. Craggy and a little stifling, it was grey in winter and not much better in summer—the one-time smugglers cove its only redeeming feature, but for the Italian Gardens... where Dad seemed intent on my working.

I remembered them from my childhood—regimental formality and precise colour, so at odds with the garish, excessive fashion of the day—and it was true that they, at least, *were* beautiful. I remembered looking down on it from a high pathway, crouching between the comfortingly wild undergrowth and wondering how they got Nature to run in such abnormally straight lines. It had seemed obscene, somehow, even to the naïve, seven-year-old me, and, yet, it had nevertheless been impressive and, yes, beautiful.

I smiled to myself when I recalled how, later that day, Mam had encouraged me to smell the flowers—still convinced that the Anosmia I've suffered for as long as I can remember could be cured by simple perseverance. "Sniff up, love," she had said. "No, harder. There. Did you get anything?" I hadn't liked to give her straight 'no'. It had seemed cruel. And so I had shrugged and told her maybe.

False hope. It's that, not money, that makes the world go round.

"Why don't you give me his number, Dad," I said. "I'll give him a bell and drop by to see him."

He cast me a sideways glance, smiling ruefully and raising an eyebrow. "Oh, I think we can do better than that, don't you?"

At this precise point in our conversation we passed a road sign. I didn't want to look at it, but I was unable to help myself. *Redburn*, it said. *Two Miles*.

We found Tony Fraser the Former Fridge Fixer in a disconcertingly modern brick building to the south of the Italian Gardens. From the outside, it looked like a public toilet—square and squat, perfectly situated for the cottaging hordes and the weak of bladder and bowel.

Dad opened the door and leant in, shouting Tony's name a couple of times before the volume finally lowered. Looking over Dad's shoulder, I saw a man approaching from the shadows at the back of the room. Tony Fraser, I guessed.

"Cliff Waters," Tony Fraser said, with all the volume and enthusiasm of the Bach symphony he'd been listening to. "Fancy seeing you again so soon, you old sod. What can I do for you?"

Stepping out into the light and very pointedly closing the door behind him, Tony Fraser took one look at me and his face broke into a huge, undeniable smile, and he nodded knowingly. "Ah," he said. "Of course. Say no more. The prodigal son—right, Cliff?"

Tony Fraser was a tall, slender guy in his mid-sixties. Hair shoulder-length and grey, thick as a lion's mane, he gave off the impression of an old hippy that was 'done with all that foolishness'. When he stepped towards me, I expected him to shake my hand but, instead, he hugged me, slapping my back vigorously and laughing heartily.

"Bloody good to see you, Price," he said, standing back to get a better look at me.

"You, too, Tony." I said it as if we were long lost buddies. The truth was, I couldn't remember the bloke. I dimly recalled hearing Dad mention the name a few times over the years, but that was about it.

"That's Mister Fraser to you," Dad said—with a nod to Tony, just to let him know that he knew how to keep the young 'uns in their place. "Mind your manners."

I was about to tell him that I'd do whatever the fuck I wanted with my manners, thank you very much, when Tony rolled his eyes, shook his head and said, "Tony will do just fine. Jesus, Cliff, you can be one uptight son of a bitch, at times." Turning to me with a sympathetic look, he asked, "How old are you now, Price?"

"Thirty-seven." It sounded ridiculous and we all knew it.

"And he's reminding you of your manners?" he said. "He still wiping your arse for you, too?"

"He'd like to think he was."

"I fix you up with a job interview, and that's the thanks I get?" Dad said, sounding a bit put out. Turning in my direction, he cleared his throat and looked me directly in the forehead. "I'll leave you here, then," he said. "I'm sure you are more than old enough to find your own way home."

I was about to point out that it was positively chucking it down—thunder rumbling in the east like a percussive harbinger of doom—but before I could say anything, Tony stepped in and told him that that wouldn't be a problem. He'd be finishing up himself in half and hour and would be more than happy to drop me back off at my flat.

"I take it you do have a flat," he said to me, once Dad had gone. "You don't still live..."

"Perish the thought."

"Pleased to hear it." He patted me on the back and then flicked his hair from his face, rather effeminately, and started leading me by the arm to the door to the, as he described it, "administrative hub of my little kingdom." Pausing before the door, he looked at me gravely, the gardens suddenly still and quiet around us, but for the sound of the rain. "If you're going to work for me," he said. "There's someone you have to meet, first."

I didn't say anything, merely followed him into the gloomy, windowless building. It felt damp inside and my eyes itched a little. I wondered what delightful smells I was missing.

As my eyes adjusted to the darkness, I was surprised to see that this was more than just a storeroom. Yes, there were the spades, forks, lawnmowers, bags of bleeding compost and terracotta plant pots that I'd anticipated—but there was more than that. A good half of the building's single room had been turned into a remarkably comfortable-looking lounge area. I saw a couple of sumptuous settees, a footstool and standard lamp (which Tony now turned on, after first closing the door behind him), a portable widescreen television, a rack for newspapers, piles of romance novels, dusty rugs on the floor and, even, a microwave oven. All of this paled into insignificance, however, when Tony stepped aside to introduce me to the person he'd brought me to meet.

"Price," he said. "This is Claudia. Claudia Aslett."

In her mid-forties, Claudia was beautiful. Her dark hair tumbled over her right shoulder to her breast and her eyes seemed to suck in the light—holding it within, feeding off it and unwilling to share, but all the more enchanting for it. She stared past me at the far wall, in no way acknowledging me, and her hands remained limp and motionless in her lap. Tony leant over and kissed her on the forehead, lovingly—with a sadness that made me want to look away.

Claudia shifted slightly in her wheelchair and made a tiny, indecipherable sound in the back of her throat. Tony wiped a spot of saliva from her chin with a paper tissue, and then turned to regard me.

"Three years ago, Claudia was driving home from work," he said, filling the kettle at the sink by the door. "Minding her own business, like we all do. She was a solicitor with a firm in town. Banks, Jaudice and Aslett. She was the Aslett. A full partner and highly thought of. She had a good mind, you see – one of the best in the business, Banks and Jaudice later told me. Plus she had principles. Too many, at times, though she would have said that too many still weren't enough." He stopped and smiled to himself. A memory stirring, but quickly banished. "Anyway, she was driving home, minding her own business, and, *wallop*. She gets hit by one of those fucking four be four monstrosities. She was driving a Porsche—which, incidentally, she never took above fifty—and... it was a right mess."

"That's awful," I said, speaking directly to Claudia, just in case. "I'm so sorry."

"Even worse when you consider that the other driver was three times over the legal limit and escaped without so much as a scratch," Tony said. "Son of a bitch got a couple of years. Claudia... well, she got life."

When I had left George's earlier that afternoon, I could never have imagined that an hour and a half later would find me sitting with Tony Fraser and Claudia, sipping Twinings Assam tea and listening intently as Tony told me all about her—the struggles and sorrows they had had, the little victories that kept them going.

"We'd been friends and neighbours for many years," he said, the two of us on one of the settees, Claudia pulled up close to Tony. "We got on like a house on fire, but I couldn't stand that husband of hers. Right pompous little turd. Anyway, when Claudia got a bit of sense—this is before the accident, you understand—and sent him packing, I started doing the occasional odd job for her... don't look like that. It's not a euphemism."

"Sorry. I didn't mean—"

"That didn't come till later," he added with a smile and a wink. Patting Claudia on her knee, he said, "We were good together, isn't that right, love? Still are, if you want the truth. You don't find that shocking, do you?"

"No. No, I don't. I... "

Tony seemed to approve of my answer, even if he didn't entirely believe me. He sat back and looked up at the ceiling. "It's been hard, Price," he said. "There's no denying that. But it could have been a hell of a lot worse." He took a sip of his tea and sniffed, blinking rapidly and clearing his throat. "Still want to work for me?" he asked.

Chapter Two

Sitting in George's kitchen earlier that day, I had never envisaged that by evening I would have a job. It had been the most unlikely of propositions—ranking up there with alien abduction and speed of light travel. I hadn't wanted a job. I certainly hadn't been looking for one. It wasn't so much that I was idle and unwilling. Not really. It was more that I was a realist. I understood that, whatever people might tell me to the contrary, sometimes I just wasn't capable of work. My Anosmia was the root cause of this—as implausible as that might seem —the depression it on occasion inspired was utterly debilitating and all encompassing. The pills never helped and so I refused to take them, and the well-meaning, pinafore-dressed therapist I had seen had had all the insight and ability of a badly stuffed mole (which the poor, short-sighted, mousy love more than resembled.) And so I had muddled along, killing time and believing that I was missing nothing by not having gainful employment—when all the while the truth was waiting for me in a squat little building in the Italian Gardens at Redburn.

Closing the door to my flat (which was actually more of a bedsit), I turned on the light and surveyed the scene before me. An unmade bed. The cracked portable television. A microwave oven that, I imagined, still exhaled the heady, stale scent of last night's ready-meal tikka-masala, which I would never smell. A DVD player with heaps of pirated DVDs and CDs beside it. Second-hand books by the dozen and newspapers galore. It wasn't exactly the most welcoming of rooms and, yet, tonight it seemed a far brighter prospect than it had for a good while. The dirty sixty watt bulb overhead shone a little more brightly, and when I crossed the six or seven short paces to the window in order to close the curtain, I felt an inner warmth that I'd never experienced in the flat before.

I felt so good, in fact, that I put Ray LaMontagne on and sang along to Three More Days at the top of my inexpert voice—the lyrics curiously apt—only stopping when the old tart next door started banging on the wall. He never had struck me as the type of person who liked to see others having a good time. It was evident in his tight, tiny nostrils and the headmasterly way in which he clasped his arms behind his back.

Even he couldn't upset or anger me tonight, though. I shrugged him off like an old donkey jacket and opened a couple of tins of beans—hungry as hell and intent on leaving the bottle of Stella for later that evening... a good book, Parkinson on the telly and a bottle of lager. All on a full stomach. What more could a bloke ask for?

But something wasn't quite right. It had been niggling away at the back of my mind ever since I'd arrived home, but I hadn't managed to put my finger on just what was bothering me. Now, however, I put the tin of beans down on the counter and turned to look about the room. The television and DVD player were still in their places—as were the microwave and the little fridge beside it. The DVDs and CDs formed their disorderly piles and ranks, just as they had when I had left that afternoon, and my books... they were where they should have been.

All but for one.

The night before, I had felt particularly miserable. The world had seemed an especially unfamiliar place to me—a world of five senses, a world of secrets whose weight I could only begin to grasp. Outside, it had been dark and windy—the glass rattling in its frame, as if someone had wanted to get in—and as I had curled up under my duvet, I had known that something very distinctive had been called for... not something that would rid me of my mood and sense of dislocation but, rather, something that would flatter it. And so I had found the Hardy novel that I had bought for ten pence at a car boot sale, Jude the Obscure, and had settled down, determined to complete the job of thoroughly depressing myself.

I had fallen asleep a couple of hours later, whispering half-sentences to the memory of a girl I had known over twenty-five years before, the book on the empty pillow beside me.

And there it had remained, a token of longing and loss, still in place when I had left for George's that afternoon.

Squatting down, I picked it up from the floor—turning it over in my hands as I tried to fathom out how it had got there. It was on the floor at the end of the bed, so there was no way that it could have simply slipped from the pillow and landed there. I knew from the numerous times I had thrown it across the room in despair that Jude did not bounce. It was the kind of book that hit the ground like a dead pigeon, and stayed there, happy to rot.

So how, I thought, had it ended up over here?

My bookmark—a tattered piece of paper—was sticking out at an unusual angle, and as I replaced it I realised that it wasn't my bookmark, after all. It was pink notepaper. Pink notepaper with, I saw as I slipped it from the book, something written on it.

Be careful, the note said. Please.

Perhaps a little stupidly, I looked over my shoulder—half-expecting to find someone standing in the corner of the room, watching me. It occurred to me that maybe the note had been in the book all along, ever since I'd bought it, but I quickly dismissed the idea when I remembered that I'd read the book a number of times, and thrown it across the room in exasperation even more. No, the note had most definitely been placed between the pages of the book some time that afternoon, while I had been out.

Checking the door, I found no sign of forced entry. The obvious culprit was my landlady, Margarite Hamshaw. Letting herself into people's flats behind their backs was, frankly, just the kind of thing I could imagine her doing. A large, oily woman—with a retroussé nose that looked at odds with her flabby face—she was always on the lookout for an advantage. Anything that could be used against her tenants was not only welcomed, but hunted down with all the tenacity of a bloodhound. That my life was so safe and, well, boring had been an obvious disappointment to her. All her prying and 'scrutinising' had revealed nothing (something she would no doubt find suspicious in itself) and it was no great leap for me to imagine her in here, looking among my books for Class A drugs or child porn.

But that wouldn't explain the note. If Margarite Hamshaw came into my room when I wasn't there it most certainly wouldn't be to put a note for me within the pages of a Thomas Hardy novel. And in the highly improbable event that she had, it most certainly would not have been a warning on pink notepaper. And nor would she have said please.

Sitting back on my haunches, I studied the note again—turning it over in my hand, just in case I'd missed something. I realised that I should possibly feel threatened, someone had been in my room, after all – but I didn't.

Standing at the window—my favourite place for thinking—the light out, I pushed the curtain aside and looked out at the street below. The rain was still falling fairly heavily and the orange, sodium streetlights reflected off the slick roads and pavements. A car shushed by, it's stark headlights cutting through the night as though it were a physical form—something solid and rich. In spite of the evidence that I'd had an intruder, I was glad to be in my flat, rather than out there on the street. It didn't do to be on the street on a night like this. These were the times when the likes of my good friend George Ruiz flourished. Cold, dark times when the susceptible were more startlingly revealed. I didn't doubt that he would be out there, somewhere, wandering from one lonely, seedy dive to the next—seizing whatever rare opportunity might come his way.

Over the road from my flat was a doctor's surgery. An old, converted Victorian three-storey house, the ailing front garden had been rehabilitated into a small car park, with a regimental line of conifers partially concealing it and the front of the building. Far from interesting, I seldom paid it all that much attention. Tonight, however, I found myself staring intently into the shadows at the end of the conifers. I saw movement there—movement that might well have been an urban fox, or merely my imagination. It shifted left to right, and then right to left, and as I moved my face closer to the window—holding my breath so as not to steam up the glass—the shadow started to take on a recognisable form. It was not a fox. It was not merely my imagination.

I recognised the Wellingtons before I recognised her, even in the poor, orange-tinted light. She stood looking up at me, in clear view, now, and I felt a chill run the length of my spine. She had been in my room. The old young woman I had seen outside George's had been in my flat. She had been the one who had put the note between the pages of the Hardy novel. It had been she who had, for some peculiar reason, felt the need to tell me to be careful... felt the need to ask me to be careful.

I took the stairs three at a time, almost falling near the bottom, but saving myself with a shoulder against the damp wall, bursting out onto the street as if I had just discovered water displacement or, at the very least, that my flat was on fire. Running straight across the road, dodging a passing car in the process, I ran into the grounds of the doctor's surgery, past the line of conifers where I had seen her. I expected to find her hiding among the shrubbery. A shadow consumed by deeper shadow. But, perhaps predictably, she was nowhere to be seen.

Back on the street, I searched its length, hoping to find her waiting for me beneath a streetlight—smoking enigmatically and humming Lilli Marlene—but found no sign of her. I looked behind garden walls, in wheelie-bins the same shade of green as her wellies, and even looked under a few parked cars, just in case she'd been looking for her lost cat. All to no avail.

Once more in my flat, I stood by the window with the lights turned out—the note held in my hand as I watched for her, hoped for her return. This time I would not race after her, questions spewing prematurely from my mouth, I would be content just to know that she was there, watching over me in her green Wellingtons and raincoat.

But she did not return, and eventually I went to bed—falling asleep with her note on the pillow beside me.

I found Tony sweeping up some litter in front of his little love nest. It was my first day on the job and, rather uncharacteristically, I was eager to impress—turning up half an hour early in a pair of neatly pressed jeans, a white shirt and heavy bomber jacket. I'd slept well, in spite of the events of the night before, and felt alert and ready for anything he might throw at me. What I wasn't prepared for, however, was the solemn way in which Tony straightened from his task to greet me. His faced etched with gravity, I understood immediately that something was wrong.

"Price," he said, forcing a smile. "Good to see you." He leant the broom against the wall and sat down on a deckchair that he'd brought outside. He looked a hell of a lot older than he had the day before. His hands flopped down between his knees and he shook his head a little bitterly. "You look like the direct opposite of everything I am today. Young and vital and ready for whatever the world might have in store for you."

I leant against the wall beside the broom, folding my arms and trying to look sympathetic. "I wouldn't read too much into appearance," I told him. "On the inside, I'm three times your age and have the damnedest time tying my shoe laces." I considered telling him about the note I had found in Jude and the mystery woman that I believed had put it there, to take his mind off his troubles, but that seemed too self-centred even for me and so, as he smiled sadly back at me, I lowered my voice and said, "Want to talk about it?"

Tony sighed. It came out as a barely suppressed shudder. Shaking his head, he thought better of it and nodded instead. "Close the door, lad," he said, indicating that he didn't want Claudia to hear. "Every now and then it just gets the better of me," he said, once he was happy that the door was firmly shut. "The things I have to do for her... that's a walk in the park. I can do all that with my eyes closed. But what gets to me... it's nothing but it's everything, you know—the not being able to hold a proper conversation with her."

I mumbled a quiet little "ah" of understanding, but said nothing more—to let him continue.

"I talk to her all the time," he told me, shoulders slumped. "And I have to imagine her replies, imagine that old wit and intelligence falling out of her with that familiar ease I loved so much. And I can do that, too. Most of the time."

"It can't be easy for you, Tony." Sometimes the hackneyed replies are all we've got.

"It's not, Price, it's not. I know she's in there, you see, whatever they might tell me to the contrary—but if I'm to keep believing that I..."

"You have to maintain your faith in the accuracy of the replies you imagine her giving."

Squinting at me, Tony gave me the most credible smile I'd seen from him today and put his head back in his deckchair—looking up at the sky, eyes twinkling, close to tears. "That's about the long and short of it," he admitted. "And as a rule that's fairly easy... only... well, sometimes I get tired. I get tired and trying to think up what she'd say under specific circumstances becomes difficult, you know? And then I start to doubt and... that isn't good, Price. I can't allow myself to start doubting."

I wasn't sure just what I could say that would help. The truth was, were I in Tony's position, I thought that I would be inclined to believe everything the doctors had told me and, however reluctantly, accept that the Claudia I had known and loved was no longer there. It would be a tragedy, there was no doubt about that, but it had to be better than the interminable suffering that Tony was inflicting on himself.

I knew enough to understand that he wouldn't want to hear this and, so, I merely waited the moment out—letting him talk his way through to the other side, which may well have been all he needed.

"We had this conversation last night," he told me—his voice little more than a whisper. "It started off ordinary enough. A film we were watching in bed together. How bad it was. You know the kind of thing. We were warm and, I thought, content, and conversation came easily. I even got a smile out of her. A real smile. Nothing made up or imagined. But things started to change, Price. We talked and... the conversation got darker. We started talking about things we've never touched on before and... she asked me something." He closed his eyes against the memory, hands clasped together tightly in his lap. "She's asked me things before. Many times. But never anything like this. I didn't know what to say—I mean, what do you say? One minute the two of us are talking about a lousy film on telly, the next she's asking me something like that... asking me to do something like that."

"What did she ask you to do?" I said softly.

Tony didn't speak for what seemed a very long while, staring into middle space and chewing the side of his mouth. I felt the moment stretching out, elastic and grim, and began to wish that I had never asked the question in the first place. It was too personal. I started to tell him to forget I'd asked – it was something I didn't need to know and I shouldn't have been so intrusive in the first place – but he merely held up a hand to silence me, letting me know with such a precise, conservative gesture that, under the circumstances, he thought it acceptable and even appropriate that I should ask this question. He just needed time. Time to judge how best to frame his answer for me.

"I'm not sure that I should tell you this," he finally said. "Claudia... well, she would say that it's something that should remain between the two of us, for my own protection, if nothing else. But it's too heavy a burden for me to carry on my own, Price. To have to consider something like this without having the opportunity to discuss it with someone... it just isn't fair. No one can ask that of another person."

"What is it, Tony?" I quietly said.

"I was holding her close," he told me. "We were in bed—I told you that—we were in bed but I'd turned the television off by this time and... we were getting ready to go to sleep. Saying our good nights and... being close. You know. I kissed her. I held her. I told her how much I loved her... and then I felt it—I felt it and saw it reflected in the sadness in her eyes... warmth where my leg pressed up against her."

Tony regarded me with all the weight and longing of the sincere, loving man I imagined him to be. "It doesn't happen often," he explained. "Normally she has excellent bladder and bowel control. We have a good little regime going and there are rarely any accidents. But every now and then... well, whether it was cold in her bladder or what, I don't know, but she wet the bed, Price. She wet the bed and she asked me. She said, 'Help me, Tony. Help me die.'"

Alone in my flat later that evening, my own mystery to grapple with, I would nevertheless find myself wondering why, exactly, Tony had chosen to tell this to me. It was not as if we were old and trusted friends. For all intents and purposes, we had known each other for less than twenty-four hours, whatever Tony might say to the contrary. So why me? My conclusion, as I ate my chip-shop chips and drank a cup of tea, was simple enough. I was there. As I stood there beside him, however, I felt that there was something more profound going on. I was aware of a closeness growing between Tony and me. Whether it was imagined or not, I don't really know—but at the time in seemed real enough, and Tony sharing such a personal story with me certainly underscored this.

I therefore wanted to say something meaningful in return. Taken a little aback by this odd revelation—and its various implications—I felt that resorting to the hackneyed phrases was no longer fitting. And so I clenched my buttocks and dug deep for some rich, philosophical insight and said:

"Sometimes... it isn't always as... you know, we have to be able to... I'm not sure I'm making sense, but what I really mean to say is..." I took a deep breath and said, "You imagined her saying it, Tony. That doesn't necessarily mean that it's something she'd want."

"I understand that," he said, his voice croaky with emotion. "But... that's the fundamental principle on which we've built our relationship, Price. That faith in my belief that I know what she wants. If I just disregard this... well, then all that other stuff was just a sham."

"I don't know what to tell you, Tony." More than that, however, I was growing afraid that I might inadvertently say the wrong thing. I didn't want to put myself in a position where I might be accused of being in some way complicit, however much I wished to help him.

"I know, mate—I know. I really shouldn't have mentioned it to you. It's not fair of me." He stood, flicking his hair out of his face, and forced a smile. "It'll all come out in the wash, as my old mam used to say. Now, come on. We better get you sorted."

Walking over to the door of his and Claudia's love-nest, he looked over his shoulder at me and tapped the side of his nose with an index finger. "Not a word. Okay?"

The tour of the gardens he gave me was wholly unnecessary. I knew the place well enough, remembering most of it from my childhood visits, and found as he led me past the disciplined borders and carefully sculpted topiary, Tony pushing the drooling Claudia in her wheelchair, that what I wanted more than anything was to be doing. There had been enough talk for one day, and now I wanted to get my hands dirty. As I'd already told Tony half a dozen times today, I knew virtually nothing about gardening, and couldn't tell a Pelargonium from a pergola, but I was ready to learn and relished the prospect of returning home with soil beneath my fingernails.

We wandered into the densely wooded area just to the north of the gardens, Tony telling me that my job would include the general maintenance and care of the gardens and surrounding landscape, heavy lifting (apparently, he had to watch his back, what with caring for Claudia and everything), helping with the planting, cutting back and weed control, and occasionally sitting with Claudia when he had to be elsewhere. "I know that probably wasn't what you were expecting," he said. "It's not exactly your typical gardener's assistant job description but I trust you won't have any problems with it?"

I didn't know if I was imagining it, but there seemed to be just the slightest hint of a challenge in this. I couldn't help but think of the note I had found. Was this what it had been referring to? Was Tony and his strange relationship the thing I had to watch out for— the possible danger on the horizon? As we walked the tarmac path up to the rocky overlook known as Lover's Leap, which seemed to cast the gardens in shadow at certain times of the day, it seemed a preposterous proposition. Tony was one of the good guys. Surely. You only had to look at the way in which he took care of Claudia to see that—ever attentive, wiping the drool from her chin and doing whatever else was required of him (something I didn't really want to think about).

And yet... what did I really know? Listening to the story of Claudia wetting herself and the resulting question she had 'asked' had been a strange and difficult experience, and while I had probably dealt with it rather well under the circumstances, it was certainly true that I had felt a considerable unease at his mention of her supposedly wanting him to 'help' her die. The whole idea of him believing that he knew what she wanted—that he knew her well enough to supply her part of their conversations—was, on the surface at least, quaint and touching. But as I looked at it more closely, I saw how open to abuse the whole process was.

When they made love, was it really consensual or was Tony in effect raping her?

"You've heard the story, right?" Tony was saying. I glanced at him, frowning. A little bewildered and lost. He gestured to the rocky ledge before us. "Lover's Leap. You've heard the story?"

The ledge was railed off—warning signs insisting that it was highly dangerous (not to mention forbidden) to pass beyond the barriers to the cliff edge... as if this wasn't already strongly implied by the notable drop on the other side. I'd seen it many times during my childhood, but only ever from a distance—Mam holding my hand tightly just in case I should be overcome by a moment of madness. Now I stepped a little nearer, shaking my head in reply to Tony's question, but also somewhat in awe of what, really, was a relatively unspectacular sight.

I heard Tony put Claudia's breaks on before joining me at the railing. "It's not much to look at," he said, reading my thoughts. "But its history... well, even if you don't know the details, you can nevertheless sense them somehow—don't you agree?"

I looked down at the gardens below, my eyes dropping to the

edge of the rocky outcrop and then readjusting. I nodded, feeling a little weak at the knees, and gripped the railing rather too tightly. It wasn't the height. That didn't bother me in the least. It was more a sense of something that I couldn't quite put my finger on—the history of which Tony had spoken, and yet something else entirely.

"They were both only fourteen," Tony was telling me. I listened through the gentle, sea-shell rushing sound in my ears, fighting the urge to close my eyes. "Rodney and Juliette. This was about 1869. Something like that. The two of them were madly in love. Met up whenever they could—which was nigh on impossible, at that time. But they managed it. Quite successfully, for a while."

"But it couldn't last." It had to end in tragedy. Stories told on the edge of a rocky drop always did.

"No," Tony said. "These things never can, can they? Soon enough, they were discovered. Two Victorian children, lost in each other's embrace—making love with a portentous urgency. Well, there was a scandal. Two of the better families in town suddenly found themselves shunned. They had brought depravity into a world where there, if the morally superior were to be believed, had been none. And as a consequence, the two families were made to suffer—socially and financially."

"So what of Rodney and Juliette?" I said, wanting the conversation to stay on track—the sooner to have it over and done with.

"They were bright kids," Tony told me. "They knew just how close to the wind they were sailing, and because of this, they also understood that there was a fair chance that one day they could well get caught. And so they'd planned for just such a contingency."

"They met here?"

"Yes." Tony looked over his shoulder, checking that Claudia was alright. Staring down at the gardens with me, he continued. "They'd been forbidden from ever seeing each other again," he told me. "Watched constantly, it can't have been easy—but somehow they both found a way. They got out and came here, as they must have arranged months before."

"They planned on running away together?"

"I don't suppose we can ever know what they planned," Tony said. "But, ultimately, that wasn't what happened."

He went on to tell me what I suppose I already knew—on some level, at least. The couple had been followed. Their escape had not been as clever and unobserved as they had thought, and as they had held onto each other—making the foolhardy promises that all young lovers make—a figure had stepped out of the shadows and approached them. Juliette's father, his cane in his hand. Rodney had backed away, trying in vain to reason with the gentleman, but it would have been easy for him to see just how futile his efforts really were. This was the girl's father. The girl he, Rodney, had loved and taken—befouled in the eyes of good society. And if he had needed proof, the steadily rising cane would have provided it. And as I listened to Tony tell the inevitably tragic final instalment of the story—wondering at the commitment to each other that the two young lovers had shown, something so unfamiliar to me—I felt their fall as surely as if I had taken those final steps myself, the wind rushing through my hair, the icy, hollow dread and certainty in the pit of my stomach. Hand in hand, they had jumped, no doubt staring into each others eyes... reverentially whispering their love for one another.

When I finally turned away from the drop before me, an unexpected sight greeted me. I don't think Tony caught it, and I certainly didn't say anything to him about it—it was too fleeting and difficult to grasp.

Claudia was staring at me. Her intelligent eyes met and held mine, and she blinked slowly—once—before dropping her head and drooling onto her breast. A strikingly pale shade of blue, those eyes had seemed so vital and aware, but just as quickly she was gone again... so quickly I doubted that she had been there in the first place.

"We'd better be getting back," Tony said. "Looks like rain again."

Chapter Three

The following Saturday evening would change my life forever. It would be a night when a part of me died so that a greater, more complete part might live—and when I look back to that time, I think how different it might have been, how I could so easily have told George to stuff it. How finely balanced it all is, I would later think. The difference between widely opposed outcomes no more than a single thought.

Standing outside his Aunt Martha's ex-council house—which she had bought in 1978 for a pittance and which was now worth a fairly healthy sum, according to George—my closest friend leant in close and sniffed liquidly. "Think I'm getting that thing that you've got," he said. "Can't smell a fucking thing."

"It's a cold, mate," I said. "Take a Lemsip and get over yourself."

"Nice bedside manner you've got there."

"For an assistant gardener."

"Do you talk to Claudia like that when you're nurse-maiding her?" I was already regretting telling him the more unusual details of my new job—I really should have known better but... well, I had been excited and enthused, and if I hadn't told him, who was I going to tell? My landlady, Margarite Hamshaw?

"Are we going in, then, or what?" I said, determined not to rise to it.

George leant back against the small wall at the front of the house, his hands in the pockets of his jacket. "You tell me," he said. "Are we?"

"Well I was under the impression that we were. Was I mistaken?"

Shrugging, he said, "I'm not sure. I mean, that was the plan but... well, frankly, your heart doesn't seem to be in it."

"That's because it isn't."

"You don't want to be here?"

"You know I don't."

George looked deeply disappointed in me. He stared at the dog-shitted pavement, sucking his top lip and shaking his head. I could hear the sound of music coming from inside his aunt's house, but this didn't make the proposition anymore attractive.

"I really don't get you," he said. "Why on earth would you say you'd come if you didn't want to?"

"Because you'd have broken both my legs if I hadn't."

His chin tucked into the collar of his jacket, he frowned at me— before breaking into a big, shit-eating grin. "I would have, wouldn't I?" he said. "I forget how bright you are, sometimes." He pushed himself off the wall and slapped me hard on the shoulder. "So," he said, "are we going in, then, or what?"

George's mother was alone in Martha's kitchen when we finally entered. Propped up in the corner formed by the sink unit and a wonky-looking cupboard, we found her puffing on the black cigarette in her holder and alternately chugging on a cheap bottle of vodka. Her grey-blonde hair was a back-combed mess and she was wearing a stained white blouse and black slacks. I noticed her right leg from the knee down was missing.

"Oh, for fuck's sake," George said. "Tell me you haven't done it again, Mam."

"It keeps them quiet, George," she told him. "And you know how I hate noise."

"But... your leg, Mam."

"I can hop."

"With a fag in one hand and a vodka bottle in the other?"

"You underestimate me."

George turned away from her, pulling an exasperated face. He sighed and beckoned me through to the hallway.

Once there, crowded with jardinières, battling coats on insufficient coat-racks, a stand occupied by a couple of dead-bat umbrellas and a pile of dirty laundry at the far end, George leant back against the wall and did his best to compose himself. I could understand his frustration. Carla Ruiz was not the easiest of people to talk to. In a perpetual drunken haze—at the very least—she appeared to see the world around her in a very particular and obscure way. Her sole motivation was to live just long enough to get to the next drink, and beyond that – well, it didn't warrant consideration. I saw all this only occasionally; George, however, had to live with it, day in, day out.

Anyone else and I would have felt sorry for him. But this was George—and I couldn't help feeling that this was no more than he deserved. I remembered all the times he had made my life a misery... all right, all the times I had allowed him to make my life a misery, today being a perfect example.

"She just never fucking listens," he told me. "I tell her, time and time again, don't do that. But does she take any notice? Does she buggery. She just keeps right on doing it, fucking clueless to the fact that they're all taking the piss out of her."

"And you are concerned why, exactly?" He frowned at me—a knife-glint of anger flashing momentarily behind his eyes. "She's you're mother," I explained. "Not your daughter. What she does doesn't have to reflect on you so... just let her get on with it. At least when she's like that she isn't giving you hell over Martha's money."

There was never any way of knowing how my antagonistic friend would take a piece of unsolicited advice. I'd seen him leave people physically and/or emotionally scarred for much less, and so I was certainly on my guard. In junior school I remember little Joey Walters had once made the mistake of helping him with his sums, without being asked, and to this day he still walked with a noticeable limp.

This time, George merely took a deep breath and nodded thoughtfully—running a hand down over his face and chuckling to himself. "That's what I like about you," he said.

"What?"

"You always see past the shit." He roughly ruffled my hair and put me in an unexpected but blessedly short-lived headlock, before leading me along the hallway, saying excitedly, "Something to show you, mate. Prepare yourself for an oddly nostalgic interlude. You're going to love this. If you aren't as dead from the crown down as your pitiful life often suggests."

He rushed me past the crowded, noisy living room, hyperactively regaling me with further insults. I caught a fleeting glimpse of the other family members gathered therein; a dusty, crumpled bunch, serenely tapping their feet along to the mellifluous melody of the Sex Pistols performing Anarchy in the UK. I wanted to stand in the doorway and watch, but George pulled me after him—telling me that I would be as calcified as them soon enough.

On the upstairs landing, we dodged past three children—two girls, one boy, all between the ages of five and seven—playing with Carla's false leg. I heard the boy tell one of the girls "You can't put it on like Aunty Carla does unless you let us chop your leg off first", but then George was pushing me into a small bedroom at the far end of the landing.

He slammed the door shut behind him, laughing and panting like a rock star who'd just escaped the backstage attentions of a horde of ugly fans. He then slapped the wall with the palm of his hand, turning on the light.

I almost wished he hadn't. The cramped little room was by far the most uninviting in the house. The floorboards were carpeted only with the filth and dust of decades—piles of used tissues at the side of a collapsed, darkly stained mattress. Looking at the brown-streaked potty in the corner of the room, I thanked the Lord for my Anosmia.

"Ta-da," George fanfared ironically. "Kim and Aggie would have a fucking dickey-fit—don't you agree?" I was only distantly aware of who Kim and Aggie were, but I nodded anyway, in awe of the springy coating of fur on the floorboards beneath my feet.

"This used to be my room when I stayed over as a kid," George explained. "It was a bit more habitable then. Not much more, but better than this. Can't say I cared, anyway. This room was too much fun for me to worry about a little bit of dirt."

"That's the first thing that hit me when I entered," I said. "This room promises to be a lot of fun, I thought."

"Was, Price," he said. "Pay attention."

"You mean it's not anymore?"

"Turn the light back out," he said—his patience wearing thin. I did as I was told, refraining from telling him how much of a pleasure it was for me, and before my eyes had had chance to readjust he grabbed me by the arm and dragged me to the window. He pushed the curtain aside and pointed in the direction of the house next door. "There," he said. "That's why this room used to be so much fun."

It was just an ordinary semi-detached council house, nothing more, nothing less. Set at a slight angle ordained by the bend in the road, it was possible to see the back garden and the bedroom windows from certain angles. Unremarkable and badly cared for—nothing that I could see to hold the interest of a young boy.

"I was about thirteen," George was telling me. "I used to come here quite a bit because Mam was with that bloke with the clapped out old Jag. You remember him? Moustache and permanently erect? We used to laugh at him 'cause you could always see the fucking thing standing to attention beneath his trousers."

I nodded, barely concealing the shudder of revulsion.

"Anyway," George continued, "he tried to feel my cock one day, filthy fuck, so whenever he was around, I tried not to be. That's when I came here. Last Resort Avenue. Don't get me wrong, Martha's pretty cool in her own acquisitive little way, but, you know, I was a kid and I didn't much like the idea of being pushed out of my home by some perv with a Jag and a hard-on.

"Then one night, I was up here alone." He smiled at the memory, his fingers lightly brushing the window pane, leaving trails in the greasy dirt. "It was about eleven o'clock and I was just standing here looking up at the few stars I could see above the light pollution. Twinkle-fucking-twinkle. I think not. Anyway, there I was. In a world of my own, trying not to think of Mam and old prick features, and suddenly there she was, staring right back at me."

"Your mam?"

"What? No. Jesus, no, not my mam. Does that even begin to fit? For fuck's sake, Price, use your sodding head for a change. It was a lass called Sharon Jones. She was about eighteen and I'd never seen her before in my life—and she just stood there, staring back at me and smiling as if... as if she knew every single fucking thought that was going through my head. I could see right into her room, because the ground's actually a little higher here, and she couldn't have cared less. I looked at her and she looked at me... and then she did it."

"What did she do?" I really didn't want to know; I asked only because I was a little afraid of what George would do if I didn't.

George sniffed long and hard before turning back to the window and continuing his story.

"She took her top off," he said. "She took it off and stood there, letting me look at her. She wasn't wearing a bra, Price. She stood there with these hard, neat little tits. And I just couldn't help myself; I got my cock out and started banging one out. And she knew. She must have because she then took off her skirt. And her knickers. Rubbing herself and feeling her tits, she was."

His laughter was a little shaky. Looking at me, his face flushed, he sneered and pointed at large stain on the wallpaper beneath the window. "My spunky little shrine to the memory of Sharon Jones."

"She's dead?"

"As far as I'm concerned, she might as well be," he said. "It went on like that for months, her in her room with her fingers up her cunt, me in mine pulling on my cock. Whenever I saw her outside it was like I wasn't there. That fucking rankled a bit, but I was okay about it. I understood that it was our secret. That made it even better, somehow. Just the two of us, alive in a world of dead twatting nobodies. I could really get off on that—and I imagined she could, too."

George fell silent, continuing to look out of the window at the house next door, his hands, suspiciously, in his pockets. I didn't know why he was telling me this, but one thing I did understand was that George seldom opened himself up in such a way without there being a good reason.

"Happy days," he said, winking at me and closing the curtains again. Leaning against the wall, careful to avoid the stain, he sighed. "She went away about six months later. The whole family did. A moonlight flit, Aunt Martha reckoned—though I tend to think it was a straightforward move. The council sticking them somewhere else, probably because her brothers were a pretty rough lot and, you know, they were always getting up to some pretty heavy shit and annoying the neighbours."

"So you never saw her again?" I said.

"Only in my dreams."

I nodded. "Which is all very interesting but..."

"Why am I telling you all this? Simple. We're mates and it's only right that mates should share stuff like this with one another. It's a male-bonding thing. Healthy and right."

I raised an eyebrow. Very Roger Moore, I liked to think. "Male-bonding?"

Shrugging, George grinned. "Yeah, okay. Maybe that's pushing it a bit. The fact of the matter is, I need a favour."

"Another one?"

"Who's keeping count?"

"Me."

"You need to see someone about that. That's how people end up with ulcers."

It was as inevitable as the sun rising and setting. I pinched the bridge of my nose between finger and thumb in order to express my fatigue and said, "What do you want me to do?"

Grinning that appallingly predatory grin of his, George walked past me to the door—hands still in his pockets, a smug air about him. Taking one hand out, he placed it delicately on the door handle. He winked once again and said, "I'll tell you later."

As thoughtless as ever, George left me alone in the lounge with a bunch of his aging relatives, all of whom I'd never met before. Before leaving, he had at least had the courtesy to introduce me to his Aunt Martha, a pale old prune with breasts that hung like sad sacks beneath the tent-like dress she wore; but now I found myself alone with someone who introduced himself as George's Great-Uncle Francis.

Francis dressed like some wannabe 1930s spiv—hair slicked flat to his head, a square, white silk scarf over his shoulder, beautifully pressed three piece suit (with lapels to die for) and, of all things, a pair of immaculate spats. Sitting beside him, his bulk was impressive and somewhat overbearing. I wanted to get up and leave with the others, but at least this room was relatively quiet, now, which gave me the time I needed to worry at the little problem of just what George might have in store for me next... just what this favour might be.

I realised fairly quickly, however, that I wasn't going to get much thinking done. Not with Francis there.

"Wonderful times, they were," he said, apropos absolutely nothing. "Times like you wouldn't believe. I practically ran the whole of the East Side, son. And ran it good! Believe me when I say. Like clockwork."

"You were in politics?"

Francis found this amusing. He rocked back and forth in his chair, gurgling his delight, and only when he'd dabbed the tears from his eyes with a red silk handkerchief did he continue. "Politics," he snorted. "Ha. Yes. Yes, that'll be it. Politics. Of a kind, anyway, and, well, nothing really changes, you know. Whatever they tell you. There's a certain amount of crossover. Always was, always will be. No. Not politics. Not really. I was more influential than that—although I certainly had a lot of friends in politics, you could say. No. I was a—what's your name again?"

"Price."

"Price? How much did a name like that cost you, then?"

"With George around, always more than I'd care to pay."

"Ah, yes." He nodded sagaciously. "That little shit. He gives you any trouble, you let me know, yes? I'll soon sort out that little turd for you." He slapped out a hasty, improvised rhythm on his thighs, collecting his thoughts, and then said, "Now, where was I?"

"You were—"

"That's it. Got it.... You could say I was a bit of a bad lad, Price, old chap." He held up a crooked, arthritic finger. "Bad but fair. I only took what people could afford, and for that they got all the protection they could wish for and the right to trade freely. For the good of the community, it was. Kept things ticking over—and the little people. You know. They didn't have to worry about a thing because Uncle Francis—that's what the little cripples used to call me, may God Above bless them—Uncle Francis would take care of everything, even if it meant offing a few no-hopers in the process. That's how I got things done, you see, and good or bad, it worked."

There was no stopping Francis, once he got started. He rattled out story after story about his gangster days (apparently, he also all but invented the unions... without him the working man would have remained down-trodden and helpless), keeping up with the rapid flow impressively for someone who, by the look of him, must have been in his late-eighties, and I'd be lying if I said that I didn't find my attention drifting.

He moved on to the post-war years, telling me how difficult it was to keep a handle on things, and I looked out of the window at the solid, oppressive night. Next came his prison years (he ran Wormwood Scrubs for six whole years) and I stared at the wall for a bit. This relatively violent period was followed hot on the heels by 'The Vegas Years'. He told me how he had seen Elvis in a casino and got the hell out of there right away. "Gave me one hell of a funny look. Sorta sneered at me. And it was common knowledge he was a special agent. Him and Nixon." He crossed his fingers. "Like that."

I glanced longingly at the living room door.

And saw her.

I didn't recognise her immediately, but I did recognise that she

was someone I needed to speak to... someone who held my interest
in ways that dear old Francis (may God Above bless him) never
could. She was the spur I needed. In more ways than I ever could
have imagined.

I jumped to my feet and excused myself and raced after her.
Outside the living room, I looked along the hallway and saw her
just disappearing into the kitchen. Immediately, those who had
been assembled there (Carla, now with her false leg reattached,
included) started milling out. I pushed past them, nodding and
smiling politely, and finally found myself in the kitchen. Alone
with my mystery woman.

She wasn't wearing her wellies or her raincoat today, but I knew
it was her the minute I looked into her hesitant eyes—the minute
I saw the defensive posture and the look of surprise on her face.
Up close, she was beautiful. A little plain, but beautiful
nonetheless. The dress she wore was on the old-fashioned side, not
helped by the cardigan she wore over it, but it touched in all the
right places and underscored her latent sexiness.

I took a step towards her.

She took a step back.

"It was you," I said.

"What was?" Her voice was soft—childlike in its lack of
confidence. Fluid, and yet broken and restrained.

"You know."

She shook her head. "I don't."

"You do." I felt sure that we could have gone on like this all
night. There was something comforting about it. An intimacy,
almost, that I didn't want to let go. She took another step back and
bumped up against the sink unit, determined to keep as much
space as possible between us and, yet, still seeming somehow
protective of me. As the note had suggested, she was concerned for
me, and however hard she tried to conceal it, it was there behind
her eyes... there in the way in which she held herself against the
sink unit, rigid but unafraid, quietly assessing.

"I don't," she insisted, following my impeccable lead.

I decided to try another approach. Taking a few steps towards her, as tentatively as if I were approaching an anxious, young horse, I tried to ignore the fact that she flinched and said, "You came into my bedsit when I wasn't there. You left me a note telling me to be careful."

"Why would I want to do a thing like that?" she said, turning her chin away from me.

"That's what I'd like to know."

She turned her face back towards me, the set of her jaw oddly noble and proud. Her eyes sparkled with what I could only think of as a static discharge—the residue of anger and passion, the weight of a hundred convictions. "Walk away," she said. "It's what they do. What they all do. I'll understand."

"I'm going nowhere," I told her.

"Then you're a fool."

"I've never claimed to be anything else." I paused, wondering if I dare risk another step towards her but ultimately deciding against it. "Tell me about the note," I said, as tenderly as I could manage.

"I've told you, I don't know anything about it."

"I don't believe you. You've been following me and... you put that note in my room. Just admit it and I won't ask you anything more."

She didn't trust me on this point—that much was evident in the snooty (and quite sexy) little sniff and the way in which she clenched her jaw. She closed her eyes, shaking her head and smiling bitterly. "You won't ask me anything more?"

"I won't ask you anything more."

"Too kind."

"One of my many failings."

"Do you have an answer for everything?"

I made a point of not replying. She insisted that that was an answer in itself, and I decided that this was one argument I wasn't about to win. She was quick-witted and adept at throwing up obstacles and diversions, but I wasn't going to let her avoid the issue that easily. "It was you, wasn't it?" I said.

Her cheeks flushed and she swallowed hard. She pulled the

cardigan close, wrapping it and her arms around her. Pushing past me hurriedly, almost knocking over a kitchen chair with her hip, I heard her say under her breath, "Yes. Yes, it was me."

Chasing after her, I collided with George in the hallway. He grabbed me by the shoulders, steadying me and preventing me from going any further. Looking back at my escaping friend, he chuckled to himself. "Perfect," he said.

"What?" I tried to push by him, but he held on tightly, his fingers painfully digging into my upper arms.

"Never mind," he said. "That favour."

"What about it?" I couldn't see her anymore. She had either disappeared up the stairs or left by the front door. I gave George a frustrated shove and he pinned me against the wall. His face inches from mine, spittle spattered against my face when he spoke.

"Time for you to do your stuff," he said, whispering threateningly. "Calm down, Price. Jesus, you're uptight." He gave my face a little slap and chuckled. "What is it? The love bug bite you on the arse, did it?"

"Let go of me, George." I tried to sound menacing but it didn't really work. Especially when I tagged please on the end.

"She's always loved your manners," he said, stepping back and brushing me off. "She says to me, George, why can't you be more like Price? And I tell her, Mam, it's your fault. Because that's the reality of the situation. I have her genes. That's why I am the way I am."

"Forget it. I'm not in the mood." I started to walk past him but he caught me by the arm—pulling me back so that he could whisper in my ear.

"Her name's Tara," he told me. "Tara Pearson. She's my cousin and you probably don't stand a snowball in hell's chance. However, you help me out and I'll put in a word for you. How does that suit you?"

"You won't tell her anything embarrassing?"

"That wouldn't exactly count as putting a word in for you, now, would it?" he said. "No, Price, mate, I won't tell her anything embarrassing. I'll make you sound like a god. A saint. By the time

I've finished, she'll think daisies sprout where you shit."

"Roses."

"What?"

"I think roses would be more appropriate."

"Okay. Whatever. She'll think roses sprout where you shit. Better?"

"I'm not sure. I mean horses –"

"Look, do you want me to put a word in for you, or what?"

"Naturally."

"Well shut the fuck up and listen, then." He proceeded to outline what it was he wanted me to do for him—flattering me ad nauseam and throwing in a few childhood memories to sweeten the brew a little. "I just want you to talk to her," he said. "Get her away from Martha. Take her outside. Take her upstairs for a bit. Whatever. Just keep her away from Martha so I can do my magic."

I was tempted to question his use of the word 'magic'. It seemed incongruous, to say the least. However, I felt suddenly quite exhausted—the excitement of finding Tara no doubt taking its toll—and merely nodded obediently and went off in search of Carla Ruiz... but only after George had delivered his final body-blow.

"That isn't the real favour, by the way," he told me.

I rolled my eyes. "Now why doesn't that surprise me?"

"Because you are a bright guy," he said. "For an assistant gardener."

I walked a few steps back towards him—my shoulders feeling as if they were weighed down by the sins of all humanity. "And what if I said you can get stuffed?" I asked him, already knowing the answer.

"Tara."

"Do I need your help with her?"

"Will we ever know?" He leant in close, whispering ominously in my ear. "Is this the kind of chance you wish to take?"

"What do you want me to do?"

It was becoming my mantra, and I hated him for this. I hated him with every fibre of my being, wishing on him every vile illness imaginable, but I hated myself more. I should have had more faith in myself. As I listened to him tell me how he wanted me to help him find Sharon Jones, his own mystery woman, I felt my face flush and the muscles between my shoulder blades tauten as I thought of all the ways in which I could bring this to an end with George. It wouldn't be difficult. Not really. Granted, there would be a little pain. But pain was temporary, and with Tara by my side I was sure I would be more than capable of enduring anything George might throw at me. I could have done it. If I'd really wanted to, I could have brought it all to an end there and then.

Instead of doing that, however, I gave in and said, "Sharon Jones? The girl from next door?"

"Got it in one."

"What do you want to find her for?"

"You'll see soon enough." He patted me on the cheek, winking. "Now," he said. "The matter at hand. Operation Distraction. Move yourself, fuckface."

Sitting at the top of the stars with her almost empty vodka bottle and a forlorn look, Carla Ruiz seemed pleased to see me when I ascended and sat down beside her. She was flushed, her eyes droopy and glazed, but she was nevertheless more alert and cognisant than I ever remembered seeing her. She smiled and patted my leg, moving away from the wall and deliberately bumping her shoulder against mine. A companionable act, and one that immediately put me at my ease.

"I thought I'd see you here sooner or later," she said. "It was written in the stars."

"That I'd find you on the stairs?"

"Nice. I like that. Poetic, but let's just say that you'd find me somewhere. Not necessarily on the stairs, but possibly."

"You look tired."

"Sweet boy, that's just my natural look," she told me. "It takes me hours to get it just right." She laughed and I smiled patiently, wondering just why George had felt it necessary to get me to distract his mother. It seemed fairly obvious that she was quite content to keep out of the way and drink herself into the woodwork.

"I'm sure that isn't true," I said.

Her mood grew darker, however—cavernous and smoky, distorted around the edges. "Oh, you don't know the half of it, Price," she told me. "A constant struggle not to go under... not to show weakness. That's what my life is. That's what all life is. Survival of the fittest—like that Darwin bloke said. Natural election."

"Selection."

"Natural selection. Got to keep fighting all the time or it all just slips away. The whole bloody sorry mess. Not that it would be a great loss." She elbowed me and chuckled. "Would get to see the back of our George. That has to count for something."

"No arguing with that," I said.

Carla studied me long and hard, sitting back to see me a little better. "He's as spineless as I am legless, you know," she finally said, clunking the vodka bottle against her prosthesis to highlight the point. "Scared shitless of me, though he'd never admit it. Knows I can see right through him, and he doesn't like that. I could bring him down..." she clicked her fingers "...like that if I wanted to. And, more to the point, so could anyone, if they set their mind to it. You included."

"He's my friend," I told her. "I don't know that I'd want to bring him down."

"He's not your friend." She blew her cheeks out and made a puffing, dismissive sound. "George's only friend is George, and if you haven't seen that by now, Price, then your eyes are as fucked up as that nose of yours."

"It's not as simple as that," I mumbled.

"Isn't it?"

"I don't know."

Carla placed a gentle hand on my leg. I was pretty sure it was meant to be a maternal gesture, but it was always difficult to tell with the likes of Carla. "Listen, Price," she said. "Don't think I don't know why you're here. He's using you to distract me while he sucks up to Martha—right? Don't lie to me. I can see the answer in your eyes."

I started to at least attempt to explain myself, but she held a finger against my lips. "Sometimes it's easier to just go along with it," she said. "I know. Believe me, I do. But... you want my advice, my dear, sweet boy?"

I nodded, thinking that she was as difficult to resist as her son.

"Leave me here," she said. "I give you my word I won't spoil his little plan. Leave me here and you go and talk to our Tara."

"Why?"

"Because you want to. Because you can."

"I don't know where she is."

"You'll find her."

I was starting to grow tired of George and his family. As far as evenings go, with the exception of meeting Tara, it had been one of the most pointless I ever recalled. Had it not been for the prospect of sitting down and talking to Tara again, just being with her, I would have made the push that Carla had implicitly referred to and got the hell out of there.

As it was, however, I left Carla and went off in search of Tara Pearson—careful not to bump into George or, for that matter, his great-uncle Francis. I half-expected her to have left, even though Carla had assured me that she wouldn't do that without saying goodnight to her, and I didn't like to think what I'd do if she had. I wanted to find out more about why and how she had left me the note—but George, in his attempt to find leverage, had been right. In my way, I had indeed fallen for her, and it was this more than anything else that now motivated me.

She wasn't in the kitchen, but I noticed the door to the back garden was open and, sure enough, I found her out there—sitting on the cracked concrete patio with her back against the wall of the sectional garage, huddled in her raincoat. It was dark and, had it not been for the light that spilled from the kitchen, I probably would have missed her. Even with the light, she was difficult to see... she seemed that inconsequential.

I sat down on the patio beside her—immediately feeling the icy dampness seep into my bones, the cheeks of my arse already protesting.

"You'll get piles," I said. "Sitting on this damp concrete."

She didn't reply, but I thought I saw the faintest flicker of a smile. Emboldened by this a little, I looked up at the stars with her, wishing I'd put my jacket on, and said, "I didn't mean to upset you. In there."

"I know."

"I just wanted to understand. I'm not angry with you."

"I find that hard to believe."

"Believe it."

She moved, rocking from one buttock to the other as she tried to make herself more comfortable, and her leg brushed against mine. I remained stock-still, willing the moment to last, but it was over in the blinking of an eye. The most profound of losses.

"Why do I need to be careful?" I said softly. Every word and gesture had to be measured and calm, so as not to spook her. That was how I felt.

"We all need to be careful," she told me. "It's the principle state of human existence. Have a care, or suffer the multifarious consequences."

"Multifarious."

"You disapprove?"

"On the contrary. An excellent word." Now it was my turn to try to make myself more comfortable; I let my leg brush against hers. She didn't pull away. "It struck me that yours was not a general warning, however." I turned to look at her. "There was something very specific about it."

"You think?"

"I do."

She shrugged and I thought for a moment that she was about to get to her feet. I felt her tense, before relaxing and saying, "You seem nice, that's all. I've seen you with George a few times. From a distance. He isn't nice. You should watch out for him."

It was getting a little monotonous, people telling me stuff about

George that, at some level at least, I already knew. It was vaguely offensive. "I've known George since junior school," I told her. "I'm more than aware of what he's capable of, believe me."

Tara Pearson sighed and laughed quietly. I'd been a little abrupt, and now all I wanted was to put my arm around her, for the conversation to be over and for she and I to just sit quietly, looking up at the stars and waiting for our piles to drop. Tara had other plans, however. She was going to make her point if it killed her.

"My dad died a few years back," she said.

"I'm sorry, I didn't –"

"I'm not telling you for that," she said, snapping. "It happens. People die. That's just the way it is. It hurts, but it's done with... The point is, he needn't have died. He was a steeplejack. Like that bloke on the telly with the flat cap and the steam engine. Heights didn't bother him. He worked with them. He rigged ladders that, when I was little, he told me went all the way to Heaven, and he swung on ropes like he was Tarzan or someone. And he was safe. He was safe because it was his job and he did everything by the book—checking and double-checking."

Emotion started to creep into her voice. A brittle kind of desperation that she had to swallow hard before continuing. I felt for her, and wanted to show it, but this was too personal and I was still too much the stranger.

"Then one day," she said. "Not working. A nice summer's day off and Mam... poor Mam... she asks him to clean the upstairs windows. And it's just a little ladder, Price. Nothing compared to what he's used to. So he's up there. Merrily whistling away to himself. And he sees this mate of his."

She stopped again—and this time I risked it; I took hold of her hand, squeezing it tightly in mine.

And she let me.

I felt her tense. Oddly aware of, I imagined, all the things she had felt that day when—as I knew he inevitably would—her father had toppled from that ladder, I struggled to find something to say... something that would not only ease her pain but would also somehow assure her that I would take care, that whatever happened I would keep my wits about me and not let George involve me in anything dangerous. She inhaled deeply—her breath catching like a sticky zip fastener—and I felt her moving closer to me. The night grew colder, but together we were warm in a way that went beyond heat.

"He got complacent, Price," she told me. "It was just a little ladder and he wasn't at work. He saw his friend. He saw his friend and he waved—and in waving he leant just that little bit too far. Too far and the ladder toppled and he went with it."

She was quiet for what seemed like minutes, but may have only been seconds. I said nothing, merely continued to sit there holding her hand—oddly grateful to her father.

"That's what happens," she finally said. "When you forget what life's really like. When you forget just how dangerous it is. That's what happens. A broken neck. Fractured skull. A hole in the ground, Price."

She resisted, which was pretty much what I'd expected. I'd arrived with George, she insisted. It was only right that I should leave with him. Her reasoning was flawed, she knew this as well as I, and so I persisted, moving in closer to her and telling her that this was just the way it was going to be, and that she should accept it.

We were still in Martha's back garden. I had my jacket, now, having successfully retrieved it from the living room without encountering George or Don Francis, and I held her against the garage wall, delicately, enjoying the closeness and warmth, determined to never let her go. The music had started up in the house, again. A throbbing bass line, wailing voices that sounded crass and synthetic. It was as out of place as The Sex Pistols had been, and I resented its intrusiveness. The night called for Sinatra or, better still, Dean Martin. Something sultry and Italian. Moons hitting eyes like big pizza pies, that kind of thing.

"There's no need," she said, letting me kiss around her words. "I walk it all the time. There's never anyone around at this time of night to bother me."

"It's not going to happen," I told her. "Not now I'm here. I'm walking you home."

"Old fashioned."

"You like that."

"I suppose I do."

"I come from a long line of gentlemen," I told her. "This is something you'll have to get used to. I'll probably even open doors for you."

"Whether I want them opening or not?"

"Exactly."

Her smile was uncertain but infectious. Brushing the hair back from her brow, I told her again that this was just how it was going to be. That she would have to get used to it. "You've been watching out for me," I said. "Now I'm going to do the same for you."

She searched my eyes for the longest time, something shadowy and heady briefly between us, before nodding. "We better get going, then," she said.

Looking back, I see now as I saw then just how alive that night was for the two of us. The air was crisp and invigorating, filling our lungs and hearts with hope and optimism, and our footsteps echoed back at us, rich with encrypted meaning and subtle form. Tara was not beside me as we walked that walk. She was not a separate person, plucky and self-determining. She existed within me, just as I imagined I existed within her. Tara Pearson had been in my room. She had seen the books I read. Whatever she might say to the contrary, she knew me. I felt her, alive, in my very being. It was impossible for her not to feel the same.

"How did you get in?" I asked her as we walked down Holly Avenue towards her mother's house.

A little shrug and a flick of her eyebrows, a shake of her head, as if to tell me that I should know better—the answer was that obvious. "Growing up around the likes of George," she said. "Well. You learn more than just your times tables."

"You picked the lock."

"It wasn't difficult," she said. "Your, erm, security measures leave a lot to be desired. Anyone could have got in there."

"As it would seem they did."

"I'm not anyone," she said.

"You're not?"

"No."

"Who are you, then?"

She thought about this for a few paces and then said, "I'm the woman you'll eventually walk away from. Just like they all do."

I remembered her saying this in Martha's kitchen. I hadn't liked it then, and I liked it even less now.

"I'm going nowhere," I said. "Stop saying that. It's insulting."

"Is it? I'm sorry. I didn't mean it like that."

"Then how did you mean it?"

Pausing beneath a streetlight, she turned to look at me—holding my hand. Her eyes met mine searchingly and confusion furrowed her brow. "You really don't know, do you?" she said.

"No, I don't. And I'm not even sure there's anything to know beyond your unwarranted insecurity."

"Oh there is."

"Well I for one don't see it."

"I don't expect you do," she said, walking again.

Her pace slowed somewhat and I sensed that we were nearing her house. Almost home, she wanted this walk—this evening—to last as long as was humanly possible, even if, as she insisted, I was destined to leave her eventually. The conversation had stalled, but we were nevertheless comfortable with each other. The night was growing colder, and as we stopped outside of what I took to be her front gate, Tara moved closer to me—wishing for warmth even as she shared her own... and I thought that maybe that was all any of us really wanted or required, to be warm with someone who cared. I listened to her breathing and heard my own in oddly sympathetic counterpoint, and in the eerie silence of the street it was as if we were the only two people on the planet. She rested her head on my shoulder and I put my arms around her—tentatively, still not sure if this was something she wanted. There was tension in the muscles around her neck and back—humming and hard—but I felt it gradually dissipate, relaxing along with her as I waited for her to speak, as I knew she would.

"I don't want to move," she told me. "I'm cold and it's late, but I want it to be like this forever."

"It can be."

A quick look up at me. "Can it?"

"If we want it enough."

"And do we?"

I think even then I understood that Tara's had not been an easy path through life. It wasn't difficult for me to believe that more than just the death of her father had impacted on her in a negative way. I didn't need to know the details. Not yet. All I needed to know was that, as she had warned, I had to be careful—careful not to make promises I couldn't keep.

"I think we do," I said.

"You've just met me."

"I feel like I've known you all my life." I smiled, wallowing in the cliché, and she giggled girlishly before putting her head back on my shoulder.

It was all so simple. The world continued to turn—it's trial and turmoil as evident as ever, the ignorance of the masses driving us ever onwards towards annihilation and self-destruction—but we had the answer, a global panacea in the form of an embrace, a kiss, a few kind and amusing words. I was probably not in the best position to judge, but then if love was not the answer, I for the life of me didn't know what was.

"It's silly," she mumbled into the shoulder of my jacket, "but I know exactly what you mean. That's why I... you know, watched you and everything. I only knew you through what George said about you, but it was... well, what you said."

"How long?"

That turn of the head again. Eyes upturned, almost pleadingly. "How long what?"

"Have you been watching me."

"Not long." She pulled away, wiping make-up off my jacket and avoiding my eyes. "A few months, on and off. I know it's weird but... it just made me feel better—knowing that you were out there, that I could watch you and make sure you were okay."

"You should have come up to me and introduced yourself," I told her.

"You'd have thought me odd."

"Maybe," I conceded. "But I like odd."

Our kiss goodnight lingered, and yet it seemed such a fleeting thing. We held onto each other tightly, but it could never be tight enough for either of us. When we parted with the promise that we would see each other the following day, the physical gulf between us seemed daunting and somehow impossible given the way we felt. Tara smiled and blushed, and I moved closer to her again, kissing her once more and making sure she had my mobile number. A hand held against her cool face, I looked at her, still very much aware that I should be careful not to make promises I could not keep.

"I'm not going to walk away from you," I said.

Chapter Four

The following morning was one of those early winter mornings that made it feel good to be alive. The low sun shone through the crystal-clear air, the sky as blue as the movies George was fond of watching, and seemed capable of lifting the spirits of even the most despondent bum on the street. Standing by my window in my shorts and an old t-shirt, I wiped the sleep out of my eyes and grinned down stupidly at the world below, thinking that, yes, it was indeed a stunning day, but that it would be just as beautiful if it was grey and overcast, the rain beating down interminably.

Drinking coffee as I dressed, not wanting to be late for work, I replayed the events of the night before—looking for things I may have missed, some clue that it might all be some great big Cosmic joke. It couldn't be real. This kind of thing just didn't happen to me. I was the man voted most likely to die the sad old git with piss running down his legs and no one to call his own. Love was for others.

However hard I tried, though, I found that I just couldn't dampen my mood—and as I headed out of the door and down the stairs, I had to consciously make an effort to stop grinning. If I turned up at work like this, Tony would assume that I'd slipped my moorings or, worse still—

The thought was interrupted by the ringing and vibrating of the phone in my pocket. I stopped by the side of the road, taking it out and checking the caller ID, hoping that it was Tara but finding, much to my dismay, that it wasn't.

"Tony," I said. "Just on my way. Not late am I?"

I could hear background noise. Voices and a hollow clanking. Footsteps that seemed a little too loud and authoritative.

"No, you're not late," he said quietly. "Not late at all but... I don't need you at the gardens today, Price."

"You don't?" I was rather disappointed, until I realised that this might mean that I could arrange to meet Tara earlier than expected—always assuming she wasn't doing anything.

"No." A pause. A crackle on the line. Someone calling urgently to someone else in the background. "Can you do me a favour? Would you mind?"

I heard something in his voice that made me, for the moment at least, set aside any thoughts I had of meeting Tara. His words were weighty with disquiet and fatigue, and I felt his mood bleed into mine, the silly grin no longer a concern.

"What is it, Tony?" I said.

He inhaled deeply and then let out a shaky breath, saying, "I'm at the hospital with Claudia. She had a fit this morning and fell out of her chair. Hit her head. I'm waiting to hear what they have to say, how she is, you know, and..."

"What do you want me to do?"

"I could do with some company, actually," he told me. "It was horrible, seeing her like that, and... I don't know what they're going to tell me, Price, but I'm fairly sure I don't want to be on my own when I hear it."

"Which hospital are you at?"

He looked unexpectedly old. Fit and tanned from all the outdoor work he did, he nevertheless sat in the casualty waiting area of the Matheson Memorial Hospital like a deflated, husk of a man, staring into a cup of machine coffee and chewing the inside of his mouth. I walked over and sat in the chair beside him, mirroring his posture and waiting for a mythical time, a time when it would feel right to speak.

"I really appreciate this," he said, by way of a greeting.

I nodded. "Have they told you anything, yet?"

He set the coffee on the floor beneath his chair and sat back, rotating his neck and stretching. Only when he had done this did he assume his former position and answer me.

"Been here two-and-a-half-hours," he told me. "And nothing. Not a dicky-bird. I've asked at the desk a few times, but they just keep telling me that the doctor'll be along to see me when they know something. You know what they're like. They've got their job to do and we... it's our job to sit here like good little boys and girls until they can be arsed to share their wisdom and insight with us."

"Would you like me to try?" I said.

Tony patted my knee and smiled sadly. "Nice of you, mate, but it wouldn't do any good. They're the doctors, we're the gardeners. It does to know your place in this world." He chuckled and held his coffee up to me. "Want one? It's good."

"I think I'll pass," I said.

"Probably wise. Not good for the old ticker, too much caffeine."

"Ironic, under the circumstances."

I was just about to distract him with my story of how, ironically, the dreaded party of the night before had actually been something of, as Dad would have said, a 'humdinger', when a young male doctor with a skilfully fixed hairlip and a clipboard came over to us.

He must have been in his mid-twenties but nevertheless seemed highly professional and, more to the point, suitably compassionate. Sitting down in the chair opposite Tony, he rested his forearms on his knees and let his hands and clipboard dangle casually.

"No preamble, Mr. Fraser," he said. "Claudia has a mild concussion, and that's it. The seizure you described was probably just a manifestation of her pre-existing condition but... well, we're going to keep her in to monitor that concussion, and while we do that we'll run a few more tests, just to be sure. I don't think it's anything to worry about, for what it's worth."

"She's going to be all right?" Tony said. I saw the tremor start somewhere around his Adam's apple, quickly spreading to his chin, and I took the coffee from him, just in case emotion overtook him altogether.

"Well," the young doctor said, carefully covering himself, "Claudia has significant problems, carried over from her car crash, Mr. Fraser. You and I both know this. But from what we've so far been able to ascertain, this seizure and the ensuing head injury don't seem to have exacerbated that. The seizure itself may have been a one off, but if not, I'm sure we'll be able to adequately control them with medication. We'll be able to tell you more about that tomorrow."

He smiled sincerely and got to his feet, offering Tony his hand. "You can pop in and spend a few minutes with her, before you go," he said. "The receptionist will tell you where to find her and... well, if there are any questions, don't hesitate. Hunt me down and ask away."

Tony stood, shaking his hand, and I swear by all that I hold sacred that I thought he was going to hug the man—his gratitude oddly disproportionate. The doctor blushed and nodded, retrieving his hand and holding the clipboard protectively to his chest. He was conscientious and sincere, but lines had to be drawn somewhere.

After Tony had spent a few moments with Claudia (something which lifted his mood somewhat and made me wonder just who was dependent on whom in their relationship), he drove us back to the bungalow he shared with her—insisting that the Italian Gardens would have to take care of themselves today.

"I think I'm due a little time off," he said, pouring us a scotch each at the crass little 1970s corner bar in the living room. "And if I'm not there." He raised his glass to me. "No point you being there, now, is there?"

I smiled and sat down in an armchair by the picture window, looking around at the room. It was not in the least what I had expected. Clean and ordered, it was nevertheless cluttered—along the back wall, especially—with about a dozen desktop computers, laptops and related peripherals. Most seemed in good working order, new and high-end, but a couple of the desktops were in pieces by the door.

Tony sat down on the floor in the alcove nearest the television—back against the wall as he sipped his scotch and nodded thoughtfully. "My hobby," he finally explained. "Or one of them, anyway. I build them for people, occasionally, and do a bit of hard drive recovery. That kind of thing. Just makes a change to be doing something that doesn't require a fork and spade." He laughed through his nose and rested his head back against the wall. "Claudia hates them," he told me. "Telephones and televisions are bad enough, she reckons, but computers... they bring people into the home, strangers, and she doesn't like that... values her privacy, does our Claudia."

"I can understand that."

It was far too early in the day for me to be drinking whisky, but I sipped it nonetheless, thinking about Claudia and her accident, Tony's imagined conversations with her and how he believed that she wanted him to help her die. It seemed ludicrous that the two things might somehow be connected and, yet, I couldn't help trying them together—just to see how they fitted. I imagined Tony standing over Claudia, a heavy, blunt object in one hand, hitting her as her eyes pleaded with him. Do it. Don't do it. Help me. Kill me. He hits her once, I thought, and then loses the strength to continue—drenched in remorse and self-loathing.

Truly an utterly preposterous proposition. Tony loved Claudia. If he had indeed decided to carry out her dubious wishes, acting on the faith he had in their highly individual relationship, he would have at least ensured the chosen method was painless and peaceful. Looking at the humming computers, I had no doubt that if Tony had set out to kill her that morning, Claudia would have passed away quietly and would now be in the morgue rather than lying concussed in some hospital ward.

Tony was studying me and I thought for one dreadful moment that my expression had somehow betrayed me. However, he merely nodded at my empty whisky glass and asked me if I wanted another.

I laughed. "How the hell did that happen?"

"All too easily, from what I saw," he said.

"I told myself it was too early."

"Never works. Time loses all meaning when you have a whisky glass in your hand. That's the beauty of it. So. You want another, then, or what?"

"I better not."

Stretching his legs, Tony set his own glass on the fire hearth beside him, looking up at the ceiling. "I owe you," he said— holding up a hand to silence me when I started to contradict him. "There was no one, you see, Price. No one I could call. Not really. Certainly no one who would have done what you did for me."

"I didn't do anything, Tony."

"You were there for me." There was an edge of impatience to his voice. I held my tongue and let him continue. "They all drifted away," he told me. "After her accident. Friends, family—they just... I don't know... they saw how I was living with her and... they didn't think it was right. The two of us sharing a bed, I mean. They told me. They said, 'She can't say no, Tony, so you can't ever assume that she's saying yes.' And I saw their point. I really did. But they... they could never understand how connected we are, Price, so... I suppose I let them drift, really. Building a relationship of this kind is hard enough without dissent."

I remembered that day on Lovers' Leap. The look Claudia had given me while Tony had still had his back to her. Had there been intelligence there? Had there been knowing? The arguments against his relationship with Claudia were not new to me. I, after all, had had similar thoughts myself. But that look—if it were real—suggested to me that Claudia could possibly communicate, and if that were indeed the case I certainly didn't know what to make of this at all.

"Have you got someone, Price?" Tony suddenly asked me. "Someone special." He grinned, a mischievous glint in his eye. "A boy or girl to curl up with in front of the fire?"

Setting my doubts and questions momentarily aside, I said, smiling at the returning memories of the night before, "A girl. Yes. I think so."

"You think so?"

"We've only just met."

I told Tony all about the night before, leaving out the bit about how she had broken into my room and left me the note—not to mention the various eccentricities of George's family. Comfortable with him, I had no problem being truthful about how I felt for Tara, how it had been immediate and complete... something I hadn't experienced before, not on this level. All through my heartfelt outpouring, Tony sat there on the floor, regarding me earnestly as I told him how we hadn't wanted to leave each other when the time had finally come to say goodnight.

"It was like," I said. "I don't know. These things can't be put into words. But. You know. We weren't two people. We were, but we weren't. It was just us, not Price and Tara. Us. A single unit and for a minute—it didn't last long, but it sealed the moment... sealed everything—briefly, nothing could touch us. That's how it seemed."

"Nice feeling," Tony said. He didn't have to say anything else; I knew he was more than familiar with it. It drove and shaped him—fashioned the finer points of his life in ways that nothing else could. When the world had turned against he and Claudia, it had been this that had kept him going—this that had assured his love and commitment, highlighted the salvation he no doubt saw in her. Seeing it and feeling it, he had held on to it determinedly, unwilling to ever let it go. A lifebelt. A reason to keep going. That feeling.

When I had finally finished, the silence embarrassed me. I'd said too much. Tony was a relative stranger—I had to keep reminding myself of that—and while it was true that our friendship was growing, in some ways at least, I now saw just how presumptuous I had been. He didn't need this. He didn't need to have to listen to some love struck old fool who should have known better, not when the woman he loved was concussed in a hospital bed.

I started to apologise, but Tony held up a big hand, smiling. "Don't," he said. "It's refreshing to hear someone talk so openly about how they feel."

"Maybe—but you don't want to be listening to me waffling on like this. Not today."

"I've waffled on enough to you," he told me. "I don't see why I shouldn't have a little of my own medicine now and then." He folded his leg under him, trying to find a more comfortable position. "And apart from that, it was a pleasant story. Just what I needed to hear, truth be known. Something hopeful and uplifting." He finished his scotch and then added, "She is obviously very special. Don't let her get away, Price. Whatever you do, don't let her get away."

I returned home at what was now becoming my regular 'knocking off time' to find Tara sitting on the doorstep, waiting for me.

She looked waif-like in her raincoat and wellies, as small as she could make herself with her head low and her arms wrapped around her waist. I noticed she was wearing a little make-up, however. Her lips a delicate shade of pink, her eyes a little darker than I remembered. When she spotted me and stood, I saw that her auburn hair was tied back. It made her neck look longer.

I kissed her and said, smiling, "You should have let yourself in."

"I didn't like to. It seemed wrong—now that we know each other."

"I'll get you a key cut."

It was raining again. She moved in close, seeking inadequate shelter. "Isn't it a bit early for that?" she said.

I opened the door and started leading her up the stairs. "I'll get you a key cut," I repeated.

It was good to be back 'home'. The bedsit was still grotty and cramped, damp and, at times, pretty bloody dire, but it was a relief to return to it after a day spent with Tony—and doubly so now that Tara was with me. I closed the door and stood with my back against it for a moment while Tara made herself comfortable on the bed, picking up a copy of Anna Karenina that she found on the floor and leafing through it. Everything seemed unusually quiet.

Cut off and distant. Just how I wanted it to be. As the rain started to fall with greater urgency outside, the world grew darker, and I felt the sense of seclusion deepen. It was like the night before, only more intense. We were all there was. The closing of the door had been the beginning.

"You have a depressing taste in books," Tara said, snapping me out of my reverie. I sat down on the bed beside her, taking the book. "Don't you have anything more cheery? Something that'll give you a bit of a giggle. Terry Pratchett—he's funny."

I turned to a random page and read a passage some previous owner had underlined in pencil. And death, as the sole means of reviving love for herself in his heart, of punishing him, and of gaining the victory in that contest which an evil spirit in her heart was waging against him, presented itself clearly and vividly to her.

Tossing it over my shoulder, I said, "It made me feel better to read about people who had a rougher deal than me. I think. Or maybe I just liked to wallow."

"Nice tense."

"Thank you."

"It speaks of a brighter tomorrow."

"The triumph of optimism over pessimism." I moved in closer.

"Noble and true." Tara pulled away, splayed fingers on my chest. "You weren't planning on kissing me, were you?"

"Well, actually, yes, I was. Why?"

"I was kind of hoping we could have something to eat, first. I'm starving."

"Food."

"Yes," she said with mock patience. "That's what I normally eat."

"You don't fancy, you know, living on love?"

"Not just yet."

"It's that or cream of tomato soup."

She was loving every minute of this, and I must admit, I wasn't exactly hating it myself. I had spent a lifetime longing for these teasing exchanges, without ever realising it.

"The cream of tomato will be just fine," she said, smiling.

Obediently, I got up and started on the soup—stealing the odd glance at her over my shoulder as I opened the tin and poured it into a bowl. I still couldn't quite believe my luck. It could so easily never have happened. If I had just had the necessary gumption to say no to George—or if I had never been his friend at all—Tara might never have come into my life. It really was that simple, and once I'd put the soup in the microwave, I turned and watched her silently as she perused my collection of second-hand books.

My mother had once told me, one dreary Sunday afternoon of Battenburg cake, sweet tea and torrential rain, that there was someone 'out there' for everyone. She'd said this in the way of, I suspect, all mothers to hopeless cause sons—more as an attempt at reassuring herself than anything else. I had sat patiently and nodded politely, close to telling her just how wrong I thought she was, how naïve she seemed and how I knew deep down that I had been brought into this world as an example... an example of just how extreme loneliness could really be. I was the one at whom other mothers would one day point. The dribbling old eccentric with flies in his hair. "Do you want to end up like him?" They would say as I growled and slapped at my invisible demons. "Do you want to die on a commode with only strangers to clean you up and bury you?" But I had said none of this to my mother. Why? Simply, she didn't deserve it. She had tried. She had encouraged. When I had wanted to stay at home, alone, and watch The Six Million Dollar Man on telly as a boy, it had been she who had talked me into joining the Boy Scouts—quickly rethinking it and taking me along to the local youth club, instead, because there were girls there as well as boys. That it had all been an unprecedented disaster had not been her fault. She had made the effort. Looking at me, she had seen something in me that clearly had not revealed itself in any mirror that I'd looked into, and she had tried in vain to do something about it.

A twelve-year-old George had told me that it was a 'pre-emptive strike' because she knew I was queer and just couldn't bear the thought of me with some sweaty bloke's cock up my arse. And maybe there was an element of truth to that. Doubts and questions concerning my Lee Majors obsession and my reluctance to watch Charlie's Angels—I don't know. But whatever her motives, I had certainly known as we had passed around the Battenburg that I could not say the things I thought. I could not hurt her because, as doomed to bachelordom as I imagined myself to be, she had given it her best shot and tried to turn me into a social butterfly.

Tara was frowning at me, a copy of Steinbeck's *Of Mice and Men* in her lap. She had moved up the bed and was now sitting with her back to the headboard. She looked comfortable. At home.

"Penny for them," she said.

"I was just thinking how quickly things can change."

As we ate our soup, side-by-side on the bed with a Ray LaMontagne CD playing, Tara marvelled at the fact that I had added some curry powder and lots of salt to mine. She pulled a disgusted, just-stepped-in-shit face and told me that I needed my head looking at. "That's got to ruin the taste, surely," she said.

I shrugged and slurped up another spoonful. "Wouldn't know," I said. "But at least this way I can taste something. My Anosmia means I don't get the flavour as well as most people."

"Your whatosmia?" I caught a crackle of concern, a slight deepening of tone. She set her bowl on the floor by the bed and jiggled about so that she could more comfortably face me.

I had thought she had known. George was such a dyed-in-the-wool big mouth that it seemed inevitable that he would have mentioned it to her—mentioned it and then went into the my dog's got no nose joke... endlessly.

"Anosmia," I told her. "I can't smell things. Never have. It means... well, it affects my taste, too. Most flavours just don't get through."

"You can't smell anything?"

"That's right."

"Nothing at all?"

I smiled, amused by her reaction. "Nothing at all."

Tara stared off into space, a dimple-like crease between her grown-out eyebrows. Sucking her bottom lip, she sat back and let her hands rest in her lap as she thought this through. My amusement turned to anxiety as I waited. I watched her absorbing this new information, and I imagined that this was how the end was destined to begin. One simple little olfactory inadequacy and her idea of me would be turned on its head. She would study and she would draw conclusions—and the imperfect me would be left alone once again to prove Mam wrong.

But instead of getting up and walking out of the door, Tara looked at me earnestly and said, "Do you believe in God, Price?"

This caught me with my theological pants down. I didn't know how to answer her for what I considered to be two very good reasons: one, after all these years, I still hadn't made up my mind; and, two, I didn't know whether Tara was religious. I didn't want to proclaim myself an atheist if she was a staunch Catholic, and so I said, "I don't... maybe... well, you know. Do you?"

Tara sat quietly, watching me sip my soup, awaiting her answer. I noticed that she had this thing she did when mulling over something especially demanding. Her hands in her lap, she methodically ran the index finger of her right hand over the edges of the fingernails of her left, as if feeling for imperfections and rough corners. There was something fascinating about it—I'd never seen anyone do anything quite like it—and as she watched me, I watched her... a cosy balance, an observational yin and yang.

"I don't know," she finally said. "I like to think there might be. It's comforting. But... no, I don't think for one minute that there is a god. Not really."

"So why did you ask the question?" I said.

"It's just that sometimes something comes along that makes you wonder." She smiled and took my empty bowl from me, setting it on the floor with her own. Moving in closer, she linked my arm and rested her head on my shoulder. "Last night. At Martha's. I thought you were going to be really horrible to me. After what I did and everything. I deserved it because... whatever my intentions, coming in here wasn't the right thing to do. But you weren't horrible to me, at all, were you?"

"I like to think not," I said.

"You weren't," she insisted. "You were as nice as pie. And now..." she teetered on the brink of something I could only just sense, "... this," she said, pulling away somewhat, even as she held me more tightly. "It's all just so unexpected."

I thought of my mother, again—how I now saw that I possibly owed her a huge apology—and let my head rest against Tara's, thinking that it would all come in time. Whatever there was to be said would be shared, but there was no immediate urgency. Now was all that mattered. Now, with food in our bellies and love in our hearts.

Later, side-by-side on the bed—still fully clothed but kissing and unbuttoning—she asked me about my day. "Did you work up a sweat?" she said.

I laughed. "You really don't want to know," I told her—not wanting to think about Claudia and Tony. Not at a wonderful time like this.

"Yes I do," she said, "or I wouldn't have asked."

Reluctantly, I told her all about them—the dedication and slightly disturbing love, the degree of disability and what had happened earlier that day. She listened intently, her nose inches from mine as I filled in the details, and by the time I had finished we had stopped our kissing and unbuttoning altogether. A development I definitely didn't like.

I took hold of her hand and placed it on my shirt button, but still she didn't take the hint.

"That kind of altruism," she said. "That kind of altruism usually conceals a complexly layered and selfish agenda."

"You think."

"Dunno," she said, grinning. "He seems nice enough, I suppose. This Tony. But... I wouldn't like him looking after me. From what you've told me of him."

"Why not?"

"He just doesn't strike me as being all that well balanced. I mean, all that stuff about the imagined conversations he has with her. We all do stuff like that to one degree or another. It's the way we are made. But the completeness of his belief in it... that's just unnerving."

I hadn't mentioned the bit about how Tony believed that Claudia had 'asked' him to help her die, and this omission now seemed a bad start to what promised to be a good relationship, so I did the only thing I could in good conscience do and told her all about it.

"You think this morning was...?" she said, once I'd finished.

I shook my head quickly. "No... No, I don't. I think if Tony was going to do a thing like that—and that's a big if—if he was going to do something like that he'd definitely find a kinder way of doing it."

"Even if that meant that it didn't look like an accident?" she said.

It was a good point, and one that hadn't fully occurred to me. I laid there beside her, staring into her hazel eyes (which, in this light, seemed flecked with sparks of emerald, reminding me of the mint cracknel I used to eat as a boy), and thought through what she had said before answering—holding her hand, enjoying her warmth and the oddly reassuring feeling of having someone there with me, someone to question and, even, cast doubt.

I held off from answering her for as long as I could, determined to savour the moment, but eventually said, "I'd never thought of it like that."

"So you think it's a possibility?"

"Anything's possible."

"But not likely."

"I don't think so." I wove my fingers in and out of hers, and she smiled. "I don't know. It would be such a big thing to Tony, being without her. I just can't see him being all that concerned about covering it up. Always assuming he decided it was something he had to do in the first place."

"What if it isn't real, though?" she said.

"What if what isn't real?"

"His love for her. What if there's something else behind it?"

"Like what?"

"I don't know but..." She paused, gathering her thoughts before continuing. "You haven't known him all that long—and all you do know about his and Claudia's life is what he's told you. Maybe there's more to their situation than he's letting on."

Having seen Claudia and Tony together, the way in which he looked after her and saw to it that all her needs were catered for, I couldn't help but feel that Tara had this all wrong. Whatever—if anything—was going on between them, I felt certain that his love for her, however obsessively dangerous, was sincere and complete. I didn't really want to talk about this anymore, though. We had a whole evening ahead of us, one with which we could do anything we chose. The last thing I wanted was to spend it talking about Tony and Claudia.

"Then what do you want to talk about?" Tara said.

"Who says we have to talk?"

"You have other things on your mind?"

I nodded, smiling, running the backs of my fingers across her cheek and down her neck. Tara returned my smile and rolled her face into my caress—catlike and appreciative—asking me just what my plans were, and saying that she hoped they were honourable. Giving her my word that she would be treated with the utmost respect and that my only wish was for her to be happy and fulfilled, I slowly undressed her, stopping every once in a while to kiss or caress, taste and nibble. Tara a little tense, more insecurity creeping in the further we proceeded, she nevertheless responded—showing me what she liked, guiding me with a touch of her hand, a gentle nod. Our hands between her legs, waxed smooth, honey-warm and receptive, she showed me precisely where to place my fingers, how to gently rock and rub. But as we progressed she stopped me, pulling away from my erection, not with distaste or fear, but rather with a look of sympathy and love.

"We will," she said softly. "Just not yet, Price. I'm not quite ready." I was about to protest, but I stopped myself. I wanted her. I wanted her in every conceivable way—physical and spiritual— but more than anything I needed her to want the same things as me.

"I love you," I told her—and it was just a statement of fact, nothing more.

"Do you?"

"You know I do."

She briefly considered this while my fingers continued to play, and then nodded. "It doesn't mean we can't do everything else," she told me.

Afterwards, we lay in each others' arms, staring up at the ceiling, talking quietly. I'd pulled the duvet over us, and now Tara snuggled in—an excited child, content with her place in the world. I kissed her on the forehead, remembering how she had got the hiccups after she had come, and I smiled. My mother would have told her she was thriving. It was her pat response anytime anyone got the hiccups. "You're thriving, love," she would say, and I would groan at the predictability of it all. Now, however, it seemed curiously apt, and not a little flattering—and I wanted it to always be this way. It was how it was meant to be. I would love Tara and make her come, and she would get the hiccups.

You're thriving, love.

"Promise not to get spooked," Tara suddenly said.

"Halloween's still a week away."

"Not that kind of spooked."

"Then?"

"I don't want to scare you off."

I pulled away from her a little so that I could more easily see her face. Her features were flat and grave, her mouth open a little, as if awaiting a kiss. Her legs moved restlessly and she looked away, embarrassed.

"You used to be a man." This was intended as a joke, but then I realised that it was as real as any other possibility. It had never happened to me before but I was fairly sure that it must happen quite often. Probably every day. Or night. In some parts of the country. "You didn't, did you?" I asked.

Tara smiled. "No, I bloody well didn't." She slapped me on the chest. "Now shut up. There's something I want to ask you."

"It's not a favour, is it?"

"No, it's not."

"It's just that I've had a lot of favours asked of me recently and I'm really not sure –"

"It's not a favour, Price."

Her voice had dropped an octave and I deduced that now was probably a good time to stop going on about favours.

"Ask away," I said.

"I was wondering." She looked a little flushed. "I was wondering if you'd like to come round for Sunday lunch on..."

"Sunday?"

Again she smiled. I hoped I'd never lose my fascination with such a basic show of emotion. It said so much about her—revealed both her joy and that hint of sadness beneath the surface.

"Yes, Sunday," she said.

"Sunday coming?"

Tara nodded, eyes flicking from left to right as she tried to read my features. "It'll just be me, you and Mam," she said. "No big deal. It's always nice and relaxed. Informal. But she does a lovely roast and... well, you look as if you could do with a good feed."

"Are you implying that I'm puny?"

"I'm saying a diet of baked beans and spiced up tomato soup isn't good for you. Yes, I am implying you're puny."

"I prefer the term 'wiry'," I told her.

"I'm sure you do," she said. "So, are you coming, then, or what?"

I'd never been invited home to meet a girlfriend's mother before—a realisation that I found both startling and rather depressing—and the prospect was unnerving, to say the least.

"Isn't it a bit early?" I said.

Tara, very delicately, reminded me of what we'd just been doing, the frantic kissing and touching, and the hiccups that had followed. Moving in closer to me, her breath warm on my face, she told me that I would enjoy it—that her mother was nothing like the rest of the family. She was normal. "You ever watch *The Munsters* when you were a kid?" she said, and I nodded. "You know the cousin or whoever she is? Marilyn? The girl who lives with them? That's my mother. Or that's who she's like, anyway. The family thinks she's odd, everyone else thinks she's utterly ordinary and nice."

"Just like you?" I said, holding her close.

"Just like me." She moved her arm so that I could put mine around her. I noticed how sweaty she was as my hand brushed her armpit and thought that maybe she was too warm. Before I could say anything, however, she said, "So are you coming, then, or what?"

My voice soft, I said, "Absolutely."

Chapter Five

We were walking down a long, seemingly endless path, rising woodland on either side, the paradoxically beautiful white flowers of Deadly Nightshade visible in among the undergrowth. Our only light was a gibbous moon, a little too stark, unforgiving in the world of shadow it revealed around us, and as we walked, silently and with an odd connection, I felt the world again slipping away from me, even as the woodland closed in on us. High up somewhere, a breeze soughed through unseen trees—trees that could have been thousands of miles away in some threatened rainforest, struggling in the alien state of destructive mortals—and I felt it like dread in the pit of my stomach. Heavy and torrid, an element frighteningly alone... cut off from its brothers and sisters as it lived out its fleeting life in self-imposed exile. I heard a murmur—gods moaning in their slumber—and realised that I could smell rain on the breeze. I could smell rain. I could smell. Smell.... That couldn't be right and, yet, I could. The unexpected, wholly new sensation lifted my spirits; I stopped and turned Tara to face me, grinning idiotically.

I drew her closer to me, burying my face in her hair, inhaling her delicate perfume. I smelled what I imagined were roses, the cold night air... remnants of the time we had spent together in my bed. My purpose was clear. To inhale and keep inhaling. To understand her through smell. To grasp the meaning behind subtle cipher and nuance. The trees closing in overhead, the moon blotted out by cloud, I understood why my mother had tried so hard when I had been a boy. Holding flowers to my nose and making me breathe in. Primroses and violets paraded before me, carnations and a highly perfumed rose. I returned to Tara's hair, the finer strands tickling my nose... tickling... tickling...

I pulled awake with a start, disoriented, the warm form in the bed beside me a shock... a surprise... a delight. Her hair was in my face, but I was disappointed to realise that I couldn't smell it. Tara fed my four remaining senses. Just by being asleep in my bed, quietly snoring, she brought me to life. I listened and watched, I carefully touched and tasted. But at that moment, I wanted the dream back. I wanted her smells to come again; at the very least, I wanted the memory of those smells.

Tara stirred in her sleep, rubbing against me. A wave of warmth swept up from beneath the duvet, and I wondered what it would be like to smell it as well as feel it. What did we smell like alone? What did we smell like together?

I had to be grateful for what I had, I told myself, as I had so many times in the past. The difference was, however, that this time it actually seemed to work. I counted my blessings and they added up to a hell of a lot more than they had a couple of days ago. The sum total was Tara, plain and simple, and when she stirred again, I had to stop myself from waking and telling her.

I saw now that her inviting me to Sunday lunch with her and her mother had been the right thing to do. We had solved something for each other—I didn't quite know what, but that much, at least, was obvious. We neither of us wanted this to end. I was sure of that. But maybe for Tara it was especially important that we formalise what we had together, that we make it public in some way. This was her way, I saw, of making it more difficult for me to walk away from her—and I couldn't resent her for that..

Nestling in closer to her, I ran a hand over her hair and thought of my own parents. I didn't see them anywhere near as often as I should. Something that, quite frankly, was just fine by me. It was true that they had helped me over the years - without their support I probably wouldn't have made it through some of the tougher times. But it was also true that I too often got from them a sense of my own failings. Dad's casual insistence that my life had all but fallen down the back of the settee and Mam's driving urge to make things better. With Tara on my arm, however, I imagined that it would be somehow different—and I knew that I wasn't going to be able to hold off parading her in front of them for too long. I smiled to myself, slipping my hand between Tara's legs, relishing that damp warmth as I thought about how they would receive her.

Imagining their initial suspicion (someone apparently foolish enough to take up with me must be up to something, surely), I saw how they would quickly warm to her—the two of them fussing endlessly, Dad reeling out his quirky (and bad) jokes, Mam telling him to stop being silly. And all the while I would sit there on the settee, smiling my self-satisfied smile and wondering when I was going to wake up. There would be hope. Indeed, there already was, but this would be of a breed only imagined prior to this. Huge and overwhelming, elevating and glowing.

"Did I give you permission to do that?" Sleepy and clearly content, Tara opened her eyes slightly and squinted at me.

"My hand was cold," I said, smiling through the darkness at her.

"You could have put it between your own legs." Her protestations were just all part of the beautiful game.

"That wouldn't have been as much fun." I wiggled my fingers and she responded by chuckling and pushing into them. "See? What did I tell you?"

"I was having a nice dream," she told me, doing her best to sound stern and disapproving. "You woke me from it."

"This is a better dream."

"You can guarantee that?"

I kissed her, rolling her onto her back and covering half of her body with mine. "Satisfaction or your money back."

"I'm paying for this?"

"Only if you want to."

Caressing my face, Tara pulled me down into another kiss— keeping me there for a long time, her tongue skilled and, it seemed, newly liberated. Aroused, I pushed against her and she moved her leg, making it known to me with this one gesture, with this yielding, that it was all right, that this was what she wanted, too. I had to be certain, though. I didn't want to force her, however subtly. Thinking of Tony and Claudia, I believed that a silent yes could never be taken for granted.

"Are you sure?" I said, and she nodded, kissing me once more.

"I couldn't be more sure if—"

I thought for a moment that the roof was falling in. I felt more than heard a loud banging, its heavy, urgent bass reverberating in my gut, and I jumped out of bed quickly, slapping at the wall for the light switch. Finally finding it, I turned it on and looked over at Tara; she was huddled with the duvet beneath her chin, an annoyed frown and tightly clenched jaw.

Again, the banging came—someone thumping heavily at my door. I stepped away from it, feeling dislocated and oddly confused. It had never done this before. It was a good door. A well behaved door. It opened. It closed. It locked and unlocked.

"Are you going to open it, then?" Tara said, bringing me back to my senses.

"It's the early hours of the morning," I whispered. "It could be anyone."

Tara rolled her eyes and then said, very loudly, "Who's there?"

Silence from the other side of the door. Silence and, more than that, complete stillness. I waited, stomach gurgling with expectation and, I have to admit, fear. I had a bad feeling about this. Phone calls and visitors in the middle of the night always meant bad news.

"Price?" The voice, immediately recognisable, was uncharacteristically unsure of itself. I felt my shoulders sag with both relief and disappointment. Mine and Tara's night together was all but over.

I looked at her and she shrugged her shoulders, resigned. "You better let him in," she said. "He isn't going to go away."

"I could tell him to fuck off. Come back in the morning."

"Could you?"

She had a point. Even if I did manage to say something like that to George, there was no guarantee that he would take any notice. In fact, it was far more likely that he would completely disregard what I said. If George wanted to be in, he would be in. He wasn't about to let a little thing like a door come between him and a 'friend'.

Tentatively, I opened the door and, sure enough, George came barging in like a bargain-hunter at the sales, elbowing me aside and plonking himself down on the end of the bed.

"Fuck," he said. "Fuck, fuck, fuck. I thought you were going to keep me out there all night. Thought I was going to have to break the fucking door down. Do you know... do you know how not-nice that is, Price?"

I didn't especially feel like tip-toeing around him. He sat on the end of my bed—the bed I had only moments before been sharing with Tara—staring up at me with that petulant look of his, all blood and piss, and I felt an overwhelming urge to stamp my authority on this conversation. Very much aware of Tara watching me extremely closely, I knew that I couldn't merely stand here and take whatever it was that he thought he could say to me. It wasn't an honour thing. It was nothing as grand or noble as that. Looking at George, it was more that I wanted to make up for lost time. With Tara by my side, I didn't feel stronger or braver—just suddenly quite tired by and disappointed in this whole bleak interdependency I shared with George. I wasn't all that convinced that it would end tonight, but end it most certainly must.

"Do you know how late it is?" I said. "You need to get it into that bloody thick head of yours, George, you can't just come around here any time you like. Some of us have work in the morning."

George held up a finger to silence me. Totally disregarding what I had just said, it seemed, he frowned, sniffing the air like a tracker in the wild waiting for rain. "Is that bullshit?" he said. "Ah. No." He turned to Tara. "It's you, cousin, dear."

"Oh, you crack me up," she told him.

"Pleased to hear it, my favourite little bint. You been letting old Pricey snuffle around your snatch, then, have you?" He looked back at me, grinning lecherously. "Finally got the taste of minge on your lips, have you mate? After all these years. Tell me, was she good? Did she, you know, give as good as she got? 'Cause the way I hear it, she's a wee bit on the frigid side. Nothing been up that old whizzoo of hers since... oh, when was it, Tara, love? Your eighteenth birthday party? Something like that, right? You see, Price, we're talking ugly duckling scenario. Tara was the ugly duckling that turned overnight into a wonderful, big fat ugly duck—and, you know, it was a bit like that film, now what was it called?"

I took a swing at him and caught him square on the jaw. He saw it coming and pulled away as best he could, but it still held more force than he was able to contend with. It rocked him and he put out a hand to steady himself, missing the edge of the bed and toppling to the floor. Tara shouted to me to stop, but I'd already grabbed George by the shoulders and was dragging him to his feet, intending to spin him around and thump him a couple more times. I should have known better, though. Past experience should have taught me something.

George came out of his crouch swinging, catching me hard in the stomach and quickly following up with a sharp slap to the ear. Winded and partially deaf, my balance suddenly precarious and my head buzzing, static-like and organic, I tried to retaliate, but couldn't, succumbing to the vertigo and nausea, crumbling to the bed where Tara held onto me, hurling abuse at George that I only half heard, such was my discomposure.

"He fucking hit me first," I heard George say as I slowly regained my senses. "What do you expect me to do? Lay there and let him beat me to a fucking pulp?"

"You provoked him," Tara said. "You went on and fucking on until he had no other option."

"I was just having a laugh."

"Jesus, George, you are such a prick."

"Don't push it, Tara."

Lifting my head, doing my best to ignore the nausea, I looked him squarely in the eye—hoping I appeared a little more intimidating than I felt. "Leave her alone, George," I said. "Leave her alone or I swear I'll take another pop at you."

"Shitting myself, mate." He took a step towards me and I flinched. Instead of hitting me again, however, George merely sat down on the bed beside me, looking suddenly depleted, head low and shoulders sagging. "Look," he said, his tone uncharacteristically conciliatory. "Maybe I was a little out of line."

"Maybe?" I said.

"A little?" Tara added.

"Okay, okay," he admitted—rather too willingly for my liking. "I was a lot out of line. I shouldn't have said what I said. I was being a complete and utter twat and all I can do is apologise."

Tara and I exchanged puzzled glances. George seemed oblivious, however. Back on his feet, he paced from one end of the room to the other as he continued, lighting up a cigarette and scratching anxiously at his neck.

"You see," he said. "It's just that... I've had a lot on my mind. I know that doesn't excuse my behaviour but... that's just... well, that's just the way it is. Things prey on my mind and I act like a twat."

"Because you're such a sensitive soul," I said. Tara caught the sardonic tone. George seemed to miss it entirely.

"That's it exactly," George exclaimed, excited at once more having—as he saw it—an apparent ally.

Tara, readjusting the sheet she had wrapped around herself, sniffed haughtily. "I like the way he says act like a twat," she told me.

"He uses the Method," I explained.

George stopped his pacing and glowered at us. I felt another wave of nausea and vertigo claustrophobically crowding in on me. "Are you two taking the piss?" he said, menacingly.

Tara shook her head quickly and I—feeling that a similar action on my part might not be all that wise under the circumstances—mumbled a quiet little "no", looking down at the floor and hoping I didn't look as cowardly as I imagined.

"Good," he said, pacing and smoking again. "Because I have things to say tonight. Important things. And I really don't need people taking the piss out of me."

"What have you got to say?" I asked him.

If I had to pick a moment when it all started to change, when everything I had previously known became something else entirely—familiar faces becoming doubtful things—I suppose this was it.

George stood before us, cigarette pinched between fingers and thumb—squinting as he drew on it, reminding me of the spiv out of Dad's Army. All he needed was a pencil moustache and a few pair of nylons to complete the picture. He went to the sink, drinking water from the tap before wiping his mouth on his sleeve and walking back to us.

"I have information on her," he said, a little too cryptically for my liking. I thought for a moment that he meant Tara and, when I felt her stiffen beside me, I realised she was thinking along similar lines. George was a bastard, I thought. But was he really enough of a bastard to invent things about Tara to make her a less attractive prospect to me? Of course he was.

"Information on whom?" Tara asked.

He peered at her, still squinting through the cigarette smoke. She shouldn't have been here, I realised. That was what he was thinking. She shouldn't have been here and he had to assess just how wise it was to discuss this in front of her. I waited to see what his decision would be, the vertigo and nausea gradually subsiding even as my sense of dread turned to a bilious lump in the pit of my stomach.

"Not that it's any of your business," he said to her, before turning to me, "but I think I know the whereabouts of Sharon Jones. The girl I was telling you about."

"Who?" Tara said.

He ignored her, speaking directly to me. "The girl I was telling you about," he said. "You remember?"

Turning to Tara, I said, "George had this walking, talking wet-dream when he was a kid. Used to live next door to Martha. She stripped and played with herself for him at her bedroom window while he had a good wank in Martha's spare bedroom. Isn't that right, George?" I said, grinning.

"My dog's got no nose," he said to me, before addressing Tara. "How does it smell, cousin dear?" he added.

She scowled at him and I felt her tense even more. I thought she was getting ready to strike—My Little Cobra—and I put a hand on her arm, just in case. She inhaled deeply, her upper lip quivering with pressure-cooker rage, but her only response was to rearrange the sheet she was wearing again and stare at the floor.

"What's this got to do with me?" I said.

"You were going to help me find her."

"And now you've found her. So, like I say, what's this got to do with me?"

George steepled his eyebrows with mock-disappointment. Squatting down before me, he pulled on the cigarette before blowing smoke in my face. I coughed and waved it away, a fresh bubble of acidic nausea assaulting me again.

"Pricey, Pricey, Pricey," he said. "What are we going to do with you?"

"Leave me to get some sleep?" I ventured.

"Sleep? At a time like this? You know—and I've probably said this to you before—for an intelligent bloke, you can be right bloody thick, at times. No, I'll tell you what we are going to do, shall I?"

"Leave him out of this, George," Tara said. "Whatever you're up to, just bloody well leave him out of it."

His smile fell away. "Now might be a good time for you to shut the fuck up, Stinky," he said to her.

"Lay so much as one finger on her, George, and I swear I'll –"

"You'll what?" he snapped. I started to tell him, stuttering my way through a very unimpressive series of warnings and qualifications, but he interrupted with a wave of a hand and a nonchalant flick of the head. "Spare me," he said. "It doesn't matter. It's all academic, anyway, because I'm not going to need to do anything like that. Am I? No. No, of course I'm not—because tomorrow... well, later today, actually, you're going to come along with me, aren't you?"

"I have to work," I told him. "I can't go with you anywhere."

George gave me that steepled-eyebrow disappointed look, again—sitting back on his heels and stubbing out his cigarette on my bedside table. "As I see it," he said. "You have two options. You can either ask for the day off or, by way of a pre-emptive strike—because you know he won't put up with your lousy work habits for too long—tell him to stick his fucking job. If it were me, I'd go for the second option. But that's just me. Either way, you're going to meet me at my place later today and we are off on a little daytrip, you and me."

"Where to?" I said, already resigned to the fact that I would go with him, whether Tony gave me the day off or not.

George grinned victoriously and got to his feet. Holding me by the face, he kissed me loudly on the forehead and then slapped me on the cheeks—just to show that he was still a man, in spite of the kiss. Just to show that he was still the man.

"You and me," he said. "We're off for a day in the country."

After George had left, Tara and I sat together in bed, silently and with a complete sense of numbness, an odd isolation. I'd lost track of time while George had been with us and, when I looked at the clock, I saw that it was four in the morning. I didn't know if I should be surprised by this, or, even, why I should be surprised. George, I imagined, existed outside of time. I'd always known that he played by different rules to the rest of us, so why should it be any different for the laws of physics? He came and went as he saw fit, with a total disregard for the patterns and regimes of the lives of others, and this impacted in ways that weren't always obvious, that couldn't easily be quantified or explained. Sitting there with Tara, knowing I should say something but at a complete loss, I struggled to make sense of this. I had resisted. I had said no. Hell, I had even hit him. And, yet, here I was, once more tied into some situation that I wanted nothing to do with. How on earth had that happened?

"You don't need to worry about me," Tara finally said, her voice broken and uncertain. "If he said something when you were seeing him out, said he'd hurt me or something like that if you didn't help him... if he did, you don't need to worry. I can take care of myself where he's concerned."

"He never said anything," I lied.

"Yes he did. You're forgetting, I know him as well as you. Better, maybe." She was still naked beneath the sheet. This now held little promise for either of us. Tara sighed, taking my hand and holding it in her lap. "All I'm saying," she continued, "is that you don't need to worry. If you want to tell him to bog off, I mean. He can't do anything to me, whatever he thinks."

"I thought you said you knew him better than me." Releasing my fingers from her grip, I put my arm around her, pulling her in close. "Tara, if George threatens something, it's always best to assume that he's willing to act on it. I've seen... he's done some horrible things over the years and there's no way that I'm –"

"You think I don't know what he's capable of?" she said quietly. "I know, Price, believe me. All I'm saying is that if you want to say no to him, it'll be fine—because I do know what he's like and I won't let him hurt me."

"You really think it's that simple?"

"It's as simple or as complicated as we make it."

I supposed there was more than a grain of truth in this. For so many years, George had been my best (and only) 'friend'. When I had had no one else, me the sculpted form intended only to be spat at and shat upon by the rest of my peers, George had taken me under his wing, protected me and, I now saw, fostered a kind of dependence from which he could only benefit. Over time, others had offered me the hand of friendship, of course—but George had always been there to see to it that I made the right decision, that I saw through their 'little games' and kicked them into touch. I had allowed this to happen. I had seen just what he was doing, how I was being manipulated and kept, but I had let it continue... I had let it continue because it had been simpler that way.

"It's all academic, anyway," I said.

"Why?" I could tell from the temperature and tone of her voice that she already knew.

"I'll do this for him and then that's it," I said. "With any luck, if he finds this Sharon Jones lass... well, it's someone else for him to spend his time annoying, isn't it? And while he's doing that, he's leaving us alone."

"I don't want you going with him, Price."

"And I don't want to go with him, Tara," I told her. "But I don't see that I have a choice."

"Sartre had a phrase for that."

"Which was?"

"I can't remember—but the point is, you have plenty of choices." She wasn't exactly annoyed with me (or, at least, I don't think she was), or even impatient, it was more that she seemed frustrated by her own inability to make me see how vital it was that I not do what George had asked of me. She looked at my stained ceiling and sighed, running the fingertips of her right hand over the edges of the fingernails on her left, and said, "We can change this. And... and sooner or later we're going to have to. So why not do it now, Price? Why not just put our foot down, take whatever nonsense he has to throw at us and wave him goodbye once and for all?"

"Because I've just had some of his nonsense thrown at me," I said. "And take it from me, it hurt like buggery."

"Then we'll go to the police." She was grasping at straws, now, and she knew it.

"I hit him first."

"It's his word against ours," she insisted.

"I'm not going to the police, Tara."

She looked at me with those green-flecked hazel eyes of hers and I saw that she was close to tears. "I don't want you doing this," she said.

"I know him, love," I told her. "What harm can it do?"

The tears coming, she said, "Short ladders are dangerous, too, Price."

I didn't have a clue where we were. Stepping from the bus into the cold, drizzly afternoon, I looked up at the road sign and recognised none of the names I saw there. When I had telephoned Tony earlier, he had happily agreed to give me the day off. It was the least he could do, he'd said. Under the circumstances. Standing beneath the sign, however, watching the bus pull away in a world of rolling winter farmland and dry-stone walls, my coat collar turned up and my chin pulled down into the scarf I was thankfully wearing, I found myself wishing he hadn't. The light drizzle was of the kind that wet more than was expected and with the added complication of George by my side, it was hard to imagine that this was going to be a comfortable afternoon.

We were at a crossroads. Literally. The bus gone, I looked around me as George looked up at the sign, and I couldn't help but think of all the stories I had read of such places. Fairies, goblins, ghosts and demons—all waiting at desolate crossroads, hungry for the weary traveller. Suicides and murderers buried in such places, witches and their rituals. Maybe much of it was nonsense. But still I didn't want to stay there any longer than was absolutely necessary. The folklore aside, it was open and flat, treeless and remote. Not somewhere I wanted to be if the rain really started to come down.

In a field at the side of the road, I saw some magpies. Four for a boy. Better than one for sorrow, I supposed, but still not two for joy.

"Almost there," George said. There was a strange light in his eyes and a flush to his cheeks that made me even more uneasy, and as he flung the sports bag he'd brought with him over his shoulder and started walking in the direction of, according to the sign, Middle Skelmthwaite. I should have listened to Tara. That look in George's eye was not the remnant of the cold that had been hanging over him since Martha's party, it was rank insanity. Nothing more, nothing less. Walking beside him as he bounced along the road, trotting to keep up, I wondered if the point of no return had yet been reached. Could I back out now without looking ridiculous. The beating would be inevitable, but would he actually allow me to turn back and wait for the next bus, or would he force me to go along with him?

It was foolish to even consider such things.

"Don't you miss this?" he said suddenly, throwing his head back and breathing deeply.

"Miss what?" I said.

"This." He waved his arms expansively. "The great outdoors. Fresh air tinged with the heady aroma of cow shit."

"I wouldn't know the smell of cow shit if you held it under my nose," I reminded him.

"Ah, yes." He looked thoughtfully at the sky. "We tried that, once, didn't we?"

"Yes, you did. It was dog shit, actually, but essentially the same."

"You imagine."

"I imagine."

"Shit is shit, after all."

George continued walking, his step springy, his chin held high. I didn't recall ever seeing him like this before. He was eager and alert, his eyes reminding me of news reports of Colonel Gaddafi from years ago. When he started whistling the theme tune from The A Team, I thought that now might be a good time for me to make my token attempt at getting out of this. Better late than never, as they say.

"I was thinking, George," I said.

"Happens to us all on occasion, mate," he told me. "I wouldn't worry about it."

Unperturbed, I continued. "It's just that I feel like I'm intruding."

"Intruding how?" There was a wary edge to his tone—but, by and large, he remained his bouncy self.

"Well," I said. "This is your story. This is about what happened between you and this Sharon Jones lass. When you find her, you're probably going to have lots to talk about and –"

"And you want out."

"I didn't say that."

"But that's what it adds up to," he said. "You're cold and damp and you just can't be arsed to put yourself out for your oldest pal. You look at the thick, dark clouds on the horizon –"

Christ, I hadn't noticed them.

" – and you think to yourself, 'What am I doing here when I could be tucked up with Tara, licking her minge and generally having a jolly old time of it?' Am I right?"

"Well I wouldn't put it quite like that."

"Of course you wouldn't," he said. "But the fact remains, that's what you'd prefer. You'd rather be anywhere than here with me— and do you know something, Price?"

"What?"

"That really bloody hurts."

I sneered and turned away from him, looking at the grazing cows to my left. "Right."

"You don't believe me?"

"Not especially, no."

George considered this and then said, "I thought you knew me better than that. I really did. You think I'm that thick-skinned?"

"Elephants consult you on how best to toughen up."

"Funny," he said, not laughing. "Funny, but just not true. Not by any stretch of the imagination."

"You're going to enlighten me?"

"I'm certainly going to try."

"I've lived all of my life for this one moment."

He scowled at me. "You want another fucking smack?" he asked.

"No."

"Good," he said. "Then shut the fuck up and listen." He took another deep breath before continuing, switching the bag to his other shoulder. "The fact of the matter is," he told me, "I'm nowhere near as tough as I like to make out. It's all a bluff, Price. I need love and friendship as much as the next man. Yeah, okay, I hide it well. But I've had to."

"Why?"

The question seemed to throw him. Walking with less of a spring to his step, he thought it through, begrudgingly—not in the least bit impressed by my unwillingness to simply accept what he had to say. I heard him mumbling under his breath, a deeply resonant sound that prompted me to look over my shoulder, expecting to see a lorry rolling towards us. Briefly entertaining the notion that he was going to completely ignore me, I considered giving him a bit of a nudge. I didn't like him when he was like this. An unexpected silence was never a good sign with George. But then, nothing was ever a good sign with him. He was a perpetual bad omen.

"You want to know why I've had to hide it?" he finally said. "All right, I'll tell you. The truth is, people take advantage of me." I started to laugh and he shot me a look of admonition. "If I let them see just how needy I actually am, how compassionate, they take advantage of me. It's as simple as that. I'm a bit of a soft touch, you see. And in my business, it doesn't do to let it show."

"Your business?" I said, with as respectful a tone as I could muster.

"Survival, mate. Plain and simple. The business we're all in. You, me, Lady Tara, that twat of a mother of mine—all of us. The day-to-day business of getting by without getting shat on. The day-to-day business of finding what we want."

"Is that what this is all about?" I said. "Finding what you want?"

"You could say that, I suppose," he said. About to say more, he suddenly stopped walking and talking—pointing to a distant hill, a huge, solar grin on his face.

On the hill, possibly a couple of miles in the distance, stood a ramshackle old farmhouse. With the low, dark sky behind it, it appeared forbidding and slightly askew, its lines and angles unnatural, out of whack, as my father might have put it. It seemed to lean towards us threateningly, about to whisper a dark secret or impart a hell-bound truth, and as we started walking towards it, I couldn't help but feel that our fate was already sealed. That whatever the future held in store for us had been decided long ago.

"I was talking to this bloke I know," George said. "In this club where I go. That little fucking dive on Kelshaw Road. Gilhooncy's."

"The one with the strict dress code."

George chuckled. "You remember."

"How could I forget?"

"Anyway," he continued. "I was talking to this bloke I know, Ray. Now old Ray, he's a bit of a drunk. In fact. No. Actually, he's a lot of a drunk. Spends hours talking to lampposts, that kind of thing. Can put it away like no one I've ever seen. But... he knows everyone. He keeps his ear to the ground and can tell you everything you need to know about anyone in the neighbourhood. He listens. He talks. People buy him drinks. All the elegance of a haiku."

"And this Ray told you something about Sharon Jones?" I guessed.

"Actually, no." He took too much pleasure in my getting it wrong, but I let it go. "He told me something about someone called Esmie Mears. I didn't see the relevance, initially. He told me she was living out here at that farm up there—Kingston Lodge— and I thought old Ray had finally started to lose his knack. I started to drift, drinking my drink and tuning him out. And then he said it. 'Maggie Mears,' he said. 'That was Sharon's mam. Her and her sister, Esmie... what a pair they used to be! Both dead now but... not to speak ill, but they were slags like you'd never believe!'"

"She's living under an assumed name," I said, little alarm bells starting to ring at the back of my mind.

"Got it in one." George stopped and sat on a dry stone wall at the side of the road, his sports bag between his feet. "You see," he told me, looking at the farmhouse a little quixotically, "That's people for you, Pricey, lad. Complex and obstructive. They never make life easy for you, forever reinventing themselves and pretending to be something they're not. Annoying, really. And ultimately futile because, as they say, the truth will out. You can't hide forever."

The alarm bells were growing more persistent and... alarming. When we started walking again, I asked him, "What aren't you telling me, George?"

He smiled a secretive smile and tapped the side of his nose with an index finger, the spring well and truly back in his step. "Nothing," he said. "Everything. All the good stuff. You'll find out soon enough."

"I'm not sure I want to find out."

"Then why did you come?"

"Because you threatened to hurt me and Tara if I didn't."

"You misunderstood me."

"I did?"

He nodded. "I only threatened to hurt Tara," he said. "Anything else was the product of too little sleep and too vivid an imagination."

"You hurt Tara, you hurt me. Same difference."

"Awww, isn't that sweet? You really have got it bad, haven't you?"

I had to struggle against the urge to take a swing at him, again. It would have been all too easy for me to grab a loose stone from the wall and brain the irritating little freak with it—but I was still smarting somewhat from the fight earlier, and it wasn't difficult to imagine that George would just as easily turn the tables if I had another go. I made do with thinking evil thoughts as he continued.

"Anyway," he said. "The choice is yours. You know that. So you're in love with my cousin the bint. It doesn't mean you have to live your life for her. All this she hurts, you hurt stuff? My opinion? It's bollocks. That's just what you tell yourself. It's your newfound get-out clause—because deep down, mate... and you know this already... deep down, you're a coward."

This hit a lot closer to home than I liked. I didn't normally take that much notice of George's insults—or, at least, I tried not to—but this caught me at a vulnerable moment. I thought of all those times when fear had overtaken reason, when the easy option had waltzed on in, presenting itself like a debutante at a coming out ball, all proper and correct, little fingers raised and cleavage delicately perfumed. Such times were too numerous to count. All through school and into adulthood, it had been one long list of the moral low ground—for the sake of a quiet life, as a way of always avoiding anything that would require too much of me. And this hadn't only been when George had been around. No. George was not responsible for my cowardice. The product of nature rather than nurture, I was sure.

I remembered the rides at the fair that came to the recreation ground every year. How I had, as a boy, always pestered my dad to take me on the Satellite and how, one year, he had finally relented and agreed. As we had walked towards it, the reality became suddenly quite overwhelming. I still wanted it. A ride on the Satellite would earn me a degree of respect at school that I otherwise didn't have. But it was real. It was real and big and I didn't want it. I remember looking at the man in the control booth. Swarthy and oily, with the bulbous, cracked-vein nose of an alcoholic. People like him fitted the rides together. People with noses and predilections. People with nagging wives back at their caravans and memories dulled and soured by the need for more Blue Nun, or whatever it was these swarthy fairground types drank. Anything could happen. I could see that. A loose nut. That was all it would take. One moment of swarthy inattention and my world would come tumbling down around my ears. Mam would be left a widow with her only child dead and significantly splattered, and I would be nothing more than a tragic headline and tired law suit. I remembered how I had looked up at dad as we had stood in the queue. Close to tears, I had willed him to look down at me—and when he finally had, he had merely nodded. I'd expected him to be disappointed in me; instead, he had only looked relieved.

"I resent that," I finally told George, but we both knew it was the truth.

"I've seen slugs with more backbone," he said. "You just take the path of least resistance every time. That's why you and Lady Tara won't last. You'll just... you'll just shrivel up at the first complication and that'll be it."

I thought of what Carla had told me as we had sat on Martha's stair. I could bring him down like that if I wanted to. And, more to the point, so could anyone, if they set their mind to it. You included. It now sounded a more appealing prospect, I had to admit—but still it seemed just as unlikely. Nevertheless, I took some courage from this and, in spite of my ingrained cowardice, said, "I won't let you hurt Tara, George."

"Won't you?"

"No."

He glanced at me, bored with the conversation, now. "Good for you," he said.

We made ourselves as comfortable as we could in among some trees and bushes overlooking the front of the farmhouse. George opened the bag and brought out a pair of binoculars and, much to my relief, a flask of coffee and some sandwiches. I was cold and starving and the rain was starting to come down more heavily, but at least now the trees offered us a little shelter and we had something to eat and drink.

"I put some whisky in the coffee," he told me as he handed me the plastic cup—and I could have kissed him. Maybe this wouldn't be so bad, after all. Maybe if I just thought of it as an adventure and got into the spirit of it, everything would seem much more rosy. I mean, it wasn't as if I had anything to lose. As I had already pointed out, this was George's story. If anyone was going to be disappointed it was him, not me.

"So what are we looking for?" I said, as we sat among the undergrowth eating our sandwiches and drinking our blessedly whisky-laced coffee.

"Sharon Jones, of course," he told me.

"You really think she's living here?"

"Old Ray is never wrong."

I thought about pointing out that Old Ray was inclined (in every sense) to talk to lampposts but I was today resigned to the fact of my cowardly nature and so, instead, I merely said, "So why don't you just go and knock on the door."

George rolled his eyes and lit a cigarette, already done with his share of the sandwiches. "That would be the obvious thing to do," he admitted, "but it isn't as simple as that, me old mucker. You see," he exhaled a plume of smoke, "I need to be certain before I go hammering on her door. I need to know the lay of the land."

I quite liked the idea of 'the obvious thing to do', but George wasn't having any of it. This was what had to be done, he insisted. It was the correct course of action under the circumstances. As he saw it, he was unprepared to go down in history as a fool who rushed in. We would wait here for the right moment—even if that meant we had to sit among the bushes all night long.

I reluctantly went along with this. The whisky-laced coffee helped a little, but even that soon began to lose its attraction. We sat and watched, George scanning the farmhouse with the binoculars and telling me how he had been made for this kind of environment and situation. The way he told it, he was, in his heart, a special forces kind of guy. He had what it took and the only probable obstacle that he had ever foresaw had been his unwillingness to take orders. "I can think for myself, you see," he said—and I thought of his uncle, Francis. George wasn't a one-off. He wasn't unique. Others like him had walked this planet many times over—and, in that, I was sure there were lessons to be learned.

Just as he was telling me how he had always enjoyed camping, as if this were some kind of proof of his special forces eligibility, an old Ford Mondeo rattled its way along the road and parked in front of the farmhouse. George stopped mid-sentence, bringing up the binoculars so quickly that I thought he might black both his eyes. He grew rigid and focused, the binoculars an extension of who he was and what he wanted, and I felt suddenly quite redundant. I saw that, quite typically, George would dump me whenever he saw fit. I was not along for the ride; I was here to fill the silence between moments.

A man got out of the car and approached the front door of the farmhouse. From what I could see, he was in his fifties and carried what appeared to be two bags of groceries. He looked around sheepishly as he waited for the door to be answered... as if he could feel us watching him. George breathed heavily and I tried to work out if Mondeo Man's arrival was significant.

"Here we go," George said, up on his knees now to get a better look. The front door opened and I squinted in vain, seeing nothing but the back of the man's head and a whole load of shadow.

George squeezed the binoculars more tightly, shifting to his left, trying to get a clear line on whoever it was that had answered the door, before throwing down the binoculars in frustration when the man entered and closed the door behind him.

"Fuck, shit and fanny juice," he said, grabbing the flask angrily and pouring himself more 'coffee'. "Couldn't see a bloody thing. Would you sodding credit it? All these years and I'm that close..." he held up his finger and thumb, half an inch apart, "... to seeing her and some dolt with a too-big head, a fucking hydrocephalic head, he gets in the way. And they say there's a god. Sick fuck."

I tried to think of something safe to say—something safe and, yet, not too obviously so. Although George wasn't in the mood for listening to anything I had to say, anyway. He mumbled and cursed, drank his coffee, picked up the binoculars, put them back down again, checked his watch, shook his head, slowly, in disgust and finally—finally—he said, "You know what Old Ray told me after he said Sharon was living out here? Last night in the club. After he'd given me all of the details, three times over, just to be sure I had everything straight, he told me to watch out for myself. 'Such quests are often inconclusive,' he told me. 'Protect your heart, my friend.' I thought he was talking bollocks, at the time. But now... I'm not so sure. Maybe I shouldn't have come here, after all."

Solemn and strangely sympathetic, George hung his head and lit another cigarette. He sniffed, and I briefly thought that he was crying—but it was only his cold making itself known. I spoke to him as compassionately as I could, filling silences that were never meant to be filled, and when he nodded and started packing up his things, I foolishly entertained the notion that victory was mine. We were on our way home.

But just as we stood, something caught George's eye. He quickly dipped down again, grabbing the binoculars from his bag and peering through the bushes at the farmhouse. My spirits taking a dive, I reluctantly turned to see Mondeo Man coming out. This time, a woman came with him. Grey-haired and thin, she looked as though she could have been in her fifties. I knew, however, that if she was who George wanted her to be, she could only be in her early forties.

They kissed and the man caressed the side of her face—saying something to her, body-language reassuring and sincere. George made a tight little grunt of disgust and then turned to me, having apparently seen all he needed to see. His lips curled in a sneer and he spat into the bushes.

"It's her," he told me.

"You're sure?" He nodded. "So what do we do now?"

"We go pay her a visit."

I felt curiously vulnerable, standing in the open courtyard at the front of the farmhouse. We paused for a moment, looking up at the building—the worn brickwork and filthy windows, the missing ridge tiles on the roof and the crumbling chimney. All in all, it had the air of a place unloved and uncared for. It seemed somehow to go beyond mere neglect, however; this was a resented place... one that had absorbed too many malcontent histories, people confined behind its walls and routines who had wanted more and had grown to understand, with much bitterness and longing, that they would never get it. The wind whistling around the courtyard, flicking grit in my eyes and causing them to tear, and the sky perceptibly darkening by the second, I tried not to think too much of the lives that had inhabited this place—turning to George, instead, sure that he would have some appropriately flippant remark to eradicate my oppressive mood. However he was as mesmerised as I, his eyes fixed on one upstairs window in particular, as if he somehow hoped to catch a glimpse of his future there.

I nudged him and he looked at me—slowly, like an automaton—his eyes struggling to focus. "What?" he said.

Nodding in the direction of the front door, I said, "Shouldn't we knock?"

George studied the front of the building again, the sports bag held limply at his side, shoulders rolled forward slightly in an exhausted stoop. He looked on the verge of saying something, but instead shook his head against the very notion and simply started walking towards the farmhouse... or, more to the point, towards the front door of the farmhouse. I waited a second or two, and then followed, jogging a little to catch up.

We stood on the doorstep, staring at the flaking, encrusted paintwork on the door. Like the rest of the building, it carried that air of resentment. I didn't like it. No home, I thought, should be made to feel like this.

"Are you going to knock, then, or what?" I said. George didn't reply. He didn't even look at me. "It's just that we've come all this way and endured sitting in those bushes back there for what seemed like forever... it strikes me that it would be a bit, well, odd not to knock after all we've been through."

"I shouldn't have to knock," he told me, quietly... sombrely. "She should know I'm here. She should be able to feel me, standing here, and she should fling the door open in expectation and welcome me with open arms."

This was a very un-George kind of thing to say, and I chose my words with great care. "I'm sure she'll be over the moon to see you, mate," I said. "But we are none of us mind-readers. Knock on the door."

He was like a little boy on his first trip to see Santa. The anticipation positively buzzed through him, but he was also afraid... afraid that this would be a let-down, that he wouldn't get the present he wanted and that the big, fat bloke with the cotton-wool beard would, upon closer inspection, turn into some tired old drunk with a huge hard-on for pretty little boys. First putting the bag down at his feet, he raised a loosely clenched hand. It hung there, poised for action and, yet, not. Looking at me pleadingly, he truly was a pathetic sight. Sad and hopeless, no longer in control, he was a man to be pitied.

I couldn't wait to tell Tara about it. We would piss ourselves laughing.

"I can't do it," he whispered. It just got better. "I want to but... I can't do it, Price."

My instinct was to drag this out as long as possible—make him suffer—but at that very moment, the rain started to really come down heavily, bouncing off the paving and overflowing the guttering. I pulled up my collar, to no avail, and, without really thinking it through, knocked on the door on George's behalf. I thought I saw a shudder of gratitude, but he was probably just cold.

I waited thirty seconds or so and then knocked again. Still no reply. The rain continued to bounce, soaking us to the skin no matter how close to the building we stood, and it didn't take a genius to see that George was growing irritated. His eyes narrowed and his jaw tightened, fists clenched as he peered at the door—as if daring it not to open. It was such a contrast to his mood of a few moments before that even I, with all my years of experience, was rather unnerved. He told me to knock again, which I did. He told me I wasn't doing it hard enough, so I knocked harder. Pushing me aside, he leant into the door and started hammering and kicking at it, shouting Sharon's name over and over, telling her that he knew she was in there and that he just wanted to talk to her, just wanted to talk to her...

He then glanced at me and it seemed to take him a moment to recognise who I was. "That's all I want to do, Price. I just want to talk to her. She... she owes me an explanation, you see. That's all. She owes me an explanation and, once I have it, everything will be hunky dory."

Just when he seemed to be calming down, his anger flared once more. He started hitting and kicking at the door again, and I placed a hand on his shoulder in an attempt to calm him. "She must have seen you coming, mate," I said. "You have to accept that she doesn't want to see you... not while you're like this, at least."

This wasn't exactly the best thing I could have said. George spun towards me, eyes fiery and livid—practically nose-to-nose with me. He breathed heavily in my face, and I thought of Tara, of the contrast between this and the time I had spent with her last night and earlier that morning. She had been right. She had been warm and loving, and she had been right. I should be back at my flat with her, once more oblivious to the world around me, and George... George should have been left to deal with the world he had on his own created.

Rage radiating from him, coming in slow, steady pulses—throbbing and barely contained—I waited for the blow, knowing that I could never prepare myself for it... that no matter how much he telegraphed it, it would still be a surprise. But the blow never came.

"Don't," he said. "Just don't ever fucking assume that you know what I should do and, more to the point, don't—don't—ever assume that you know what she's thinking. You don't know her. You've never known her. All you know is that it's pissing down, she isn't letting us in and you want to go home so you can give my little cousin a damned good seeing to. So don't. Not ever. Just fucking don't."

George slammed his fist against the door once more and then started marching purposefully away—heading around the side of the building, head bent against the rain and his shoulders hunched. I tried to decide what to do, the rain running down my neck distracting me somewhat, torn between leaving him to his fate and seeing that he didn't get himself into any trouble. I shouldn't care. George was not my concern. So what if he ended up arrested and, ultimately, serving a stretch in prison? Wouldn't that benefit the rest of us? I imagined what it would be like to have him out of our lives once and for all. The freedom. The knowledge that he wasn't going to pop up at any moment and stir things up.

But there was a woman in this house—a complete innocent, for all I knew. I saw the possibilities unfolding before me and as abhorrent as it was, I knew what I had to do.

I found George clambering over a fence at the side of the building. His jacket caught on a post and he yanked it free—ripping the lining and almost falling in the process. Grabbing his arm, I steadied him and did my best to encourage him down, but he was having none of it.

He cocked his leg over the fence and jumped down onto the other side. All I could do was follow him.

"I thought you'd be off home," he said, once I'd negotiated the fence.

"And leave you to get yourself into more trouble?"

"You're not my nanny."

"I never claimed to be."

George was having doubts of his own. I could see it in the way he appraised me and in his flat, emotionless expression. He gave the fence a long, sideways look—as if contemplating throwing me back over it—and then took a steady step towards me.

"Just don't get in my way, Price," he said. "Whatever happens, this is my call. We play it how I say, not how you in your infinite fucking wisdom think it should be played. Is that clear?"

Foolishly, I nodded—trying not to think of Tara and what she would say if she had been with us.

"Good." He grinned and patted me on the cheek. "Follow me, then, my good man. And remember. My rules. Don't dick me about, Price, or I just might have to do unspeakable things to the Delectable Lady Tara."

"Stop it," I said. "Leave her out of this."

There must have been something in my tone—something I'd missed completely. George stopped and regarded me with that appraising look again, and then nodded. "All right," he said. "Do this my way and we'll leave Tara out of it. No more threats."

I didn't believe him, of course. Not really. But if it shut him up about her for the time being... well, that was good enough for me.

There were no ground floor windows around this side of the farmhouse and, so, I went with George, however grudgingly, to the back of the building. We stepped over old milk crates and broken paving slabs, a little more sheltered from the rain round here, and George pointed at a window, rather too victoriously for my liking, before stepping closer and peering in.

Shielding his eyes, he pressed his face to the glass, giving me a running commentary on what he saw. "Living room," he said. "Dark. Messy. You wouldn't want to live here. You really wouldn't. Makes Martha's spare bedroom look luxurious in comparison. Fucking plasma TV, though. Right big cunt. Must be at least fifty inches. Plasma TV, DVD player... and..." He pressed his face harder to the window, trying to block out more of the light with his hands. "Looks like toys. Little kids' toys, scattered all over the floor. Fisher Price, Price. That kind of shit.... Why the fuck would –"

He stopped suddenly and took a step back, glancing warily at me before beckoning me over and approaching the window again.

"Far left-hand corner," he said, whispering. "By the door. What do you see?"

Obediently, I pressed my face against the window and looked into the room—more anxious than curious.

I saw darkness, overall. A consistent gloom that seemed to have little to do with the poor quality of light outside. As my eyes adjusted, I saw all the things George had described—the plasma TV, the toddlers' toys and the filth—but it was a struggle, and as I strained to see into the far left-hand corner of the room, I thought that my efforts were futile. Whatever he had seen (or imagined he had seen), I saw nothing. Shadowed and distant, it was a place of stories to which we would never be privy, a corner in a room to which we, I was sure, would never be admitted.

I started to step back, about to tell George that he was seeing things, when I caught a movement in those deep shadows. It could so easily have been missed. A grey-black flicker among the greater black. It was there, and then it was gone, but I was certain I had not imagined it.

Someone was watching us from the corner of the room.

"Did you see it?" George said, his face pressed to the window beside me. "You did, didn't you? You saw it. Don't tell me you didn't because I know you did. You saw it."

"I saw something," I admitted.

"Something." He rolled this around his mouth, to get the taste. "Something. Yes, I like that. Something about covers it."

"Suitably vague," I said.

"Beautifully vague," he corrected.

"Praise, indeed."

"Put it down to uncharacteristic generosity."

We both turned back to the window at the same time—sensing something or seeing it on the periphery of our vision. A blur. A thumping bang and roar. Violent, spastic movement that, at least initially, defied explanation. George and I jumped back, grabbing hold of each other like the couple of cowards we actually were, ready to run if the window should break and the something should get out.

With the benefit of hindsight, it was a sad scene. The young, deformed man—one side of his face tumour-swollen, his limbs ill-matched—hammered and drooled on the window, enraged and afraid. His hair was blonde and greasy, and his eyes rolled with confusion... and George and I held onto each other, equally afraid and confused. Now I know enough to pity the young man. I understand all that he had been through and see all too clearly the weight and volume of his suffering, the Divine Nature of Cruelty. But then I had been a quaking child—a child led by a fool, accepting and ridiculous. I had felt the fear like something alive and venomous, coursing through my veins and consuming me from the inside out. He was coming through the window. It simply could not keep him in. The monster (had I really thought that?) hammered even harder at the glass and there was just no way that I saw that it could keep him in. It would shatter, and then he would be on us in all his insane glory.

I barely registered it, at first. More movement, but not yet enough to distract from the horrific sight before us. George gasped and blubbered, mumbling something under his breath that may have been a prayer, or may have been an obscenity. And then she was there with him. The woman we had seen at the front of the building.

Sharon Jones.

She placed a hand, delicately, on each shoulder and spoke to him, calming him impressively and leading him away from the window. I could hear her voice, distant and muffled, but with a lullaby rhythm—soporific and kind... maternal. She took him back into the depths of the room, but once she had him settled, she returned to the window.

The look she gave George was precise and brief. It spoke of hatred and history, pure resentment and loathing. Her lips curled back from her teeth and George broke away from me, stepping back towards the window.

Sharon Jones was no fool, however. Not today, at least.

She reached up as he approached, grabbing the edge of a raggy curtain in each hand and drawing them together—sealing him out as surely as if she had brought down a portcullis. George stopped dead in his tracks, and I expected a violent reaction... something suitably George. He only stood there, though, staring at his hazy reflection until the message hit home. And then... then George climbed back over the fence without saying a word.

And he didn't speak all the way home.

Chapter Six

There wasn't a cloud in the sky and it was cold enough to make me wish I'd taken Tara's advice, after all, and worn the woolly hat she had bought me, but it was nevertheless good to be outdoors and working—even if said work was only clearing up litter.

It was the Saturday after my eventful visit to Kingston Lodge with George, and by rights it should have been my day off. However, it had only seemed fair and right that I should at least offer to make up for the time I'd taken off, and when I had, Tony had unexpectedly said that there was quite a bit of catching up to be done.

Straightening up and stretching my back, I saw I was more or less directly beneath Lovers' Leap. I stood there with my black plastic bag and my spike on a stick, looking up at the craggy outcrop of rock, a little disappointed. It didn't seem all that impressive or dangerous from down here.

An icy wind blew through the gardens and I suddenly longed to be away from that place. I didn't like The Leap, as Tony was inclined to call it — and I certainly didn't like the sensations it stirred up. This was a tragic place, I thought, as I shuddered against the cold, a place where people, two at least, had died with love in their hearts for each other and nothing in the way of hope. Bleak and strangely commonplace, it made me think back to the day with George at Kingston Lodge. I didn't see a connection between the two—or nothing direct, at least—except maybe for their gothic nature and stink of grief, but that didn't stop me returning there, to that grim farmhouse and the highly disturbing image of the disfigured man hammering at the window.

George hadn't yet given me an explanation and, frankly, I wasn't expecting one. His silence on the subject had, however, spoken volumes. It told me in no uncertain terms that he had been seriously wrong-footed out there. Whatever he had thought had been going on, whatever his and Sharon's story actually was — that was only a part of it. There was a thread about which he knew nothing.

I had wanted to go back. As we had waited at the bus stop, my main concern, I'm pleased to say, had not been for George or myself but, rather, for Sharon Jones. She was alone in that place — night falling, the rain coming down heavily, remote and unaided with only the deformed man for company. We couldn't just leave her like that, not after disturbing them in the way we had. What if, I had said to George, what if we had frightened that guy so much that she was unable to calm him? What if he attacked her? There was no one there to help her. She was at his mercy – and, when you got right down to it, were such people capable of mercy?

George hadn't responded. Standing there with his hands in his pockets, his bag between his feet, he had merely continued to stare at the distant horizon. Now, alone at the bottom of Lovers' Leap, I shivered again and told myself I had done all I could. Sharon Jones was not my concern, and that I had remained with George instead of returning alone to the farmhouse was sensible, given his uncharacteristic state of mind. It niggled, though, and deep down I knew that this was just another manifestation of my cowardice.

Tara had assured me that I had done the right thing. As I once more started picking up the litter, I smiled at the memory of this — holding her close to me, Ray LaMontagne singing Can I Stay? in the background, the distant taste of her on my lips and the essence of her in my very being. It was George's mess, she had insisted. That I had gone along with him didn't have to mean that I was committed. Sharon Jones, Tara had told me, was a big girl. She had taken care of herself this long without my intervention, and she was sure she could continue to do so in the future. "What you have to remember," Tara had told me, "is that she clearly has friends, people she can call on, or she simply wouldn't have survived otherwise."

Even now, I wasn't completely convinced that she hadn't just said this to make me feel better. She didn't want me to be hurt. She wanted to protect me. George was—

"Ah, here you are."

I jumped, almost dropping the bag of litter, and Tony stepped around in front of me. Putting a hand to my chest, I smiled at him and rolled my eyes. "Tony," I said. "You just about scared me shitless."

"You looked like you were miles away." He'd been in a much better mood since Claudia had been discharged from hospital a couple of days earlier, but he was still showing tight little signs of strain around the eyes and mouth. "But still working effectively. A man after my own heart."

"The mind goes into freefall," I said. "The body does its thing and I just drift. I like it."

Tony nodded. He had something else on his mind. He took a step closer and said, sotto voce, as if someone might overhear, "I hate to tear you away from something you clearly find spiritually rewarding, Price, but I need you to sit with Claudia for a short while. I have an appointment that I really can't cancel. I swear, if I could, I would but –"

"No problem, Tony," I said, sensing that he was anxious about something and wanting to make it a little easier for him (he wasn't George, after all). "I could do with a cuppa, actually."

Smiling, Tony said, "Try the Twinings' Assam & Kenyan Blend. It's to die for."

It was the first occasion I'd been left alone with Claudia for this length of time and, sitting down on the settee in the squat brick building, mug of tea in hand, I didn't quite know what to do. Claudia sat a few feet away, chin on her chest, hands limp in her lap, a Bach concerto on the stereo, and I realised that this was nothing like picking up litter with a spike on a stick. My body was unoccupied and my mind didn't know quite know what to do with itself. Tony had assured me that I wouldn't actually need to do anything for Claudia, "everything" had already been taken care of and all I had to do was sit with her and, if I felt like it, talk to her.

Easier said than done. I couldn't think of a single thing to say.

The music continued to play and I sipped my tea. I found myself thinking of the conversations I'd had with Tara about Tony and Claudia. Tony hadn't again mentioned Claudia's 'request' that he help her die, and I'd assumed that he'd finally found a way of denying it without undermining his faith in the truth of the rest of their 'conversations'. But, sitting there sipping my tea and looking at Claudia, so isolated and unreachable, I couldn't help thinking that maybe I had got it wrong. Maybe every element of my interpretation was fundamentally flawed.

Leaning forward and putting my mug on the floor, I then shuffled along the settee so that I could be nearer to Claudia. I wanted that look, again—just so I could be absolutely certain that I hadn't imagined it—that fleeting look she had given me at the top of Lovers' Leap. I sat forward, bending so that I could see her face more clearly, perhaps make eye-contact with her.

"Why won't you look at me, again?" I said, my voice soft and, I hoped, encouraging. "Tony isn't here, now. You can do whatever you want. If you want to look at me, you can. You can look at me all you want and I won't tell him. I won't say a word."

I waited, letting the silence build—a desperate void in need of filling, and one I was prepared to leave hanging, if it looked likely to achieve the desired result. I sat back, hoping that this would more fully communicate my infinite patience... but quickly got bored and sat forward again, placing a hand on her knee and repeating what I had said, enunciating clearly, praying that the rhythm of my words would lull her, mesmerise and lead her out of her pit of silence.

"You have nothing to be afraid of," I said. "Listen to me, Claudia. I will do whatever you want. I'll help you or leave things as they are. Whatever you wish. Just look at me."

Still nothing. I didn't know how Tony did it. This was so frustrating. I tried to imagine her reply, the way he did, but nothing would come. I didn't know her well enough. I'd never heard the tone of her voice or the no doubt highly individual way she had had of phrasing a sentence. She had been a clever woman and now she wasn't. As reluctant as I was to do so, I had to admit that her 'look' at the Lovers' Leap had probably been a fluke.

I couldn't let it go, though. Not yet. This was an opportunity I probably wouldn't have again for quite a while and I was determined to make the most of it.

"What do you really want, Claudia?" I asked, quite sharply this time. I thought I saw her twitch, but it may just have been an involuntary reaction to the tone of my voice—either that or my imagination. "Do you want to get away from him? Is that it? Because that can happen. That can happen easily. All you have to do is say the word... say the word or give me some sign that that's what you want and it's as good as done. If he hurts you, Claudia... if he does things to you that you don't want him to do... we can stop him. It doesn't have to be this way."

I stopped, delicately lifting her chin so that I could see her face more easily. Her eyes stared at things I hoped I would never see. Distant things. Lost futures and the absence of memory. Her world, now—and wholly different to the world we inhabited. She coughed a little and spluttered saliva onto her chin. I wiped it away with a paper tissue, wishing I'd never started this... wishing that my father had never brought me to this place.

Feeling suddenly quite depressed, I sat back with a hopeless sigh. The world was a cruel place. I didn't need Claudia to make me see that. Nevertheless, she unwittingly underscored my feeling and I struggled with the reality of her situation—the unfixable reality of all our situations. The all too familiar, smoky edges of despair approached and only by thinking of Tara, of the wonderful, unexpected nature of our love for one another, could I hold them at bay.

"It's scary," I said to Claudia. "The way I feel about her. About Tara, my girlfriend. I don't know how I got by without her. It's only been a matter of weeks and already she's such a big part of my life that... it's hard to remember what it was like without her.

That's a little frightening, but in a good way—if that makes sense."

I was no longer looking for a reaction from her. A good thing, really, since she still showed no sign of having heard a word I'd said.

"I suppose I just find it hard to believe that..." I paused, framing the words as best I could. "I find it hard to believe that someone wants me. I mean, I'm not exactly the catch of the year, am I? No, I'm not. I'm a pretty bloody sad case, truth be known, but Tara can see right past that. She sees something even I can't see."

Claudia still sat there with her chin on her chest, apparently unmindful of my inane rambling. I sighed again and shook my head, thinking how potentially soul-destroying this could be.

"Is that how it is for you and Tony, Claudia?" I said. "Do you love him the way I love Tara? Does he love you the way Tara loves me? Or is that just what he wants everyone to believe?" I put a hand on her knee, again, my voice so low it cracked. "Did he try to kill you, Claudia? Is that what happened? Is that why you had to go to the hospital?"

I imagined she was about to speak. She showed no visible signs of doing so, and, yet, I felt it, somehow, deep inside—a knot of promise and hope, a disinclination to accept that Claudia didn't have something she wished to communicate to me. I tensed, knowing on some hitherto unknown level that it was there, that she could do this if she only wanted it badly enough. I squeezed her knee a little, believing that this would encourage her and give her the strength she needed. Like some American Bible Belt faith-healer, I laid on my hands and willed her to speak. I pushed and, briefly, I felt something return. A movement in her leg. A spasm, perhaps, or something more intentional.

"Did you move your leg, Claudia?" I asked. "Did you do that?" I waited, relaxing my hand. "Do it again. If you did it, do it again."

Nothing. I kept my hand on her knee, staring at it—trying to work out if I had imagined this as well. Should I just leave it be, or should I pursue it further—perhaps talk to people who knew Tony and Claudia? I couldn't help feeling that I might become too involved in whatever it was (if anything) that was going on here.

And this wasn't my business. I also had Tara, now. Tara to love and focus on, George to complicate my life as much as I needed. This was a concern that should be left to others.

However, as I started to draw my hand away, I felt it again. More definite, this time, there was no doubt in my mind that this was a very deliberate, conscious movement. I placed my hand more solidly on her knee again, not wanting to miss the slightest tremor, and leant in towards her, keeping my voice low—not wanting to alarm her.

"Move it once for yes and twice for no," I said, feeling like a bad, sepia-tinted spiritualist—and a little disturbed by the implication. "Do you understand?"

Twitch.

I paused for a moment, collecting my thoughts. I didn't know what this meant, but I now understood that there was no going back for me. Feeling chosen but far from blessed, I framed my words carefully.

"Do you want to be with Tony?" I said.

Twitch twitch.

No. I was hoping for a yes. A yes would have made everything much simpler.

"Does he hurt you?"

Twitch twitch.

Well that was something, anyway. If he didn't hurt her, that meant that he hadn't been responsible for the 'accident' the other day and things were not as urgent as I'd imagined they might be. I considered my next question, wanting to ask "why" and knowing that that would achieve nothing.

"Do you love Tony?"

Twitch.

"And he loves you?"

A moment's hesitation and then: twitch.

"But you want to be away from him?"

Twitch.

I thought I was beginning to understand. This wasn't about what Tony was doing to her. Claudia had no problem with that because she loved him. Rather, it was about what she was doing to him.

"Are you worried that caring for you is... harming him somehow, Claudia?" I said.

Twitch.

I remembered that morning when I had found Tony sitting outside on the deckchair—what he had said to me and how strange it had at the time been. It was a possibility that I didn't really want to acknowledge, but I knew I had to.

"Your accident wasn't an accident, was it, Claudia?" I said, and she twitched her leg twice in reply. "You tried to kill yourself, didn't you?"

Twitch.

I was about to ask her more when I heard a noise behind me. The door opening. I quickly pulled my hand away from Claudia's knee and sat back—smiling at Tony as he entered, wanting to tell him everything that had happened but knowing that I couldn't, not until I'd had the opportunity to ask Claudia if it was what she wanted. Good or bad, she had taken me into her confidence.

Tony closed the door behind him and walked over, smiling—clearly pleased to be back with the woman he truly loved. He bent and kissed Claudia on the cheek, and then stood behind her, a hand on each of her shoulders.

"Hope my girl here hasn't been flirting too outrageously with you, Price, mate," he said, winking. "Once she gets started, she doesn't know when to stop. Isn't that right, love?"

I saw her leg tense once and almost smiled.

"Actually," I said, "we were thinking of upping sticks and running away together. Leaving all this behind us and making a new life in some place exotic. Bradford or Glasgow, somewhere like that."

Tony chuckled and sat down on the settee beside me, slapping me on the knee companionably. He seemed a little intoxicated, and I wondered if, by any chance, the urgent appointment he'd mentioned had been held in a pub. "Now, you see," he said. "That's where I know you're fibbing."

"It is?"

"Oh, yes. Absolutely. Because, you see, my Claudia is a flirt. No denying that. She's made an Olympic event of it. But one thing I do know... she would never leave me. Isn't that right, love?"

Twitch... twitch.

Under the circumstances, I could possibly have picked a better time for visiting my parents, but as it was—as preoccupied as I was with the problem of Claudia, not to mention the whole George situation—I didn't really think I had any option. Talking to my mother on the phone the night before, I had admitted that it had been too long, I just hadn't realised, and promised that I would call in after work. Apart from the obligation, however, there was something else on my mind; I wanted to tell them about Tara.

The semi-detached on Chesterlee Avenue was much the way I remembered it from my childhood. It was one of those places that was a little difficult to go back to without feeling that you'd somehow discarded the adult years you'd struggled so hard to hold onto. I stopped on the corner and took in the avenue—the row of three shops that hadn't significantly changed in the past twenty-five years, the 1950s housing, the tree on the patch of common where I'd once built a tree-house with my pre-George friends... friends who would drop away the minute he arrived on the scene. Bad choices. Childhood choices. That's what this place spoke to me of—that and the conflicting feelings of parental love and simmering, difficult to define frustration.

I looked at the oak tree, still strong after all the years of abuse and pollution, and it seemed remarkable to think that this had once been the centre of my universe. A universe of 'dens' and Top Trumps, before that, tank tops and football chews—bad haircuts and jutting rabbit teeth. Remarkable and oddly reassuring. It was and still is, I thought. A constant in a world—in a universe—of flux.

I found my parents in the kitchen, polishing their collection of brass ornaments—as they had done on every third Saturday for as long as I could remember. It was yet another reassuring sight, the two of them at the kitchen roll covered table, Dad applying the

Brasso, Mam wiping it off. I could have been eight, again, home from playing football at the rec', my cold face and fingers tingling when they hit the warm kitchen air.

"Price!" Mam put down her cloth and wiped her hands on some kitchen roll that she had on her knee before standing and coming over to me. She looked well, I was pleased to see, well and at least ten years younger than she actually was. "You've put on some weight," she said, squeezing my upper arms. "No. Wait. You've built up a little muscle tissue, there—that's what it is."

I smiled, already somewhat exhausted by her attention but still lifted by it. "You're looking good, Mam," I said, kissing her on the cheek and giving her a hug. "If you weren't my mother I might have mistaken you for Joan Collins."

She pulled back and gave me her famous one-eyed squint. "Now I know you mean that to be flattering, Price," she said, "but Joan is a fair bit older than me. You might want to revise the script before your next visit—which, by my reckoning, gives you about a year to get it right, if past performance is anything to go by."

"Come on, Mam. It hasn't been that long." I did a quick finger-count behind my back and I had it at about three months. Still nothing to be proud of, though.

"Long enough," Dad said, without looking around.

"Seems like an eternity." Mam stroked my cheek, smiling. "But never mind. You're here now. That's what matters." Sitting back down, she pulled out the chair beside her and patted the seat. "We have a lot of catching up to do."

I was sure she didn't mean to, but she made this sound like a threat. I smiled at her and then looked at the chair. I wasn't ready for this. I loved my mother dearly, and my father... well, I tolerated my father dearly, but I couldn't sit down with them. Not yet. In a short while, maybe, but not yet.

"Give me one minute," I said, heading for the hallway. "I've just got to use the loo. Won't be a sec."

Upstairs, I had a pee, even though I didn't really need one, and then, after splashing my face with cold water and taking lots of deep breaths, started to make my way back downstairs.

I stopped on the landing, however, when I noticed that the door to my old bedroom was open. It seemed like an invitation, somehow, and I couldn't resist taking a look, having a little nostalgic wallow—as tragic and pointless as that might be.

It had been decorated thoroughly a few years back and was nothing like I remembered it. It had become Mam's idea of what a room should be—all pastel colours and soft furnishings—and every trace of my funky, slightly seedy late-teen existence had been impressively eradicated. Where there had been darkness and introspection, an urge to analyse that had been spawned from earlier vistas of Airfix models and Action Men, there was now comfort and acceptability, a duvet and deep-pile carpet. And, a little worryingly, I thought I actually liked it.

Standing at the window, hands tucked beneath my armpits, I thought about Claudia and looked down at the narrow road that ran behind the house. I needed to talk to Tara. I needed to hear what someone else had to say. The whole idea of her wanting to be away from Tony, of her wanting to die, while understandable, was totally alien to me. I could see that were I in a similar situation, I might at my lowest consider the possibility that it might be better for her were I dead—but to actually want that, to pursue it... it seemed obscene. As someone who had known loneliness, wallowing in it far too often, I could only begin to understand her desire to throw away that companionship. For her, it was something she was prepared to sacrifice for, as she saw it, the sake of the man she loved. For me, it was something to be held onto at all costs.

I had known isolation. Even when I had had friends, I had felt cut off and strangely singular. For as long as I could remember, I had blamed this on my Anosmia. It had singled me out, hindered me in the strangest way, and marked me as different. But there had been more to it than that. There had to have been. Standing at my bedroom window then as I did now, I had watched the girls go by—pretty girls in hot pants and, years later, ra-ra skirts... all legs and elbows, inviting in their movements and choices, repelling in the measured look they had always seemed to give me. I approached tentatively, palms sweating, cock twitching like a divining rod, and they would pull their collective chins in, as if to say 'don't even think of it, you fucking mong'. But that had all changed, however briefly, with Squeaky Sally.

I smiled fondly as I remembered her and the voice that had inspired her nickname, wondering if things might have been different if George had not come on the scene shortly after I'd met her. Sally had been dead five years now – a simple accident, hit by a bus while crossing the road on her way home from the fish and chip shop – but I couldn't help feeling somehow responsible. It was preposterous, I knew, but as I stood there, I tried to imagine how different things might have been if I had only had the courage to deny George's time-consuming whims and stuck with her, paid her the attention she undoubtedly deserved. Would we have still been together? And if we had, would she have still been alive? It had to be more complicated than that. Maybe she'd have died earlier, I thought. Or maybe she'd have sent me out for the fish and chips and I would have been the one smeared across the road with a couple of battered cod.

You can touch it if you want. I remembered her saying that to me. We must have been about eleven and we were in her father's garage—in a little 'den' we'd made at the back from a tarpaulin and empty creosote cans. Squeaky Sally had her knees steepled so that I could see her off-white knickers beneath her skirt, but now she reached down and eased her knickers aside so that I could see the neat, slightly sore-looking cleft of her vagina. It had reminded me of my Uncle Walter's chin, and, yet, it hadn't.

"You can touch it if you want," she had told me in that ear-piercing squeak of hers. "I don't mind. Really. I want you to touch it."

It hadn't been the first fanny I'd seen. Lots of girls liked to flash them about, I'd already learned. But I'd never touched one before—and now that I was faced with the prospect of doing just that, it was a little frightening. I didn't want to offend her, though. Sally was nice. I liked her. The last thing I wanted to do was make

113

her feel bad.

And so I had cautiously reached forward and brushed my fingers over that soft, small mound—surprised by how warm it was, happy just to stroke it, run my finger along the paper cut between her labia... reluctant to take my hand away. Sally had merely continued to smile at me, her legs steepled and parted, patient and giving.

It had been the first and last time, and now, the streetlights coming on, I felt that old, familiar pang of loneliness once more—remembering how, being Mummy's Good Little Boy, I had spent the rest of the day sniffing my fingers, hoping against hope that I might at least get a faint whiff of Squeaky Sally's fanny. I sniffed so much I made myself dizzy, and all to no avail.

"Now don't get mad."

Mam was waiting for me at the bottom on the stairs, hand resting on the newel post, looking up at me with an air of expectant promise. The brass was apparently done with, either that or she'd left Dad to finish it off on his own, for once I'd descended she took me by the arm and led me into the living room.

"I have this friend in Lubbock, Texas," she said. "You know, where Buddy was from. And anyway, she's lovely. You'd like her. A bit of a Republican, but with a good heart." She stopped by the computer workstation in the corner of the room and sat down, pulling up another chair for me. "Well, we were talking, Suki Jane and me... I say 'talking', we were actually typing, but you know what I mean. Anyway, one of her cousins has Anosmia, you see, and she was telling me about this."

Mam moved the mouse to take off the English country garden screensaver and, with a little oral fanfare—ta-da!—revealed to me the web page she'd been reading.

"What do you think?" she said, once I'd finished reading it.

Of all the reasons I could possibly find to dissuade me from coming round to see my parents, this had to be top of the list. Mam was a ceaseless seeker. All my life, she had been unwilling to accept what, to most of us, had become something that simply had to be worked around and accepted. When I looked at her, I saw determination and strength—an unrealistic optimism, but optimism nonetheless. She wasn't prepared to blithely accept what someone as inconsequential as a mere doctor might tell her. No. Mam had to read the books herself, look it up on the internet— following every hyperlink until she dead-ended on some struggling server in the People's Republic of China. She wasn't content with accepted theory. She didn't limit herself to trusted medical journals and websites. She also hunted down every alternative theory, treatment and opinion—only truly happy when she was sure she had exhausted all of her leads. On occasion, this was endearing, but for the most part it was wearing and annoying. I was a case to be cured, a problem to be solved, and while that didn't affect me half as much as it once had, it did make me wish I'd returned straight to the flat and Tara.

Everything else aside, this new 'treatment' looked like quackery in the extreme—and not a little painful. As far as I could work out, the theory was based on the (possibly wrong) belief that the limbic system could get blocked up, thus impeding the flow of information from the senses in the nasal cavity. As the website put it: 'For most of us, this is a temporary occurrence that is most usually the result of residual physiological trauma brought on by the common cold, and, as such, it is merely a matter of waiting for this mild inconvenience to pass. For many, however, it is a persistent condition that requires, if a full, rewarding life is to be enjoyed, bold and drastic intervention!' This guy could have been selling snake oil and whores out of the back of a covered wagon, and, while my mother seemed quite taken with him, I just couldn't get that phrase bold and drastic intervention out of my head... or the exclamation mark that followed.

"It looks... a little unorthodox, Mam," I said, as politely as I could. "Let me see if I've got this right. They put an electrode on either side of your nose, stimulate the relevant reflexology zone on the sole of the foot—with minutely charged needles—and then... chant while they pulse a low voltage current through your nose? Yes?"

"That's about the long and short of it," Mam said, frowning and daring me with a stern look to dismiss this out of hand. "But there's a bit more to it than that. It's based on good, solid medical research, Price. The man behind this organisation has genuine qualifications. He's studied this condition and related conditions for over twenty years and –"

"I'm happy the way I am, Mam," I said. "All this... I'm sure it helps some people. Maybe. But... I don't need it anymore. It's not what it's all about."

Her mouth turned down a little at the corners, enhancing the first signs of the jowls she would wear in later years. I didn't like to see her like this. The disappointment. The frustration. It was an accusation that I couldn't bear—an icy hand around my heart.

"Then what is it all about?" she said, quietly. "We just stay where we were put and don't try to improve ourselves? Is that what you're saying?"

That wasn't what I was saying, at all, I told her. But improvement, I insisted, wasn't just about fixing things that were broken. "Sometimes, Mam," I said, "improvement is about accepting that something is irreparable and instead finding another way of making life better."

She studied me—her frown flickering and falling around her eyes. Looking back at the screen, she appeared to read some of the page again, before closing the browser window and once more looking at me.

"And have you found another way of making life better, Price Waters?" she said, smiling knowingly.

I nodded, returning her smile. "Yes, Mam, I believe I have."

Dad was the least enthusiastic of the two. Where Mam saw endless good possibilities (grandchildren among them, I was sure, though she never said as much), he only saw distraction and the potential for yet more failure.

We were all three of us in the living room, seated around the gas fire, drinking coffee as the air pressure lowered. My eyelashes were itching with the overpowering heat from the fire and I wanted to be out of there more than ever before.

"All I'm saying," Dad repeated, "is that you need to be sure that this is a good time for you to be entering into a relationship. You have your work, now. Your career. Maybe you need to concentrate on that for a while, that's all."

"A career?" I said, incredulously.

"That's what I said."

"Picking up litter and sitting with a crippled woman. That's a career?"

"We all of us have to start somewhere," Dad said, rather too regally for my liking.

"And the two are mutually exclusive?" Mam said. "The boy can't have a career picking up litter and a girl? Is that what you're telling me? Because if you are—" he made to interrupt her, but she just kept right on going, "if you are... well, that's just about the silliest thing I've ever heard. With a girlfriend to love and look after he'll have even more incentive, won't you, Price, love?"

I could have kissed her, but, instead, I simply smiled at her and nodded. She knew. For all her futile attempts to find a cure for my Anosmia, she knew. She would already be aware of the positive changes in me—changes I couldn't even begin to see in myself, yet—and, already loving Tara just a little for that, she would happily fight my corner for me.

I had to admit, incentive had always been something I had lacked. Drive and ambition were all well and good, but they needed a point. Success in and of itself could never be enough for me. Tara was my point. My mother had spotted that immediately and, as the minutes ticked by, I found myself a little surprised by just how much of an ally I actually had in her. Whereas before she would more probably have backed Dad, at least where focusing on my job was concerned, she today shot down all of his objections in flames—telling him in no uncertain terms that he was being a "prime arsehole" and that he should try looking at this from my point-of-view. I just sat back, quite happy to let them fight it out among themselves, and when it finally—blessedly—came time for me to leave, Dad merely raised an eyebrow at me and smiled resignedly. He knew he could win against me, but he wasn't really foolish enough to believe he could emerge the victor against someone as formidable as my mother.

"Bring her to tea," Mam said to me as I was leaving. "Tomorrow or whenever it's convenient. Just give us a little notice, ok? So I can have something nice in."

"I'll do that, Mam," I said, and kissed her on the cheek.

Returning to my flat had never been like this in the past. Yes, it had been my haven. Yes, it had been the one place in the world where I could be just what I wanted to be. When everything else had been against me, I had always known that this place was waiting for me—waiting for me with my books, music and baked beans. It had also, however, always been a place of isolation. I returned home and very effectively cut myself off from everything and everyone around me. Granted, that had been what I had believed I'd needed—but, in retrospect, it could only have been harmful.

With Tara now waiting there for me, however, everything was different. It was still my haven, still my safe-place in a hostile world. But now it was healthy. Now it was warm and welcoming, and when I shut that door behind me, yes, I still shut out the world, but now I had someone with whom I could share that isolation.

Tara was sitting on the bed, listening to Ray LaMontagne (again) and reading a John Irving novel she must have found under the bed. She looked up at me and smiled. I stood by the door, returning her smile and giving myself time to take everything in. How right my mother had been. This was my reason. Tara was everything I needed. I knew how that sounded, and I probably wouldn't have said it out-loud (except to Tara), but it was the truth—and I embraced that.

"Ah, the wanderer returns," she said, marking her page in the book with a piece of pink notepaper and closing it, setting it on the bed beside her. "I trust you had a nice time with Mummy and Daddy."

"It was a complete hoot," I said, kicking off my shoes and bouncing down on the bed beside her. "One laugh after another.

They just kept right on coming."

"I almost wish I'd been there with you." There was the expected irony to this, but I also thought I detected something else. It was difficult to put my finger on what it was, exactly, but as she continued, I thought I began to understand. "Although maybe not. A little early, perhaps... It wasn't too demanding, then?"

I shook my head, studying her. "Actually, no," I said. "No, it wasn't. I told them about you."

"Of course you did." She believed me, but she wasn't quite ready to let go of her security blanket.

"I told them about you," I insisted.

She squinted—reminding me, unnervingly, of Mam—and pulled back from me a little, so that, I assumed, she could get a better look at me. "You told them about me?"

"That's what I said," I told her. "Twice, if my memory serves me well."

"Twice."

I touched the tip of my nose to hers. "I told them about you," I repeated. "That's three times, now. Do I need to go for a fourth?"

"There's such a thing as overkill," she said.

"My sentiment exactly."

"But... you actually told them about me?"

This was getting monotonous, and I told her so. She nodded a little frantically, grinning inanely, and got up off the bed. She walked over to the window, thought better of it and came back, joining me on the bed, again.

"I know," she said. "Really, I do. It's just that... this changes things."

"It does?" I looked around, half-expecting to see the flat transformed.

"Now it's real," she said, speaking more to the room than me.

"You mean it wasn't before?" This was news to me. Not exactly welcome news, either.

"What? No, of course it was." Laying on her back, she looked up at the ceiling. "What I meant was, now it's officially real."

"Well that's a little better but —"

"You're not going to be a pain, are you?" she suddenly asked.

"No."

"Good. Because all I'm saying is that we're, you know, entering a new phase. That's all. Now that our parents know... it just makes it more..."

"Officially real," I reminded her.

"Yes." She stuck out her tongue at me. She still looked a little worried, but I thought that maybe I was imagining it. "So what did they say?"

"Dad was concerned that you might distract me from my career as a litter picker-upperer, while Mam believed you'd be the incentive I've needed all along. She made mince meat of Dad. I just sat back and watched."

Tara made herself more comfortable and did that thing again with her fingernails. Resting her head against my chest, her fingers then moved on to play with my shirt buttons and I put my arm around her, drawing her in close, oddly afraid that she would say something that might shatter the sense of contentment I felt.

"And that was it?" she said.

"Pretty much. They want to meet you, of course, but I didn't make a date or anything."

I wanted to tell her all that had happened with Claudia, but Tara wasn't about to be sidetracked. She sighed. "What if they don't like me?" she said. "What if they meet me and think I'm, I don't know, not good enough for you or something?"

"Don't be silly," I chuckled.

"I'm not," she insisted. "It's a perfectly valid question. What will you do if they don't like me?"

I sighed. I didn't like this kind of conversation. It was heavy with likely outcomes, some of them not all that appealing. All it would take would be one wrong word in the right place (or one right word in the wrong place) and it would all come tumbling down around my ears. The contentment I felt would be gone. Everything I'd dreamed of and wished for, the very things I now believed I was at least on the way to accomplishing, would be forever banished to a wasteland of lost love and hopelessness. I would be the sad old git who had to whack off to half-memories and imaginings again, hugging his pillow for warmth and reading Hardy for the laughs.

Choosing my words carefully, I said, "I don't see them that often, love. Their opinion doesn't impact on my life all that much."

"Which is why you're doing a job you never would have chosen to do if your father hadn't set it up for you."

"That's different," I said. "That wasn't worth making a stand over. You are. And it's all academic, anyway."

"Is it?" She didn't seem in the least bit convinced.

"Yes it is." I held her more tightly, talking into her hair—wishing once more that I could smell it. "They'll love you, Tara. What's not to love?"

"They'll find something," she said. "They always do."

"What's that supposed to mean?"

Shrugging, she pushed away from me and sat up. "Nothing," she said. "I nearly forgot. George came round."

Sitting beside her on the side of the bed, I searched her face for signs of pain or humiliation. "Are you...?" I said. "Did he...?"

"I'm fine," she said. "Which is more than can be said for him."

"What do you mean?"

Tara sighed and leant back on her elbows. Dressed in tight jeans and one of my old shirts, she looked extremely inviting beside me. I wanted to cover and become her, make everything that was wrong with her life right.

"He wasn't himself," she said. "He was practically monosyllabic, and he didn't insult me once. I even baited him a little, but he just wouldn't rise to it."

"He was like that the other night," I said. "So what did he want?"

"He left you that." Tara told me, nodding at a matchbox-sized package on the counter beside the microwave. "He said to make sure you got it as soon as you came in."

"What is it?"

"I don't know. I didn't open it."

Standing by the counter, I picked up the package, turning it over in my hand. Matchbox-sized because it was a matchbox. A matchbox wrapped in grease-proof paper. Turning it over in my hand again, aware of Tara watching me, I felt something shift inside. A shushing. Slightly metallic and very light.

"Open it, then," Tara said, sitting up and putting her chin in her hands.

Looking from the box to Tara and then back again, I finally pulled off the grease-proof paper, dropping it to the floor (Tara picking it up with a shake of her head) and opening the matchbox before my courage deserted me.

Inside I found a tightly folded piece of paper and a gold pendant on a chain. As I pulled out the chain, the folded paper fell to the floor—and Tara picked this up, too, unfolding and reading it before handing it to me.

"We really need this," she said, as I showed her the name on the pendant. Sharon, it simply stated. "Read the note."

I took it from her, letting her take the chain. The notepaper dirty and stained, I didn't like to think what George had been doing with it before writing this annoying little missive to me.

She wanted me to have this, the note read. I'm going back there. Tonight. 8 p.m. Come if you want.

Shoulders slumped and her face slack around the mouth, I didn't need to ask what Tara thought of all this. She was exhausted by it—fed up of the various ways in which George could touch our lives. There was no overt threat there this time. He hadn't come right out and told me to be there or else. But George was smarter than that. He knew that force of a more subtle kind was now called for. He'd seen my concern for Sharon. He understood it. And as he understood that, so he understood the power such concern might have over me.

"Fucking bastard," I said, sitting dejectedly on the bed beside Tara.

"He knows exactly how to work you," she told me.

"He always has."

"And you don't think it's time to put an end to it?"

"But I just don't see how I can get out of this one. There's no telling what he might do, Tara. I can't leave... there has to be someone there... someone to see to it that he doesn't do anything rash. I realise that this Sharon Jones is probably a very strong woman, with resources that we know nothing about, but I can't take that chance. I wouldn't be able to live with myself if he did something to her and I could have done something to prevent it."

"And you really think it might come to that?" Tara said, her voice soft with compassion—not for Sharon Jones, but for me.

"Don't you?"

She thought about this, sucking her top lip and looking out of the window at the cloudy sky. "I don't know," she said. "He's a complete arsehole but... would he really take it that far?"

"You know he would."

Nodding slowly to herself, she finally said, "Yes, I suppose he would." Looking me evenly in the eye, she took a deep, hitching breath before adding, "There's one thing you need to know, though—if you're going there with him tonight."

"What's that, darling?"

"I'm coming with you. No arguments. If you're doing this, I'm doing it, too."

Chapter Seven

We found George standing outside his mother's house, hands in the pockets of his jacket and leaning against an old Volvo parked at the kerb. He pushed himself away from the car when he saw us approaching—hawking up something distasteful and spitting it over the wall and into his mother's sorry excuse for a garden. I noticed the way in which he stared at Tara as we got closer, and imagined that we had yet another battle on our hands.

Surely enough, his first words were, "What's she doing here?"

"She's coming with us," I told him. "Either that or we both go home."

George opened his mouth to speak, and then thought better of it—shrugging and kicking at the car tyre. "I borrowed this pile of shite off a friend," he told us. "Best I could do at such short notice, but I think it'll get us there and back okay. If the gods are on our side."

"Gods?"

"People up in the sky. They roll dice and shit."

"Gamblers."

"And we are created in their image."

Tara looked from George to me and shook her head, muttering something that sounded vaguely obscene beneath her breath. "Spare me the metaphysical bollocks, please," she said. "It's cold and we probably have a long night ahead of us—so can we just get fucking on with it?"

I flinched in anticipation of what must inevitably come next. George liked his space, his freedom. The choices in life were his and no one else's, and if there was one thing he detested more than anything, it was someone trying to take that away from him... someone trying to disempower him. It was a little thing, a minor infraction, but I just couldn't see how he could let this one pass. If this evening was to stand anything like a chance of proceeding the way he wished, he would have to stamp his authority on it now.

Stepping forward, George opened the rear near-side door of the Volvo and reverentially lowered his head. "Just don't sweat on the upholstery," he said.

The roads should have been familiar from our earlier visit, but they weren't. I put this down, initially, at least, to the fact that it was dark this time, the full moon hidden behind pillows of black cloud, but as time went on I started to wonder if maybe George was lost.

On the back seat of the Volvo with Tara, however, I found that I really couldn't have cared less. The car's heater was in good working order and, cuddled up against her, I couldn't really find all that much to complain about—other than George's frighteningly erratic driving. We leant into each other as we rounded corners, and linked arms, Tara's head on my shoulder as she sighed her way through the ridiculousness of it all. It was oddly erotic, the two of us somehow seeming cut off from George, as close as he was, and when my hand briefly strayed beneath Tara's skirt, she welcomed it... her legs falling open as she pushed towards my fingers, happy to let me play until, with a too-sharp turn of the steering wheel, George said, "Hope you brought your map and compass, Price, cos I ain't got a fucking clue where we are."

Tara reluctantly released my hand and I, with equal reluctance, leant forward between the two front seats. "You're shitting me, right?" I said.

"Nope," he answered, sounding just a little too happy about it. "I'm about as lost as lost can be. In a world of lost, I'm the most lostest. I am loster than those beautiful but utterly fucking gormless people on that island. You know—from that TV series. What's it called again?"

"Lost."

"Couldn't have put it better myself."

"You have absolutely no idea where we are?"

"That is, I believe, the widely accepted definition of 'lost'," he told me. "I have a vague notion that we're somewhere in the north-east of England still, but that's more an act of faith than anything else."

"And, roughly speaking, how long have we been lost?"

"Roughly speaking? About half an hour or so."

"Oh for fuck's sake," Tara said.

"I thought that if I just kept driving it would work itself out," George said, with a very un-George-like chuckle. "Can't be right all the time, I guess."

I peered out at the road ahead of me without replying. It was all too easy to share Tara's exasperation. We were here to do George a favour (on the surface of it, at least) and for him to be so careless with that was potentially rather annoying. I couldn't help finding it a little funny, though. Here we were, lost and in a 'borrowed' car, whatever that meant to George, tootling around the country lanes in the darkest dark I believed I'd ever seen, and dear George had simply continued driving, convinced on some primitively naïve level that it would all come out in the wash. Coming from George, who always took great pleasure in being right, it was especially amusing.

"And I don't suppose this thing has sat-nav, right?" I said.

George twisted his neck to look at me—swerving onto the grass verge before correcting. "Does it look like it's got sat-nav? Jesus, Price, you crack my up, sometimes. The onboard entertainment system still plays cassettes and you're asking if it has sat-nav. Precious."

"It's not that unusual a question," Tara piped up, not bothering to hide her annoyance.

George was on the cusp—about to say something very insulting that I would have no other option but to respond to. His shoulders came up and he twisted his hands on the steering wheel, his palms squeaking against the luxury plastic, and I jumped in before he had chance to speak, hoping to defuse the situation.

"Maybe if we went back the way we came," I said. "Tried to spot familiar landmarks, that kind of thing."

"Like the Eiffel Tower?" Tara asked, a little unhelpfully, I thought.

"Good plan," George said. "Except that I'm not sure I remember which way we came."

"I'll give you a clue. It's behind us." This was Tara, again. Boy, was she on form tonight. "You turn the car around and, bingo, off we go."

"It's not as simple as that," George insisted.

"It isn't?" I said.

"Nope." He was chuckling again, and I was beginning to find it rather unnerving. "I don't remember which turns I took, you see. Lefts. Rights. That kind of thing. This driving business is fairly new to me and I had to give it my full attention. Directions weren't exactly my prime concern."

Something had been niggling at me ever since we had set off on this journey—something I only now allowed to creep back to the forefront of my mind. I had known George since childhood and we had progressed through life's various and tumultuous stages together but, through all that time, I couldn't once recall him taking a driving lesson or test.

"When did you get your licence, George?" I asked.

He grinned at me, steering with one hand as he scratched his balls with the other. "What licence?"

I sat back, exasperation finally getting the better of me, and Tara linked my arm, patting it consolingly.

"You're not going to get all disapproving on me, now, are you?" he said, looking at us through the rear-view mirror. "Drastic measures were called for. Surely you can both see that. I needed to get out here quick and stealing a car and driving it myself just seemed like the most obvious route to take."

"The car's stolen?" Tara said. She was anything but incredulous—merely in need of a little confirmation.

"Surprised?"

"No. I just wished it had occurred to me earlier." She sighed deeply and held my arm more tightly as we rounded a bend, tyres protesting, George having way too much fun.

"Too late now," he said, working the steering wheel enthusiastically. "We have business to take care of—top of the list being finding out where the bloody hell we are. Any ideas, Pricey?"

I had plenty of ideas, none of which had anything to do with navigating our way out of this predicament. Staring at the back of George's head, I felt the familiar resentment bubbling up. I wanted to take a swing at him again, beat his sorry face to a pulp and hang him as an example for all to see at the next crossroads we came to. I had allowed this to go on for too long. Tara was right. It could end. I could stop it. All it would take would be for me to say the right thing at the right time. Physical violence wouldn't be called for. I merely had to understand the space George and I inhabited... understand it, and know what to say in order to break the ridiculous hold he had over me.

"What's this all about, George?" I said, quietly.

He didn't reply right away, but the car slowed somewhat and I sensed that I had found a vulnerable spot. His shoulders hunched again, and then dropped—and without saying a word, he pulled into a lay-by, turned off the engine and lit up a cigarette.

"What do you mean?" he finally said.

"This," I said. "Coming out here to see this Sharon lass. In the dark. In a stolen fucking car that you aren't qualified to drive. What's it all about, mate?"

Rolling down his window, he blew his cigarette smoke outside—an oddly considerate gesture for George, and one I didn't especially care for.

"I don't want to talk about it," he said.

"You don't?" I thought he did.

"No."

"Well maybe this isn't just about what you do or don't want anymore," I said, Tara nodding beside me. "Maybe it never was."

It was cold with the window open, in spite of the heater. Tara, if it were at all possible, moved even closer to me. I could feel her breath on the side of my neck, and once again wished I could smell it. At times, the degree to which I felt cut off from the world (not in a good way) seemed overwhelming and far too complete. Now was one such time. I yearned for that added dimension in a way in which I hadn't for a very long time. I wanted to understand George's cigarette smoke, breathe it in a fully experiential way, break it down into its various chemical, carcinogenic components and truly identify its shape and shade—but more than that, I wished for a sense of its counterpoint; the cold, night air. With Tara beside me, the heater struggling against this new adversary, I tried to imagine what it must be like to inhale that refreshing brew and know it as more than just a cooling sensation in one's lungs.

"You want to know?" George said, looking over his shoulder at Tara and me. "You really want to know?" We nodded—me a little less enthusiastically than Tara—and he sighed and coughed, spitting out of his window before drawing deeply on his cigarette again. Finally, he closed the window and shuffled around in his seat so that he could see us better. "Okay," he said, as serious as I'd seen him tonight. "I'll tell you... but if it goes any further, I swear, I'll kill the both of you. And that's not fucking hyperbole, so get it into your thick skulls. Tell anyone about this, and you'll live to regret it. Or not, as the case may be." He chuckled at his priceless wit, and then said, "Do I have your word that you won't tell anyone about this?"

We both nodded sheepishly and waited for him to continue.

I never knew quite where I was with George. That was his way. He mixed truth and fiction as if it were not the oil and water of reality that some claimed it to be, sometimes with skill, more often with rank crassness. Contradiction was just another tool with which to outfox the gullible. Tonight, however, sitting in that stolen car and listening to the story of George and Sharon, I was more sure than I'd ever been that he was telling us the truth. And it was this certainty more than anything that truly disturbed me.

"I didn't tell it quite how it happened," George said. "Back at the party. At Martha's. Yes, that was how we first saw each other, and yes we did those things—but Sharon didn't ignore me. When we saw each other on the street, I mean. That bit wasn't true. I wanted her to because... I didn't want people to know what had been happening to me... but Sharon was better than that.

"The day after our first encounter, she came up to me. I was sitting on the wall outside Martha's and she just came along and sat down beside me without saying a word. She bumped her shoulder against mine, playfully, and I looked at her. She was smiling. It might not sound much, but right then, not many people were smiling at me, so it meant a lot. I smiled back at her and... well, that was it. We became friends. Good friends. We laughed and played and talked... we even fucked a few times... and then, one day, I..."

He stopped at this point, turning away from us and looking out through the windscreen at the blackness of the road ahead. Tara and I looked at each other, and I wondered if I should say something. He'd sounded a little choked and, as suspicious as this made me, I couldn't help feeling that something was required of me.

Before I could say or do anything, however, he coughed and continued. "You remember the Jag man, right, Price?" he said. "My mother's piece of shit boyfriend."

"How could I forget?"

"Quite. A right slimy piece of work. Anyway, he'd started coming round more and more often. He was shafting Mam in every room I went. I'd go into the living room, and there she'd be with her leg spread, panting like a bitch with him on top. So I was spending as much time as I could round at Martha's. It felt safe, and with Sharon there, right next door, it had an added dimension that I found hard to resist. Still, I couldn't stay there all of the time. Martha had a life of her own and... well, Mam could be a clingy fuck when it suited her. So I had to go home sometimes and, sure enough, when I did, Jag man was there, shagging the saggy arse off Mam and watching me out of the corner of his eye... always watching me."

Tara was holding my hand, now—her grip tight and moist. I felt somewhat light-headed, and realised that I'd been so engrossed in what George was saying that I'd been holding my breath. I didn't exactly know where he was going with this, but I had a vague idea—and if I were correct, I saw that it could completely alter the way in which we thought of him.

"I did my level best to just keep the fuck out of his way when Mam wasn't around," he said, voice low and as broken as the dry stone walls on either side of the road. "But one day... Mam was out and..."

"You don't have to tell us if you don't want to," Tara suddenly said.

I knew where she was coming from with this. It was so bloody alien to hear George talking this way that I could only assume that what he was about to tell us was so personal that we might not want to hear it, after all. As annoying and demanding as he could be, I found that I wanted the old George back—the George that didn't matter, the George who could get hurt without my actually giving a shit. And so I echoed Tara—insisting that this was something he needed to think about. Was he absolutely sure it was something he wanted to share with us?

"You can't undo it," I told him. "Once you tell us, it's done. We'll know and... we'll always know. No getting away from it."

"Always know?" he said, trying the idea on for size.

"Always," I told him.

"Always," Tara repeated.

George nodded thoughtfully. "Well," he said, "don't think I haven't given that plenty of consideration. Because I have. I've had a long time to think about it. Years, in fact. Decades, even. And I suppose I've always known that this time would come. It had to. Something would happen and I'd have to tell someone else. If I was to ever get the things I wanted, I would have to tell—I would have to share." He faced us, features shadowed and long. "Truth be known, I'm just glad it's you two. If I have to tell this to anyone... this is about as right as it gets."

I liked to think that I was correct when I told myself that there was nothing fabricated about this, that George was being more honest with us than ever before—but still I felt that niggling doubt creeping back. I was conditioned not to trust him through years of bitter experience, and resisting the impulse his trigger inspired was far from easy. Nevertheless, I sat back with Tara and listened, growing more depressed as the minutes passed by, more certain that George's bleak tale was taking us to places we ultimately wouldn't want to go. I listened, and I knew that Tara had been right. I should have stayed away. I should have paid heed to the note she left in my room... I should have walked away from him a long time ago.

"Mam wasn't about and I was in my room, doing my homework," George said. "Fucking Pythagoras. I can remember it to this day. The square on the frigging hypotenuse. I was growing more and more frustrated with it, wishing Sharon was there to help and seeing no other option other than to throw the book out of the window and go kick a ball about for a bit. It was one of those early Spring days and it was just too nice to be cooped up doing pointless shit like this. That was my way of thinking. So... I closed the books and stood up to leave my room. And there the fucker was. Standing in the doorway looking at me."

George paused to light a fresh cigarette off the butt of his last, inhaling deeply and staring out at the heavy night sky. I don't know what he saw out there, but it made him shudder—shudder and turn up the collar of his jacket.

"I thought he was just being his usual creepy self," George continued. "He was blocking my way and I thought, fine—I'll just push my way past him and fuck it. No problem. But it wasn't that simple. I pushed, he resisted. I was a kid. He was a lot bigger and stronger than me. But it still took me a minute to see that I was going nowhere. The Jag man was the one making the rules, and there was fuck all I could do about it.

"He pushed me back into the room and closed the door behind us. I could smell stale beer and piss, and he had his usual hard-on beneath his trousers. I didn't know what he wanted. I really didn't. I thought he was going to bollock me for scratching his car, which I'd taken great pleasure in doing the day before, but that wasn't what he wanted at all... fuck, it wasn't."

None of this made any real sense—and, yet, it made perfect sense. I just couldn't get my head around how it had happened or how I had known George all this time without ever realising that he'd been subjected to such an obscene and cruel act. If George had not always been the dysfunctional bully, it would have explained a lot.

"I'm sure I don't need to fill in the blanks," he said. "He did exactly what you think he did to me. Everything imaginable. And then he left and we never saw him again."

"Did you tell Carla?" Tara asked.

George shook his head. "No. She blamed me for him leaving, anyway. The scratch on his car. The last thing I needed was to tell her only to have her turn round and call me a liar."

"She would never have done that, surely?" I said.

"Heard the one about the boy who cried wolf?" He smiled bitterly. "Mam had had lots of boyfriends and... well, let's just say I hadn't exactly liked any of them. She had every reason not to believe me. Truth is, there was only one person I never lied to— and she was the one I told."

"Sharon Jones," Tara said.

"Got it in one. I went right round there. Still had the old fucker's come seeping out of my crack... anyway, she knew something was wrong the minute she saw me... she was good that way, was Sharon."

I was cold. The heater was still blasting away and Tara was holding on to me tightly, her head on my shoulder, her arms gripping mine—but still I felt, quite suddenly, as if someone had opened all of the doors. I shivered and Tara looked up at me questioningly. Doing my best to smile at her comfortingly, I tried not to look too deeply into myself—tried to focus on George and not dwell on the gloomy, soul-destroying frame of mind that this strange evening seemed to be inspiring. He was not who I had thought he was, I now saw. If what he was telling us was true (and that no longer seemed as big an if as it once might have), he had been as shaped by circumstance as the rest of us. There was no telling what other horrors had occurred in his life—and the more I thought about it, the more I dispiritingly saw that this reflected on me. This was a tragedy I should, on some level at least, have already known about. I was his best friend, after all. And, yet, I had been wholly oblivious to it. To me, George had been nothing more than a pain in the arse that I tolerated merely because I was afraid that no one else would put up with me. I had never been interested in his problems, not really, and I most certainly had never tried to help him... not it any real, altruistic sense. As depressing as it was to acknowledge, I had lacked insight as surely as I lacked a sense of smell, and because of that, I now felt that I owed him this evening, at the very least.

Tara checked to see if I was okay, again, and I nodded a little impatiently before saying to George, "Go on, mate. We're listening."

Without looking at me, he sighed and said, "She didn't mess about, did Sharon. There was no one home, so she took me up to her room and cleaned me up. She didn't ask me any questions, just got the residual spunk out of my crack and made me feel as clean and comfortable as she could. It was almost worth him doing that to me just to have her looking after me like that. Not really, but you know what I mean. She was so attentive, so kind. I wasn't used to it but... I liked it. And when she sat me down on her bed, legs up, pillows plumped, and sat down beside me... I cried. I cried like a fucking baby and she just held me,. She just held me until I stopped crying and she didn't say a fucking word."

"But you told her all about it?" Tara said. "Everything he'd done to you?"

"Eventually, yes," George replied. "It must have been an hour or so later. I don't know. She'd given me some of her dad's whisky and a sandwich, so I was feeling a bit more human. I didn't want to tell her. Not really. But I knew I had to. I knew that if I didn't, I might lose her as a friend—plus there would be absolutely no chance for me to exact revenge on the Jag man. If anyone would know just what had to be done, it was Sharon. She had a good head on her, that lass. She was as calm as you like and when I filled in all of the details of what had happened, she just sat back and stared at her feet, biting her fingernails as she tried to figure out what had to be done."

The car was thick with cigarette smoke and, when Tara started coughing, George considerately opened the window again for her. I had a bad feeling about this. George clearly hadn't taken his grievance to the police, which meant—as far as I could see—that some other course of action had been agreed upon.

"She suggested going to the police, first off," George said, as if reading my struggling mind. "But she knew I wouldn't be up for that. It had been difficult enough telling her, how the fuck was I supposed to tell it to complete strangers? So she didn't force the issue. This was something that had to be dealt with, she said – he couldn't be left just to get away with it. If I didn't want to go to the police, she said we'd just have to find another way of making sure he didn't do this kind of thing again."

"And that was?" Tara asked warily.

"Sharon had three brothers," George said. "Or four. I was never sure. Their number seemed in a perpetual state of flux, but she had at least three—and they were as rough as fuck. She wanted to have a word with them, arrange for him to get a right good kicking. And I wanted that, too. I wanted that, but I wanted more.

"She thought it was just her dad's whisky talking, at first," he continued. "But she soon saw just how serious I was. He had to pay, I told her. But he had to pay in such a way that ensured he would never hurt anyone ever again. I wanted the fucker dead."

George got out of the car to pee and, as he had ironically put it, "get his bearings"—leaving Tara and I alone together in the car, dumbstruck and bewildered. The moment he slammed the door shut behind him, Tara asked me if I thought he was telling the truth. Was he for real, or was this all just some complex ruse designed solely to make us do the things he wanted us to do? I was quick to tell her that I couldn't be certain of anything, but that my instinct was to believe him—and that wasn't exactly the easiest thing for me to admit to.

"I thought he was making it up, to begin with," Tara admitted. "But now I'm not so sure. I've never seen him like that before."

"Me neither."

"And I don't think I ever want to see him like that again. It's too bloody real."

I knew exactly what she meant, of course. The strength of emotion connected to what George had told us, the way it made me feel about and for him was too intense. Frankly, I didn't want to have to contend with it and, yet, I saw very clearly that there was simply no getting away from it; George's peculiar reality now dominated and, whether we liked it or not, we would have to deal with that.

"Do you think he was serious?" Tara said. "About wanting the Jag man killed, I mean."

That, at least, was typical George. "Yes," I replied. "If it had happened to me, I'd have been serious about having the old fuck killed—and I'm nowhere near as vengeful as he is."

"So you think they killed him?"

"I don't know," I said, as George approached the car.

George entered with the cold night air, closing the door quietly and then merely sitting in his seat and staring silently ahead. I waited a moment, seeing if he was going to say anything, and then asked, "So what happened, George? Did her brothers kill him, then, or what?"

Tara grabbed my hand and held it tightly in her lap. The eroticism of earlier that evening was well and truly gone now, and, in spite of everything he had been through, I couldn't help resenting George for that. When Tara grabbed my hand, I wanted it to be about desire rather than fear... I wanted it to be about me rather than George. I know how selfish and unflattering that was, but it truly seemed that so much of my life had been wasted, and this was just another sodding distraction we really didn't need. Events had so overtaken us that I hadn't even had chance, yet, to discuss with Tara what had happened with Claudia earlier that day. And now we were faced with this. The possibility that George had been an accomplice in someone's murder. And the depression loomed ever larger as we waited for George to answer.

"She said that something that extreme was out of the question," George finally told us. "She didn't want any part of anything quite so excessive. Whatever he had done, it was wrong, she told me, just not wrong enough to justify our breaking the law—but I could tell she didn't really believe that. She had this habit of looking away when she was trying to conceal her true feelings... glancing out of the window, that kind of thing... and that's what she was doing then. I knew I had her. All I had to do was retreat a bit but keep the emotional pressure there and she would crumble. She'd have to. She cared, you see. That's what I saw. She cared about me and... she cared about other people, too. Sharon didn't want him doing this to anyone else. But I was the key. I was the leverage. And while she patiently explained just why we couldn't do such a thing, I sat there on the bed, trying to get comfortable—grimacing occasionally just to underscore the fact that only a few hours earlier I'd had that twisted fuck's cock up my arse.

"When she'd finished, I let the tears come," George told us. "Manipulative, I know—but that was all I had, and I didn't see that there was any choice. I cried and she held me, and I said again that I wanted him dead. He'd hurt me. I felt dirty. The things he said to me. How I was nothing. Never would be... all that would be true, I told her. If he didn't die."

For a few seconds, all we heard was George's breathing above the hum of the heater—rasping and drawn-out, liquid and heavy with hidden depth—and then he turned in his seat to look at us, again.

"Long story short," he told us, "she came round to my way of thinking. She said that she'd have a word with her brothers and see what they could come up with. She promised me, Price. She said that whatever happened, she would see to it that the Jag man got what was coming to him. He would die for what he'd done to me. She would see to it.

"She promised and then three days later, her and her entire family disappeared."

"So let me get this straight," Tara was saying, somewhat obstreperously. "All this driving about in the countryside at night and getting lost—it's all about a broken promise?"

We were moving again, George having had something of an epiphany while having a pee and now wholly convinced that he knew exactly where we were. "Got it in one," he said, merrily swerving from one side of the thankfully deserted road to the other.

"And your intention is what? To punish her for this?"

"Now come on, Tara, love," he said. "You can do better than that. Think, cousin. Don't pretend you can't, because we all know you can."

I watched Tara working through this, my own conclusions already drawn. It seemed to take an abnormally long time for her to figure out just what it was that he was saying—and I could only imagine from this that she simply did not want to believe the clear truth. It was ludicrous – on that we could be agreed. But it was pure George, and it certainly should not have surprised us.

"You're holding her to her promise," Tara said, her tone thick and laboured. "After all these years... you're holding her to her promise."

"Bingo!" George yelled, taking both hands off the wheel and clapping enthusiastically. The car started to swerve towards the hedge to our left, but George quickly corrected it—getting the hang of this driving lark—adding, "See. I told you you had a head on you, cousin. Wasn't that difficult, after all, now, was it?"

Tara didn't answer. From her sombre look, she had said all she was going to say for the time being. My hand still held in hers, I felt the tension strumming through her—and as dark as my own mood was becoming, I couldn't help but feel for her. George, as I believed we both knew he would, had drawn us into something we saw to be dangerous and bizarre, and short of abandoning George and Sharon to whatever Fate had in store for them, neither of us, I believed, saw a way out of this. George had held onto this for all these years. Nothing we could say or do was about to change that. But that wasn't about to stop me trying.

"Don't you think that's a bit ridiculous?" I said. "You were both kids. She made a promise that she just couldn't keep. There's no way you can reasonably expect her to honour that."

"You don't think so?"

"I don't, no."

"Let me tell you something," he said, taking a right at a vaguely familiar crossroads. "This is how it was, okay? Sharon was there for me. She was there at a time in my life when I needed someone. Even before the thing that happened with the Jag man, she was supportive and kind and giving — and I loved her for that. I loved her and I would have done anything for her. And then she went. Just disappeared, the whole lot of them. No letters, phone calls — nothing. And I had to find a way through it all on my fucking own. I had to deal with what old shit-for-brains had done to me and cope with being let down by her. But you know what? I didn't hate her. That's a biggie for me because I find hate pretty fucking comforting. No. I didn't hate her. I was worried about her. I couldn't believe that she wouldn't find a way of getting in touch with me unless something really bad had happened to her... I would have done anything for her, Price. Even then... even now."

"Then don't you think it's maybe time you let her be," Tara said, kindly.

"I can't," he said. "He's still out there, and a promise is a promise."

We did nothing to try to conceal our arrival at Kingston Lodge. George parked bang-smack in the middle of the front courtyard and we all three slammed the doors closed behind us when we got out.

Tara came to my side immediately and I took her hand — the two of us looking up at the unlit façade of the building.

Either Sharon and her deformed friend were all tucked up in their beds, I thought, or there was simply no one home. No lights shone at any of the windows and there was a stillness about the place that made me want to back away. Tara stepped forward and then thought better of it, returning to my side, pressing her shoulder against mine. On cue, I heard an owl off in the distance—the most hackneyed of harbingers, and, yet, oddly beautiful and appropriate. A few feet away from us, George stood with his hands in his pockets, a fresh cigarette hanging out of the corner of his mouth. Now he was here, again, he looked as if he didn't quite know what to do.

Something felt wrong. The awareness passed over me as quickly as the skipping, heavy clouds had passed across the face of the moon upon our arrival, and I knew immediately that I had to say something—I had to try once more to make George see that this wasn't the right thing to do.

"We shouldn't be here," I told him. He squinted at me through his cigarette smoke. "I'm sorry, mate, but I just don't like the feel of this."

"Me neither," Tara piped up.

"Maybe we should come back when it's light," I suggested. "It looks like she's in bed and –"

"We'll just have to wake her then, won't we?" he said, striding towards the front door.

We had no other option than to follow him, not really. Granted, we could have got back in the car and simply waited this out, but there was no telling where this might end if George was left to his own devices. And so Tara and I jogged after him, still holding hands—still staying as close to each other as was humanly possible.

"Do you remember Raintree Hall?" George said, suddenly turning to face me, grinning inanely. "1983. Remember, Pricey-babes?"

I didn't know what he was talking about to begin with, it was that out of the blue, and then it clicked and I found myself nodding slowly as I remembered that humid summer night of all those years before.

I hadn't wanted to go camping and, truth be known, neither had George. It had all been a scam to get me to Raintree Hall at night—and I had fallen for it like the gullible fool that I was.

I never particularly liked looking back at such times—but

tonight it was especially hard, standing in front of Kingston Lodge with Tara beside me, looking up at the gloomy building and wishing that that night long ago had never happened and that, similarly, this night was nothing more than a dim and distant recollection of something that might have been. I closed my eyes against the memory of Raintree Hall, but that only made it stronger—and, try as I might, the depression weighing down on me like mortality itself, I couldn't stay away from that place.

In its heyday, Raintree Hall had been just about the poshest hotel in town. Everybody who was somebody had stayed there at one time or another, living the high-life and, local lore had it, enjoying the multifarious delights the management had on offer (which, if the rumours and histories were anything to go by, included cocaine and whores by the bushel). By the time George and I visited it, however, camping in its grounds and generally, on George's part at least, looking for trouble, it was a derelict shadow of its former self. Windows were broken and one whole wing had been burned out. The ivy that had at one time decorated its exterior walls had run amok—reaching in through broken windows and giving the place a look of somewhere reclaimed... somewhere that had been taught a lesson it had long been asking for. George had been full of himself. I remembered that, now, waiting before Kingston Lodge... waiting for him to say whatever it was he wanted to say... whatever point it was he wanted to make. He had been bristling with energy and enthusiasm, his eyes darting about as he held the torch under his chin, shining it up spookily into his face. This hadn't been a random choice for our campsite. I was as aware of the stories as he was—the tales of the numerous ghosts and ghouls that inhabited this place—and I had very quickly understood that this was some kind of test. It wasn't a prospect that I relished, but that boy that I had been had in many ways been stronger than the adult me gave him credit for; as we had put up our tent, I had determined that this night would be the one when I would not let George make a fool of me.

"It was so funny, watching you," George said. "You had this set grimace on your face... like a kid waiting outside the headmaster's office. You knew you were going to get a fucking good caning, but you weren't about to let anyone see that you were scared. But it was obvious. You were shitting yourself and it was there in the tightly clenched jaw for the whole world to see." He chuckled again, and I sensed that he was merely putting off the moment when he would have to knock on the door of Kingston Lodge. It was he who was scared tonight, and we all knew it.

"Do you remember what happened that night?" he said, and I reluctantly nodded. "The act didn't work, did it? You saw one shadow too many and ran off home with your tail between your legs. Terrified. Scared shitless is, I believe, the technical term. And I stayed on, all on my own—camping in the grounds of that fucking place like some comic book hero. Right?"

"That's what you told everyone," I said.

"Exactly. That's what I told everyone." Solemn and unable to look at me, he stared at the front door of Kingston Lodge and added, "The reality was quite different. I was as scared as you were. The only thing that made it easier for me to cope with the whole frigging thing was having you there to tease. I sorta dumped all my fucking fear on you and then pointed my finger and laughed. And it worked a treat, until you buggered off, then... I was five minutes behind you. I just couldn't stay there. Not on my own."

I wasn't completely sure just what it was that George was trying to tell me, but I thought I understood—and I think I was a little bit flattered. That he had picked this particular moment to say this to me didn't really surprise me; it was that kind of night. What did surprise me, however, was his uncharacteristic generosity.

George glanced at me sheepishly and slapped me in much more familiar George fashion on the shoulder, and then turned his attention back to the front door—bracing himself as Tara leant in and whispered in my ear, "What the hell's wrong with him tonight?"

I shrugged and waited, wondering just what would happen if I did a runner now. Would he be able to stay and see this through without me, or would he be hot on my heels—panting like my true partner in cowardice?

It was too late now. George lifted his hand, paused a moment, and then knocked on the front door.

It reminded me so much of our previous visit. The sense of expectation, the heavy, turgid silence. George shuffled his feet and Tara clung onto my arm, looking up at the windows above—dark, lifeless and blind. I listened, but heard nothing, not even the owl of a few moments before. Something, I imagined, pressed against the back of my neck, and I turned quickly, seeing nothing but the stolen car, the distant hills and trees... the unfathomable night. Tara frowned at me questioningly, and I shook my head and smiled, trying to convince her that everything was all right, even though I was by now fairly sure that it wasn't.

George knocked on the door and we waited—the three of us, I believed, knowing on some level that he was not going to get an answer. The door rattled in its frame and the seconds passed. He knocked again, stepping back and looking up at the windows above... daring someone to look out... praying, I imagined, for someone to look out. Still no reply came, no sign of life, and I saw the frustration building in George, his shoulders pulling up and into his neck, feet shuffling and kicking. He took an extra step closer to the door and knocked one final time, more as an attempt to keep his bubbling anger under control than anything else, I believed. His effort, however, was in vain. He knocked and with this action there seemed to come an overpowering release of energy—his right foot kicking out hard and fast against the base of the door. The rotten wood rattled in its frame and then, ever so slowly, it opened.

We all looked at one another, before once more regarding the murky sliver of hallway we could now see through the opening. No one looked back at us and I knew immediately that it was too much of an invitation for George to resist. Not exactly unaccustomed to illegal entry, he would, I was sure, see nothing wrong with our walking into Kingston Lodge as if we had been invited.

George ran a hand through his hair and then threw his cigarette away, casting me a sideways glance (as if daring me to voice reservations) before stepping over the threshold.

"What should we do?" Tara asked.

"Go with him, I suppose."

"Do you think?"

"I don't know." George disappeared inside and Tara squeezed my hand more tightly. "We can't leave him to his own devices in there. Isn't that why we came?"

"We came because I couldn't talk you out of it." There was just a hint of blame and accusation to this. I chose to ignore it.

Without saying another word, I stepped over the threshold after George—Tara trailing behind me.

At the far end of the hallway, we found the living room—where we had last seen Sharon and her deformed friend. It was empty, but for a few toys, furniture, the plasma TV and a pile of women's underwear, washed and folded, stacked on the arm of a nearby armchair. George stood by the chair, fingering the knickers thoughtfully before calling out Sharon's name, as he had done a number of times since we had entered.

"It stinks in here," Tara said, holding her fingers to her nose.

"Then go outside," George said absently, momentarily his old self again. "That should cure it."

She ignored him, describing what she smelled for me, even though I hadn't asked. I didn't have the heart to tell her that her description meant little to me. It was just so many words. "I can smell vomit and urine," she said. "Those are the two obvious ones. Then there's something like... yes, it's fried food. Chips, that kind of thing. But worse than all that... damp. The place smells damp and feels damp. Do you feel that?" she asked me.

I nodded. She was right. This place made my bedsit seem snug and cosy in comparison. The air in that room was so damp and chill that it felt almost painful. How Sharon and that poor guy lived here like this was beyond me. It felt as if it hadn't been heated in years.

"We need to look upstairs," George insisted, pushing between

Tara and I and heading out into the hallway. "Sharon's a private person. If we're going to find any clues, they'll be in her room."

"Clues?" Tara said to me as George took the stairs two at a time. "He thinks he's Scooby Fucking Doo."

"More like Scrappy Doo, if you ask me," she said.

"Are we going up?" I was quite happy to stay there and talk about bad childhood cartoons.

"I suppose we'd better."

We found George on the landing, outside the open door to a room we took to be Sharon's. He just stood there, arms hanging limply by his sides, and as I took in his exhausted-looking form, I felt dread knot itself more tightly in my gut—a cramp threatening to shit it out. I couldn't see what he was looking at, not from where I was, but I imagined all kinds of things. Ransacked rooms, dead bodies, a scene of BDSM terror and depravity—you name it, in those brief seconds, I imagined it.

As we approached him, however, George spoke. "It's how it used to be," he said. "It's exactly how it used to be. All those years ago."

I glanced past him into the room, but couldn't see what he meant. It was too dark for me.

"The room," he clarified. "Her room. It's how it used to be at the other house. She's... she's—this one's the same. She's decorated it just like her old bedroom."

As I moved towards the doorway and my eyes started to adjust, I gradually saw just what he meant. Granted, I hadn't seen her old bedroom—but this most definitely didn't resemble the bedroom of a woman in her forties. Posters of long-forgotten pop stars hung on the walls, and when I reached inside and turned on the light, I saw just how faded and torn they were. Like the rest of the room, with its cheap, girly furniture and vile 1970s throws, they showed not only the marks of time, but also a wish so seldom beheld; the desire to hold onto something that deserved to be let go, simply because it was by far preferable to the world she inhabited today, as grim as it might have been. Stepping over the threshold with George and Tara, I tried to imagine what this Sharon woman was

145

actually like. She had been a friend of George. She had known him in a way that I never had. Hers had been a complicated life—this room and the things we had seen on our last visit had testified to that—and I couldn't even begin to imagine where that life had now taken her.

George sat dejectedly on the edge of the bed, picking up a discarded nightie from the floor and holding it to his face—breathing in a wealth of information to which I would never, could never, be privy. He looked misplaced and, whatever conflicting feelings I might have had about him, I didn't want to see him like this. He sank deeper into himself as we watched, struggling, as Tara and I were, to make sense of this, and when he stood and went to the window, still holding the nightie, I felt his longing and confusion pulling at me—creating a void that begged to be filled.

Before I could make a fool of myself by saying something utterly banal, however, George spoke. His hands resting on the window ledge, he placed his forehead against the glass and said, "I should have stayed. She knew I'd come back. I should have stayed and talked to her—made her talk to me. But I didn't. I was fucking stupid, just like I've always been." He straightened and stared out past his reflection at the ghostly image of the distant moorland, reeling in the thoughts and memories, fighting to make sense of the way he was feeling. Weeks later, he would tell me that at that precise moment he had believed it was all over for him. He had seen no way forward and had, however briefly, considered suicide. But I didn't see that. All I saw was a man who couldn't understand the hand that had been dealt him, a man who couldn't figure out what to do next.

"Maybe we should just go home," Tara said softly. "We can get some sleep and then... then the three of us can sit down and work this out—see if we can't find her and get you two talking." I wondered if she had forgotten what this was all about or if this was just her subtle way of getting us out of this place. "I'm sure everything will look better in the morning. A good night's sleep. It works wonders."

She was rambling, now, and I touched her arm to stop her.

George had stiffened, standing straighter and suddenly filled with purpose. I didn't want him taking his anger out on her, and I knew that the longer she talked, the more likely that was.

But he wasn't in the least bit concerned by Tara. In fact, he didn't seem to have heard a word she'd said. He stared out of the window, his face close to the glass, and only when he told me to turn out the light did I began to understand.

George beckoned us closer, pointing to the distant moor and chuckling to himself. I couldn't see anything. It was as black as tar out there, the moon behind heavy cloud, and without any other form of lighting I couldn't be sure that George wasn't just having us on.

"I don't see anything," I said.

"You aren't looking hard enough," George told me. "Try letting your eyes go out of focus, then it'll just jump right out and hit you."

"Why don't you just tell us what we're looking for? That might help," Tara said.

"I've got a better idea." He stepped back, grinning. "Why don't I just take you out and show you?"

Maybe this was the jolt I needed—I don't know—but suddenly, there he was, as plain as day. I muttered a sibilant curse and peered more intently out through the window, feeling George and Tara's eyes on me, alarmed and annoyed all at the same time by what I was seeing.

"It's him."

"Who?" Tara said.

"It is indeed," George agreed.

"The man we saw when we first came here. The deformed man that Sharon was looking after."

He danced under a sky that seemed endless and preternaturally low—arms held high as he spun like a dervish, stumbling and swaying, head back, rolling from side to side like Stevie Wonder getting off on one mother of a riff. He disappeared and then returned, and I blinked hard, trying to understand how he had done that. A man on a moor. There and then gone and then back again.

I watched and, sure enough, it happened again, the effect only making sense when I realised that the moor wasn't as open as the night made it appear – he disappeared behind the bush again, and then re-emerged on the other side, still dancing his strange dance.

"I've never been more certain of anything in my life," George said. "If he's out there like that, Sharon won't be too far away."

Chapter Eight

Having found our way round to the back of Kingston Lodge—this time without having to climb a gate—we proceeded out onto the moor, taking great care on the uneven ground. Visibility was appalling, a mist coming down and, together with the cloudy obscurity, complicating matters considerably. Tara kept putting a hand on my shoulder in order to steady herself, and every time she did so I became more aware of just how precarious this could be. Nobody knew we were here, we were heading out into god alone knew what—and George hadn't even remembered to bring his torch. As Tara stumbled along beside me, the two of us doing our level best to keep up with a distressingly hyper George, I saw that anything could happen.

Once, George looked back over his shoulder at us, and I thought I saw that unsettling grin of his again—nicotine-stained teeth catching what little light there was and reminding me of a Cheshire cat. All that was needed was a Sammy Davis Junior song and we'd be fucking made.

"Not far now!" he yelled, and we yomped on towards the now visible figure on the distant horizon.

"How did we get here?" Tara whispered, and I told her that I didn't know. "I promised myself that I wouldn't let this happen. Even that day. When I went into your flat and left that note. I promised myself that I wouldn't let him pull you into anything like this. Make sure nothing bad happened to you."

"Nothing bad's going to happen to us," I panted—my heart thumping in my chest, as if to challenge this. "We'll just see that this bloke... we'll see that he's okay and then... we'll phone for a taxi or something. We'll tell George, if he wants to stay and sort him out, find out where Sharon is, that's fine—but he can do it by himself."

"We will?"

I nodded emphatically, breathing more heavily now and stumbling twice as much as Tara. "We will," I promised. "Enough is enough. We can only do so much and this is above and beyond the call of duty."

George stopped suddenly and we almost walked into the back of him. Tara cursed under her breath and held onto me, steadying herself. He stepped away from me, staring ahead at the deformed man (who I could not stop thinking of, much to my own disgust, as Monster Man), now only a few yards away from us. Looking at us hopefully, George asked us what we thought we should do next, how we should best proceed. "I've never had to deal with an imbecile," he said. "Well, I have—but never one that's so fucking big and ugly. Do you think he's violent?"

"Probably," I said. Monster Man was still turning in circles and looking up at the sky. As he did so, he made a low, steady growling sound in the back of his throat. "He sounds a bit pissed off to me."

"Maybe you should try to calm him down," he said, looking at Tara.

"And maybe you should kiss my moisturised arse. I'm not going anywhere near him, George."

"We can't just leave him out here," he insisted—and he was right. For all my talk of phoning for a taxi and leaving him to it, I for one could see that something was amiss. Sharon had left Monster Man to fend for himself, which could have meant any number of things—but what it said most of all to me was that something had to be done.

"He's right," I said. "We have to do something."

"I'm not going anywhere near him, Price," Tara insisted—as if I would even suggest such a thing. "Not on my own, anyway."

"I know that," I told her. "But George is right. We can't just leave him out here. We have to do something."

"Like what?"

"Like find a way to get him inside and then phone someone...
the authorities."

"The authorities?" She resented the fact that we'd allowed
ourselves to get dragged into this ridiculous charade and, if she
were inclined to apportion blame, I was sure I was getting more
than my fair share. She wanted to have a go at George, but it
seemed I was a safer bet.

"Social services," I said. "I don't know. Whoever it is you
phone under such circumstances."

"This is after we've got him indoors?"

"Yes."

"Which you propose to do how, exactly?"

"I don't know." I sighed exasperatedly, turning away from her
and then turning back, wishing I'd never left my bedsit. "That's
what we're trying to work out, aren't we?"

"We are?" She softened ever so slightly and moved closer to
me, again—delicately touching my arm, rubbing it soothingly to
show that there was no harm meant, that she was just frustrated
and annoyed with this whole predicament. "Look," she said. "I
know we have to do something. I know we can't just leave him
out here. But he looks dangerous. I don't want any of us getting
hurt. Not even him," she added, nodding at George. "It might be
better to just phone someone now and let them take care of it.
You know, keep an eye on him until they arrive, and then step
back."

"Could work," George conceded.

"Brought your mobile?" Tara asked me.

I told her that there were normally only two people I really used
my phone to keep in touch with, and they were both with me."

"I only keep mine with me when I want to be disturbed,"
George said. "A night like tonight is not one for ringing phones."

"I don't suppose you brought yours, either," I said to her.

Much to my disappointment, she reached into her jacket pocket
and pulled out her neat little Sony Ericsson. She tossed it in the air
and caught it, before returning it to her pocket. "No credit," she

admitted. "Might as well have left it at home."

"You could still call the emergency services," George pointed out.

Tara nodded. "Does this really count as an emergency, though?" she said. "No one's died, no one's hurt..."

"Sharon's missing and this guy's been left out here to fend for himself," I said. "Sounds pretty close to me."

George watched her. It was rather strange, actually. As unlikely as it may have seemed, Tara had now become the pivotal member of our little cabal—and I didn't think it was because she was the one with the mobile phone. She had insecurities like the rest of us, most I hadn't even begun to understand, yet. She was a relatively uncomplicated girl who was probably still convinced that I would one day walk away from her. But tonight she was different. It was as if she had grown into this new part that she felt she must play— as if that kernel that had always been there had come to fruition the minute we had stepped out onto the moor. Her fate, whether she liked it or not, was to ensure that George didn't get me into any more trouble than was absolutely necessary—and tonight she truly embraced this, the acceptance empowering her in a way that even George had to recognise.

She reached into her pocket while watching Monster Man as he turned in ever slower circles—finally growing tired, it seemed, his footsteps faltering, his head drooping forward. She tossed her phone to me without looking. I caught it awkwardly, almost dropping it, and swore to myself while George—ever the piss-taker—sniggered at my ineptitude.

"You do remember the number, right?" he said.

"Fuck off, George."

"Jesus. Lighten up." He said this more loudly than was perhaps advisable. As I thumbed in the first nine, I noticed Monster Man flinch out of the corner of my eye. It was a subtle movement, but obvious nonetheless, and something about it made me understand that this wasn't a good thing. And as I moved closer to Tara, Monster Man yelled out "Lord's name vain!" ran and took a cumbersome swing at George.

George, of course, had a fairly well tuned street instinct. He was by no means the local hard man—far from it—but he did know how to survive, and a good part of that was as uncomplicated as knowing when to duck. Our deformed friend came at him from the left and a little behind, but George heard that battle-cry yell and knew exactly what was about to happen. Without bothering to look at his approaching attacker, he crouched and turned, coming up behind Monster Man as he hurtled past and giving him a good shove to help him on his way. Tara and I side-stepped to let him pass by—all steam, spit and flailing limbs—and watched as he disappeared into the darkness.

"The fucking ingratitude of it," George said. "Would you credit it? We're out here trying to help that ugly fucking thing, and that's the thanks we get."

"And while you're whining on," Tara interjected, "he's getting away from us. Don't you think we should at least make sure he's all right?"

And so we headed off in pursuit of Monster Man—somewhat reluctantly, to begin with, and then with more enthusiasm as it became apparent that finding him might not be so easy after all. At one point, George staggered and fell, and in the process of trying to help him back to his feet, I almost went with him. As we jogged along, growing more tired by the minute, I finally allowed myself to believe that he'd got away from us, that we were never going to find him and that tonight would simply end with us returning to Kingston Lodge and calling the police.

Sure enough, that was when I tripped over and found myself staring into the terrified, sorrow-stricken face of the Monster Man. Sharon Jones lay unconscious on the ground beside me, Monster Man sitting over her—rocking and whimpering. I thought at first that she was dead, but her breath came in very audible rattles and hisses and, much to my relief, when I hurried to my feet, her eyes flickered open for a few moments. There was a black patch down one side of her face that Monster Man (I really must stop calling him that) kept dabbing at with his fingers. I didn't want to think about that, but I knew I would have to sooner or later.

"I don't ever remember seeing her so still and quiet," George said. "Do you think she's going to be okay?"

"Not if we stand around here all night, no," Tara said. She cautiously approached Sharon and her guardian, squatting when allowed and trying to get a better look at her injuries. "She looks as if she's taken a bit of a beating. I think we need the police and an ambulance."

Sharon stirred again, her eyes opening and her mouth and throat clicking as she tried to form words. Tara leant in close to listen, and Monster Man emulated her—his lumpy, ugly face mere inches from that of my lover. He was calmer, now that we had found Sharon, but I still didn't like the idea of him being so close to Tara.

I squatted down with them. "No," Sharon said. She shivered, so I took my coat off and put it around her. "I'm... I'm all right. No police. No ambulance. Just help me... help me get back inside."

"You're hurt, Sharon." This was George, from behind me. His voice was flat, with a twist of authority that didn't quite fit the circumstance. "You need to get checked over."

"No," she said, sounding stronger now. "What I need is for you and your friends to help me inside and then go and leave me alone. Stop... stop bothering me, George. Just get me inside and then... go."

"I want to help you the way you helped me," he said.

"I know what you want." She looked pleadingly at Tara, placing a hand on her arm and lifting her head slightly. "Get me inside, please. I'll be fine once I've rested and washed the muck out of my hair."

Tara glanced at me and I nodded. Whatever George might say, we were getting her back to Kingston Lodge. Then we could decide what needed to be done next.

I started to help Sharon to her feet and was surprised when Monster Man jumped up and helped me. Sharon's lolling head lifted and I thought I saw her smile. "Good man, Richard," she mumbled and Monster Man (Richard) grunted his satisfaction.

We did our best to make her comfortable on the settee in the living room—the long haul up the stairs seeming too much for any of us—Tara finding pillows and a duvet, George watching with folded arms from the corner of the room. Now that it was fairly clear that we were behaving in a friendly manner towards Sharon, Richard was far more amenable. Content to sit on the floor in the middle of the room and play with his toy cars, he was no trouble whatsoever. I almost wanted to sit down and play with him... and I had a feeling that, before the night was out, I probably would.

For now, though, I did my best to see just how badly Sharon was hurt. I didn't know where to start. She was still drifting in and out of consciousness, which alarmed me most of all. There was blood down the right side of her face that seemed to have come from an injury on her forehead. It looked worse than it was, I was sure, but I had no way of knowing what internal damage there was. As much as I wanted to respect her wishes, I knew that if she didn't show some radical signs of improvement very soon we would have no option but to call an ambulance.

"I should be doing that," George said. Tara had brought in a bowl of warm water and a cloth, and I was now perched on the edge of the settee, carefully wiping the blood from Sharon's face. Up close, and even after such a traumatic night, I was surprised by how young she actually looked. The grey hair was misleading. Granted, she was no spring chicken, but neither was she a tired old horse. There was, potentially, plenty of life in her yet, which begged the question—what the hell was she doing living like this?

"So why aren't you?" Tara said to George. "Price." She gestured for me to get up. I wasn't sure I trusted George with such a delicate act, but I doubted Tara would look kindly on a refusal.

Getting to my feet, I handed the cloth to George and then, at her beckoning, followed Tara through to the kitchen.

It was more repugnant than Carla's kitchen, even without the cats and litter trays, and I could tell right away from the look on Tara's face that it smelled even worse than it looked. She recoiled visibly and grimaced, closing her eyes and bracing herself before pushing forward. For my part, I strolled in after her and thought how incongruous it all seemed. Cleaning the blood from her face, I would never have thought that Sharon Jones would be someone who would be happy to live in such squalor.

"How do people get like this?" Tara said, wrinkling her nose.

"A bit at a time," I guessed.

"And there's only the two of them?"

"As far as we know."

I watched as Tara found the kettle and, pulling a face at how much limescale there was inside (not to mention how much grime there was on the outside), filled it from the gurgling cold water tap. She set it on the worktop and plugged it in, before turning to me and folding her arms. As much as she wanted to be away from this place—away from George and his ever-evolving life of complexity and complication—I could see just how involved she had become. Her frown lines deepened and she chewed at her bottom lip, and, cliché or no cliché, I could have sworn I literally heard her mind working.

"How much do you know about Richard?" she finally asked me, chin low, peering at me from beneath finely furrowed brows.

Resting back against the worktop, thinking better of it when my hand touched something furry and damp, I shook my head and shrugged. "About as much as you do," I said. "Why?"

Her mouth twitched dismissively. "Oh, it's nothing," she said. "Not really. I'm just trying to get my head around all of this. It's even more complicated than we've been led to believe; you do realise that, don't you?"

"I'm beginning to get that impression. Not that it surprises me. Not the way George is."

Tara nodded thoughtfully, and glanced at the kettle, which was taking forever to boil. "I can't help wondering where this is going to go," she said. "And whether or not we have any right to walk away from it."

"We only came along to make sure George didn't do anything stupid," I said. "Now we've done that, as I see it, we can do whatever we damn well please. We're under no obligation, here."

"Not even a moral one?"

"I don't think so."

"Sharon's been beaten up," she pointed out. "She's living in this shithole with a man she may not be capable of looking after, and George... George wants her to fulfil a promise she made to him years ago—a promise that involves killing another man. And we're not morally obliged to make sure this doesn't all go terribly wrong?"

I went over to her and held her, knowing she was feeling the strain of this evening as much as any of us—maybe more. She rested her head against my shoulder and I kissed her on the forehead.

"Now that we're involved," she said, "I just want to make sure we aren't left with any regrets. I can't live with guilt, Price—it just eats me up."

"We can't live other people's lives for them," I told her, and she looked up at me—her eyes searching my face for something beyond me, something I suspected I would never see in myself.

"Then what are we doing here, Price?"

I didn't know how to answer her. Now, I see that it was all simply a matter of degrees—that we could help to a point, but once that point was reached, it was time to step away. Standing in the kitchen, holding her, I couldn't articulate this, because the thought wasn't there to articulate. I wanted to walk away from this. Hell, I wanted to run. But at the same time, I felt bound to the whole strange series of events.

"And I thought the new Claudia and Tony development was complicated," I said, thinking out loud.

"What new development?"

Of course. I still hadn't had chance to tell her. "Long story. And one that's probably best left until later. Let's just say that it's something else I really need to think about—and that I'm going to need your help with."

Sharon was looking a hell of a lot better when we returned to the living room with the tea. Sitting up with the blood gone from her face, she looked much more in command—and even less happy to see George. As I handed her a mug of sweet tea, I noticed a muscle twitching rhythmically in her neck—her pale blue eyes sharp and icy—and wondered if perhaps Tara and I should have legged it while we'd had chance. Wrapping her hands around the mug, she shivered, and this seemed to me to be more about her revulsion at being in this bizarre situation than the mere fact of her being cold.

George sat in an armchair in the corner of the room. As far away as he could get from her. They eyed each other suspiciously, and the air in the room grew steadily thicker. Only Richard, all cranial lumps and drool, seemed happy.

Sharon shivered again, almost spilling her tea, and George said, "I think she's in shock. That can be dangerous, can't it?"

"I'm not in shock," Sharon insisted. She looked at Tara. "Tell him I'm not in shock. I'm just bloody freezing."

I thought Tara might take the line of agreeing with George. It seemed fairly clear to me that Sharon needed looking at, however improved she might seem. But Tara could never be that predictable. Rather than reply to what Sharon had said, she merely lifted her head, tilted it with a compassionate air, and said, "So what happened here tonight?"

Sharon stiffened and sipped her tea. I noticed her hands shaking. "None of your business," she said. "As far as you're concerned, nothing happened here tonight. You were never here. You saw nothing. Understand?"

"Maybe we should call that ambulance," Tara said to me. Cute. I had to hand it to her; I didn't think George could have done any better.

"That's beneath you," Sharon told her. "You wouldn't."

"You don't know me. Wouldn't I?"

"No, you wouldn't." We'd forgotten about George, sitting quietly in his own little corner—his own little world. When he spoke, however, we turned and looked at him. "You would never do a thing like that, Tara," he said. "Admit it. Not to someone like Sharon. It's that gender sympathy shit you've got going on. More to the point, you empathise. Me, on the other hand, I'm a different matter entirely. When I say that I'll do something like that, I'll do it. Whatever the consequences for you, Sharon, or me. So why don't you just tell us what happened here, tonight, Sharon? Then we can all get on and enjoy the rest of our evening."

"What's it got to do with you, George?" she said. She didn't look about to relent, all tension and petulance, but then her head lowered and she let out a heart-rending sigh. "You don't need to know this," she said. "None of you. It's about me, no one else. Me and Richard and the fucking shit life insists on throwing at us."

"We just want to help, Sharon," Tara told her, laying a hand on her leg.

She laughed bitterly. "Maybe you do," she said, "but he doesn't." She nodded in George's direction. "All he wants to do is find a way back in."

"I have a way back in," he told her. "I don't need another."

"That's news to me," she said.

George chuckled to himself. I wanted to slap the little fuck every time he did that. "It shouldn't be." He sat forward and put his mug on the floor at the side of his chair. "I take promises very seriously," he told her. "Especially broken ones."

"That isn't a way back in," she insisted. "That's a dead end, and well you know it."

"What happened?" Tara interjected, her voice so milky and smooth that I wanted to drink it. "Forget that, for now—just tell me: what happened?"

I sat on the floor beside Richard and listened, determined to leave this to Tara and hoping that George had the good sense to do the same. What she had to say was vague and unremarkable, but I couldn't help but feel that it was merely the tip of the iceberg. Like George, she knew how to say just enough.

"I had a disagreement with one of my brothers," she finally said. "It was nothing out of the ordinary, but it got out of hand. Richard... he tried to defend me, and I just didn't want him getting hurt, so I ran out onto the moor. It seemed a good idea at the time. It was all I could think of to do. Get away. Run. I knew my brother wouldn't give up. He'd still get me. But at least it was less likely that Richard would get hurt this way..."

"Which brother was it?" George asked.

"Does it matter? It could have been any of them. One's much the same as the other."

"So what was the fight over?" Tara said. I thought that this might just be one question too many, but now that we'd got her talking, Sharon actually seemed disinclined to stop.

"They don't like the way I live," she said. "I don't like the way they live. It's inevitable that something like this should happen every once in a while." Close to tears, now, she watched Richard, utterly oblivious, playing with his cars. "They think I should dump him," she told Tara. "As they see it, the only sensible thing to do is hand him over to the authorities and wash my hands of the whole 'sorry mess'."

"And you can't do that."

"I'd rather cut off both my arms," Sharon said — and I thought of Tony again, selflessly caring for Claudia while she cared only how his selflessness might cause him harm. The sacrifices we make; the pain we are willing to endure. When I looked at Tara and considered the way I felt about her, I thought I understood it. But maybe I didn't. And maybe I never would.

"For them," Sharon said, "life is one long series of quick and dirty fixes. They see me out here and they don't get it. As they see it, it reflects on them."

This I couldn't quite grasp. I was about to ask just how it could reflect on them, and what was bad about it if it did, when George butted in.

"Why do you live like this?" he said. I was again surprised by the concern I heard in his voice. He sat on the edge of his chair, forearms resting on his knees and his hands clasped together, and once more I was convinced of his sincerity — and of the still-forming suspicion I had that this was about more than just his wish to have his promise fulfilled.

Richard made a purring sound, running one of his toy cars around the toe of my trainer, and as Sharon looked at him, her eyes misted.

"I have no choice," she said. "This is where I ended up. This is where we ended up."

"Who is he?"

"My salvation," she said. "My salvation and my damnation."

I welcomed the quiet—the cold air and the late-night stillness that came with it. We stood outside the back door, both drinking some cheap scotch we'd found in one of the kitchen cupboards, George chain-smoking and, as he put it, "pondering". I was exhausted, and it was fair to say that the alcohol wasn't really helping, but I needed something, and this was the best we could find in a kitchen that looked as if it should have carried a health warning. Tara, Sharon and Richard had fallen asleep in the living room, and after we'd covered them with throws and duvets from upstairs, we'd slipped away to get a breath of fresh air and, I imagined, talk through the evening man to man.

So far, however, George had been extremely unforthcoming. He squatted down against the wall, pulling on one cigarette after another, and closed his eyes, hands drooping below his knees, and remained like that for a good ten minutes. He seemed to be collecting himself, and I didn't like to interrupt. Instead, I stood a short distance away, trying to make my own sense out of this.

I could have oh so easily washed my hands of the whole 'sorry mess'. George couldn't do that, though. He was tied into this in ways too numerous to imagine. He wanted the promise Sharon had made him honouring, that much was true—but there was so much more going on here. That he loved her, in my mind, was beyond question; I also saw hatred and loss in his eyes when he looked at her, questions in need of answering and... recalcitrant hope, even. The old, calculating George was still there, his mind working endlessly on how he might best turn this to his advantage, but everything was more finely tuned, now, more multi-layered and considered. I think I pitied him, right then. Pitied him that soul-destroying drive and need.

"Should we be letting her sleep?" he said, and I knew what he meant right away. "She's had a pretty hefty blow to the head. We should be keeping our eye on her, shouldn't we?"

"She hasn't been sick or anything," I said. "We'll keep waking her, just to be sure, but she should be okay."

"You think so?" A little boy in need of reassurance.

"I think so."

He was satisfied by this, and fell silent again with a nod and a drag on his cigarette. Now that he had spoken, however, I was determined to keep the ball rolling. Sitting down beside him, the cold, damp concrete reminding me of that first night I had spoken to Tara, I took a courage-inducing swig of the scotch and said, "So you're going to hold her to that promise?"

He shrugged. "Has anything changed?" he said.

"You tell me. Has it?"

"Not that I can see."

"Of course." I shook my head, indignantly. "That's right. Silly me. She's got a deformed, backward guy to look after and everything's just as it's always been. How could I not see that?"

"A minor consideration," George insisted. "I'm sure, with a little imagination, she could even work Richard into it, if she wanted to. Keep her brothers out of it and get Richard to do the dirty deed for her. She could make it look like he was protecting her. No one would ever blame him for that, now, would they?"

"You are joking, of course."

"I'd never joke about something this serious," he said, lighting another cigarette.

"You really don't care if you destroy their lives, do you?"

"What lives?" he said. "Jesus, Price, look around you. They're living in a fucking hovel in the middle of no-fucking-where, for Christ's sake. They haven't got lives to destroy."

"I doubt Sharon would agree with that."

"I'm sure she wouldn't. Who would? But... look, Price, mate. I don't want to destroy their lives. Really I don't. But look at her. She needs a change. She needs a new beginning. A fresh start. And... and sometimes the only way of doing that is to go back — go back and tie up all the loose ends."

"You're doing this for her own good?" I said.

George laughed. "Now you're just being fucking ridiculous."

"It's the company I keep."

"There was a time when I wouldn't have put up with a comment like that from you," he told me, with just the slightest hint of warning. "And you perhaps need to bear in mind that that time may not necessarily be gone forever."

I thought again of Sharon and the way in which her brother had sought to impose his will on her through violence. Such a crass and basic way of impacting on the world, and yet so effective. Maybe it didn't always achieve the desired results, but there had to be some degree of satisfaction in it nonetheless. I'd seen it in George — seen it in the way in which he glowed and twitched after taking care of someone. It was something that had always repulsed me, something I'd always tried to avoid but, sitting beside George that night, I briefly entertained the notion that maybe it was the way forward. Would I have to hurt George to make him see just how stupid he was being? Remembering that night in my flat when I had swung for him, I hoped not.

"Do you think it really was one of her brothers that hurt her?" I said, not wanting to dwell on what might happen if I ever had to take another shot at overpowering George.

"No," he said. "They're right nasty bastards but... she'd have had to have done something really bad for them to hurt her like that."

"So she lied?"

"People do," he told me. "I think it's about time you got used to it."

"I have," I said. "I've had plenty of experience."

He flicked his latest cigarette butt into the darkness and sniffed haughtily. "I've never lied to you, Pricey-babes. I just play with the truth a bit. That's different to lying."

"My mistake. Forgive my stupidity."

"Already done, mate." He necked the rest of his scotch and then lit up yet another cigarette, squinting through the smoke before saying, "Sharon, on the other hand. She's lying. No playing with the truth there. I wouldn't be surprised if her brothers didn't even know where she was."

"So why tell us it was one of them?"

George smiled. He liked it when I asked the right questions. "Two reasons," he said. "One: she knows I won't want to cross them. They're bastards, like I said, and more than even a tough little fuck like me can contend with."

"Hard to believe."

"Thank you."

"I was being sarcastic."

"I know."

"And two?"

"Ah, yes, two," he said. "That's even more simple; she doesn't want me to know who really did it."

"Because she wants to protect him?"

"Yes." He looked at his cigarette. Sneering distastefully, he stubbed it out on the floor beside him. "And because she knows I'll know him. This is someone I've at least met, and she doesn't want to tell me who it is."

"Because of what you'll do to him."

He shook his head. "I think it's more about what she thinks I'll do to her," he told me. "She's ashamed, mate, and I'm not sure she should be. Whatever happened here, I don't think it's her fault— and I need to make her see that."

"You think she'll let you help her?"

When he spoke, I saw again the depth of feeling he had for Sharon Jones. He shivered and pulled up his jacket collar. "I don't know," he told me. "But I mean to try."

Chapter Nine

"I don't know. That was all she said."

We'd been back home for a couple of hours, but neither of us could sleep. George had dropped us off at about 4am, before dashing off to dump and burn the stolen car before the sun came up. We'd both been more than glad to see the back of him, but I think it fair to say that we were also concerned. The night had taught us many things about George Ruiz, not least that he was as lost and vulnerable as the rest of us.

"She must have said more than that," I said. We were in bed together, drinking hot tea and listening to Ray. I was aware of Tara's sweaty heat beside me, but was far too tired to make the most of it.

"Not really," she said. "You and George had left us alone, asleep, but we both woke a short while later. We could hear you talking outside and we just fell into a conversation of our own. When she said that, I pressed her—but all she'd say was that some things can never be taken back. We live with our mistakes until we die."

"Nice."

"Cheered me right up, I can tell you."

When it had finally become time for us to leave, Sharon, looking much stronger and determined, had walked us to the door. George had wanted to stay, but she insisted that Richard needed his routine re-establishing, and that was something she'd never be able to do with strangers around. George had refused to take this sitting down, however, and, ultimately, Sharon had buckled and suggested a compromise; George could return, and they would talk. Properly.

"Who do you think he is?" I said to Tara now. "Richard, I mean. Who is he?"

"That's easy." Tara grinned.

"It is?"

"Of course it is," she said. "Only a mother would put herself through that. You didn't see that?"

"No." Now that she'd said it, it seemed so obvious. "I guess I was a bit preoccupied."

"There's more, though," she said. "You really haven't given this much thought, have you?"

She snuggled into me, grinning, and said, "Think about," she said, as if I hadn't already. "How old do you think Richard is?"

I shrugged. With all those lumps and bumps, not to mention the vastly reduced mental capabilities, it was difficult to tell. He played and behaved with all the enthusiasm of a three-year-old, but his body was strong as... I couldn't say for definite—someone in their mid-twenties?

"That's what I'd say," Tara agreed.

"So, he's about twenty-five," I said. "And that proves...?"

She rolled her eyes, laughing at my stupidity. "How long ago?" she said. "When did George last see Sharon, do you think?"

"I don't know," I said. "Over twenty-five years or so, that's for sure. If everything George is telling us is true."

"Good. Now we are finally getting somewhere. Beginning to see where I'm going with this?"

I studied for a few minutes, the tiredness slowing me down and the depression I had felt approaching earlier that evening threatening again. I saw a sense to what Tara was implying, that much was true, but the closer I got to it, the more ridiculous it seemed and the less I wanted to acknowledge or accept it.

"That can't be right," I said. "It's absurd. The very idea that George could... it's preposterous."

"We know they were in a sexual relationship," she told me. "And, let's face it, if you had to put money on someone knocking up a lass while he was still in his early teens, it would have to be George, now, wouldn't it?"

"You really think that George is Richard's father?" One of us had to say it out loud, just to be one hundred percent certain that we were reading off the same page. Now that I had, however, I couldn't get over just how obvious it all seemed. Tara was right. It was just the kind of situation George would have got himself into. Buggered by the Jag man and then fathering an imbecile. It had a perversely poetic quality about it that I couldn't fail to appreciate.

"I'm certain of it," she said. "And when you think of it, it all fits with her brothers' attitudes towards her. She's brought a shameful, illegitimate imbecile into the family and the best way of dealing with that, as far as they are concerned, is to dump it—get rid of it and pretend it never happened."

"George thinks she's lying about that," I said. "About it being one of her brothers that did that to her. He reckons it's someone else. Someone he'd probably know."

Tara tutted and shook her head. "It all has to come back to him, doesn't it? He's so bloody arrogant at times, it's unbelievable."

"Maybe," I said, "but I'm inclined to go along with him on this one. Don't ask me why, but I just feel that... well, he knows her better than any of us, and if anyone's going to know when she's lying, it's him. We have to remember, George is from a dodgy background—but he's not the only one. Sharon promised to help him have the Jag man killed, let's not forget that. She plays by a different set of rules, too."

Before I had got to the bit about the Jag man, Tara had looked on the verge of objecting. She had frowned, and her mouth had opened as she had sat up, eager to contradict me. Now, though, she sat back—looking rather disappointed—and carefully considered what I had said.

"I just took everything she said at face value and... I didn't question it. It wasn't that I was just blindly accepting whatever she told us, it was more that I believed she was just trying to protect her privacy and get rid of George. But there could be more to it than that, couldn't there?"

"Very possibly."

"What do you think's going on, Price?"

"I don't know, love," I said. "And, if I'm totally honest, a very significant part of me is hoping we never find out."

I remember the walk to Tara's mother's for all the good and right reasons. However brief, it was the respite we needed—the time alone in a cool, crisp world that revived us and restored our humour. Her arm linked through mine, head resting on my shoulder, I felt the looming depression lift and thought that, yes, maybe everything was going to be alright, after all. Fellow pedestrians, out on their Sunday morning strolls to and from the paper shop, nodded their greetings with rare elegance, and we in turn nodded back, half in a world of our own, half in their world of the Sunday Mirror and roast beef.

"I feel like this is the best sleep I've had in ages," Tara said, and I knew exactly what she was getting at. "We should do this more often. Just get out and walk. Even if we haven't got anywhere to go."

"That sounds like something my parents would do."

"Then I like your parents already," she said. "They have clearly reached a level of wisdom that we can only aspire to."

I told her that, as much as I loved and respected her, and however much I felt I had to protect her from such harsh realities, she didn't have a bloody clue what she was talking about. "They're nutty as squirrel shit," I said. "Okay, they're sweet enough, and generally well-meaning, but... they're caught up in this miniature world of their own where I'm, contrary to what their five senses might tell them, still seven-years-old and boisterous. They really don't get that I've matured significantly since then."

"Matured?" she said.

"I like to think so."

"Significantly?"

"Okay," I admitted. "Maybe that's stretching it a bit. But the fact is, I'm not the person they imagine me to be, and no amount of effort on my part can make them see that."

"I think it's sweet," Tara said—as much to annoy me as anything else, I was sure. "You're still their little boy and they love you. What more could you ask for, Price?"

"Foster parents?"

She laughed, even though she tried not to, and then slapped my arm. "Now you're just being cruel," she said. "I'm sure they can't be that bad."

Shrugging and pulling her into me more tightly, I rested my cheek against the top of her head and said, "I don't suppose they are. Not really. Truth be known, I probably wouldn't be here today were it not for them."

"Well that kind of goes without saying."

"I don't mean like that," I said. "I mean what with my Anosmia and everything."

"The gas leak you failed to smell?"

"No. Well, yes. There are always instances like that. I was sat in the living room for three hours one time with this steadily growing headache. Then Dad comes in and tells me he'd painted it earlier that morning and it might be an idea if I didn't stay in there too long. But that's not what I'm talking about. I mean the depression that sometimes comes with it. I probably couldn't have got through the worst of that without their help."

"It gets that bad?"

"It has done," I told her. "It doesn't happen that often, and by and large there has to be some kind of trigger. It isn't just the Anosmia, you know. Although that feeling of being cut off in such an indescribable way is certainly a major contributing factor."

Tara didn't say anything, and I wondered if she was having second thoughts about our relationship. I'd been here before, a couple of times. The pause. The delicately put questions. The gradual stepping away. She'd never exactly struck me as that 'type', but what did I know?

"It's the worst thing imaginable, isn't it?" she finally said. "The depression, I mean. After Dad died, I was clinically depressed for a while. A reactive depression, they called it. Oh, yeah. That about covers it—except that it makes it sound just too fucking dynamic for my liking.

"I felt as if it had all fallen away. Meaning, sense, order—the need to move, to function. All of it was gone and all I had left was... I don't know. I thought of it as this black hole. Inside me. Sucking everything into it."

"You felt like you were going to implode."

She stopped walking, prompting me to do the same, and looked up at me. An old man and his Labrador passed by, grumbling to himself because we were taking up so much of the pavement. Tara waited for him to get out of earshot and then said, "I love you, Price." She kissed me. I kissed her. We kissed. And then she linked my arm again and said, "Now, come on. Enough about depressing depression. You were going to tell me about Tony and Claudia."

"I'd rather tell you about it later," I said. "Let's just be alone while we can. I've had enough of other people's problems for the time being."

"Fine by me." Her voice held a sleepy quality. If I moved away from her I felt sure she would fall to the pavement, curl up in a ball and sleep the rest of the day away. "I'd be happy if it was like this forever. No Tony and Claudia. No George and Sharon and poor, poor Richard. Just you and me, in our own private world, just like your Mam and Dad."

"Snuggled up in our very own fallout shelter," I offered. "The only people left alive on the planet. The new Adam and Eve, eating their tinned fruit in lieu of an apple and talking about how it used to be before and the world was blown to kingdom fucking come."

"So, we're in our fallout shelter?"

"The place to be."

"No television or radio?"

"Probably not. Plenty of books, though. Thomas Hardy, just so we can see how lucky we are."

"You'd get bored with the company," she said. "You'd walk away from me."

"With all that radiation?... I'll never walk away from you, Tara. Stop saying that. What do I have to do to make you see that I'm going nowhere?"

"Stay right beside me. No matter what."
"I think I can manage that."
"I'm counting on it, Price."

Tara stepped into the hallway and I followed, closing the front door behind me and smiling as Bernice, Tara's mum, almost sprinted along from the kitchen to greet us. Wiping her hands on a tea towel, she looked a little flustered, but otherwise perfectly ordinary, unlike the rest of their family. Her greying blonde hair was arranged neatly but with style, and her jeans and plaid shirt, if a little too 'country' for my taste, flattered her well-maintained figure. I recalled how Tara had referred to her as being like the cousin in The Munsters, Marion, and thought that that was as apt a description as I'd ever heard. She moved with old-fashioned grace, and her honey-brown eyes oozed warmth and welcome.

Taking her hand, I shook it gently—remembering what my father had taught me ("A woman isn't a man, Price. Easy does it.") But this wasn't enough for Bernice. She leant in and kissed me on the cheek, one hand on my shoulder as she said that it was lovely to meet me after all this time. "Tara has told me so much about you," she said. "Come on through to the dining room. Lunch will be half an hour."

When Bernice, or 'Bernie', as she insisted I call her, went through to the kitchen for our drinks—a scotch for me and white wine for Tara—Tara reached across the table and took hold of my hand. She smiled and her eyes positively sparkled. It didn't take a genius to see just how happy she was.

"See," she said. "I told you that you'd like each other."

"She's lovely," I said, giving her hand a supportive squeeze. "I didn't really know what to expect but... she's just like you, only older. A little older."

"She likes you, too. I can tell."

"I pass the test?"

"There is no test, but I'm sure if there was, you would. With flying colours."

I didn't think that Tara would ever have admitted it, but she was as relieved as I. No matter what she might say to the contrary, a part of her had been worried about this meeting.

"I hope that's okay," Bernie said, handing me a fairly hefty measure of whisky in a crystal tumbler. "It's only the blended stuff, I'm afraid. Tara's dad used to like a nice single malt, but I'm afraid the last of that went a good while ago."

"Blended is fine," I said. "The harsher, the better."

Bernie frowned, puzzled, but before I could explain, she twigged—nodding and saying, "Ah, yes. Your Anosmia. Tara told me it affects your sense of taste, too?"

"That's right." I smiled. "But it's no big deal. Not really. I've never known anything different. Probably would have been a lot more difficult to bear if I had."

"You've always had Anosmia?"

I sipped my scotch and nodded. "As far as I know," I told her. "I don't recall ever smelling anything, let's put it that way."

"And they don't know what caused it?"

"No. There are lots of possible causes, but mine's atypical to all of them." I winked at Tara, and smiled. "I'm unique, right, love?"

An eyebrow raised, Tara said, "Oh, you're that, all right. I've never met anyone quite like you in all my life—and I'm not always sure that that's such a good thing."

While we ate, Bernie told us of her morning. She had got up early, she said, determined to get well ahead in her preparations for lunch and our visit. Her plans were scuppered somewhat, however, when her friend Paula decided to call in unannounced. "She claimed she wanted to borrow some sugar," Bernie told us, "but we all know that's the oldest trick in the book, don't we. Turns out—and this was only a surprise to Paula, the poor short-sighted love—it turns out that that husband of hers has been putting it about again."

"Who with this time?" Tara asked, shovelling roast beef and Yorkshire pudding into her mouth.

"The hefty lass from the Co-Op," Bernie said. "That's not the worst of it, though. He's only gone and brought the crabs home to Paula."

"He hasn't?"

"Oh, I'm afraid he has." She chuckled then said, "I shouldn't laugh, though. It's absurd, because Paula just lets it happen time and time again—but it's like I said to her, this time it was crabs, what's it going to be next time?"

"Lobsters," Tara ventured, and the three of us broke up, laughing.

"No, stop," Bernie said, wiping her eyes with her napkin. "No. It isn't funny. Really it isn't. In this day and age you just can't be putting up with stuff like that. There's no telling where it might end. I said to her. I said, 'Paula, put a stop to this now. Before it's too late.' Not that she'll listen, of course. The silly love never does."

"That's friends for you," Tara said, very pointedly looking at me. Bernie caught this and sat back in her chair, glancing from Tara to me and back again, appraising us. "George," Tara said. "Took us on quite a little adventure last night, didn't he, Price?"

"Adventure wouldn't be my first choice of word," I replied, "but... yes, last night was certainly interesting. Not to mention exhausting."

"What happened?" Bernie said. She sat forward, pushing her plate away and folding her arms on the table. "I hope he hasn't pulled you two into another of his illegal schemes."

"Other than driving around the moors in a stolen car, he hasn't," Tara replied. I thought of reminding Tara that George was in the process of trying to get a man killed, but I suspected that this might be something she would rather her mother didn't know about. "He's been looking for an old girlfriend, and last night... well, he found her. It was a long night. What time did we get in, Price?"

"About two or three, I think."

"And then we couldn't sleep. You're actually very lucky to see us today. The way we were feeling, it's a wonder we managed to get out of bed at all."

"You want to watch him," Bernie said. "George. I'm sure I don't need to tell you what he's like."

"You don't," Tara and I said in unison.

"I'm not saying he's a wrong 'un," she continued, regardless, "but that lad hasn't exactly had the best of upbringings. It was okay for a while. Carla... she wasn't exactly equipped to deal with a kid. She was all movie-star daydreams and boyfriend mad. But when George came along, she really put her best foot forward for a while... until she lost her leg, at least."

"How did that happen, anyway?" I said. It was a story George had never told me. Which, when I thought of it, was suspicious in itself.

"Her leg? Oh, well, that's a long story but, basically, she's always blamed George for it. When he was a toddler, he could be really hyper. Fun and happy, but positively buzzing with energy. You had to run him around the park for five hours before you could get the little tyke to sleep. Carla was young herself, though, and by and large, she coped. Some of the time, she even looked as if she was enjoying herself.

"This one day, though, she just wasn't feeling well. She owed some people some money, George's dad had just told her that he reckoned George wasn't his and he didn't want anything to do with him, and, to top it all, some kids had got hold of a stray cat she'd been looking after and spray-painted it pink."

"Not a good day, then," Tara said, trying to move Bernie along.

"You could say that." Taking a sip of her wine, she shook her head and then sighed. "I really felt for her back then. Don't get me wrong, she was by no means perfect—but she was a tryer. She was determined to make the best life she could for herself and George, with or without his father, but everything just seemed to conspire against her.

"On this particular day, George just wouldn't let up. He was excited—God alone knew why, but I suppose when you're three it doesn't take a lot. He zipped around the house, Carla later told me, like a thing possessed—running from room to room, banging into furniture, slamming doors behind him... you get the picture. It was more than she could bear. She tried reasoning with him. She tried bribing him. She even smacked him—a form of discipline she abhorred, believe it or not. But none of it did any good and, so, as

174

a last resort, she let him play out in the back garden... once she'd made him promise he wouldn't run off."

"Which was the first thing he did," Tara guessed.

"More or less," Bernie said. "The next thing she knows, she looks out of the front window, trying to figure out how she was going to raise the money to pay her debts, and there's George running up and down the pavement, waving his arms about like he's an aeroplane.

"Well, this was back before they built the bypass, so it was still a fairly busy road. So Carla screamed his name and ran out as fast as she could. The way she told it, she ran like she'd never ran before and she was there in a few seconds, though it seemed to take forever. But she wasn't quick enough. Just as she got to him, George—no doubt thinking it was some kind of game—ran out into the road, still waving his arms about. Carla didn't take the time to look or think. She just ran after George—grabbing him and diving when she saw the bus bearing down on them."

Bernie smiled sadly and took another sip of her wine before continuing. "If she'd been just slightly quicker, it would have all been so different. As it was, though, the bus caught her leg. It hit it hard enough to almost sever it at the knee—spinning her around and leaving her in the gutter, screaming and holding onto George. The doctors tried to save it, naturally, but the damage was too extensive. She'd never have been able to walk on it."

The three of us grew silent. In the past twenty-four hours, I had learned more about George than I had in the twenty-odd years that I'd known him. Did he remember any of that day, I wondered? And if he did, how much did he blame himself? He by no means lacked intelligence, and I was sure that he was more than capable of reasoning with himself—insisting that he had just been a child. But it would be difficult for him to be entirely rational where this subject was concerned... especially if Carla still insisted on holding it over his head.

"Like I say," Bernie continued, "after that... well, dysfunctional doesn't even begin to come into it. It's easy to feel sorry for George, but I don't suppose I need to tell the two of you that it isn't to be recommended."

I nodded solemnly, the mood around the table weighing down on us like an old and sodden duvet. I felt suddenly quite claustrophobic, glancing at the door hopefully and swigging back the last of my scotch. I liked Bernie. I liked her a lot. But I didn't want to be here, talking about George and his mother. I wanted this to be about Tara and me.

Bernie wasn't obtuse, though. She also felt the oppressive atmosphere, it seemed, and so moved the conversation on. "How are you enjoying your new job at the gardens, Price?"

"It's proving interesting," I said, smiling at Tara.

"You were going to tell me about the 'latest development'," Tara reminded me—and Bernie raised an eyebrow, intrigued.

"Whatever you say won't go beyond these four walls," she promised, holding up three fingers of her right hand. "Scouts' honour."

And so I told it all from the very beginning for Bernie's benefit and then filling them in on all the latest details. I didn't feel like I was breaking a confidence by sharing this with Bernie—although I suppose that's exactly what I was doing. I trusted Bernie. And apart from that, she was a good, intelligent listener. Not sharing my story with her seemed unthinkable.

"She talked to you?" Tara said.

"You could say that, I suppose. Yes. Yes, she did."

"And you didn't mention any of this to Tony?" Bernie asked.

Shaking my head, I said, "No. He sort of interrupted us, so I'm really not all that sure how Claudia would want to play it. I want to speak with her again, first. See what she wants me to do—if anything."

Something was bothering Tara. She sat back in her chair, hands on the table. She was doing that thing with her fingernail, again, and as I frowned at her, she looked up and met my eyes.

"What's up?" I said, and Bernie turned to look at her.

"I don't know," she said, sighing deeply. "It just seems... odd."

"It's that, all right," Bernie agreed.

"It just seems especially odd that she'd talk to Price but not the man she's meant to be so concerned about."

"I think it's more a case of her never having had the opportunity to talk to him," I reminded her.

"What?" she said. "In all his years of looking after her, he's never once had his hand on her knee?"

"Good point," I conceded. "But there are other things to consider."

"Like?" Tara said.

"Like, I was trying to communicate with her."

"And Tony never has?"

"I'm not saying that."

"Then?"

Bernie was smiling behind her hand. Oddly, I quite liked it.

"Maybe he wouldn't see a twitching knee as an invitation to talk," I said.

"I don't buy that, somehow." Tara inhaled deeply and rubbed the back of her neck. "If you're right, Price, you have to remember that this is the second time she's communicated with you."

I frowned.

"That time on Lovers' Leap. The look she gave you. If you weren't mistaken, that means she has at least two ways of showing that there's something still going on in that head of hers. So, if that is the case—if communicating is easier for her than we previously believed and she's made a choice not to communicate with Tony—you have to ask yourself why. Why she made that choice, and why she decided she could 'talk' to you?"

I didn't know how to reply. While I would have flapped about for hours on end trying to find such depth and understanding, Tara went straight to the heart of the matter. She wasn't distracted by the scenery. The familiar and accepted landmarks were of no concern to her. She looked at the map and asked the questions that no one else would think to ask, let alone dare. And she found the answers more readily than anyone would have thought possible.

"What are you suggesting?" Bernie asked her.

"I don't know. Nothing, I suppose... except that maybe in this case Price needs to be careful not to take too much at face value.

It's probably nothing, but there may be much more going on here than we could ever imagine."

Bernie smiled. "And you don't think that it's merely the case that you've been spending too much time around George? In the habit of questioning every little thing?"

I thought I saw a little flash of annoyance behind Tara's eyes, but it was gone before I could be absolutely certain. Returning her mother's smile, she shrugged and slumped further down in her chair, suddenly looking as if she wished she could disappear altogether. Sheepishly, she pulled in her hands and hid them under the table. "Maybe," she said. "I don't know. I just want Price to be careful, that's all. It's bad enough that we've got George leading us a merry dance. Helping people is all well and good but... you're not the town sin-eater, Price. These aren't your problems."

Her voice caught and I saw just how worried she was. Maybe it was the tiredness of the night before catching up with her, I don't know, but however disproportionate I may have thought her concern to be, I didn't like seeing her like that. She was my girl. She was the single most important person in my life.

"I know," I said. "I know, love."

Sunday afternoon was for curling up on the settee and watching old black and white movies, Bernie insisted as she herded us, post-lunch, into the living room. Both Tara and I had offered to help her with the washing-up, but she was having none of it. "After the night you had last night," she said, "I think you deserve a little together time. There's a good film on BBC2. A right old weepy but you'll love it. Like I say, it's what Sunday afternoons were invented for."

She sat us both down and surrounded us with cushions — as if we were babies sitting up for the first time and she was afraid we might fall. I grinned at Tara, overwhelmed by the attention but loving every minute of it, and she pulled an exasperated face. She nevertheless seemed pleased and was especially impressed when I lifted my arms for Bernie as she took a throw from the back of the armchair and placed it over our legs, tucking it in neatly before standing back to admire her handiwork.

"As snug as two bugs in a rug," she said, chuckling. She and Tara exchanged a glance, and I thought I understood what was going on here. This was all part of their little game. See how fussy Bernie could be before Price started to get scared. What they didn't seem to realise (or maybe they did) was that I was loving every minute of it. Watching telly under a throw with Tara was my idea of heaven, and no matter how hard they might try, something like this was never going to spook me.

When Bernie finally left us alone, exiting the room with a cough and a chuckle, Tara turned the television up and snuggled into me. The afternoon rolled slowly along. We watched the film (a cheery thing about a woman who believed her lover had died in the war and therefore became a prostitute... all fog and bridges) and dozed, savouring every minute while Bernie distantly clattered pans in the kitchen. It was so far removed from the night before that the whole Kingston Lodge episode now seemed like a dream, a nightmare even, that we had awoken from with relief into Bernie's welcoming and reassuring arms.

Tara snored quietly at one point and I simply sat and watched her, turning down the volume on the television and wondering if this was it—if this was what we were all looking for... that elusive someone to share the quiet moments, that sense of balance and completion. I would never have claimed to be a great thinker, but for a short while I believed that, however fleetingly, I had touched upon something rare and nigh on Divine. We had purpose—and that purpose was, plain and simple, to each complement the other. She was left; I was right. I was up; Tara was down.

She snored more loudly and woke herself up—looking at me, confused, before smiling. "Did I miss anything?" she asked.

"Only a terminal depression. Don't get me wrong, your mum is a wonderful woman, but she really has got terrible taste in films. I don't think I've ever seen anything quite so gloomy. Maybe she would enjoy Hardy, after all."

Tara smiled and shuffled about, making herself comfortable. "You like her, then?" she said.

"How could I not?" I lifted the comforter to make my point. "Anyone who spoils me like this is always going to be in my top five favourite people—take my word for it."

"She's never been like this before," she admitted. "Never fussed quite this much. I suppose it's partly because I let her but... it's more than that."

"In what way?"

"She knows," Tara said.

"I'm pleased to hear it... Knows what?"

"She knows how much you like it," she explained. "How much you like being looked after and... she knows you're like me. You need it. The simple things like this. Sitting curled up with someone you love in front of the telly—it's all you really need, and she admires that."

"She admires my lack of complication?" I said.

Tara sighed, trying to find a way of explaining this without making it sound like an insult. "People today," she told me. "Most of them... or a lot of them, at least—they want everything yesterday. They want their LCD televisions and –"

"I'd like an LCD television."

"Shut up." Her hands were under the throw, but I knew she was doing that thing with her fingernail again. I slid my hand over and took hold of hers, letting them rest in her lap. "The point is, you don't measure the success of a life by these things. You're not materialistic."

"I can't afford to be."

"I'm gonna clobber you, if you don't stop that," she said. "You know what I mean." She pressed my hand more firmly into her crotch, moving herself again so the she could better position it, and when she continued, her voice had dropped an octave. "Intimacy," she said. "Love. Sharing. Being with someone you care about. These are the things that mean something to you. And Mam can see that. That's why she likes you."

"I thought she'd resent me," I admitted. Though it wasn't something I'd been quick to acknowledge, even to myself up until this point, it was true.

"Resent you?" Tara said, flabbergasted. "Why on earth would you think that?"

"Because it's just the two of you," I said. "You're all she's got, now, and it just seemed to me that she might think that I was taking you away from her."

We heard the living room door open too late, both of us turning to see Bernie standing there looking at us. There was a gentleness around the eyes, though I prayed that she had not overheard something that had inadvertently offended her.

Holding what appeared to be a photo album to her chest, she stepped further into the room and smiled. "Don't worry, Price, love," she said. "I'm not about to turn all evil and clingy. I'm happy that you and Tara have found each other, truly I am.

"Anyway," Bernie said, patting the navy-blue, vinyl-bound book on her lap. "I've got something I think you'll enjoy seeing, Price. A little piece of history, you might say."

"How did I know you were going to do this to me, Mam?" Tara complained (though her heart didn't seem entirely in it.)

"Because it's a mother's duty and obligation," Bernie said, rather grandly. "And apart from that, you love it. You know you do. You want Price to know everything about you, however embarrassing—because that's what being in love is all about. Right, Price?"

I wasn't all that convinced that it was, but it seemed impolite to disagree with her—and so I merely smiled in reply, hoping this would be adequate as she opened the album to the first page of photos.

Tara, quite unexpectedly, had been a chubby baby. Pretty but perpetually distressed, she had toddled her way into childhood with birthday candles and chocolate cake, surrounded by balloon-popping brats that she may or may not have thought of as friends. Bernie and the man I assumed to be Tara's now deceased father had been ever present in those earlier years—or that, at least, was what the Instamatic photographs told me. They fussed over her in much the same way that Bernie had fussed over us this afternoon, and held her aloft with beaming smiles for all the world to see.

There was nothing perfunctory in those early photos. This was not merely a family going through the motions. Pride oozed from each and every page. This is our daughter, that album said, and she will accomplish great things.

The further through we proceeded, however, the more I began to notice a change. As Tara approached adolescence, she seemed less inclined to take centre stage in the family snaps. Instead, she cowered on the fringes, eyeing those around her with suspicion and, in a couple of cases, outright hostility. If I hadn't known her so well—hadn't seen the photos that had come before—I would have guessed that she was an unlovable brat, spoilt rotten by her parents and determined to take it out on the rest of the world. Knowing Tara, she had simply become less confident in herself. Why, I could never have said, but it had affected her deeply enough for the residual vulnerability to still be present today.

"People started to make less sense to her around this time," Bernie was saying, and I thought that this was only half of the story—if that. "She looked at them and they puzzled her—didn't they, love?"

"They still do, on the whole." Tara linked my arm and rested her head against mine. "Everyone has an opinion on everything, and most of them don't know their arses from their elbows."

"Can't argue with that," Bernie said, turning the page and smiling. "And you had such a delightful way of letting it show."

Tara chuckled and we moved on into her teen years—a time, it seemed, when fashion meant even less to her than it did now... her clothes plain and practical, any makeup she wore glossy with antipathy. It didn't take a genius to see that she hadn't been happy, but what teenager had? Dislocation and depression were, as far as I could recall, the two constants of adolescence—and I suppose I didn't see anything all that unusual in these images of Tara skulking in corners with her cardigan wrapped tightly around herself. With me, it had been dark glasses and a grunt in reply—for Tara it had been bad clothes and greasy hair. It didn't make a difference; she was still my Tara.

The rest of the album saw Tara growing into adulthood and

moderating somewhat. Over the space of a few pages and approximately fifteen photos she developed into someone I more easily recognised. There was still that hint of petulance, but by and large she smiled more readily.

The final photo took me by surprise, however. It was grainy and dark, difficult to discern. Taken at night, I made out a lamppost and two figures, framed from above, embracing—but only after careful study did I realise that it was Tara and me. It must have been taken on that first night we met, and when I looked at Bernie, she seemed somewhat abashed.

"Call me sentimental," she said, "but seeing the two of you that night, it just melted my heart. I just had to take a photo. Even if it didn't turn out very good. The two of you looked so perfect together."

Anyone else, and I might have found this creepy and intrusive. But for the three of us, it marked the end of one era and the beginning of another—the photo uniting the two with an embrace—and while some may have balked at the pressure this added, I didn't; I wanted that night marked, too, because it had been the night when meaning had returned.

It was time for me to be heading back to my flat, but Bernie was intent on making this day last as long as was humanly possible. I told her that I had to be up early for work the following day, and that I really needed to get some sleep after the night we'd spent with George, but this apparently wasn't the obstacle I thought it would be.

"You can sleep here," she insisted. "We can have a bite of supper together and then all get an early night."

"But I'd still have to go back to my flat in the morning for a change of clothes," I explained. "It'd be too much of a rush."

Bernie rolled her eyes. "Come on, Price," she said. "I thought you were a man of vision. Run back and get a change of clothes now, then we can all relax for the evening."

I glanced across at Tara. "I don't know," I said. "It feels like I've imposed enough already. I don't want you getting fed up of me before we've even had chance to get to know each other properly."

"I don't think that's going to happen, do you, Tara?"

"Oh, I wouldn't bet on it," she said. "He does try one's patience at times—as this proves."

"Thank you for your support."

"You're welcome," she answered with a playful smile.

With a resigned shrug, I finally accepted that there was nothing more for me to do other than go along with it. I was getting the feeling that this was something they had hatched together—perhaps as a way of seeing that I had a good feed and a good night's sleep—but that just made it all the more endearing.

"Okay," I said, scratching the back of my head again, my cheeks feeling flushed. "You win. I'll be quarter of an hour."

Closing the door behind me, it was as if I had somehow stepped back in time. The room was exactly as we had left it that morning, not messy though clearly lived-in but, as hard as I looked, I couldn't see any immediate evidence of Tara having been there. I knew she kept clean underwear in a bag at the side of the bed and a few clothes in my rickety wardrobe, but that was all there was of her here. This was still my flat. Still the place where I had spent far too many lonely hours. It was true that it had at times seemed a refuge, my haven in a world of heartache and ambivalence, but with the contrast of the lovely day I'd just had (a day which wasn't over, yet, I reminded myself), this place could only ever be a sad place... a sad place heavy with memory and the threat of loss.

I didn't like being there on my own. Having Tara here with me made it bearable. I could live through just about anything with that girl at my side. But with her back at her mother's the contrast was stark and oppressive.

Sitting on the edge of the bed for a moment, collecting my thoughts and generally trying not to let the gloom get the better of me, I breathed deeply and looked about me—knowing now that this wasn't somewhere I could live forever. Apart from it not being practical now that Tara was in my life, it just wasn't healthy. It had given me all I had asked for over the years—seclusion, a sense (however fallacious) of safety and that feeling of having somewhere wholly my own—but it wasn't difficult for me to now see just had bad for me that had been. Finding somewhere else, somewhere I could be with Tara, had to be a priority.

Finding my work clothes for the following day, I pushed them into a carrier bag – I didn't want to stay there any longer than was absolutely necessary. The Black Dog of the night before was snapping at my heels again, and I knew that if I didn't get out of there soon I would find myself battling with it more strenuously, and increasingly in vain.

Closing the curtains, I told myself that it was just a flat, just a room. It couldn't affect me, not now that I had so many positive factors in my life. I occupied it. It did not occupy me. But no matter how hard I struggled against it, it weighed down on me— pushed into me and tried to shape me to its nefarious will.

I paused by the door, carrier bag of clothes in hand, looking back at the curtained window. It hadn't registered. Not immediately. Closing the curtains, it had been there and I had seen it—but I hadn't paid it any mind, because it had been outside, and outside didn't matter.

Except now it did. Now, outside was where all the things that mattered to me resided. Outside was where Tara was. Outside was where I wanted to be.

Slowly, I walked to the window, placing my bag of clothes on the bed as I passed by. It was nothing. I was sure it was nothing. But it niggled at me, that image of what I thought I had seen, and I knew that the only true way to disempower it was to look at it again.

Standing to one side of the window, I carefully eased the curtain aside and looked down at the road below.

The car was still there—a nondescript old Renault that, as far as I knew, I'd never seen before. It sat at the far kerb, silent and dark, and had it not been for the shadowy figure sitting in the driver's seat, I probably wouldn't have given it a second thought.

I watched him. Largely unseen, little more than a silhouette, he seemed innocuous enough. Someone waiting for a friend or lover, picking up a relative, perhaps, or dropping off a business associate. In a world of threat and unexpected developments, I saw nothing overtly disturbing... and, yet, something made me stay there in the darkened room, peeping out at him from between my shabby curtains, making up stories even as I tried not to make them up.

Finally convincing myself that there was nothing here for me to worry about, I started to step back from the window and—sure enough—that was the moment he chose to look up at me. Our eyes met (or, at least, I imagined they did—for I couldn't actually see his) and for the count of about ten, neither of us moved. I held my breath, totally unmindful of the fact that Tara was back at her mother's waiting for me—thinking only of the car and its driver, of what it meant to me, if anything at all.

I thought about going down there and confronting him... but what would I say? It was just a driver sitting in his car, when all was said and done, and I had no real reason to believe that his presence had anything to do with me. So him being there like that gave me a bit of a funny feeling. What did that prove, other than that I was a bit of a prat who'd probably been spending too long in George's company? I was jumping at shadows, missing Tara already and filling the gap she left with demons and bogey men. The best thing I could do, I reasoned, was close the curtain and put it out of my head—go about my business like the sane man I purported to be and get my hairy, flatulating arse back to Tara.

The man in the car nodded to himself and looked down. The headlights came on and I heard the engine shudder to life. Without indicating, he pulled out and drove off—leaving me staring like a knob at the space where he had been.

Alone again, I dismissed my inexplicable feeling of foreboding, picked up my carrier bag of clothes and—telling myself that I was a complete prat—left, looking forward to my return to Tara and her wonderfully hospitable mother.

Outside the door to Tara's room, Bernie wished us both goodnight—first kissing Tara on the cheek and then me. She gave my arm a little squeeze and she beamed at my sleepy Tara—pride and satisfaction flushing her cheeks—and in that moment I thought that maybe, just maybe, I wasn't as pointless as I'd always imagined myself to be. That I wasn't another George Ruiz, pinballing from one false and criminal start to another, I was Price Waters, charmer extraordinaire, and I was about to spend my first night in my girlfriend's bed.

"I still can't believe she didn't stick me in the spare bedroom," I said, when we finally stepped into Tara's room and closed the door behind us. The room was done out in rich shades of burgundy—heavy, sumptuous quilt on the bed, deep-pile carpet underfoot—and being here seemed somehow more intimate and personal than any of the wet and lingering acts of love she had allowed me to share with her. Suddenly out of my depth, I stood by the wall and waited for permission to move.

"We're not teenagers, Price." She was already starting to undress—removing her clothes with an automatic grace and letting them drop to the floor, as she must have done for all those years before I came on the scene. "But... well, even if we were, she'd still probably let us sleep in the same bed. She's that kind of woman. A realist. A romantic, too."

"Something for which I'm eternally grateful," I said.

Down to her off-white knickers and bra, Tara turned to look at me—the little vertical frown between her eyebrows reminding me of her vulva. She smiled with one side of her mouth and tilted her head questioningly to the left. "Are you going to stand there all night?" she said.

"I feel a little odd."

"You look a little odd." She clasped her hands together in front of her fanny. Too late. I'd already spotted the dark, damp shadow on her knickers. "Is there... is something wrong?"

It was horrible, watching her confidence ebb away like that. One minute she was intent on taking me to her bed and having her wicked way with me, the next she was inhibited and wholly unsure of herself. And I had done that to her. Welcomed, I had foolishly wavered, not knowing what to do and Tara had read that to mean... well, God alone knew how she had read it.

Quickly, I took her in my arms—telling her that there was nothing wrong and that I merely felt a little strange, being in her room for the first time. I kissed her and told her that I loved her, laying her on the bed and removing her knickers. Still fully-clothed myself, I parted her labia, tasting deeply, inhaling with all my might in a desperate attempt to smell her. My nose pressed against her clitoris, I breathed in again... and again... and again, Tara whimpering softly as I worked at her, my cock painfully hard in the confines of my jeans.

Tara glanced down at me and, seeing my futile efforts to know her completely, caressed my face. "It's all right," she told me. "It doesn't matter. We have everything else."

"I want to smell you."

"I know, Price." She kissed me and said the only thing that, under the circumstances, could really help. Nothing.

I didn't recall ever feeling warmer. It wasn't that cloying, invasive heat of summer but, rather, the welcome heat of winter—the kind of heat that said you were where you should be and that, huddled in bed beneath a duvet with the woman you loved, was what you had been looking for all along. Simple warmth. I'd thought it before, I know, but its sense struck me again as I held onto Tara in our post-coital haze and savoured this new place, this new sense of belonging.

"Do you really have to work tomorrow?" Tara said softly.

"I'm afraid so."

We listened to the rain pattering against the window for a while and I thought of the car I had seen—the Renault. It all seemed especially ridiculous, now that I was safe and warm with Tara. Cars parked at kerbs every day of the week. That was, in part, what kerbs were for. If the driver had done something unusual, then it might have been understandable—but, as it was, I had merely allowed my imagination to run away with me, and as I held Tara in my arms, I smiled at my own silliness.

"He wouldn't have let us sleep in the same room," Tara said a few minutes later. "Not when we were younger, at least. And not without a lot of argy-bargy."

"Your dad?"

"My dad. He was a wonderful dad, Price. Probably about the best I could have wished for. But he had this urge to protect that was so strong... it was so difficult for him to just let things happen, just let me find things out for myself. He wanted to wrap me up in cotton wool... a bit like I do with you, I suppose. Keep me safe and perfect."

"But he knew he couldn't," I said.

"Not at first. It was something he had to learn." She grew quiet, falling into a memory, and when she finally spoke again her voice was syrupy and low, dripping with dream and recollection. "I remember this one time," she said. "He took me to the swimming baths. I was about thirteen. Turning into a woman, with breasts and hair and a bit of a fear of being seen in a bather. I wanted to go but I didn't want to go, you know? I loved swimming but... I was self-conscious, and Dad knew it. His instinct was to just take me home. Truth be known, I don't think he wanted the whole world looking at me, either. But he knew I had to do this. For me and, I suspect, for him. So he sent me into the women's changing rooms and he went into the men's."

Outside, the rain was coming down more heavily. I knew that if it persisted, tomorrow might be a complete write-off and Tara might actually get her wish of my having an extra day off. Knowing my luck, though, Tony would ask me to come in anyway and have me alphabetising the seed packets ready for spring.

"It was a good afternoon," Tara said. "Once I'd settled myself. I bumped into a couple of lads I knew from school and... well, while Dad swam lengths, I mucked about with them and generally enjoyed their admiring glances. The water was colder than usual and my nipples could have taken their eyes out, but I wasn't in the least bit embarrassed. I loved it. We splashed and laughed and at one point one of them brushed up against my leg and... the poor lad was hard, Price. I'd made a boy hard and I was over the fucking moon. My self-esteem was going through the roof and then..."

"Something happened?" I said.

With a twitch of the eyebrows, she answered. "Oh, yes. Something happened all right. We started to get rough. You know how it is with teenagers when they don't quite know how to express their sexuality. They want to touch and explore, but the boundaries are difficult to find and comprehend. So they push and grab at each other, wrestle and slap. I was unaware that Dad had stopped swimming his lengths and was watching us. Frankly, I was having too much fun to be bothered. Something was happening, you know, downstairs, and the only way I could think of to deal with it was to try to hold this boy David's head under the water. I jumped on him and he laughed and pushed me away. I splashed water at him and he grabbed at me... and the next thing I knew, my bather was torn and my right tit was hanging out."

I laughed and Tara slapped at me lazily.

"It wasn't funny," she said. "No. Actually, it was. Even at the time I wasn't especially concerned, which shows just how far I'd come in the space of that hour or so. I covered myself up as best I could, telling a very apologetic David that it was okay, it was just an accident and everything, and started heading out of the pool — meaning to return to the changing rooms as inconspicuously as possible.

"Before I could, though, Dad came over. He'd seen everything and he was livid. He started shouting at poor David like he'd tried to rape me or something, and no matter what I said, he wouldn't stop. He just kept on and on, and when I tried to explain again he sent me to the changing rooms. I'd never been so embarrassed in all my life."

I heard Bernie moving about a couple of rooms away, and wondered as I had earlier if she had heard our love-making. It must have been harder for her than she cared to let us see — so much happiness and satisfaction in a world that had denied her such a lot. First her husband had been taken from her with cruel irony, and now her daughter had found someone who Bernie would have to share her with. No matter what she said to the contrary, that had to trouble her, on some level, at least.

"By the time I'd showered and got dressed, he'd calmed down," Tara was telling me. "But I hadn't. I was fuming and the minute he set eyes on me, he knew I wasn't going to make it easy for him."

"I feel sorry for him already," I said, and she smiled.

"I wanted to shout at him and hit out," she said. She was speaking in a whisper, now—as if her father's ghost might be lurking in these rooms somewhere, listening in on our conversation. "I wanted to behave like he'd behaved and make a fool of him in front of all the people in the foyer. It would have been so easy to just let rip. Tear a right fucking strip off him and really make him feel as bad as he had me. But I suppose I grew up a little that day. I saw so clearly that his little display had accomplished nothing—apart from making me resent him and question his behaviour. So I didn't kick off. I decided to walk quietly to the car with him and got in, closing the door gently and calmly buckling up. I knew just how small I was making him feel, and as much as I loved him, I liked it. I liked that I could make my point so effectively, without having to say a word.

"As he drove us home, though, my silence really started to get to him. He tried to talk about neutral topics, but I only stared coolly out of my window, determined not to respond—as difficult as that was becoming. I was beginning to feel like a complete shit by this time, Price. You know that feeling where one minute you feel completely justified in your actions and the next you start to look at the reasons behind them and it all starts to fall to pieces?"

I nodded.

"Well that's what it was like. I thought about what he'd done and I saw beyond it. I understood that, however wrong he'd been, he'd only wanted to protect me. I swear, if he hadn't spoken up when he did, I would have turned around and apologised to him in a matter of minutes."

"Daddy's little girl."

"I suppose I was, yes."

"What did he say to you?"

Tara moved deeper into the bed, encouraging me to follow and pulling the duvet up over our heads. I couldn't be sure why she did this, but it certainly leant our conversation a conspiratorial edge—and as peculiar as it might have seemed, I liked it.

"He told me he was wrong to act the way he had and he apologised," she whispered. "Parking at the side of the road, he turned in his seat and looked at me—telling me that while it didn't justify the way he'd been, his intention had only been to protect me. He couldn't do that forever, though, he said. He had to learn to trust me to protect myself. He smiled, then, and... I was so bloody glad that I hadn't apologised, Price. It wouldn't have done either of us any good. He smiled and he told me that I'd probably do a far better job of it than he ever could, anyway."

In our dark cave, we both smiled at one another and I said, "I think he had a point."

"I think you're right. He stepped back after that. Didn't crowd me quite so much. He never embarrassed me like that again, but I could tell he had to fight it. I don't think he ever really let go."

"Would he have liked me?" I asked.

"Oh, yes," she said. "He would have liked you. But he would have hated you, too."

Chapter Ten

Four days later, I finally got my chance to be alone with Claudia, again.

It had been a fairly monotonous few days of sporadic work interspersed with heavy showers and, on a couple of occasions, fairly impressive storms—and it was fair to say that both Tony and I were growing rather frustrated. We'd so far only managed to do about half of the work on the trees we'd wanted to and, to top it off, the latest storm had done more damage and it now looked as though we might have to take another tree down completely. Tony blamed it on bad management prior to his taking up the post and, by the fourth day, he looked like a man on the verge of blowing a gasket. I didn't know if there was more to this, and I wasn't about to ask, but when he excused himself for a couple of hours to take care of "a bit of business", I was more than happy to sit with Claudia.

Making myself a coffee while she sat patiently in her wheelchair, drooling onto the right breast of her cream blouse, I thought about what Tara had said, and asked myself if this was something I really wanted to do. If she could talk, why on earth hadn't she talked to Tony? It seemed odd that she'd chosen me— if 'chosen' was the right word—and I couldn't help feeling that maybe she had spoken to Tony and he had decided to keep it to himself.

Sitting on the settee beside her wheelchair, cupping my mug of coffee in both hands, I knew that she understood what I was about to do. I could almost feel her tensing with excitement or expectation—and as I placed my coffee on the floor by my feet, she moved her head slightly to look at me. It was fleeting, but there was such keen intelligence in those eyes. I shivered and reluctantly placed a hand on her knee, trying not the think of the doubts I had and the peculiar feeling that Claudia might be playing me.

"Once for yes," I reminded her. "Twice for no."

Twitch.

"Last time we talked," I said, "you told me that you wanted to be away from Tony—that you didn't like what looking after you was doing to him. Do you still feel the same way?"

Twitch.

The answer I was expecting, but it seemed only right that I should give her the opportunity... I was hoping that she would at least have second thoughts regarding my involvement. No such luck.

Her leg was virtually humming with the tension of waiting for my next question. She struggled to look at me, again, but I wasn't about to be rushed. If I had to do this, I was going to be sure to do it right and frame my questions as carefully as possible.

"Have you had the opportunity to talk to Tony the way you are talking to me?" I finally asked her.

Twitch. No hesitation—an urgency, almost, as if she wanted to get these formalities out of the way as quickly as we could and get onto the important stuff.

"And you chose not to?"

Twitch twitch.

"You've tried to talk to him?" I said, sounding rather more incredulous than I'd intended. Again, she twitched her leg once in reply and I sat back for a moment to think about this and sip my coffee. She'd tried to talk to him.

"Was it just an opportunity he missed?" I said. "Did you twitch your leg and he just didn't see the possibility for communication?"

Twitch twitch.

"He knew the two of you could communicate using this method?"

Twitch.

"And he wilfully ignored the opportunity?"

Twitch.

"Because he prefers the answers he thinks up himself." This wasn't intended as a question, but she twitched her leg once as I worked at making sense of this. What did this say about Tony? Was he a bad man or had the strain of looking after Claudia, the woman he claimed to love so deeply, simply taken its toll on him? Given that he controlled all the physical aspects of her life, wasn't it just a natural extension of that for him to think that he could, and, indeed, should, control the answers she gave?

"Is this one of the reasons why you want to be away from him?" I asked on a whim. "Because looking after you is making him believe that he knows what's best for you?... It's making him do things he would never have done before?"

Twitch.

She strained to lift her chin to look at me again, and when our eyes met, I saw that intelligence once more—sharp and precise, as aware of her predicament as anyone could be. I didn't want to think what it must be like for her. All that knowledge and mental ability, and only one knee with which to express it—and even that was dependent on the knowledge and awareness of the 'listener'. What disturbed me more than anything, however, was Tony's behaviour. As damaged as he might be by their relationship, he had made the choice to silence her. Hell, with all his knowledge about computers he could even have rigged up a system to allow her to write complete sentences—or books, even, just like Stephen Hawking. She probably still had a good legal brain and, as I saw it, there was no telling what contributions she might still make.

"Do you still want to die, Claudia?" I asked her.

Twitch.

"Even though there's still so much you could do?" No answer. I explained that, with the right equipment, she would be able to communicate as effectively as the rest of us—possibly more effectively, given her impressive intelligence. "You could write law books, keep in touch with people all over the world via the internet... do you really want to throw all that away?"

A pause, during which I held my breath, and then... Twitch.

"You still want to die?"

Twitch.

"But you don't want Tony to help you?"

Twitch twitch.

"So the first step is... what? To get you away from Tony?" It seemed we were reading from the same page. Her leg twitched quickly and she waited for the next question. "This isn't something I can do for you, you do know that, don't you? I can't help you die—you know that, right?"

Twitch.

"Is there someone I can contact for you?" I said. I wanted to do all that I could for her, but, at the same time, wanted to hand over responsibility. Even though I was fairly certain that it was probably the right thing to do, the thought of going behind Tony's back was unnatural to me.

Twitch.

"A friend?" I said.

Twitch twitch.

"Family."

Twitch twitch.

For a moment, I couldn't think of an alternative, and, then... "Social services?" I found it remarkable that a knee could communicate so much disdain. "Then who? I'm sorry, Claudia, I just can't..." And then it came to me. Not family. Not a friend. But people she could trust. "Your ex-work colleagues."

Twitch.

I finished work at two-thirty—grateful that the weather had once more shortened our day, my head spinning after the conversation I'd had with Claudia and also preoccupied with concerns about George. It was unusual for me not to hear from him and, however foolish, I couldn't help but feel that I somehow owed it to him to make sure he was all right. Talking on the phone to Tara earlier that afternoon, I had mentioned that I might drop by his place on the way home. I'd expected an argument from her—an insistence, at the very least, that we had done enough and should now leave him to his own devices. But even she had agreed that it was unusual not to hear from him. "Just don't stay around there any longer than is absolutely necessary," she said. "And if he's there, don't let him drag you into anything else. I'll be round Mam's when you're done. She's out for the evening, so I'm cooking us something."

With the promise of a pleasant evening with Tara ahead of me, I stood on the front step of Carla's house and knocked on the door—determined not to let this go anywhere I didn't want it to go but knowing in my heart of hearts that I was asking for trouble by even thinking of coming here. I knocked again, the rain belting against the back of my coat, running down my neck, and a minute or so later, I heard a clatter and the unmistakable sound of Carla— swearing like an Irish navvy. It took her another minute and a considerable number of expletives to open the door, and when I finally laid eyes on her, I could understand why.

Drunk as the proverbial skunk, she stood before me—swaying like a skyscraper in a severe gale. Wearing only a stained pink bra and her artificial leg, seeming oblivious to the fact, she absently scratched her shaved vagina and grinned at me. I'd seen her drunk before, of course, most recently at Martha's party, but I'd never seen her quite this drunk.

"Price!" She remembered my name, at least—that had to be a good thing. "My favourite boy. My favourite drinking buddy. How are you, sweetheart? Come to see how your old friend Carla's doing, have you? Isn't that nice? A gentleman, I tell you. The last of the few!" She wobbled and grabbed hold of the door for support, grinning and winking at me. "What are you doing standing out there like that? Come on in, Price, love—you're getting all wet."

I was suddenly rather fond of the rain running down my neck. "Actually," I said, "I can't stop. I was just wondering if George was in." I struggled not to look at her vagina, but it was difficult. Appearing bruised and raw, it looked as if it was about to fall out. My instinct was to neatly tuck it back in for her – something I easily resisted.

Her nose crinkled with distaste and, before I knew what was happening, she grabbed me by the coat and dragged me into the hallway, slamming the door shut behind me. "George?" she said, still scratching herself. "Don't talk to me about that little runt. No... no bloody regard for others. One minute there's no getting rid of him, the next he disappears for days on end. I mean, tell me, Price—is that any way for a son to behave?"

I wasn't really in a position to comment on mother-son relationships, and this didn't exactly seem like the appropriate setting for a right old chin-wag. I wanted to be out of there, but leaving Carla to her own devices when she was so clearly in no fit state just didn't seem the right thing to do. And, so, I delicately steered her into the untidy living room—telling her that I was going to make us both a nice mug of coffee each, and then we'd talk about George until the cows came home. She seemed satisfied with this, patting my arm and settling onto the settee without complaint as I found an old, discarded dressing gown with which to cover her.

Once this was done, I went through to the kitchen and called Tara on my mobile.

"Only a bra and her false leg?" she said.

"Yes," I replied. "And I think her fanny's about to fall out. It looks like an overflowing wheelie bin in need of stamping down."

Tara seemed to like this. The line crackled with her laughter and she said, "Not that you were looking or anything."

"I did my best to keep my eyes averted at all times but... it's like when you meet someone with a bloody big wart on their face. I pulled my eyes away and the next thing I know, I'm staring at it again."

"And this has nothing to do with your being an old perv? Do you want me to come round?"

"Frankly," I told her, "I'm a bit sick of other people right now. I just want to walk the fuck out the door and get back to you—but I don't think I can leave her like this."

"I'll come round."

"You don't have to."

"I want to," she said. "Unless..."

"What?"

"Unless you'd rather I left you alone with Carla and her itchy vagina?"

"Perish the thought," I said, laughing grimly. "When you put it like that... get your arse around here as fast as you can—before I succumb to her subtle charms."

"I'm on my way."

The house was quiet. Alone in the kitchen with only one of Carla's moggies for company (one of the ones that wasn't Gemini), I listened to the silence—the stillness—and found myself relishing it. Moments like this had become so few and far between since the Sunday we'd spent with Bernie that I was fast learning to appreciate them at every opportunity. The cat sat on the table, squinting at me through its off-white fur, and I stared back at it, absorbing its calmness and knowing that, if I could just hold this mood, Tara would be with me before I could say furry feline friend. I breathed deeply, glad I didn't suffer with allergies, and thought how different the kitchen was without George in it—and only when I heard a dull thud from the living room did I snap out of my reverie.

I found Carla on the living room floor in a pool of her own steaming vomit. It was clumped in her hair, and bits of what looked like celery were stuck to her face. She struggled to get to her feet as I stepped towards her—making it halfway before her bladder gave way and an impressive stream of piss splattered onto the carpet a few inches away from where I was standing. Carla squatted there, watching it pour out of her as if it belonged to someone else—transfixed, a satisfied sigh escaping her lips.

When the last drop had been squeezed out, Carla dried her fanny with the hem of the dressing gown she'd dropped on the floor and slumped back on the settee. Closing her eyes, she brushed the sick off the side of her face and made a guttural sound She shivered and I considered putting the dressing gown over her again. That meant getting closer to her, though, and with all the piss and the vomit that was lying about, I didn't much fancy that.

"What must you think of me?" she finally said, sounding much more sober, now. "I'm ever so sorry, Price. You really... you don't need to see this."

"A little late now," I said—smiling to show that I wasn't fazed by it. "What caused it, Carla?" I added compassionately. "I mean, I know you like a drink, but this..."

"I've really surpassed myself, eh?"

"You could say that." Like toothpaste from a tube, Gemini squeezed out from behind the settee and started taking too much interest in the piss and vomit. I picked her up and threw her into the hallway, closing the living room door before turning back to Carla. "This have anything to do with George?" I said.

Looking down at her prosthesis, she pulled a pained expression. "You should know better than to ask such silly questions," she told me. "One way or another, everything in my life has something to do with George. I expect it's getting much the same way for you and our Tara by now."

"I wouldn't say that, exactly," I said.

"You both went with him to see that lass, didn't you?"

"Yes, but that doesn't mean that—"

"And you're round here now why?"

"We were talking about you," I reminded her, and she put her head back—closing her eyes and chuckling again.

"No," she said. "We weren't. We were talking about George. Because that's what we do, Price. Whenever the likes of you and I get together, however hard we try to avoid it, we talk about George. Because that's what he wants."

I'd known George for too long to feel entirely comfortable jumping to his defence but, given what I knew about what had happened to him with the Jag man, not to mention that Carla had always blamed him for the loss of her leg, I felt I had to say something.

"It hasn't been easy for him," I said, rather lamely I must admit.

"What hasn't?"

I shrugged, wishing Tara would hurry up. "I don't know," I said. "Life, I guess. Granted, he hasn't exactly made it any easier for himself, but he's had his pain, too, Carla."

She studied me evenly. It was difficult taking her seriously with the bits of sicked-up celery still stuck to the side of her face and in her hair, but I did my best. "You're a good friend, Price," she told me. "He's lucky to have you. But... I can't see things quite how you do and... I'd still advise caution. Everything in his life is about him. You know that as well as I. And while you are on-side I have no doubt that he will be the George we so rarely see. He will be sympathetic and, on occasion, even quite grateful... but underneath all that, you've still got the same George. He'll do whatever he has to do to get what he wants and, trust me, Price, he won't let a little thing like friendship stand in his way."

"You once told me that you could destroy him if you chose to," I said. "That I could, too, if I set my mind to it." She nodded, her memory obviously better than her boozed-up state suggested. "If you feel the way you do about him, why haven't you?"

Pale from the top of her head to the tips of her five toes—her artificial leg far too pink to ever be convincing—Carla grew paler still. I thought she was going to be sick again and, by way of a precaution, I took a step back. Once more scratching at her vagina, she finally realised just how naked she was; she pulled the dressing gown over her legs, her chin dropping forward as she closed her eyes and struggled against something that I wasn't entirely sure I understood. Her breath hitched and I realised that she was very close to tears.

"He's my son," she told me. "I hate him. I resent him. I wouldn't give him the time of day. If he died tomorrow, I would see it as a relief and welcome it." She looked up at me. "But he's my son, Price. He's my son and I love him. I couldn't do that to him, no matter how much he deserves it—not really. I want to, and sometimes I even kid myself that I could do it, but I just can't." She smiled bitterly, her shoulders sagging and her hands limp in her lap. "Is it any wonder I drink?"

"What happened, Carla?"

"We had another argument," she said. "Just before he went off with you and our Tara to find that lass of his. He told me that if everything went the way he expected it to, he wouldn't be living here too much longer. He would be out from under my foot and I wouldn't have to look at him again was how he put it. I would just have to fend for myself, because that's what he'd always had to do.... He was cruel, Price, and you know just how bad he can be. He told me I should have died when that bus hit me. Apparently it would have been better for us both."

When Tara finally arrived, I met her in the hallway I filled her in on all the details. "She's extremely lucid," I said. "But she looks like death warmed up. She really needs to be in bed, but I was a little afraid to move her."

"Didn't want to jiggle up the juices, eh?" she said, grinning.

"It's no laughing matter," I told her. "I'm betting you'll wish you had Anosmia, too, when you go in there."

"That's what I love about men like you." She kissed me on the cheek as she passed by into the living room. "So bloody squeamish."

As I followed her in, I hoped that the sight would stop her dead in her tracks—forcing her to eat her words and admit that it was pretty bad, after all. But Tara was Tara was Tara, and she just marched into the room without giving the piss and vomit a second glance, plonking down on the settee beside her Aunty Carla and taking hold of her hand.

"Well," she said, "I'm not saying you look like shit or anything, Aunty Carla, but if you were on my shoe, I'd pretty sharpish scrape you off. What on earth were you thinking of?"

"I was thinking about not thinking," Carla said quietly. Her nose wrinkled and she turned away from Tara. I thought she was going to be sick again, but, as far as I could tell, she was just embarrassed. "You're a good girl, Tara," she continued. "We none of us give you enough credit for that. But you can never know. You can never know what it's like to have to live with what I have to live with. Sometimes alcohol is the only way."

"Awww." She patted Carla's hand and I suddenly saw that she wasn't going to play this quite how I'd expected. "Feeling sorry for yourself? Jesus, Aunty Carla, do you know how old all of this is getting? You've had plenty of opportunities to change things and you've chosen not to. If you don't like your life, you've got no one to blame but yourself."

Carla didn't react—she merely stared at the far wall and inhaled slowly. I didn't know how Tara could stand to be so close to her. She must have smelt to high heaven. But Tara remained on the settee beside her—still resolute, still a little cold and, even, cruel around the eyes. Rather hunched, she seemed to realise this and straightened herself up, glancing over at me uncertainly, before saying to Carla, "It's time you did something about this. Whether you do or not is completely up to you, of course, but you need to admit that you've got a problem and do something about it. In the meantime, though, I think we should get you to bed, don't you? Let you sleep it off for a bit and then we can discuss this some more."

A sulky Carla didn't reply. No doubt seeing that she wasn't going to get anywhere with Tara, she decided to not even bother trying.

Once we had finally got her up the stairs and into bed, Tara cleaning her up with a faded face cloth while I stood in the doorway looking, and feeling, pretty useless, we returned downstairs and regarded the mess. Both the piss and the sick were well on their way to completely drying into the carpet—and I didn't much fancy the prospect of having to clean it up. Nevertheless, it appeared that that was exactly what we were going to do.

Tara looked at me and smiled sneakily. I felt my stomach drop an inch or two, and clenched my buttocks—just in case. The dread must have shown on my face, for she chuckled to herself and rubbed my arm. Who was I to argue? And so we cleaned. We scraped and scrubbed and did our level best to remove all trace of what Tara was already calling "Carla's Embarrassing Incident".

Once the thick of it was out of the way, I got down on my knees and worked at the stains with a scrubbing brush and hot, soapy water. There was simply no way that we were ever going to remove all trace of The Incident, but we tried—Tara even mixing a little vinegar with the water in an effort to neutralise the stink of the piss, which I was blessedly spared.

Some of Carla's piss had splashed under the front of the settee, so I pushed the sofa back out of the way so that I could do a thorough job. As I did so, however, I heard a rustling sound and looked up to see a sheet of pale blue notepaper falling from the arm. I caught it before it landed on the damp carpet and, as rude as I knew it to be, read a little of what was written on it.

Tara, noticing that I had stopped scrubbing, came over and joined me, sitting down on the edge of the settee and removing her yellow Marigolds. "What is it?" she said, and I held up a finger to silence her.

Once I had finished reading, I lowered my head and sucked my bottom lip, thinking. "Well?" Tara said.

"It's a letter," I told her—looking up and handing it to her.

"Who from?" She turned the letter over and read the signature first. "Victor. Who the fuck's Victor?"

"Who was Carla seeing when George had his thirteenth birthday?" I said, sitting beside her so I could read the letter through again.

She thought for a moment before answering. "The Jag man?" She looked at me questioningly and I nodded. "Victor's the..."

"Read the letter," I told her.

My Carla,

It has been too long. I should have written this letter years ago, but you know what a stubborn old fool I can be. It's all too easy to become entrenched with a personality like mine—and digging oneself out isn't always easy. Especially where pride is involved. Hah! Pride. A young man's vice if ever there was one!

But, of course, I'm no longer a young man. I'm old and lonely and sad for the things I have lost... sad for the things I so carelessly tossed aside.

I'm a different man to the one I once was, Carla. Many things have happened to me since last we met. I won't bore you with all of them, but I will tell you of the most important event in my recent life. I almost died, Carla. I crashed the Jag and, while my injuries were fairly superficial, the shock and stress of it all caused me to have a heart attack. I don't tell you this in an attempt to garner sympathy, you understand. I tell you only that you might grasp more easily the reason for my reassessment of my life.

It scared me, Carla. It scared me like nothing had before and nothing has since. I was suddenly quite old and ill, so far from the man that I had been that I found it difficult to recognise myself. More than anything, though, it was the extreme sense of being alone that scared me. I was going to die, I realised, probably sooner rather than later, and I was going to do it by myself, without anyone I truly cared about to hold my hand and ease my passing. It was a terrifying time, but it was also one of personal growth.

While I was in hospital, slowly recovering, I had time to think. Not just in a superficial, what have I done with my life kind of a way—but in a real, in-depth way. I looked at all the expectation and disappointment I'd ever experienced and, with time, understood them anew. Over the weeks, I slowly saw that I had constantly striven for more. I found what I wanted, was happy with it for a while, and then grew disillusioned and had to start looking for something else. I'd always believed that it was because, ultimately, people disappointed me. But now I saw that that wasn't it at all. I was the weak link, Carla. I was the one with unreasonable expectations. In that hospital bed, I saw just how arrogant my world-view was. Better late than never, yes? Ha ha. All those years I'd... I suppose I'd seen myself as a social climber, someone destined to be better than everyone else. But I was a nobody, Carla. I see that now. I was a nobody who, frankly, didn't know just how lucky he was.

Do you remember little George's thirteenth birthday? What a wonderful day that was. We treated the boy to a day at the park and then tea at that burger place on the High Street. I'd expected George to be his usual, hard to please self, but he was a star. The boy actually enjoyed himself and showed it! That in itself was remarkable and I wondered if perhaps he'd been starting to accept me. I never stuck around long enough to find out, of course, but that had been a glorious day—the night that followed even better.

Do you remember it, Carla? Do you remember how we put George to bed later that evening and then went dancing? I'm sure you do. It was the most magical evening we spent together. Music, champagne and the most athletic love-making I've ever experienced in my life! We were so connected. I just knew what you wanted without your having to tell me. I touched you where you wanted to be touched, how you wanted to be touched—and I think I understood that night that that was how it was meant to be. That was the pinnacle, for me, Carla. I wasn't going any higher. But I didn't see it that way. I was arrogant enough to believe that I had more to do with my life, and I couldn't allow myself to be held back by a woman and her child.

I was stupid, and I'm not sure that the damage caused by my exalted view of myself is something that can ever be repaired. For me to expect you to forgive me is probably asking too much. But I do want you to know that I am sorry. I am sorry and I miss having you in my life.

So many years have passed and so much time has been wasted. I am not the man I once was, Carla—and I tend to think that that is a good thing. I am by no means perfect, of course. I doubt I will ever be able to make such a claim, and don't think I would wish to anyway. But one thing I do wish for is to have you back in my life. I have missed you.

I love you, Carla Ruiz,
Victor Pynchon.

Tara rolled her eyes and sat back, holding the letter in her lap. I took it from her and looked at it again, checking the date and seeing that it had been written on the previous Thursday. I pointed this out to Tara and she nodded.

"George has probably seen it," she said, solemnly.

"Which possibly explains the state Carla's in," I added.

Again, she nodded. "I can't say I blame George," she said,

however reluctantly. "If he kicked off, I mean. Even without the whole sodomy thing, this Victor bloke sounds like a slimy piece of work. Carla takes him back, she's a bigger bloody fool than I thought she was."

"You don't think she's as much the victim in all of this as George?" I said.

"No," she said sharply. "No, I most certainly do not. As little time as I have for George, he didn't ask to be fucked up the arse by some pathetic old git who should have been drowned at birth. Carla let him into their lives and if she does it again... well, she deserves everything she gets."

"And we still think George is telling us the truth about that, do we?" I asked her.

"We?" She was a little angry, now. With me or Carla, I couldn't say. "I don't know what we think, Price. All I know is what I think."

"Which is?"

Tara studied me—and as inaccurate as I knew this to be, I felt that I could only prove a disappointment to her. She stared, and I felt myself all but withering under her scrutiny. I was an anxious little boy, again, waiting for my balls to drop.

She blinked slowly and very calmly said, "George is an oddity in a world I already have difficulty understanding, Price." That vulnerable girl I saw when first we met was back. She rubbed at her fingernail and, as wrong as it might have been, it was good to see her again. "Making sense of who he is... of what he is—not only is it something I struggle with, it's also something I'd simply rather not have to think about. All my life, I've known George— and all my life I've known him to lie, manipulate and bully. When I was little, he used to scare me. Just the look of him was enough to send me running upstairs to hide in my room. I wrote you that note because of all that. And I still think you have to be careful... I still think we have to be careful. But that doesn't mean that I think he's lying about what this Victor bloke did to him. I believe him, Price. I've told you that before, and nothing's changed. I believe him and I know he's telling the truth when he says he wants the

Jag man dead. George could only ever be serious about something like that. And as far as I'm concerned..."

She trailed off, staring at the letter in my hand—her brow furrowing. I asked her if everything was all right, but she just shook her head dismissively, following a train of thought, it seemed. Swearing under her breath, she snatched the letter from me to look at the front page... and slowly I began to understand.

"Victor's address," I said.

"Yes."

"Victor's address, on the letter that George may have seen."

"Got it in one."

We neither of us said anything for a few moments, letting the implication fall into place. I recalled just how impulsive George could be, remembering the time in our teens when he had heard that a boy called Brian Copeland had been saying things about him behind his back. He had acted swiftly and without mercy, not in the least concerned with checking his facts—merely marching round to Brian's and beating the shit out of him... in the kid's own front garden. It hadn't mattered that he'd got caught. It hadn't mattered that he'd had to endure a severe talking-to from the local bobby. All he'd been concerned with had been taking care of Brian Copeland—or, more accurately, being seen to take care of Brian Copeland. In George's view, one fight fought and won was five more confrontations he wouldn't have to waste his time with.

"We should go round there," Tara said. "We should go round there and make sure everything's all right... make sure George hasn't done anything stupid and... just check everything out."

"George wouldn't do this himself," I told her—directly contradicting my initial conclusion. "There's more to it than George just wanting the Jag man dead."

"There is?"

"Of course there is," I told her. "If that were not the case, George would have taken care of it himself years ago. This is about him making sure that Sharon fulfils her promise. Look at the address," I told her. "This Victor is living—what? Half a mile away? Chances are, he's never been more than a stone's throw away. George could have offed him anytime he wanted if that had been his only concern. But it wasn't. We know that from the other night."

Tara was nodding slowly. "I'd still prefer it if we went round there," she said. "For peace of mind."

"It won't achieve anything," I insisted.

"Maybe it won't." She tucked a stray clump of oily hair behind ear and looked out of the window. "You're probably right, Price. But I'd just feel better seeing for myself that George hasn't well and truly got himself in the shit, you know?"

We could have been sitting down to a nice meal together. A half-decent bottle of wine, my food spiced up the way Tara was learning to do it, something romantic on her mum's old stereo, and quiet conversation about things that didn't really matter. Instead, we were contemplating going for a walk in the rain to make sure someone we knew hadn't killed someone we didn't know, all the while knowing that the dreaded event was highly unlikely anyway. And the more we struggled against this ridiculous net, the tighter it became—activity and involvement only serving to cause us to reveal to one another that we cared more than we were willing to admit. I said something about Carla being right—we were getting drawn further and further in—and Tara nodded.

"I thought we had a say in the matter," she told me. "I thought we could just choose not to be involved. But life isn't like that, is it? It has a habit of making you do things you never thought you'd do."

"We can at least choose to wait until the rain stops," I said. "I've been soaked to the skin once today already; I don't much fancy having it happen again."

"I'd rather we do it now," she told me. "You're a big boy. You'll cope."

"If I catch a cold, I'll make you suffer."

"When a man catches a cold," she said with a smile, "women always suffer."

Thirty-one Mount Drive was ten minutes walk from Carla's. The rain had thankfully eased up somewhat, and Tara had had the good sense to find Carla's umbrella and bring that along. It was cosy, almost, the dark fabric over our heads setting us apart from the rest of the world.

Standing over the road from number thirty-one—a nineteen-fifties semi-detached, neglected and forlorn, the garden overgrown and the curtains at the window dirty and hanging down—I asked Tara what we should do next, and she said she didn't know. The tone of her voice told me that she had finally realised just how pointless this was. We didn't even know what this Victor bloke looked like. How on earth were we meant to identify him and ensure he was all right?

There was a beaten up old Jaguar in the driveway—clearly unroadworthy after the crash he'd mentioned. An emotional attachment to something that could no longer serve its purpose. I could almost have liked him for that. Tara said that at least we could be fairly certain that we had the right house, and I nodded—trying to think of the best way to achieve what we had set out to do. The last thing I wanted was to have to stand out there like a lemon until we saw some sign of life. I briefly entertained the notion that we could peep in through the windows, but it was still too light, and Mount Drive looked like it might have more than its fair share of busybodies. If we'd had his phone number, we could have merely called him and waited for an answer—the most annoying thought of all, since it made me realise that thinking of it earlier could have prevented us from having to come here in the first place.

The idea that occurred to me next was not exactly the best I'd ever had but, as the old saying goes, desperate times called for desperate measures. I looked at Tara and she seemed to sense that I had a plan. An eyebrow raised and her head tilted. I said, "Does Jesus want you for a sunbeam?"

She frowned. "What on earth...?"

"Never mind," I said. "Just follow my lead."

We crossed the road and went up the drive ("Careful you don't scratch the car," I joked) to Victor's front door. Tara glanced about nervously, as if we shouldn't be there, and I told her to pack it in. "We're not breaking in," I told her. "We're just going to knock on his front door. So try to stop looking so bloody suspicious."

"I can't help it. I just feel like... like everybody's watching us."

"Well they're not."

"How can you be so sure?"

"I can't. But they're not—and even if they are, it doesn't matter. We aren't doing anything wrong."

"Aren't we?"

I knocked on the front door. "No," I assured her. "No, we aren't."

We waited only a matter of thirty seconds or so before the door was answered. It was snatched open, as if we had caught Victor in the middle of something important—and I knew right away that I had to play this one very carefully.

He might only have been in his late-sixties, but Victor Pynchon looked much older. Pigeon-chested and arms skinny in the tea-stained vest he wore, I knew right away that his days of being any kind of a physical threat were well gone. Nevertheless, his bloodshot eyes and grey, stubbly beard told me enough to prompt me to proceed with caution.

"Yes?" he snapped, his few teeth stained and as crooked as ancient headstones.

"Mister Pynchon?" I said, as serenely as possible. "Mister Victor Pynchon?"

He nodded and then stuck his head out of the door, hawking up a wad of phlegm and spitting it on the pavement by my feet. "Yes," he said. "What is it?"

"We represent the Non-Aligned Church of the Greater Good," I explained. "And we are just taking a few moments to introduce ourselves to your good self and the other members of your community." I was already running out of steam. I'd expected him to slam the door in our faces at the first mention of the word 'church', but it seemed I had misjudged him.

Victor Pynchon folded his arms and leant against the door jamb. "Can't say I've heard of it," he said. "You Anglicans then, are you—or what?"

I stammered something about how, yes, in a manner of speaking, we were and then, blessedly, Tara jumped in ahead of me. "We prefer to avoid those kind of terms," she explained. "Our church prefers instead to focus on the practical application of Christianity. We leave the politics of interpretation to others. Our primary goal is to live like Jesus—to be as good as we can be in a very real and observable way."

Victor Pynchon looked Tara up and down, his bloodshot, red-rimmed eyes thin and assessing. I believed I knew what he was thinking, and I didn't like it one little bit. At that moment, I understood George better than I ever had. I saw the cruelty in the way in which Victor licked his lips, and I found myself wanting to take a swing at him.

"Sounds very laudable," he said-sneered. "Can't say it appeals all that much to me, though—seeing as how I'm a self-centred old fuck who doesn't really care who he hurts. All sounds a bit showy, actually. Like you want to be seen to be doing good, while all the while you just want to suck cock and call God the lying piece of shit that you know him to be."

I was about to step in and get Tara the hell out of there. Suddenly highly protective of her, I had to restrain myself. He continued to stare at her, smirking, and just as I was about to take Tara by the arm and lead her away, she spoke.

"Have you got no shame?" she asked him.

The smirk faltered a little, and then, after a minor readjustment, came back in full force. "I have found it to be of little use," he told her. "It only serves to hold me back—and I don't like being held back."

"That surprises me." Tara now took a moment to look him up and down, mirroring his smirk and apparently enjoying every minute of it. "Judging by your appearance, you don't seem to have progressed that far. Must have been difficult for you, living with the knowledge of your own failure."

"You assume."

"So I'm wrong? Your life has been one big success after

another?"

"I have regretted nothing." He was just a little too smug to be convincing. I thought that Tara just might be getting to him—and I wasn't entirely convinced that that was a good thing. Our only concern when we had arrived here had been to ensure that he was indeed the man we thought him to be, and that George hadn't done him in—and now here was Tara having a full-blown conversation with him. Silently, I willed her to say goodbye and walk away with me, but, unsurprisingly, my efforts had no discernable effect.

She smiled at him and nodded thoughtfully. "Not even after your heart attack?"

I tried not to groan, but it was difficult. Victor Pynchon was visibly taken aback. He pulled away from us a little, as if considering shutting the door, and his bloodshot eyes narrowed. Gripping the door jamb, he all but snarled at Tara, spittle forming at the corners of his mouth as he said, "How do you know about that? Who are you?"

"It doesn't matter who we are," she told him. "The only thing that should concern you is that Jesus sees everything. Nothing goes unnoticed, Victor Pynchon, and no sin goes unpunished. Think about that when you have your next heart attack."

As I finally managed to lead her away, Pynchon hurling insults after us, I asked her just what she thought she'd been doing. Pynchon slammed the door, with the promise that he was going to call the police, and I rushed her along the pavement as quickly as possible, away from his house—putting up the brolly again in an effort to conceal us from onlookers—waiting for an answer.

Only when we got to the end of the road and we stopped did I get one, however. "I don't know," she said, looking anxious and flustered. "Just... seeing him standing there like that—knowing what he'd done to George and what he's probably done to lots of people in one way or another... it was more than I could bear. I wanted him to suffer. I wanted to see him suffer. A part of me wished George had got to him, Price. Seeing him standing there, looking so bloody sure of himself... I could have killed him myself—or that's how I'd felt at the time. Is that awful, Price?"

My Tara. A creature of such contrasts. As I looked at her, the two of us huddled face to face beneath the umbrella, tears forming in her eyes, I thought again just how remarkable she was—and just how remarkable it was that we had found each other (or, at least, that she had found me.) There were so many layers to her, so much still to learn, that it might well have been far too daunting a prospect—had I not loved her as much as I did. She shivered, no doubt cooling down rather too quickly after her rage against Pynchon, and I held her to me, telling her that it wasn't awful and that I understood completely how she was feeling.

"He should be dead and if no one else is willing to do it you just feel... however briefly... that it would be so easy. So easy and so right."

"I couldn't do it, though," she assured me—or tried to.

"Yes you could," I told her. "Under the right circumstances, we all could. But that doesn't mean we will, and it certainly doesn't mean that we'd sit back and let George do it, either. The truth is, the Victor Pynchons of this world aren't worth the additional grief and, however much he repulses us, the likes of you and I can see that."

"I wanted him to know that we knew something about him," she said, her voice fluttering like the heart of a frightened sparrow. "But I knew I couldn't come right out and mention what he had done to George, so I mentioned the heart attack. I thought... I don't know what I thought."

"You thought it would let him know that he wasn't a complete stranger to us," I said. "You wanted to unnerve him and, if it's any consolation, I think you achieved that."

"I did?"

"He won't sleep a wink tonight."

"Good."

Satisfied that she now felt better about the whole situation, I started walking again—leading Tara through the deepening dusk back towards Carla's. My mood somewhat lighter, even if my headache hadn't improved, I told Tara all about Claudia as we walked, how she wanted me to contact her work colleagues and how relieved I was to be almost rid of the burden.

It was hard for me to admit, but that was indeed how I now thought—and that in itself made me wonder if she were not right in wanting to end her life. If I, someone relatively untouched by her predicament (at least when compared to Tony), could feel like that about her, what did that say about others? I said all of this to Tara—and though she nodded in all of the right places, I could tell she wasn't really listening. She linked my arm and stayed close to me beneath the umbrella, but she was somewhere else entirely, and even though I knew I might regret it, I eventually asked, "You all right, love?"

She looked at me questioningly and I told her that she seemed a little distant—that I hoped the incident with Victor Pynchon wasn't playing on her mind too much.

"I'm just tired," she said, and I knew her well enough not to force the issue. "Every now and then... I just get this feeling that... that we can't keep doing this indefinitely. Something's got to give, Price—and I don't want that to be us."

"Us?" It seemed such a ludicrous proposition that I couldn't help but question it.

"Our relationship. I don't want other people being the source of problems between you and me. It's got to happen eventually, but when it does, I want us to at least know enough to recognise it and try to do something about it."

"We don't have to go back to Carla's," I said. "We've done more than enough to help her—we'd have nothing to feel –"

She interrupted me, a little impatiently. "That's not what I'm saying," she told me. "I'm talking about how other people affect us. How we let them affect us. At the moment, we're both pretty much in agreement about what has to be done—and even when we aren't, we can still see the sense of what the other's saying. What I'm on about is when that starts to change."

"It won't change."

"Maybe not—but if it does, I want us, like I say, to be able to recognise it and take care of it."

I stopped and turned to face her. We were on a corner, not

far away from where I first saw her—the young old woman holding a cat.

I stared into her eyes, which appeared grey-brown and diluted in the poor light. She was beautiful in a way, I thought, that maybe only I could see, and just about the brightest person I'd ever met, but still she didn't understand—still she didn't see that I was committed to her in a way that I'd never been committed to anyone or anything in my whole life.

"If I never succeed in anything else in my life," I told her, "I'll still have achieved far more than most men in having you love me. I'm not going to do anything to jeopardise that."

She seemed satisfied with this (until the next time she needed my reassurances, at least.) We embraced and kissed beneath the brolly, and I felt my heart lift somewhat. My optimistic mood soured, however, when I pulled away from Tara; parked down a side street was a familiar Renault. The driver looked at me and seemed to smile, before checking his (her?) mirrors and pulling out.

I thought about telling Tara about this, but apparently communication only went so far.

Back at Carla's, we had a surprise waiting for us.

I knew something was different the minute we entered the hallway, but I couldn't immediately pinpoint what it was. Tara glanced at me, somehow picking up on the fact that my four good senses were working overtime. "What is it?" she said, and I shook my head, holding a finger to my lips—still not sure if this 'difference' was a good or bad thing. Scanning the hallway, everything seemed pretty much the same. It still had the air of somewhere that had seen better days but something had changed. I remembered the time I had returned to my flat to find the note from Tara waiting for me. This felt very similar. A sense of dislocation. The angles of the room looked askew.

My eyes lighted on the newel post at the bottom of the banister. The stairs stretched up to the neglect that was Carla's bedroom. Last time I'd entered the hallway, the newel post had been exposed. Its paint had been cracked and browning, and I recalled putting my hand on it to steady myself as Carla had dragged me over the doorstep. Now, however, it was covered—covered by a familiar jacket.

Turning to Tara, I said, "Looks like George is back."

We found our formerly absent friend pacing back and forth in the living room. Unshaven, his hair greasy, his eyes had a manic look about them – a burning intensity that seemed to seep from somewhere deep within his mind or soul. One of Carla's cats got in his way and he aimed a kick at it, missing and almost losing his balance. So distracted was he, it took a couple of lengths of the living room before he even noticed we were there.

Stopping, he finally looked at us. We were still standing in the doorway—only a few feet away from him—but he nevertheless seemed to be having trouble figuring out who the hell we were and just what we were doing there. He took a step towards us—chin jutting forward, a perplexed frown just visible through his long, lank hair. I thought for a moment that he'd been drinking, or that he'd maybe sampled some of the shit he was occasionally known to sell, but that didn't fit, somehow; George didn't look high, he looked extremely anxious.

"Thank fuck," he said, once it had sunk in just who we were. "I thought for a minute... well, never mind what I thought. I was wrong. That's all that matters. Wrong about that like I was wrong about so many other things."

"Where the hell have you been, George?" I said, and he turned away from me—making a sound like steam escaping from a broken pipe. "Everyone's been worried about you."

"Sure they have," he scoffed. "Had the search parties out looking for me and everything, I'm sure."

"We've been worried about you," Tara clarified. There was a warmth to her tone that made George look over his shoulder at her. "It's not like you not to be in touch. We thought something had happened to you."

George studied her, and I thought for a moment that I saw

something about him soften—the piercing stare or something less easily identified. The manic quality drained from him and he went over and sat on the edge of the settee, hands hanging between his thighs.

"Something did happen to me," he said. "Sort of."

"What?" I asked. Tara and I sat on a chair together, just across from him, waiting to hear what he had to say.

Calmer now, he stared at the damp patch on the carpet and scratched at his beard. "I was there," he said. "Up until a couple of days ago, at least."

"Kingston Lodge?" Tara asked.

George nodded. "With Sharon and Richard. We were getting on really well. I didn't think we would, but as it turned out... it was as if we'd somehow rediscovered the people we were way back then, you know? In part, at least—because some things were different. So many years have passed and she has the responsibility of Richard. But... well, all things considered, we were talking and working things out—so much so that she asked me to stay."

"That's wonderful, George," Tara said.

"It would have been," he said. "Except things never got that far."

"Tell us, George." I expected a tale of how he'd overstepped the mark and completely ruined his chances of any kind of permanent reconciliation with Sharon. What I got was something very different.

"I'd been there most of the day," he said. "We'd gone through the whole nostalgia kick and we'd moved into a quieter phase altogether—filling in gaps, talking about all the things we had or hadn't done in the intervening years. I asked her why her and her family had disappeared so suddenly, and she told me that it had been 'drugs related'. Apparently, her brothers had got in too deep and had seriously pissed off one of the big local dealers. Almost fucking poetic. It was either get them away or start making the necessary arrangements with the Co-Op."

"They fuck up," Tara said, "the whole family suffers."

George looked up at the ceiling. "That's the way it usually

works, I'm afraid." He laughed through his nose and looked at the floor again. "Anyway," he continued. "Sharon asked me to stay, I said I'd like that and we decided to have something to eat. It would have all been very cosy, but for the fact that there was nothing in worth mentioning. I was in a good mood, though, and as far as I was concerned, it wasn't a problem – I said I'd walk into the village and get us all something."

George pulled his cigarettes and lighter from his shirt pocket and lit up, drawing deeply before continuing. Squinting through the smoke in a way that was quintessential George Ruiz, he regarded Tara and me earnestly, seeming to dare us not to believe what he was about to say.

"It was all bollocks," he said. "That's what I would have once thought—and maybe I still should, maybe I'd be better off thinking that way. I don't know. But when I walked down into the village, I felt... I felt as if I'd finally found a way to put everything where it should be. I walked down to the village and I bought practically everything in the shop. The old biddy thought her fucking birthday had come. Seventy-five squid, I spent—and I didn't resent a sodding penny of it. I handed over the cash with a bloody big toothy grin, picked up all of my carrier bags and headed back to the lodge feeling like a right knight in shining whatsit.

"I knew something wasn't right the minute I got back," he told us. Tara was holding my hand, now, squeezing it so tightly that my fingers were nigh on turning blue. "The front door was open and when I called out, I got no reply. I put the bags down in the hallway and all but ran through the house looking for them. I couldn't find them anywhere but..." He pulled on the cigarette and held it in for a good thirty seconds before letting it out. "In the living room... it looked as if there'd been a struggle. A chair had been knocked over and there was a pile of books on the floor. Richard's toys had been scattered about and there was a hole in the door where something had hit it. I knew it was bad but... it had all been going so well that I just didn't want to believe it. I convinced myself that it was Richard. He had simply had one of his turns and he was out on the

moor, wailing at the moon while Sharon tried to calm him down."
He looked at me, his chin quivering slightly. "But they weren't out
there, Price. I looked everywhere, but they were nowhere to be
found and in the end I just had to accept that –"

"Someone had taken them," Tara said.

He nodded. "While I had been down in the village, someone
had come in and taken them. While I'd been buying groceries,
Sharon and poor, poor useless Richard had been..."

He trailed off, close to tears—and I saw just how exhausted he
really was. Any façade he might have relied upon in the past was
now wholly insupportable. He shuddered and struggled, but he
was in no fit state to fend off such an unaccustomed emotional
assault. He stubbed out his cigarette against the soul of his shoe
and slapped away an errant tear before looking out of the window
as he cleared his throat.

"I've been searching for them for the past couple of days," he
said. "I asked everywhere but... nothing came of anything. It's as
if... I don't know. It's like they were just sucked into some fucking
vortex or something, and all I had to go on was a fucking car."

I stiffened and Tara frowned at me. "A car," I said.

"Yes. A shitty old Renault. Not sure of the model, but I've seen
it a few times in the past week. I didn't think about it much until I
saw it in the village after Sharon and Richard were taken." He
looked up at me. "Why?"

"I've seen it, too."

Tara let go of my hand. "What?"

"I thought I was just being paranoid," I explained. "But I've
seen it a few times. An old Renault. Kind of a mucky grey colour."

"That's the one," George said.

Tara moved as far away from me as the chair would allow.
"And you didn't think to mention this to me?" she asked.

"I couldn't be sure it wasn't just my imagination," I insisted.
"It's a small town, love. Things like that happen."

"You still should have told me." Her initial anger was already
waning. Now I could mainly hear disappointment in her voice.
That was somehow worse.

"I know," I said. "And I'm sorry. It's just that so much else has been going on and it seemed... inconsequential. Relatively speaking."

"Inconsequential?"

"Yes."

"You still should have told her," George interjected. I thought at first that he was taking the piss—but one look at his grey, saggy-eyed face told me that he wasn't. "We can't afford to have secrets from one another. Not now. Isn't that right, Tara?"

They held each other's gaze for a moment too long. I felt a bubble of anxiety shift in my gut. Tara nodded slowly and said, "Yes, George. Yes, that's right."

"What he doesn't nose won't hurt him," George chuckled. "Except maybe it won't always be that way, correct?"

"What are you talking about, for Christ's sake?" I said—really scared, now.

George started to explain, but Tara cut him off. "I have a condition that I haven't told you about," she said, her voice hard and resentful. "Axillary Hyperhidrosis. This means –"

"You have extra sweaty armpits."

I remembered seeing a documentary on the condition but, that apart, it was something I'd already noticed, anyway. As intimate as we'd been, it would have been difficult not to.

"I've heard of it before."

"And you know about the related problems?"

Initially, I didn't understand what she was saying. When she spoke of 'related problems', I automatically assumed that she was referring to something far more serious than anything I could ever have guessed at. Did Axillary Hyperhidrosis perhaps make her more susceptible to certain cancers or heart disease, I briefly wondered, or was it something more complicated and esoteric than that?

She watched me, and when I told her that I was afraid I didn't have a clue, she rolled her eyes and looked away from me.

"I smell," she said, ever so quietly. "No matter how clean I keep myself, no matter what deodorants I use or medication I take, I smell. I walk into a room full of people and, unless they're an especially smelly bunch or the room itself smells, within a few minutes they start to leave. One by one, they drift away—and I'm left on my own, Price. I'm left on my own because I smell and there's nothing I can do about it."

I should have known. All the clues were there. The sweaty armpits I first noticed when we were in bed together, George continually calling her names like 'stinky', even the conversation we'd had about believing in God—it had all been about this. Her insecurities, however valiantly she fought against them, stemmed from her condition, and when she expressed concern that I might walk away from her, it was only because so many others already had—because she smelled.

However, none of this had been immediately obvious to me, as it otherwise might have been, for one very good and slightly spooky reason – I had Anosmia. But I like to think that it wouldn't have mattered, anyway. I like to think that, however off-putting it may have initially been, I would have quickly got beyond it and got to know Tara as the beautiful woman I now knew her to be. How likely that was, I can only guess; I have never experienced any kind of smell, good or bad, so it's difficult for me to know how it might affect me.

Tara was afraid. It didn't take a genius to work out that much. It didn't bother me that she had kept this from me. I knew that, without George's prodding, she would have told me eventually. What concerned me, however, was that my knowing was something that had clearly been worrying her. All this time, she'd been carrying it around with her, keeping it to herself and, yet, still managing to be there for me. The strain must have taken its toll, but I'd seen nothing of it.

Putting my arm around her, I drew her to me. I couldn't love her any the less because she had kept the fact from me, and I told her as much. "It's just another way for Nature to show us how perfect we are for each other," I said, determined to make light of it. "You should have told me sooner, though, love. It just... it isn't even an issue."

"It is for me," she said. "And it will be for you. It hasn't happened, yet, Price, because we haven't been around many people together—but sooner or later someone's going to walk away from me when you're with me, and, when they do, they're going to be walking away from you, too."

"You know what my life was like before I met you," I told her. "Do you really think that I'll be troubled by something like that? I don't care, Tara. As long as I have you by my side, that's all that matters to me."

"You say that now."

"I mean it. It doesn't make a difference. It will never make a difference."

"You can't say that," she told me. "Not for certain. We none of us know what's going to happen from one moment to the next."

"Very true." I kissed her on the head. "One thing I do know, though. I love you—and nothing that anyone can say or do will change that."

"Which is all very bloody touching and everything," George said, sounding a little disappointed, "but there are more pressing matters we need to address here."

"Sharon and Richard," Tara said.

"And the car," I added.

"Yes. Sharon and Richard and the car. I need to rest." He lit another cigarette, clearly happy to be the centre of attention again. "I need to rest and then I need to figure out how best I should do this. I need to find them and get them away from whoever it is that has them, and the car—I need to find out who the fuck it belongs to and put the word out that I want to speak to them... yes, that's it. They either speak to me or the next time I see them I rip their fucking heads off and shit down their necks. Can't say fairer than that, right?"

"Go to the police, George," Tara said.

"The police." He smirked. "Do you even know, cuz?"

"Do I even know what?"

"Just how ridiculous a proposition that really is? Christ, Tara, they just wouldn't want to know. Oh, yes, they'd probably go through the motions, if we were lucky. Fill in a few fucking forms, that kind of thing. But something like this... even if I wasn't involved, they wouldn't give a shit."

"I think you're wrong," she said.

He shrugged and exhaled cigarette smoke through his nose. "Fine," he said. "You're quite welcome to think whatever the hell you like—but as far as I'm concerned, I know the terrain better than anyone and this is my call. So, if it's all the same to you, we'll leave the police out of it and... this is what we're going to do."

Chapter Eleven

The room was small and dreary—damp and poorly heated. Standing at the window and looking out at the swatch of sea and sky between looming houses, I unthinkingly placed a hand on the window ledge and instantly regretted it – dead flies left over from the summer and grey grit soiled my palm, and I quickly brushed them off against my jeans.

Tara was seated on the bed, eating an apple, and when I looked over at her I saw the tiredness in the dark welts beneath her eyes. We should never have come here, I thought. We should have refused, told George that it was a wild goose chase and nothing would come of it. We were doomed to failure—doomed to damnable disappointment—and all this imbecilic running around would guarantee us only one thing: further aggravation. But, now listening as George outlined his latest theory, I couldn't help but think that maybe this would be the end of him. Maybe, without Sharon (who I was suddenly quite certain we would never find), George would simply never make it beyond this point.

"She used to come here on holiday with her parents," he told us for about the tenth time in the past three days. He was pacing again, even though the size of the room didn't really allow for it (he took a couple of steps and turned, took another couple and turned once more—the rapidity of it making him appear all the more manic and disjointed). Tara crunched and slurped at her apple and tried not to look at him. "She hated the place, but they loved it because there was none of the shitty tourist trappings—no amusement arcades, no gift shops, nothing like that. Just a little fishing village with a beach and a few fossils. Nowhere for the kids to waste their pocket money on trivial things like having fun, you know?"

"You've told us all this, mate," I said.

Turning to me sharply, he said, "Well I'm telling you again, aren't I?" He took a breath and looked around, as if seeing the room for the first time — and then, mumbling and looking down at his shoes, apologised before continuing. "You see, she's got to be here. It's the natural place. If her brothers have her — and I think it is them, this time... don't ask me why... this is where they'll be. I even discussed it with Old Ray when I borrowed the car off him, and he agreed that it made sense. It's remote. No one ever comes to Everburn. They'd be able to bring her and Richard here and no one would be any the wiser because they have contacts here and..." He leant against the wall — the past three days of hunting through Everburn finally seeming to take its toll on him — and closed his eyes. "This place used to be a smugglers' cove, you know. Just like that place where you work, Price," he said. "Redburn. Similar names, similar histories. Contraband. Got a right fucking romantic ring to it, hasn't it? Not as pretty as that makes it sound — but that was why her brothers loved it here so much. Their parents brought them as kids, and they were as bored as Sharon to begin with. But as they grew older they started to see the possibility. Once a smugglers' cove, always a smugglers' cove."

"They brought stuff in through here?" I said.

"According to Old Ray, yes. And I'm beginning to wonder."

"Wonder what?" Tara asked him.

"I'm beginning to wonder if they take things out this way, too."

Tara and I glanced at each other before looking back at him. He was still leaning against the wall with his eyes closed. "You think her brothers have taken the two of them out of the country?" I said.

"Maybe not her brothers," he said. "Or not just her brothers. But, yes. They've either taken them out this way, or they're going to. Soon."

"There are simpler ways to get people out of the country," Tara pointed out, clearly unconvinced.

"Not if they don't want to go."

Three days and seventy miles from home. The more I thought about it, as George continued to bombard us with theories and explanations, the more difficult I found it to believe that we'd actually gone along with this. I'd risked losing my job and, possibly, Tara (although it was fair to say that she had been as willing as I to come here)—and all for what? So that George could fill us in on Sharon's family history and lurk in alleyways watching innocuous buildings and their equally innocuous occupants?

That day, Carla had sobered up and was also downstairs. Dressed (thankfully) and seated on the settee, she had looked up as George had come into the room. She appeared scared, and I couldn't help but think of Victor and wonder if George did actually know about the letter and Victor's wish to be a part of Carla's life again.

Meeting his mother's eyes, George had quickly looked away—turning his attention to Tara and me, instead. "Everburn," he had said, grinning. "I've thought about it and thought about it some more, and it's the obvious conclusion. She can't be anywhere else."

"Forget about her," Carla had said, looking out of the window. "She's no good to you, anyway. Never has been, never will be."

It had deteriorated from there. George had continued to talk about what needed to be done, how he was determined to rescue Sharon and Richard without anyone getting in his way, and Carla kept on at him, insisting that "this Sharon lass" was the last thing he needed. "She'll stifle you, lad," she had said. "Believe me, I've seen her type before. They take all the air out of the room and before you know it, you're dead. Or might as well be. They want everything you've got, but they give nothing in return. They tell you they'll do things, make grand promises, but they never deliver, because they're all self. They change the rules, George. They change the rules to suit themselves, whenever they feel like it, because fools like you let them get away with it."

I had seen George's anger growing all through this little

diatribe—a vein in his neck pulsing, wormlike and oddly fascinating—and I was ready for what came next. His fist had come up and he pointed at her, calling her all the noxious, vile bitches under the sun, and he lurched forward, clearly meaning to make a grab for her. Tara and I were quicker than either of us might have imagined, however, and we had reflexively placed ourselves between the two—Tara talking him down while I did my best to physically hold him back. Carla had continued to taunt him, however. On and on she had prattled and cackled, and, finally, Tara had apparently realised that more drastic measures had been called for; turning quickly, she had slapped Carla sharply across the face.

If silence truly is golden, then in that moment we had been the richest three people on God's little blue planet. None of us had spoken. Staring at each other, as if trying to fathom out just what it was that had happened, I listened—as I imagined the others did—to that nothingness and relished it. Oddly at peace, I had wanted to sit down with Tara and close my eyes, the fatigue suddenly overwhelming, but instead I had walked with George and Tara into the back kitchen, leaving a dumbstruck Carla on the settee.

And in the grimy room, overflowing with unwashed dishes, litter trays and cats, George had finally confirmed what Tara had suspected all along.

"I have an obligation," he had told us. "That's what that one-legged bitch in there doesn't understand. And normally I'd run from something like this. You two know that as well as anyone. But I owe them, Price. I owe Sharon and I owe Richard... shit... you know, that lad's just about the biggest fucking retard I've ever come across but..." He had looked up at us both, at this point, his eyes moist and lost-looking. "He's a retard, but he's my retard. He's my son and I owe it to him to be there for him the way no one has ever been there for me."

Pulling out a chair, he had sat down at the table—overcome with emotion and exhaustion. "This is a chance, Price. Maybe my last. I have to find them."

"This isn't about the promise any more, is it?" I had said.

"No."

Tara had looked at me and I had known what she was going to say even before she opened her mouth to speak. "Then we'll help you in whatever way we can," she had told him.

We had reached something of an impasse. George wasn't entirely sure what he wanted to do next, but he was adamant that he couldn't simply do nothing. I sat on the bed with Tara, and we watched him continue to pace and mutter. "What am I forgetting?" he kept asking himself, knocking the heel of his hand against his temple like some two-thirds crazy Jack Nicholson character, and around the twentieth time of his asking this, I did the only thing a sensible and compassionate man could do—I excused myself to go to the toilet before I clocked him one.

Out on the landing, I paused to compose myself. I was sweaty and unshaven and my clothes felt like they needed a good wash, but at least I wasn't George. That had to be some kind of consolation. I smiled and shook my head. Too cruel. Much too cruel. But if the thought kept me going through all this ridiculousness, then so be it. In this bizarre world of ours, beggars most assuredly couldn't afford to be choosers.

I started walking across the landing in the direction of the toilet, feeling somewhat better now that I was out of that room—but I stopped halfway, at the top of the stairs, hearing voices below. People talking. Two men and a woman, if I wasn't mistaken. Nothing unusual about that, except... call it instinct, if you will, but the minute I heard those voices, I knew it was in my best interest to stop and listen.

Holding my breath, I still only caught some of what they were saying. One of the two men cleared his throat and said, in a voice gritty from too many cigarettes, something that sounded like, "Scruffy little fuck. Looks like he's found a lump on his bollocks and doesn't know quite know what to make of it."

I moved a little way down the stairs and heard the second one say, "Got another bloke and a lass with him. The bloke's going bald on top and the lass looks like she walks dogs for a living."

I didn't need to hear any more. Moving quickly but quietly, I returned to the room and whispered urgently for Tara and George to follow me. George being George, he started to question and argue, and I angrily hissed at him, "There are two blokes downstairs. Looking for us. And I don't think they're a fucking welcoming committee."

This got his attention. Nodding seriously, he, begrudgingly, made it clear that I should lead the way. I mugged at Tara, who looked about as anxious as I felt, and opened the door a crack to see whether the coast was clear. Once I was completely sure that the two men were still downstairs, I led them stealth-like out onto the landing and across to the toilet. The plan was simple, but I was hoping that it would be all the more effective because of this.

Once the three of us were in the cramped toilet, I closed the door behind us, leaving it open a crack so that I could peep out, and said, "Once they're in our room, assuming she lets them up here in the first place—"

"I doubt she'll have a choice," George whispered.

"My point exactly. If they want to come up here, they will. So. The minute they're in our room, we're out of here and down the stairs—as quickly and quietly as possible. We get in the car and we drive and keep driving until we're absolutely certain that we're safe and—"

I stopped. Two burly figures, dressed in black leather jackets, black jeans and dark glasses, appeared at the top of the stairs. They paused, seeming to sniff the air, and then approached the door to our room. I held a finger to my lips to silence George, and peered through the crack, willing them to enter the room and close the door behind them.

The larger of the two men said something to the other one and he obediently knocked on the door. They waited a polite interval and then knocked again, this time more forcefully. Unless I was seriously mistaken, the door rattled considerably in its frame. Only when they were absolutely certain that no one was going to answer did they try the handle and very cautiously enter.

"What's happening?" Tara asked, and I told the two of them to get ready.

"They're just going in," I said. "Any second... right, come on. Let's go."

I swung the door open, almost catching George on the shoulder with it, and stepped purposefully out onto the landing—making a point of keeping myself between Tara and the bedroom door. If one of those pseudo-Men-in-Black came out, I didn't want her to be the first thing they saw within grabbing distance.

Blessedly, the door had swung partway shut behind them, and we made it to the top of the stairs without attracting their attention. I could hear them rummaging about in our room; thankfully, we hadn't brought a whole lot with us, so I was confident that they would find nothing of use to them.

Bundling Tara and George down the stairs before me, I willed them to move faster. There was no way we could get away with this. These men were probably professionals. They hunted people down and snapped limbs for a living, I was sure. Three bumbling idiots like us were bound to fail in our attempts at escape.

We made it to the bottom of the stairs without incident, however—only to be faced with the ample-bosomed, folded-armed form of the disapproving, toe-tapping landlady. Tara groaned and George, ever the gentleman, pushed past the old woman, telling her to get her "fat fucking retarded arse the fuck out of the way," before assuring her that he'd settle up with her later, if the thugs she'd sent upstairs to see us didn't get us in the meantime—"In which case, send the fucking bill to them."

Before she could respond with anything more than a haughty sniff, we were past her and out onto the street, running in the direction of Old Ray's thirty-year-old Austin Allegro. It wasn't exactly my first choice of getaway car, but judging by the drive out here, I knew it to be reliable and well cared for. Something that had come as a surprise to me, until George had explained that Old Ray was never sober enough to drive it anywhere.

As we got into the car, I heard voices behind us—shouting obscenities and generally making suggestions about where we might find our heads once they'd finished with us. I wasn't entirely sure just what it was we'd done to piss off these two lumbering, pumped up mounds of vitriol, but I was fairly sure that I didn't much fancy sticking around to discuss it with them. With this in mind, I slammed my door firmly shut, made sure Tara was safely in her seat beside me, and told George to start the engine, put his foot down and get us the hell out of there. Blessedly, George duly obliged and only when I looked out of the rear window and saw Little and Large squeezing themselves into a Porsche did my spirits start to drop again.

It was fair to say that George's driving had improved somewhat since our last outing together. I wondered, a little sardonically, if he'd been taking lessons. Tara and I pinballed off the doors and each other in the back of the car, and, try as I might not to, I couldn't help but steal another glance out of the rear window. The Porsche sat on our tail like a patient beast of the Serengeti, waiting for just the right moment to do its stuff. I got the distinct impression that it could do this all day, without breaking sweat. And all the while, George practically had the Allegro's accelerator floored. It didn't bode well.

The little big guy in the passenger seat of the Porsche gave me a cutesy wave and before I knew what I was doing, I waved back.

"What on earth...?" Tara said.

I blushed and shrugged, facing front and holding onto the back of George's seat. "Do we have a workable plan?" she said.

George nodded his head enthusiastically. "Oh yes," he told her. "I's got a workable plan, boss. You bet I do."

"And you intend on sharing it with us any time soon?"

"I'm going to outrun them."

"I think it only fair to point out," she said, "that they're driving a sporty little German number while we... aren't."

George checked his rearview mirror as if to confirm this, and then shrugged. "A minor detail," he said, before adding, "Maybe I should find a police station and park in front of it? If we run really quickly we just might be able to get to safety before they off us— or whatever it is they intend on doing."

"I like that plan," I said. "It sounds pretty perfect, if you ask me."

"Except we happen to be driving out of Everburn," Tara pointed out. "I don't think you get many police stations out on the moor."

Far in the distance, on the horizon, I saw a snaking, almost lonesome passenger train. As grimy and crowded as I was sure it must be, it looked positively idyllic from where I was sitting. George hit yet another considerable bump and swerved to bring the car back under control—momentarily veering into the oncoming lane and scaring the bejesus out of a pretty little thing in a purple Mini.

"Nothing for it, then," George said. "I'll just have to lose them. Can you see any side roads we can use to cunningly double back on them?"

We actually looked, that's what amazed me. Myself and Tara looked left. We looked right. We squinted hard. We squinted harder. And then we both sat back in our seats. Idiots. Complete bloody idiots.

The road ahead was flat and featureless—drab countryside on either side quickly becoming full-blooded moorland with all its heather and gorse and bracken, or whatever the fuck it was. The only thing to break the monotony was the train on the horizon, which seemed to be taking forever to pass from the left side of our field of vision to the right—and which also, unless I was seriously mistaken, seemed to be growing in size (does that mean, I wondered in my anxious state, that it's getting nearer... or just getting bigger?)

The oncoming lane was clear, and this was the opportunity the two thugs in the Porsche had apparently been looking for. I heard them before I saw them—the Porsche's revs increasing to a controlled, super-smooth hum while the tyres screeched briefly before finding purchase. The hairs stood up on the back of my neck right about the time that George started drumming on the steering wheel and shouting, "Whey-hey! Here we fucking go! Game on!" He then started singing what I believed to be the theme tune to B. J. and the Bear (something about being off to New

Orleans or who knows where). I didn't want to be on that no longer quite so distant train anymore. I wanted to be dead. I wanted to be dead in a ditch somewhere so that I didn't have to think about this.

And when the Porsche drew level with us, I thought that I might just get my wish. In that moment, I was quite sure that the word 'nonchalant' had been invented for George. He did everything short of drive with his elbow out the window. He sang a little more of the theme tune and then whistled something I didn't recognise, smiled at the two gentlemen in the depressingly fast car, winked, blew them a kiss—and, finally, after giving them the finger, rammed them.

Tara was catapulted into me, the two of us swearing and yelling and generally voicing our disbelief. My head cracked against the window, and I thought for one dreadful moment that the door was going to open and we were about to be thrown out onto the road. I glanced to my right as I bounced back off the door, giving Tara a substantial whack in the ribs with my elbow in the process. I saw the Porsche skid and swerve onto the verge on the far side of the oncoming lane. Dust and dirt flew up as its driver struggled to regain control, and then it was falling behind as brakes were applied and George was a-whooping and a-hollering.

"Did you see that?" he yelled. "Did you? Fucking idiots think they can mess with an Austin Allegro, do they? Well we fucking showed them. Those Nazi-mobiles might be fast, you see, but there's no real weight behind them. Not compared to this little beauty."

"That's your theory," Tara said, and he started singing again, this time something from Tosca, I believe.

Meanwhile, I was trying to pluck up enough courage to look out of the rear window, again. As the driver of the Porsche had struggled to get the car back under control, I had turned and watched as they had slipped behind. And I hadn't liked the look on his face. Crimson with rage, I'd expected to see steam coming out of his ears. His eyes had looked as if they were about to pop out, and his jaw had been clenched tightly enough to give a dentist nightmares for years to come. Receding into the distance, I had thought I'd seen him mouth the words 'fucking dead'—and now I just didn't want to look again... but I knew I had to.

George had caught them a good one. There was no disputing that. In all their years as thugs, I doubted that they'd ever actually found themselves in such a physical car chase. When they had pulled alongside, they'd never for one minute believed that George would pull such a stunt—and as a result, they had been wholly unprepared. George had caught them hard, and the only way in which to regain control over the car was to bring it to all but a stop. Looking out of the rear window, I saw that they'd dropped a good way back. I also saw, however, that they were quickly catching us up again.

"I have some good news," I reported. "And I have some bad news."

"They're coming back for more of the same?" George said.

"But judging by the expression on the driver's face, you won't catch them out with that one again."

"I have plenty more tricks up my sleeve," George assured me. "Just you sit back and relax. Leave it all to old Georgie."

Tara was uncharacteristically quiet. I looked at her in order to make sure she was alright. Still rubbing her rib where I had inadvertently elbowed her, she was staring out of the window at the passenger train. It was a long bugger, I now saw. Long and running at an angle to us that suggested it was...

... I looked at the road ahead and spotted the level crossing.

"Shit," Tara and I said in unison.

The crossing didn't have any barriers—merely a few flashing warning lights. As I looked and made the necessary mental calculations, I couldn't envisage one single scenario in which this could work out well for us.

"There's no way we can make it," I said to Tara, and she nodded. "Either the train hits us or we stop and let those two catch up with us and..."

She nodded again. Before adding, "I'll take my chances with the train."

George seemed to like this. "I'll tell you, Tara, love," he said, "I've never thought all that much of you. You know that. But right now? You're just going up and up in my estimation.

"There is however a third alternative," he went on. "With a little skill and extra speed, we can turn this to our advantage."

Skill, I was more than happy with. It made me think of routines well-practiced and death-defying. Extra speed was a different matter entirely, however. Apart from the obvious fact that I didn't believe the Allegro was capable of going any faster—the very notion of George propelling us along at even greater speed made me wish I'd had the foresight to bring a change of underwear.

Surprising both Tara and I, George succeeded in finding the very thing I dreaded him finding. He'd been keeping something in reserve, it seemed, and we now found ourselves hurtling towards our destiny at in excess of eighty miles an hour, compared to the sixty-five we had previously been doing. The Allegro shuddered and shook, but all in all it seemed to be holding up remarkably well.

Risking another glance out of the rear window and finding the Porsche once more hot on our tail, I mourned the lack of rear seatbelts and did my best not to think of how all of this might turn out.

Tara was holding my hand tightly. Up front, George had stopped singing and was now focused on getting as much speed as he could out of the Allegro. The train loomed, coming at us at a slight angle, and it seemed impossible to me that we could beat it to the crossing. George was committed, though. His foot was to the floor and if he didn't apply the brakes within the next fifteen seconds or so, I estimated that there would simply be no going back.

I'd like at this point to tell you that Tara and I faced our destiny with brave hearts and our chins held high. I'd like to, but I can't— because, we didn't. Wet with fear, we went from merely holding hands to huddling down together behind the front seats, eyes closed and a babbled prayer on our lips. Tara said something to me that I didn't hear above the struggling screams of the Allegro's engine, and I said "yes", hoping that this was the right response but somehow doubting that it actually was. And then, with preternatural clarity, I heard George say, "Okay. Hold tight. Here goes—shit or bust time, ladies and gentlemen." I fell into myself, at this point—fell into myself in a way that I never had before and haven't since. Eyes closed, I held on to Tara and wished the two of us away from there.

I heard the bass drone of the tyres against the surface of the road and felt it like the remnants of a bad meal in the pit of my stomach. The floor dropped away and suddenly I felt as if I were floating—a strangely euphoric feeling that made me think of clouds and harps and eternity. And then I heard the dum-dum dum-dum of the railway tracks beneath us and I held my breath, eyes squeezed painfully shut, just waiting for the inevitable moment of impact.

But it didn't come. The reliable sound of the tyres against the standard road surface resumed and above that I, briefly, heard only silence. Silence, and then a whoop and holler of elation and victory from George.

Tara sat up with me. We looked around, bewildered and wholly at a loss to explain how we had survived something that had seemed so inevitably doomed to disaster. A quick look out of the rear window told us that the train was still going over the crossing and that, blessedly, the Porsche was still on the other side.

Things wouldn't remain like this forever, however, and George's elation was tempered by the need to find a route that would ensure that we lost the thugs in the Porsche. He took a sharp right onto a side road that led down through some trees into a small valley, driving as quickly as the winding lane would allow. Tara kept glancing behind us, no doubt expecting to see the Porsche on our tail, again. But, so far, everything seemed to be going according to plan.

None of us speaking, we drove through a small village—doubling back in the general direction of the coast. The singing, excitable George of earlier had now totally disappeared. He was intent on doing this right, and I found myself actually admiring him for this. Apparently, he knew when it served him better to be serious.

Finally, George spoke. "There's a place I know," he said. "Where we'll be safe. For the time being, at least."

It reminded me of the dream I'd had, where I had been with Tara and, miracle of miracles, my sense of smell had returned. Another narrow lane wound down through crowded woodland, the trees holding hands over our heads—making me feel like a newly-wed or a child playing a macabre rhyming game. The light, filtered and watery, was difficult to see by, but George nevertheless resisted the urge to put on the car's headlights. He wanted to melt into the scenery as much as Tara and me.

Once he found somewhere that looked right, he pulled over onto the grass verge, taking the car as far into the undergrowth as he dare and turning off the engine.

Twisting in his seat to look at us, I saw that he was back in goofy-grin mode. "Nobody ever told me life could be this exciting," he said. "Are we enjoying ourselves, boys and girls, or what?"

"I can't think of another time when I've laughed quite so much," I said, and Tara nodded in agreement. "Have you any idea what you did to us back there? Christ, George, you must have taken ten years off our lives."

Chuckling, he said, "Nothing compared to what would have happened if those two fuckers had caught up with us. A little gratitude is called for, I believe, Pricey-babes—yes indeed."

"It was pretty impressive," Tara admitted. "Totally fucking nuts, but impressive."

"Thank you, cousin dear." George took out his cigarettes and matches and lit up. I noticed his hand was shaking, but thought it best not to point it out. He inhaled deeply, and the mere gesture alone looked so cathartic that I almost asked him if I could have one. But instead I sat back with Tara—holding her hand and feeling her wind down, her growing sense of ease taking me down with it.

We sat like that for a good few minutes (long enough for George to finish his cigarette, at least) and then Tara decided she needed to pee. There were plenty of available trees and bushes, but she was reluctant to go on her own. "Come with me," she whispered. "In case I get lost... or something. You know."

It was starting to get dark when we left the car, and I didn't much fancy being out here on our own—not with those two thugs quite possibly still looking for us. Sitting in the car, getting our breath back, had been bad enough, but this—wandering among the shadowy trees and bushes, looking for a fitting place for Tara to pee—this made me feel about as helpless as I had all day.

"This'll do," Tara said, dropping her jeans and knickers and squatting among the bushes, not caring whether I could see or not (I could and didn't bother looking away—enjoying the sight possibly a little too much under the circumstances.) "I wasn't really all that desperate," she admitted, her pee spattering and pattering onto the undergrowth, vaguely reminding me of that afternoon a few days ago with Carla. "I just needed a few minutes away from George. To make sure I'm still here."

"Where else would you be?" I said. I smiled though, knowing exactly what she meant.

Tara pulled up her knickers and jeans. "I don't know," she said, zipping her fly. "Anywhere where I wasn't. Or that's how it feels... It's like I've been here, been with you and George, all this time and yet... I can't quite believe it. I feel like I've been body-snatched." This made her smile and she added, "A couple of times I've almost succeeded in convincing myself that I'm actually enjoying the excitement of it all. That can't be good, can it?"

"Depends on how you look at it, I suppose."

"Give me some choices."

"Well, the way I figure it, this was always going to happen. No matter how hard we fought it, we still would have ended up here, having this conversation and trying not to acknowledge that you've just peed in front of me for the first time."

"Fate," she said.

"If you want to call it that. I just tend to think of it as George, but I suppose it all adds up to the same thing; here we are and here we would always have been, no matter, as I've said, what."

"So...?"

"So for me it's all about how we deal with it. We can be miserable and unreceptive or..."

"Enjoy it and take something from it?"

I nodded. "I mean," I said, "it's not every day you find yourself in a car chase involving a Porsche, an Austin Allegro and a train, now, is it?"

"No," she said, smiling. "Thank God." She walked over and linked my arm. I held her, then, and we kissed, and then I held her some more as she said, ever so quietly, "Tell me it won't make a difference, Price."

I didn't know what she was talking about, at first, and then she took my hand and held it to her damp armpit. Her eyes searched mine in the poor light for some indication that this was something that would condemn us, something with which we simply could not contend. I didn't know what she saw there, but I hoped it was as reassuring as I tried to sound when I said, "You know it won't, Tara. It could certainly never come between us, if that's what you're thinking. I've told you."

What with George and all the excitement, we hadn't had as much time to discuss this as I would have liked. I could see that it was going to take a good while (and quite possibly a lot of patience on my part) before she was going to be wholly convinced that this would not tear us apart—but I was prepared for that, and underscored this for her.

"I don't smell all the time," she said. "I wash and use strong antiperspirants, and that helps, but as soon as I get hot or anxious or excited... I got these pills from the doctor once. They worked really well but... they dried me up down below, too, Price. It was awful. I couldn't even masturbate without using an artificial lubricant—and even that... it just didn't feel right. I wasn't me, somehow. I don't know. So I stopped taking them and..."

I kissed her, not wanting to hear anymore—not needing to hear anymore. She had suffered. Like me, she understood heartache and alienation, and, while it was in my power, I intended to protect her from further pain in whatever way I could. I owed her that much, and, I was sure, a whole lot more.

I told her I loved her again, and walked with her back to the car.

We found George leaning against the Allegro and smoking yet another ciggy. He grinned at us as we approached—suggestive and sparkly-eyed. Pushing himself away from the car and drawing deeply on the cigarette, he squinted and then said, "Now that the two of you are finished with whatever it is you've been up to, maybe we can get on with the rest of our little adventure."

"I was hoping we could go home," Tara said.

"Hope springs eternal, as they say," he told her. "I've never got that. You'd think we'd learn, wouldn't you?"

"We're not going home." I said this with all the enthusiasm of a pensioner who's just realised that he's going to be spending a lot of time in the shit-smelling dayroom before him.

"We're not going home," George confirmed. "And with good reason, too. Everything comes to those who wait, right, Tara, love? And let's face it, we did a lot of waiting back there in that bed and breakfast."

"You've remembered something?" Tara said.

He didn't answer, merely flicked his cigarette into the bushes and made it known we should follow him. I didn't like leaving the car behind, but we didn't seem to have much choice; the road down which we had been driving grew steadily steeper and more narrow, the woodland rising up abruptly on both sides before suddenly dropping away and opening up to reveal a stony beach, cliffs to the north and south, and a stormy, petulant sea.

George threw his arms wide and rather foolishly fanfared. As impressive as the cliffs and sea might be, it was a fairly unspectacular place—there were dozens of similar coves along the east coast, I was sure—and Tara took great pleasure in telling his as much. George just shrugged it off, though. He was in too good a mood to let someone like Tara upset him.

"This isn't it, though," he said. "This is only the beginning. Follow me."

We started walking across the pebbles, being careful not to twist an ankle, in the direction of the north cliff face. Tara held my hand and rolled her eyes at me as the sea crashed onto the rocks and beach, its spray cold and invigorating against my cheek. I couldn't see what our being here like this had to do with finding Sharon and Richard. It seemed so far removed from that house on the moor— as did all of today's events, for that matter—that I just couldn't fit the two together. The more I thought about it, the more absurd this whole charade seemed. We had no real evidence that Sharon and Richard were even in Everburn, other than the fact that we had been chased by a couple of thugs that may have been her brothers—and I certainly didn't see how being on this beach at dusk was going to help resolve the issue.

As if he had known what I was thinking, George said, "This used to be one of their places. When they were kids, but when they were older, too. Sharon told me all about it." His voice had a quixotic quality about it that was very unlike him. He walked along the base of the north cliff, clambering over the rocky debris as I wondered just how safe this was. There were no signs about the danger of falling rock, but maybe those in authority had deduced that the chunks of broken off cliff at the base were warning enough.

George was a little way ahead of us, now—mumbling to himself and, it appeared, frantically searching for something. Tara pressed in close to me and admitted that she was now finding this rather boring. "If he could see himself," she said, "you know what he'd say, don't you?"

"Enlighten me."

"He'd say that there was a bloke in need of sectioning."

"At least we know which side of the family Richard gets his brains from," I said, and Tara slapped my arm, telling me not to be so cruel.

Sniffing first, she said, "Whatever, he's going to end up really disappointed. You have realised that, haven't you? The odds of our finding Sharon and Richard are stacked against us—and when he realises this, we're the ones who'll have to deal with the fallout."

I started to tell her that there was nothing new in that, that we'd done it before and would no doubt do it again, as long as George was in our lives, at least, but then George was shouting us over excitedly. He'd found something. He'd found something and the discovery was thrilling enough to prompt him to jump up and down, waving and yelling for us to get a bloody move on.

I couldn't see what he was pointing at, at first. The light was poor and the cliff face was craggy and shadowed. I looked at him questioningly and he pointed more persistently. "There," he said. "Jesus, Price—open your bloody eyes. Or are they going the way of your nose now, too?"

When I obediently looked again, I didn't know how I could have missed it the first time. I blinked, just to be sure, and then said, "It's a cave."

The minute the words were out of my mouth, I knew we were in deep shit. George had brought us to this beach with the sole purpose of finding this cave, I reasoned, and as I saw it, that could only mean one thing.

Tara had apparently worked it out, too. "No way, George," she said. "If you think you're getting us to go in there with you, I'm afraid you've got another thing coming."

George had impressive powers of persuasion, we both already knew that, and he had innumerable tricks up his sleeve. Today, however, he was going to surprise even us—employing not exactly the most subtle of techniques, but nevertheless doing it with such conviction that resisting him became nigh on impossible.

"Well," he said, so quietly that we could only just hear him above the noise from the sea. "I certainly wouldn't dream of making you do something you don't want to do. Far be it from me to dictate under what are, let's face it, very unusual and extreme circumstances." He ignored Tara's derisive laugh and continued, "However, I feel I have to point out a couple of things you may well have overlooked." Here it comes, I thought. "Sharon and Richard are, quite possibly, depending on us. If I'm right, they have no one else looking out for them at this time but me—and before you say anything, I do know what a shitty deal that is for them. But beggers can't be choosers, right? I'm all they've got and I mean to do as good a job for them as I possibly can." He paused a moment, just in case we felt the need to say something. When we remained silent, he continued with point number two. "That aside," he said. "There are her brothers to think of. Because that's who those two were. The twats in the Porsche. Her brothers."

"You recognised them?" Tara said.

"I did. You never forget faces as ugly as those. They were her brothers, and as far as we know, they're still out there looking for us." He gestured at our surroundings. "And, of course," he said, "the longer we stand around out here, the more likely it is that they'll find us... Now, I don't know about the two of you, but I certainly wouldn't want to be standing out here on my own should they happen to come wandering by. Far better to be doing something useful—out of sight—in my opinion."

He stood back and folded his arms, awaiting our decision, but when one was not forthcoming, he apparently felt it important to add, "If I'm right about this place, there'll be a little alcove to the left, just inside the entrance, where there should be some candles and dry matches. If there isn't, it'll be too dark to go on, in which case... we'll return to the car."

Tara and I looked at each other. She shivered, and I knew from the way she looked quickly away that her mind was already made up—and I wondered if perhaps she had been right and she had indeed been body-snatched. Was I actually looking at Tara or some alien-infested doppelgänger?

"It can't be safe in there," I said. "What if there's a cave-in and we get trapped? No one knows we're here, George. We'd die of starvation or asphyxiation or some other fucking ation before anyone found us."

"Today is our day for living dangerously," he said, dropping his voice an octave and grinning. "We've survived a car chase and a game of chicken with a passenger train—what makes you think a little old cave is going to do for us?"

"You know we're going to give in," Tara said. "Why bother

even trying to fight it? Fate, remember? Or 'George', as you insist on calling it."

George liked this. "That's how he thinks of me?" he chuckled. "Fate? Oh that's fucking precious, mate. I must remember to write that one down—so I can read it when I'm feeling blue."

"I'll make a deal with you," I said, ignoring his piss-taking. "We'll go in with you on one condition; if we find nothing in there, we get in the Allegro and fuck off back home. How does that sound?"

George shrugged. He was apparently fairly confident that this cave would somehow lead us to Sharon and Richard, telling us that it was part of the whole smuggling thing—and, unless he was sorely mistaken, it would have a surprise or two up its sleeve for us. "So," he concluded. "Yes. That sounds fair enough to me."

I'd never in my life been in a cave before. And I was surprised to find that it wasn't half as bad as I'd thought it would be. Yes, up until George found the matches and candles he'd promised would be there, it had been pretty dark—the dank air tingling with promise and, quite possibly, something akin to threat. But once we had a little light with which to better judge our surroundings, I found a warmth and silence there that was actually quite welcoming. Rather than worrying about all those tons of rock above, I instead found myself thinking of them as an expression of Nature's wish to keep us safe. Maybe that was sickeningly romantic, I don't know—but I was frankly quite glad of anything that might make this whole experience more bearable.

George walked ahead with the candle, humming the theme music from The Amityville Horror, and Tara and I huddled behind, talking and occasionally glancing over our shoulders. Narrow and low-ceilinged, I realised that I was stooping, even though I didn't actually need to. I tried standing taller, but it didn't feel right, somehow. This was a place where stooping was called for... my mother would have hated it.

We'd been walking for a good couple of minutes when George stopped suddenly. I asked him what was wrong but he just held up a hand, positioning the candle so that he could look down at the floor. Bending down, he picked up something that I couldn't quite make out.

"What is it?" Tara asked.

Turning it over in his hand, our huge, deformed, flickering shadows dancing on the walls and ceiling, I saw that George was holding a toy car—a silver-blue Mercedes, unless I was mistaken. "Look familiar?" George asked me, and I nodded, taking the car from him, surprised by how cold it was.

I handed the car back to him. He put the car safely in the pocket of his jeans. "At least we know they came this way, that we're on the right track."

"Unless that's someone else's toy car," Tara pointed out.

"And you think it is?" George asked, sharply.

Tara shook her head, cowed. "No," she said. "No, I don't suppose I do."

She seemed somewhat panicked—as if she found George, or maybe our surroundings, suddenly more intimidating than she could bear. I squeezed her hand and, when she looked at me, she rolled her eyes

We walked deeper into the cave and I started to feel the damp air penetrate every cell and sinew. There was a silence above the noises the three of us made that was all-encompassing and eerie in its stifling form, and I finally allowed myself to think about where we were—to really think about it. It was quite possibly the worst thing I could have done. The walls started closing in on me and the roof of the cave weighed down more heavily, prompting me to stoop even lower. I thought of all the horror films I'd watched as a kid about people being buried alive and I finally had a real inkling of what that might be like. I had the freedom to turn around and walk towards the light (what was left of it), but what if that choice were taken away from me? What if I found myself imprisoned here—entombed here? It really didn't bear thinking about... but the more I tried not to think about it, the more solid that dark fantasy became. Suddenly quite convinced that I would die here—that we would all die here—I struggled to find a way through it, reaching for passing positive thoughts as if they were life-belts and I a drowning man. But all to no avail. The darkness closed in on me; George's candle helping little, I concentrated on breathing through my nose. Nice, controlled inhalations. No panicky gasps. Tara looked at me once, eyebrows knotting together with concern, and I managed to smile at her—fairly convincingly, I thought. I didn't want her to see how bad I was feeling on the inside. How certain I was that the three of us would die down here and no one would ever be any the wiser.

George stopped suddenly and Tara and I almost walked into the back of him. It appeared that we had come to the end of the cave. A craggy, curved wall greeted us and the sound of our breathing seemed to bounce around us—shallow and rather frantic, the soundtrack to a bizarre fuck-flick. George put his hand against the damp rock, holding out the candle with the other. He seemed to be searching for a secret doorway or something, and I was just about to tell him how bloody ridiculous that was, and how I thought we should be getting back to the car and heading off home, when he looked up at the roof of the cave and said, "Bingo. Just as I suspected."

I followed his gaze, Tara doing the same, and was surprised to see what appeared to be a trapdoor set into the roof. Made from heavy wood that had been painted to match the colour of the dark rock around it, it would have been easy to miss. If George hadn't been specifically looking for clues to the whereabouts of Sharon and Richard, he might never have spotted it. As it was, however, he grinned victoriously and handed Tara the candle.

"I'm going to need a hand," he said, and, at first, I didn't know what on earth he was talking about. Then he laced his fingers together to show me that he wanted a leg up and I realised that he was actually going to try to open the trapdoor.

"Do you really think that's a good idea?"

"I do," he said. "As I see it, we have no real alternative. Sharon and Richard were brought to this cave. They were brought to this cave and taken up through this door—and if we're going to find them, we have no choice other than to go the way we believe they went."

Tara was nodding slowly. As much as I loved her, I wanted to give her a nice, sharp slap. We should have been united in this— even though I knew that, deep down, we were.

"We don't know who's up there," I pointed out. "For all we know, her brothers could be on the other side, just waiting for us to stick our heads through so they can give us a bloody good clobbering."

"They're probably still driving around looking for us," George said. "They'll be working on the assumption that we're going to return to the bed and breakfast, mark my words. It won't ever occur to them that I know about this place. As far as they're concerned, it's their little secret."

This seemed pretty unlikely to me. Smugglers' caves (which this clearly was) were well documented, in my admittedly limited experience. Anyone with an ounce of sense would surely assume that other people knew about it too. And take the necessary precautions.

I saw that mentioning this was futile, however, and squatted down and braced myself against the wall, making a stirrup of my hands for George to step onto. He nodded approvingly, finding a suitable hand hold on the wall and then placing his scuffed and filthy shoe into my hands. I boosted him as best I could, my fingers burning when he pushed against the door, my grip only just holding. I realised that before my job at the Italian Gardens, I could never have done this, and I added this to the already substantial pile of grudges I held towards my father.

"I need a bit more..." George grunted, putting his other foot further up the wall, trying to brace himself more solidly.

"Hold on," Tara said.

"Like you don't think I am?"

She switched the candle to her other hand, stepping in and sticking her right shoulder under George's left thigh. "Any better?" she asked, standing on my toe as she altered her footing.

"A little," he said. "Yes... no, not really. I can push more but... fuck it. Let me down."

George dropped to the ground and brushed off his palms. He

looked angry and resigned all at the same time, the shadows on his face giving his complex mood an added dimension.

"Want me to try?" I said.

Shaking his head, he said, "It's locked from the other side. As you might expect. Either that or it's jammed solid. It's not going to budge whatever we try. I wouldn't mind betting they have something heavy parked on it. An old trunk or a chest of drawers."

"Makes sense," Tara said. "If you have a secret entrance to somewhere you're going to want to secure and protect it."

Tara was staring thoughtfully at the trapdoor. I looked at her. George looked at her. "Penny for them," George said.

Tara spun on her heel and started back towards the mouth of the cave, leaving George and I with a choice – since she now had the candle, we could either remain there in the dark, or follow her. We followed her.

It was good to be back in the car, the heater blasting away and that deceptive sense of being cocooned making me feel safe. Comparatively speaking, I supposed we were, but I reminded myself not to grow too complacent—for that was when, inevitably, tragedy had a habit of striking.

I looked out of my window at the dark moorland, dusk now completely fallen into night, and took consolation in the fact that the Allegro was now less easy to spot.

Tara was rigid beside me, leaning forward and purposefully looking out through the windscreen. Since we'd left the cave, she had been a woman on a mission—believing that, with a little judgment and imagination, we could find the house into which the trapdoor opened. Personally, I thought this was a rather ludicrous proposition, especially when I considered that without her insistence that the hunt for Sharon and Richard wasn't over we probably would have been on our way home by now.

Leaning between the two front seats, she pointed at something I couldn't quite make out and told George that if he took a right there she was fairly certain that we would be on the right track. I sat back and let them get on with it—just glad to be out of the cave.

I tried my hardest to block out the whole experience. I told myself that it was wholly natural to feel the way I did. We'd had two thugs in a Porsche after us and what had we done? We'd gone into a cave where we could have so easily been cornered and killed. Was it at all surprising that I just wanted to put the whole thing behind me and head home?

As we had walked back to the car from the cave, Tara had let George go on ahead so that she could speak to me privately. Her voice had been constant and exact—each word carefully measured and enunciated—and as I'd listened (for that was really all that had been required of me), I had felt myself reassured a little to find that she at least still understood that we were being pulled along in George's wake.

"Don't get mad at me," she had said. "I know I should just keep my mouth shut and let him take us home. But I can't. Not anymore. I'm worried about them. About Sharon and Richard— and about what this will do to George if we don't find them." I'd told her that George was a big boy and he was more than capable of taking care of himself.

"You don't really believe that," she had said. "Not after talking to that monster the other day. You can't. I mean, that was it for me. If I'm honest. That was the one moment that made me sit back and think about what George had really been through. I know he can't be trusted and I know that we still aren't seeing the full picture, but I think we both know we can't just leave him to cope with this on his own." I'd wanted to disagree with her, but while I could have lied to myself, I hadn't thought I could lie to her. As I sat in the car, now, listening to Tara give George directions, I saw that when Tara was around, I was more inclined to be true to my feelings. There was no hiding.

"You need to take the next left," I said, leaning against the back of George's seat and putting an arm around Tara.

"You sure?" George said, looking at me through his rearview mirror and not sounding in the least bit convinced.

"As I can be," I said. "It just feels right. Somehow."

"I'd concur with that," Tara said, smiling at me. "If there's a row of houses, I'd say the trapdoor—or the shaft the trapdoor leads to—opens into one of them."

George nodded and rotated his neck, not up to arguing, I guessed, even if he'd wanted to. It was fair to say that we were all feeling the strain by this time. My head was throbbing and Tara, in between rushes of adrenaline, looked as if she could have fallen down on the pebbles outside the cave and slept where she lay. We needed to rest, and since returning to the bed and breakfast was out of the question, I saw that, hopefully sooner rather than later, we would have to return home, possibly with Sharon and Richard in tow.

George took the left we had indicated—taking us further into the centre of the small, clifftop village through which we had been driving—and, almost as if Tara had thought it into existence, we were greeted by the sight of a row of four terraced houses.

They looked isolated and vulnerable, even though they were in the centre of the village—cut off like schoolyard misfits, one eye always watching out for danger. I looked at those houses and I knew, on some level, at least, that one of them was the house we were looking for. And I didn't especially like that, however much of a miracle our finding it was. The shaft leading from the trapdoor we had found in the cave most assuredly opened into the cellar of one of those properties—and, to confirm this, the dreaded Porsche was parked at the kerb before one of the end-terrace houses.

George stopped the car and then reversed a little, so that we were a safe distance away. He pulled on the handbrake, a little too vigorously for my liking, and then turned off the engine—twisting in his seat to look at us. His smile was one of impending victory – he had the look of a Grand Master who knew that he would have mate in three moves. I wished I could have been so confident.

"Have you ever known such a team?" he said. "Together, the three of us are un-fucking-beatable. Never thought I'd say it, of course. I'd always had the two of you down as dead wood and little more –"

"You're breaking my heart," Tara said.

"I know," he said, sadly. "But today we worked like a team and got everything right." He waved a regal hand in the direction of the Porsche, as if to underscore the point. "The question is," he said, growing rather more serious, "how do we approach the little problem now facing us without spoiling our one hundred per cent record?"

Tara didn't like being so close to the house (or the Porsche) in the Allegro. "Our first priority," she said, "has to be to find somewhere safer for the car. Perhaps leave it there and approach the house on foot once her two brothers are out of the way."

George was nodding thoughtfully, happy to let Tara do all the thinking on this. I was still rather surprised by his change in attitude towards her. It was true, she had earned his admiration (whatever that was worth) but it was so unlike him to put his trust in someone, without there being conditions. Though he merely continued nodding thoughtfully and said, "So we get the car out of sight. Yes. I like that. A good first step—self-preservation being the order of the day. After all, we won't be able to help Sharon and Richard if those two brothers of hers get to us first, right?" He winked at Tara, and then looked at me—seemingly disappointed with what he saw. Sniffing and regarding the Porsche again, he said, turning the key in the ignition, "Let's find somewhere a bit less conspicuous, then, shall we?"

George drove us straight towards the Porsche and the row of terraced houses. At first I thought he had some crazy scheme up his sleeve, like ramming the Porsche (again), or driving right into the tiny front garden of the house where we thought Sharon and Richard were being held. But George had blessedly thought this through more thoroughly than that. Instead, he took a left in front of the terrace and took us around to the back of the terrace.

It was a poorly lit space. Another blessing. I looked out of the window, barely making out the high fencing at the backs of the houses—suitable concealment in itself—and, on Tara's side, the row of shabby garages. I saw that this was actually quite possibly a stroke of genius.

George parked close to the fence and I felt myself lost in the shadows. For a brief moment, as the engine died and all was quiet, it was like being alone in my flat with Tara. I felt inexplicably safe, and content just to be where I was. I listened to the silence building around me and it seemed unthinkable that we should move from this place. It was meant for us.

I started to tell Tara this, explain to her that all that was required of us was that we remain here, that the Universe expected nothing more of us, but George began speaking again and the moment was ruined.

"We should be able to watch the house okay from the corner of the terrace," he said. "From the road that brought us round here. If they come out to the car, we'll see them before they ever have a chance of seeing us."

It seemed a reasonable enough proposition but I was nevertheless reluctant to get out of the car. It wasn't so much the cowardice that George had highlighted on numerous occasions, more the sense of belonging that had overcome me. I held Tara's hand, hoping that she would feel it, too.

"What's wrong?" Tara said to me as George started getting out of the car.

"Nothing."

She studied me through the darkness. "Are you sure?" she said, not in the least bit convinced.

"I don't want to get out," I admitted.

George rapped on the window with his bony knuckles and Tara and I turned to face him. "If this wasn't about Sharon and Richard," she said, "we really would tell him where to go. As sympathetic as we are towards him after everything, we're only really here because this involves Sharon and Richard... right?"

This was what we told ourselves in order to make the reality more bearable. Nevertheless, I nodded.

George looked impatient and pissed off with us when we finally got out of the car. He stood with his back to the fence, his arms folded, tapping his foot like a silent movie parody of himself.

"All very cosy and everything," he said. "But in case you've forgotten, we aren't exactly here for the good of our health, tonight. We have that little matter of finding Sharon and Richard and making sure that they are alright. Remember?"

"We remember," Tara said, coldly. She looked as if she was about to say more, but I put my arm around her waist and pulled her to me.

"This is as important to us as it is you," I said, knowing it wouldn't really change anything but nevertheless feeling that I had to say something. "We wouldn't be here otherwise."

Sniffing scornfully, George pushed himself away from the fence and headed around the corner—beckoning us with a half-hearted wave of the arm as he went. "This is how we're going to handle this little situation," he said, his voice no more than a whisper. "We're going to be patient. You should be good at that, Price, because, basically, it means doing sweet fuck all for as long as it takes." He chuckled to himself and I considered pushing him to the floor and giving him a bloody good kicking. I was behind him, so I had an obvious advantage. But I knew that no matter how badly I hurt him, he would see to it that I got mine.

"We wait and we watch," he continued as Tara stifled a yawn behind her hand. "We wait and we watch, and when we see an opportunity, we go for it."

"What if we don't see an opportunity?" Tara said. She wasn't trying to be obstructive. It was a question that genuinely concerned her.

He stood still for a moment, considering the question, and then said, "We make one. If we have to. I don't think it'll come to that, though."

"Why not?"

"Her brothers," he said. "They're the type that do most of their business at night. They're bound to go out sooner or later."

I'd thought that our first trip to Kingston Lodge had been bad enough, hiding in the bushes drinking George's whisky-laced coffee, but this was far worse, even with Tara by my side. We were none of us dressed appropriately, and the night was quickly growing cold, Tara already shivering. Standing at the corner of the end terrace house, taking turns to peep around the edge of the brickwork to see if anything was happening, I felt that we were more vulnerable here than we had been all day. George didn't agree, though. As far as he was concerned, we were as safe as houses.

"There's hardly anyone out and about," he said. "And the street lights are piss poor."

Then he added to Tara, "You can go back to the car, though." Reward, no doubt, for her ingenuity in finding this place. "Price and me can take care of this, can't we, Price?"

"I was hoping I could go back with her," I said. "And they're less likely to spot us if there's only one of us here, aren't they?"

George gave me a look that suggested that he was not in the least bit in the mood for such despicable cowardice in the ranks. He took a step towards me, eyes narrowed, jaw clenched, and then... and then his features softened, morphing into something quite un-George-like and... almost human—and it occurred to me that maybe he was the one who had been body-snatched, after all, not Tara.

"Well," he said. "I guess there's a certain logic to that. One person standing at the end of a row of terraced houses smoking a ciggy looks just as suspicious as three, of course—but I will be less visible. There's no arguing with that." He studied my face, smiling a smile that I just couldn't read, even after all the years of knowing him. "You want to go and keep warm with Tara?" he asked.

"Yes, I do."

"A little bit wimpy of you," he told me. "But I suppose that's something I've just got used to. You two run along. I'll give you a shout when something happens."

"You're a gent," I said, with just the slightest trace of irony.

"Don't push it. And just don't leave any sticky patches on that back seat. I'm going to have enough trouble explaining the damaged side to Old Ray without having spunk stains to deal with, too."

"Do you have to be so crude?" Tara said.

"Genetically predisposed," he answered, nodding vigorously.

I led Tara away from him before their little exchange turned into something more noteworthy. We had gone no more than four or five paces, however, when George called to us over his shoulder in a stage whisper, "Price. Tara. Get fucking back here."

Turning and walking slowly back to him, Tara whispered to me, "If I didn't know better, I'd think he was manipulating everyone involved in this, not just us."

"What now?" I asked him, and he quickly pushed Tara and I back against the wall, his hand, flat against my chest, hurting a little. I slapped him away, asking him if he really thought it was necessary to be quite so rough, and he held a finger to his lips. It was nevertheless the pleading look in his eyes that silenced me.

I then heard the resonant purring of the Porsche's engine and saw the sweep of the headlights as it pulled out and drove away.

George stepped forward and watched it go, Tara and I huddled behind him like timid kittens. I dreaded what was to come next. I didn't know what it was, exactly, but still I dreaded it. If only we'd made it back to the car for a while, things might have been different.

I looked at her and saw from the tightness around her mouth that she was as ill-prepared for this as me.

Breaking cover, George said, "Follow me."

Chapter Twelve

It was difficult to imagine it working. Not quite stupid enough to believe that Sharon's brothers would be so lax as to leave Sharon and Richard alone in the house, George assumed that somebody would be, as he put it, "guarding" them. He made it all sound very cloak and dagger, and I couldn't help wondering if we'd perhaps totally got the wrong end of the stick. What if Sharon had come along willingly, in an attempt to get away from George, I thought. We, after all, only had his word for it that they had been getting on like a house on fire. What if Sharon had actually been glad to see the back of him? I walked beside Tara on our way to the front of the house, thinking about this and so many other bizarre possibilities that I could have sworn I could feel my thoughts collecting at my temples like distressingly pressurised blood clots.

"We'll keep under cover until the door's open," George whispered as we walked along the short front garden path to the door. "Either side of the door. Yes. That's what we'll do. We'll stand either side of the door. Tara can stand directly in front of it looking all sexy and distracting... well, distracting, at least." He sniggered and I was that close to delivering a swift blow to his kidney. "Make out like there's been an accident or something down the road," he told her. "Try to get him out onto the path so we can have a good go at him."

"We'?" I said.

"Have a good go at him?" Tara asked.

We were standing before the front door now and George looked impatient to get on with it. He sighed and pushed his oily hair back from his face, keeping his voice low and standing close to the wall beside the door, trying to merge with the shadows, it seemed.

"What?" he said. "You think we're just going to have a polite conversation with him and that will be that? Is that what you think? Because it isn't going to work like that, I'm afraid. These things never do, in my many years of experience."

"I'm not sure I can do this," I told him. "I'm not... I'm not the physical type."

Before I knew what was happening, George had hold of me by the throat and had pinned me against the wall. His face about an inch from mine, he told me in no uncertain terms that it was too late for me to back out now. I'd come along with him this far, leading him to believe that I would do whatever was required of me. "If you think you can just put the brakes on when we get to the important bit, you've got another thing coming." He let go of me and brushed down the front of my shirt. "Understood?"

I nodded sheepishly, trying my level best to avoid Tara's eyes, and George gestured at the other side of the door. My heart was thumping coldly in my chest but nevertheless I did as I was told, standing close to the wall and well back from the door.

Once George was in position, he gave Tara the nod and she stepped forward and knocked on the door, casting me a sideways glance as she did so. She didn't like this any more than me but she didn't know what to do about it either. I held my breath and then forced myself to exhale. The last thing I needed was to faint due to lack of oxygen… not when Tara was right in the firing line.

This hadn't properly occurred to me until now. Tara was right there—right in front of the door. If anyone was in danger, it was her. If there was going to be the barrel of a gun, figurative or otherwise, she would be the one staring down it. But it was too late now. Just as I was about to step forward and stop her knocking again, the door started to open.

I flattened myself against the wall and watched Tara's face closely for clues about how this was proceeding. She looked panicked and shaken, and I almost intervened to put a stop to this—until I remembered that she was meant to look panicked and shaken. There'd been an accident, after all. She was a damsel in distress. She was acting, and doing a damn fine job of it, too, from what I could see.

"I... I was wondering... can you help me?" she said. Her chin quivered and she staggered slightly. "There's been an accident. I've called the ambulance but... it's my boyfriend. He's trapped and I need to get him out because... it's starting to burn. It's starting to burn and I'm..."

She stepped back—her movements unsteady—and I willed the man at the door to step out and follow her. But he didn't. Because he was no fool.

"I know you," he said.

Tara stopped, and in the light from the door I saw the colour drain from her face. She seemed to be struggling hard not to look at George and me—desperate not to give the game away, her chin trembling with the effort. I glanced quickly across at George, trying to get him to do something to help her, make a decision and act, but he wasn't looking at either of us. Instead, dear old George was studying the man's shadow on the paving in front of the door. It was big and distorted and told me nothing I needed to know. George, however, seemed to find something of value there, something he could use. He looked at it and frowned, his lips moving silently.

"No," Tara said. "No, I'm sure you don't. There's... there's been an accident. You don't know me." She inhaled deeply, closing her eyes and composing herself. I was reminded of that day on the Jag man's doorstep and was surprised to realise that I was actually, quite perversely, looking forward to what might come next.

Opening her eyes, now seemingly fully in control of the situation, Tara said, "Yes. You're right. You do know me. I'm a friend of Sharon's and I've come to make sure she and Richard are alright." A count of three and then: "I'd therefore be obliged if you'd let me in."

There was a considerable pause before the man in the doorway spoke—a pause during which I continued to look from George to

Tara. So far removed from that rainy day when I had first saw her in her green wellies, I wasn't sure I recognised the woman I had fallen in love with. Truth be known, I wasn't sure I recognised any of us. We become different people by small progressions, I thought. And there was nothing we could do to change that.

"I can't do that," the man said. "Sharon doesn't want to see anyone and... more to the point, we don't want her to see anyone."

"I can make it worth your while to let me in," she said, taking a step forward.

"You haven't got anything I want," he told her—nevertheless sounding rather unsure of himself. "Now be a good little girl, yeah? Be a good little girl and fuck off back to wherever it was you came from."

George chose this moment to act. Snapping his gaze from the bulky shadow on the pavement before us, he stepped out in front of the doorway and pushed hard against the man I assumed to be Sharon's remaining brother. "That's no fucking way to talk to a lady," he said, arms swinging now. "And it's no way to talk to our Tara, either—do you understand me?"

I turned and reluctantly looked into the hallway, Tara trotting up beside me and taking my arm; her fingers dug in as she drew air sharply through her teeth, distressed by what she was seeing.

George was rolling on the floor with Sharon's brother. He seemed to have the advantage, sitting on the brother's chest and pummelling his face repeatedly, but then a knee came out of nowhere and caught George completely off guard, their positions reversed in a matter of seconds.

"I think we should do something to help," Tara whispered.

I nodded. I had no idea how best to approach this little problem. It wasn't at all like the time I had taken a pop at George back at my flat. That time I had been fighting for Tara's honour and had had anger, adrenaline and pure instinct on my side. This time I felt... well, ambivalent is as good a word as any, I suppose. A part of me would have actually enjoyed seeing George get a right good kicking, for a change.

"For Sharon and Richard," Tara whispered, and I stepped over the threshold.

The three of us stood staring down at the unmoving form on the hallway carpet. George sighed depressingly and shook his head. My fist was throbbing as if I'd just put it through a mangle. I was sure I'd broken something.

"Jesus Christ, Price," George said exasperatedly. "Did you have to be so rough. I think you've fucking killed him."

It was true; he certainly didn't look too well. The cut over his right eye was bleeding heavily, and there had been a limpness about him when he had bounced of the wall when I'd thrown him against it. His left arm was folded beneath him at a slightly worrying angle and when Tara moved it to feel for a pulse, I thought I heard a crunching, grinding sound.

Tara felt around at his wrist and then looked up at us. "His pulse is fine," she said. "He's just unconscious and, I'm guessing, unlikely to remain that way for too long."

My sense of relief was so strong I could practically smell it (I obviously couldn't) and, as I helped Tara up, I couldn't resist giving her a hug. She nodded and held onto me. "Impressive," she said quietly. "Be afraid. Be very afraid."

George shook his head and turned away from me. "We probably haven't got long," he reminded us. "Let's get them found and out of here, yes?"

George started up the stairs and we followed. We didn't have to search through one empty room after another. There was no building frustration, no disappointment ultimately turned around by the final, unexpected discovery. Instead, we stepped onto the landing and found Sharon by a bedroom door with Richard holding onto her. They both looked afraid—Richard especially—but there was a calm resignation behind her eyes that faded to relief when she saw us, which nevertheless worried me. She'd been expecting someone else, I realised, and this was yet another unknown quantity that we just didn't need.

Tara and I gave the three of them room, staying back as George slowly stepped towards them. Richard, all snot and quivering lumps, flinched and held onto Sharon more tightly, making a sing-song, whining sound way back in his throat that reminded me of air raid sirens and impending danger and ships being lured onto rocks. George slowed, allowing Sharon time to calm Richard, and then, ever so slowly, he reached into the pocket of his jeans and brought out the toy Mercedes. When he reached out a hand and snatched it (hungrily, it seemed) from George, it seemed that a substantial victory had been won.

Sharon nodded and smiled. "He's been inconsolable since he lost that," she said. "Where did you find it?"

"In the cave," George said.

Sharon frowned at him, puzzled. "The cave?"

"Yes. The cave they brought you in by. The old smugglers' cave down in the cove."

"We haven't been in the cave."

"They didn't bring you in that way?"

"No. They brought us in through the front door."

George looked at the toy car in Richard's hand. The boy (I figured it was better to think of him as a boy rather than a monster) was spinning one of its wheels repeatedly with his thumb. The tsk-tsking sound it made was mildly irritating, but George didn't seem in the least bit concerned by this.

"Then how did that get there?" he said.

Sharon studied the toy car her son was holding—their son was holding. "I don't know," she said. "My brothers still go down there, sometimes, I think. Maybe one of them took it and dropped it there."

"Or maybe it was just a coincidence all along," Tara whispered to me. I nodded, knowing that, however ridiculous a proposition that might be, stranger things had indeed happened.

"Does it matter?" Sharon asked, and George shook his head, snapping out of it.

"No," he said, smiling. "No, of course it doesn't. We found you. That's all that matters."

"We really need to be thinking about getting out of here," I told George quietly. "Tweedle Dumbest'll be waking up any minute and there's no telling when the other two will be coming back."

"They've just gone to pick up a curry," Sharon said. "This time of night, they shouldn't be too long at all."

George started herding Sharon and Richard towards the top of the stairs, Tara and I stepping aside to let them go first. They had only covered half the distance to the top, however, when the three of them stopped. George groaned and, as I followed his gaze, I found my hope of a quiet car journey home dwindle away.

Tweedle Dumbest was slowly making his way up the stairs towards us—looking rather dazed, but still very much intent on inflicting some therapeutic pain. I stood in front of Tara and, not wanting to be outdone, George stepped protectively before Sharon and Richard—glaring intimidatingly at Tweedle Dumbest. I have to say that, in spite of everything that had happened, I was proud of him in that moment. A man who had, it seemed to me, always fought for the sake of fighting, George now had something worth fighting for. And he understood this. They were important to him, and he wasn't about to stand by and let anyone take them from him again. I could have kissed him. But I didn't.

Tweedle Dumbest stepped onto the landing before us, a little shaky, it seemed, but still more than capable of doing whatever was required of him. He put a hand to the cut above his eye and then wiped the blood on his jeans. With a smile as predatory as a paedophile's, he took another step towards us and said to Sharon, "And just where do you think you're going, sister, dear?"

"You know where I'm going, Tom, dear," she answered. "Anywhere where you aren't."

"That's not very nice."

"It's not meant to be. This was wrong, Tom, you know that. However many times you tell me it was for my own good. It was wrong."

"You think so?"

"I know so. You damn near scared poor Richard to death—and, that apart, it was wholly unnecessary."

"You could have handled this on your own?" There was a sardonic edge to this that made me want to slap him. I wondered how George was managing to restrain himself.

"Yes," she said. "Yes, I could." She didn't sound all that convinced. Nevertheless, I got the feeling that this wasn't the real issue. Fail or succeed, Sharon wanted to do it on her own terms — and this was something that was extremely easy for me to understand; my father had meddled in my life enough times for me to know how she felt.

Tom smiled sadly, head tilting to the right. "We weren't prepared to take that chance, Sharon," he said. "You and our Rich are too precious to us. We aren't prepared to just sit back and let you put yourself in danger like this."

Sharon was studying him — her frown deep and cruel, extremely unflattering, her eyes searching and bold. "That's something else I don't understand," she said. "Why is this so important to you? What is there about this that I don't know, Tom?"

"You're our sister, Sharon," he said, all treacle and bile. "We love you and we just don't want to see anything bad happen to you."

"Bollocks." She spat the word out like venom sucked from a wound and Tom recoiled noticeably. "You couldn't give a flying fuck about me or Richard, and you bloody well know it. This is about you and those other two arseholes. You mark my words — when I work out what's behind it, all, Tom... your lives won't be worth living."

Tom rolled his eyes and sighed. "Jesus Christ," he said, "you're a bloody ungrateful bitch, Sharon." He stopped, frowning — realising a moment too late just what he had said. The lamp had been rubbed and the genie was well and truly out.

"Lord's name vain!" Richard yelled, pushing past Sharon and George. "Lord's name vain!"

Tom took a step back, but it was no good. There was no avoiding the predestined and, sure enough, Richard came barrelling towards him like a thing demented. I expected him to make a dive for Tom, but it seemed Richard was smarter than I'd given him credit for. He saw the stairs and apparently understood that momentum could also be an enemy. Stopping before a positively shaking Tweedle Dumbest, he whispered "Lord's name

264

vain", again, and then, very precisely, with studied method and assured grace, he reached out with both hands and gave Tom a nice, firm shove in the chest.

I was reminded of a physics lesson I'd once had as a kid on stable and unstable equilibriums. It had bored me at the time and now I couldn't help but wish that the theory had been demonstrated as graphically as what happened next.

Tom teetered on the edge of the top stair, all but pin wheeling his arms to maintain his balance. He looked at Richard pleadingly, but there was no mercy to be had there (or anywhere else, for that matter). He struggled and strained—his very personal and quite touching battle with gravity seeming to go on forever—and then, just when I was beginning to think that he might actually pull this off and regain his balance, he fell.

It was a little disappointing, it has to be said. Something of an anti-climax. However many times he bounced and rolled and cracked his head, limbs flying hither and thither as he tried in vain to break his fall, I still wanted more—something definitive that would let him know once and for all that he was messing with the wrong people and that now might be a good time to accept that he wasn't quite the big deal he thought himself to be. But all I saw was a nobody who I didn't much care about one way or the other taking a very painful fall down a flight of stairs that would never be quite as steep or long as I would like them to be. He bounced and rolled and cried out. And then he stopped. Once more an unmoving, disappointing lump at the bottom of the stairs.

"No one can survive a fall like that, surely," Tara said.

Sharon waved her hand dismissively. "He'll be fine," she said, starting down the stairs. "He's used to the odd bump on the head."

At the bottom of the stairs, I checked to make sure Tweedle Dumbest still had a pulse. Much more of this, I thought, and the law of averages would have to work against us eventually. It was as Sharon had predicted, however. His pulse was strong and, when I gave him a little prod with the toe of my boot, he groaned.

"Satisfied?" Tara asked as we followed Sharon, Richard and George out of the front door.

"I guess so," I said. "He could have a subdural haematoma or something, though. He could be dying as we speak and what are we doing about it?"

"Nothing."

"Exactly. Nothing. Do you feel comfortable with that?"

"Perfectly. it's no more than he deserves."

"You really think that?" I was rather taken aback. She sighed again. "Probably not," she told me. "Though we don't have time to worry about it.

I knew she was right, of course, but I couldn't help but fret about it. It was still possible that Richard had dealt Tweedle Dumbest a fatal blow.

"Are you getting in, then, or what?" George was saying to me over the roof of the Allegro. I felt dazed and somewhat confused, but nodded nonetheless—opening the front passenger side door and making myself comfortable on the front seat beside George. Tara, Sharon and Richard were already safely ensconced in the back and when I turned around to look at them they almost looked as if they were waiting to head off on a daytrip somewhere. There was an eagerness to the way in which Tara sat with her hands sandwiched between her thighs, the way in which Sharon's chin jutted forward, that seemed oddly nostalgic and heartening. They were actually rather calm about this—and if they could be calm, then so could I.

"That went far better than I ever would have expected," George admitted as he drove slowly away. "I imagined all kinds of shit happening before we went in there. Guns, knives, the fucking lot."

"You thought he'd be armed?" I said, incredulously. "You took us in there when you thought there might be a chance that –"

"What does it matter? I was wrong, wasn't I? There wasn't a gun or a knife in sight and we got Sharon and Richard out of there no bother at all. What could be simpler?" He was looking far too pleased with himself. I tried to think of something to say to wipe that smug look off his face, but Sharon beat me to it.

"It would have been a lot different if our Harry and Dick had been there," she told him. "They're always armed. Don't go anywhere without their Heckler and Kochs."

George glanced over his shoulder at her before turning back to the road and saying, "You're joking, of course."

"I wish I was. Tom's the only one that never carries a gun. Harry and Dick won't let him. He'd scratch his balls with it and blow his cock off. He's that kind of bloke. Harry and Dick, though. A different kettle of fish. They like guns. They like them and they know them... and they're quite happy to use them. Coming in for us while they were out was probably the smartest thing you've ever done in your life."

George was nodding slowly and I wondered if he was perhaps beginning to question just what it was he had got himself into. I'd briefly considered the possibility of guns before we had gone in, of course, but only in the most abstract of ways.

"Your other two brothers are called Harry and Dick?" George suddenly said, grinning.

"Yes," Sharon grudgingly answered.

"I like that. Tom, Dick and Harry. But not just any old Tom, Dick and Harry. Oh no. The Tom, Dick and Harry that'd like to rip our heads off and shit down our necks. Lovely."

George continued in this vain for the next few minutes, driving along merrily and continuing with his observations regarding Tom, Dick and Harry and the absurd quality of life. I stopped listening pretty quickly. I didn't much get the joke and, that apart, I had other things on my mind. For one, I couldn't help but focus just a little on those guns Sharon had mentioned. Surely she wouldn't lie about something this serious. Not even to rattle George. Which left me with a few very important questions—not least of which was, Where were we going?

"Home," George said when I asked him. "Where you've been wanting to go all day. Why, where did you think we were going? San Francisco with fucking flowers in our hair?"

"We can't," I said, trying to be as succinct as possible. "Well, I mean, we can, if we want to—but, under the circumstances and everything, I don't think it's all that wise. Not unless you're fond of having your colon cleaned out with a Heckler and Koch."

"He's got a point," Sharon chirped up. "They're going to know where each and every one of us live. Naturally, they know where I live, but they'll have checked out you three, too, mark my words. If we return to any of our homes, they'll have us by morning."

"They won't know where I live, surely," Tara said. "I spend so much time around Price's that they'll have just assumed we live together... won't they?"

"I very much doubt it," Sharon said, a sleepy Richard echoing her word for word, his speech slurred and oddly meaningless. "They're much more thorough than that, love. They'll know where your mum lives and where Price's parents live. That's just the way they work."

Work.

I watched the cat's eyes zip towards us mesmerically as I made my way through the problem one step at a time. We needed somewhere safe to stay. Or somewhere safe for Sharon and Richard, at least. All our usual abodes were out of the question because we had to assume that they would be the first place her brothers would look. I didn't much fancy the five of us staying in yet another bed and breakfast... which left us with what, exactly?

"I think I have an idea," I said.

It was a lot to ask, especially given the amount of time I'd taken off just recently, but I didn't see any other alternative—or certainly not one that I was as yet ready to entertain. It was just possible, given his more outgoing nature, that George might have friends or associates who would put us up, but from where I was standing, this was a far more preferable solution to our problem.

I made George, Sharon and Richard stay in the car—not wanting to alarm Tony from the offset with our sheer numbers. Standing on the doorstep, waiting for him to answer, I was grateful to have Tara by my side. She held onto my arm and the two of us stared at the dark façade of the semi-detached bungalow Tony shared with Claudia—and I couldn't help thinking how, if I did what Claudia wanted of me, I would be the one to separate the two of them. Not directly, maybe, but I would certainly be playing a considerable part. And, yet, here I was about to ask yet another favour of Tony.

"It hardly seems fair," I said, my voice a croaky little whisper.

"What doesn't?" Tara asked me.

"What I'm about to ask Tony," I told her. "After all the time I've taken off. After... you know."

"Claudia." I nodded and Tara sighed. "You're just doing what you think's best," she said. "It's all you ever do. No one can blame you for that."

"Can't they?"

"No. Well, yes. Yes, they can. But that doesn't mean they're right." She shivered and I put my arm around her, pulling her in close. "You've just got to keep on doing what you feel is right, Price," she told me. "People will always question or object, but that doesn't mean they're right and you're wrong."

"Then what does it mean?"

Shrugging, she said, "That they need time to adjust to the absolute scale of your superior wisdom and intellect?"

"That'll be it," I said, nodding quickly and smiling down at her.

Tara pointed at the door and then held a finger to her lips. I could see through the frosted glass at the side of the door that the hallway light had been turned on and we could now hear the unmistakable clanking and clinking sounds of bolts being removed and the door unlocked. It seemed to go on longer than expected, but I didn't find it all that surprising to discover that Tony was so security conscious. He had something of value. Something that went beyond all his computer equipment and other sundry items. He had a life with the woman he loved. I saw now that, whatever Claudia's wishes, this was not something I could easily imagine him giving up.

Dressed in shorts and t-shirt, I guessed that I'd got him from his bed. I looked at my watch - eleven thirty-five. Pushing his long, grey hair back from his face with both hands, holding it there, elbows raised, he regarded me with slight bafflement before smiling warmly and saying, "Ah, the errant assistant returneth. Will wonders never cease?"

"Tony," I said.

"Price," he replied.

We stood like that for a few moments, regarding each other indecisively, and then Tony leant against the door jamb. Folding his arms, he apologised for not being able to invite us in—it was late, in case I didn't know, and Claudia had just got to sleep... he didn't want to do anything to risk waking her—and said, "What was it you were wanting? I assume it's something important, given the ungodly hour."

"Actually," I said, "I'm no longer all that sure you can help us. We were looking for somewhere to stay for the night, Tony, but –"

"You and the girl." He smiled at Tara and I thought I saw his nose twitch a little as he scented the air.

"Yes," I said. "And three others. I wouldn't ask, Tone, especially when you've been so understanding as it is, but we're really in a bit of a tight spot. It doesn't matter so much about us, I guess, if you could just put up George, Sharon and Richard. They're the ones we really need to find somewhere safe for."

He shook his head and looked down at his bare feet. "I'd like to help," he said. "Really I would. But I have Claudia to think of and... well, from the little you've told me, it really sounds as if this might be... well, it sounds like it's either something very illegal you're involved in, or something rather dangerous. Or both, even."

"It's nothing illegal," I told him.

"But it is something dangerous?"

I considered lying to him, but thought of Sharon's two Heckler and Koch-wielding brothers and realised I just couldn't do that to him. "Yes. Yes, it's something dangerous."

"Then as much as I'd like to," he said, "I can't help you, Price. I have a responsibility to Claudia, and that has to take priority."

"It's just for one night," I pleaded, but Tara squeezed my arm. It was pointless going on. Both Tara and I knew that Tony would not relent. He had his little world to protect, and he wasn't about to let me jeopardise it for him.

"I can't, Price," he reiterated. "Please, don't ask me again. I really don't like having to refuse you but... I have no other option, mate. I'm sure you can see that."

Of course I could, but that didn't stop me resenting him—so much so, in fact, that I very nearly told him about Claudia's knee and how she had used it to tell me that she wanted to be away from him. It would have been a vile, spiteful thing to do, but it would have been so easy. I was tired and afraid, hungry and not looking forward to the prospect of losing face in front of George. Had Tara not chosen this moment to speak, I was quite sure it would have all come pouring out.

"We both understand, Tony," she said. "It's just that... we're pretty desperate to get Sharon and her son somewhere safe. They've had a pretty trying few days and they just need somewhere to rest while we figure out what to do next."

Tony stared at her and chewed his bottom lip. There was no way he was going to take Sharon and Richard in, we both knew that, so I was a little baffled to see that he actually seemed to be thinking about what Tara had just said to him. He chewed his lip some more and stared over our heads at the Allegro, before exhaling loudly through his nose and saying, "They can't stay here." Tara started to say something but he held up a hand to stop her. "They can't stay here," he repeated. "But I think I might have a solution. A very temporary solution, but a solution nonetheless."

He asked us to stay where we were and then walked along the hall and disappeared into the kitchen, leaving Tara and I on the doorstep.

"What do you think he's doing?" Tara said.

"I'm not sure. I think I have an idea, but I don't know."

"Is it a solution like he said?"

"If it's what I'm thinking it is, yes. But he's right. It can only ever be a temporary fix. Sooner or later—well, actually sooner rather than later—we're going to have to come up with something more permanent for them."

"We?" she said. "Don't you think...?"

"What?"

"I think we've done all we can be expected to do, Price," she said. "Once they're settled somewhere relatively safe... well, I think that should be our cue to walk away."

"Can we do that?" I asked. "I mean, it's all well and good our saying it, but when it comes right down to it, can we actually do it?"

"I don't think we have a choice. We've done more than any reasonable person could ask of us and... it's time to think about us."

"I like the sound of that," I said, kissing her on the forehead.

"Then it's agreed?"

Tony was coming back down the hall towards us, a set of keys jangling in his right hand. "It's agreed," I said.

As I led the way along the sloping path past Lovers' Leap and down into the Italian Gardens, the cold wind biting through my insubstantial clothing, the night so dark beneath the canopy of trees, I thought about what Tony had said as we had been leaving. This had to be for just the one night. Two at the very most. As he told it (and I had no reason not to believe him), he was putting his job on the line. While he had a certain degree of autonomy, he had told me, there were lines that it nevertheless did well not to cross.

"I'm doing this because I like and trust you, Price," Tony had said, and I now couldn't help but think about just how misplaced that trust really was. This man was willing to risk his job for me. He had, in part, at least, taken me into his life and taken me into his confidence. And what was I planning on doing? Admittedly with the best of intentions, I was planning on betraying him. It was no good telling myself that it was in fact Claudia who was the principle figure in all of this, that it was she who was actually doing the betraying, I still felt rotten—and it wasn't as if there wasn't more to come. I would do the dirty deed, tell my story to Claudia's solicitor colleagues, and I would feel bad. But then... then I would have to face him. Assuming that nothing went wrong with George, Sharon and Richard, we would both still have our jobs and I would have to come down here and face him. Work with him. Explain to him if (God forbid) he ever found out what I'd done. The very thought of if made me feel sick. To do something like that to someone like George would be difficult enough, but someone as trusting and as giving as Tony? I now wasn't sure I could do it.

Exhausted and more than a little distracted, I stumbled and Tara grabbed my arm. "Are you alright?" she said, and although I nodded, it was perfectly clear to her that I wasn't. "It's what we have to do," she whispered, referring to the agreement we'd made on Tony's doorstep, and again I nodded. "It simply isn't possible for us to go on the way we are, Price. This—all this is going to kill us if we don't step back now."

"I know," I said. "You're preaching to the converted, love."

George, Sharon and Richard were a little way behind us, Richard needing a lot of encouragement to walk this dark and winding path, and we waited for them to catch up. Tara was holding tight to my arm and I released it so that I could put it around her, pulling her in close so that we could share each other's warmth. We'd already agreed that once George, Sharon and Richard were safely tucked up in Tony and Claudia's little love nest, Tara and I would take a taxi back to her mother's and spend the night there—and as unwise as this might be under the circumstances, I couldn't wait to get back there and for this night to be over.

"Fuck," George said as they caught up with us, "you really know how to put us through it, don't you, Price? Did it never occur to you that this place might scare the kid shitless?"

"No," I answered, coldly. "But what did occur to me was that having a gun pointed at him might scare the kid shitless, and since no one else had any other suggestions, this seemed the best way of avoiding that."

Tara gave my stomach a little pat. "Couldn't have put it better myself," she said.

Sharon joined us, Richard clinging to her like sphagnum moss. "Is he being a pain?" she asked me, nodding at George.

"No more than usual." I smiled at her to show that everything was okay, that I was accustomed to George's ingratitude and complaints. "It's not far now," I told her. "Richard going to be alright?"

"He'll be fine," she said. "He just needs a little sleep. He gets especially edgy when he's tired."

"Don't we all?" George muttered to himself.

Rather than continue the conversation, I got the five of us moving again, picking up the pace somewhat, and within a couple of minutes we were standing outside Tony's storage and 'administrative' building.

Unlocking and opening the door, I reached inside and turned on the light before stepping back to let the others enter first. "It's a lot more comfortable than you might expect," I told Sharon as she passed by me, and she smiled, not in the least bit convinced.

Inside, something struck me right away—taking me by surprise and making me question once more the decision I had arrived at regarding Claudia. This was her place. Whether she realised it or not, this simple, wholly unexpected room might never have existed had it not been for her. And when she wasn't in it, it died a little bit, lost some of its vitality... in such a way that made me see, to an admittedly lesser degree, what it would be like for Tony to lose her. We define our worlds by the people with whom we share them, I thought. And to remove someone of such integral importance is to risk losing all meaning.

George was perusing the selection of teas on the shelf over the sink. "Bit gay," he said. "He keep anything stronger here?"

"Try the cupboard under the sink," I said. "I think that's where it is."

It took Sharon a good half an hour to get Richard settled and off to sleep on the sofa, but once she had, we all sat where we could and drank the tea Tara had made. Even George relented and poured his scotch down the sink—grudgingly admitting that he needed something hot and "... well, you know." Looking around, I saw the paleness in the others' faces, the darkening slackness of the flesh around their eyes, and I knew that exhaustion had caught up with them, too. It was a physical thing, almost, pressing down on us and robbing us of the will to move, to function—to make the most basic of decisions—and, when Sharon finally spoke, I was amazed by her will to overcome, her ability to do the one thing I couldn't currently imagine myself doing.

"I think in part they do want to protect me," she mused, and George sniffed noisily. "Perhaps. There's definitely something more going on but... there's also plenty I need protecting from, let's put it that way."

"Not least of which is your brothers," George said.

Sharon shrugged, too tired to argue, and I asked her just what else it was that she needed protecting from.

Looking from me to George, she rubbed the side of her neck and sighed hollowly. "You remember the promise I made you all those years ago?" she said to George. He nodded, his anticipated sarcastic reply silenced by the obvious gravity of what Sharon was about to tell us. "Well, I acted on it."

None of us spoke for a moment. That wasn't possible, I remember thinking. We—Tara and I—had spoken to the man she had been meant to have had killed. Before I could say any of this, however, Sharon proceeded to fill in the blanks.

"I couldn't ask my brothers to do something like that for me," she said. "I didn't want to be indebted to them because... well, there was no telling what they would ask of me in return. They were into some really heavy stuff at the time and they wouldn't have hesitated in using something like that against me, to make me do whatever it was they wanted me to do."

"So you tried to do it yourself?" Tara asked.

Sharon shook her head. "No," she said. "I could never have done something like that. It was just beyond me. That kind of thing... it needed the right type of person—preferably someone who'd had a similar experience to George—and I thought I knew just who would do it for me."

She took a sip of her tea, cupping the mug in her hands and shivering. "There was this girl I knew," she told us—very deliberately avoiding eye-contact with George. "We were lovers, on and off, and I knew that she'd been raped, too, by her cousin, and it seemed like something... well, let's just say that it was something that I knew Donna wouldn't be in the least bit reluctant to do."

"Donna Kesey?" George said, simmering and threatening to come to the boil. Sharon nodded and George rolled his eyes. Getting to his feet, he walked angrily to the corner of the room, putting his forehead to the cool plaster and fighting to rein in his powerful emotions. Remaining in this position, his anger for the moment in check, he asked, "What happened, Sharon?"

"Donna wasn't big on traditional justice," she said. "I mean, she didn't believe in our judicial system. She'd been hurt, in the worst way imaginable, and there was no justice in people who did that kind of thing being locked away. She wanted them all dead. Rapists. Paedophiles. The lot. So when I told her about you and about what the Jag man had done to you and what you wanted done about it... well, at first she wanted to meet you. She liked that you wanted him dead. You had a common bond and simply had to meet. I knew you wouldn't want any part of that, though—"

"Damn right I wouldn't," George said, still with his forehead pressed against the plaster. "She's a fucking headcase, Sharon." He turned to face her. "Surely you must have known that."

"I did," she said softly, nodding. "But I wanted it sorting for you, George. I'd made you a promise and I wanted to at least try to fulfil it. So I talked to her. Worked it out with her. And she agreed that she'd do it without meeting you because she understood how you must be feeling. She said that she would take care of it—for all his past victims and all his future victims. It was like she was on a fucking crusade."

"So what went wrong?" I said, avoiding looking at George. "Given that the Jag man is apparently still alive, I assume something did go wrong."

Sharon nodded again and the darkest, most despondent of looks fell over her face. "She killed the wrong man," Sharon told us. George started laughing, swearing under his breath, and turned to face the wall again. Sharon ignored him and continued. "It was terrible," she said. "I never would have believed it if it hadn't happened. There was this known kiddie-botherer on the same estate where the Jag man lived, and, as unlikely as it may seem, he also drove a Jag. I'd given Donna a name and address, but, Donna being Donna, she just assumed that I'd made a mistake. Not that it ultimately made that much of a difference to her. One kiddie-botherer was much the same as any other, as long as they ended up dead."

Tara and I sat absorbing this, holding hands. Richard snored and twitched in his sleep, saliva dribbling down the side of his face. The sound of the wind through the trees outside, so unremarkable in the daytime, seemed to move around and through us, sharing arboreal secrets we would never understand. I watched George as he sat down on the floor in the corner of the room, knees steepled, hands arranged limply at his crotch. None of us spoke, knowing that Sharon would continue in her own time. She shifted, trying not to disturb Richard, pulling up the collar of the cardigan she was wearing, and fought to find a way of expressing whatever it was she had to say next.

"It was awful," she finally told us. "Donna was... she wasn't as tough as she liked to make out, you know? Once it was done, she all but went to pieces. Oh yes, the bravado was still there. She went on about how her actions were morally defensible and how it didn't matter which one she'd killed, as long as she'd taken another one off the street, but I could see how rattled she was and I was scared. I was scared for her but, more to the point, I was scared for me. The full weight of what we'd done came home to me and I knew it had to end badly. I'd conspired to murder and, even though Donna had killed the wrong man, I doubted that the law would see me as any the less culpable."

"But you nevertheless got away with it," Tara said.

Sharon nodded. "Yes," she said. "I did. But Donna didn't. They found her within a couple of days and took her in, and she confessed to everything—telling them she was proud of what she'd done and that she'd do it all again given half the chance. She told them everything, but she didn't tell them of my involvement. I don't think I've ever been so relieved about anything. I knew by the time of the trial that I was pregnant with Richard. We'd moved away. It was like I'd been given a second chance and I... I just wanted to hide, be myself without all the pressures I felt I'd had imposed on me. My family. My parents and my brothers. They knew I'd been involved in some way. Donna had been around our place nearly every day in the run up to the murder and I suppose they put two and two together. They were good, though. They watched out for me and made sure I was okay, and when Richard came along they helped in every way they could—or my parents did. At least until they found out Richard wasn't normal and that I planned on keeping him."

She fell silent, looking down at Richard, and George asked, "So how does this fit in with all that's been happening?" I had a feeling he already knew. He just wanted to hear her say it.

"Donna served her time without ever once mentioning my involvement," Sharon told him. "And then she got out. About a month ago. She got out and she somehow managed to find me."

"Not easy," George conceded.

"She knew me a lot better than you," she told him. "She knew the people I'd turn to for help, my friends and the people who owed me. Getting my address wasn't difficult and, when she did... it was horrible. I thought I was pleased to see her, at first. It had been so long, and in spite of having been locked away for close on twenty years, she looked well. We chatted for ages and, well, pretty soon I started to see that things were different now. She hadn't changed, but everything else had. She'd been in a state of stasis, sitting in her cell waiting for everything to start up again, and she just couldn't get it into her head that it hadn't been like that for me. Granted, I hadn't exactly been living the most dynamic of lives, but my life had moved on and... I didn't want Donna anymore. It took me three hours to get rid of her, but she pestered and pestered me, by phone and letter, and eventually she came back. That's how I got to be on the moor like that when you found me. It wasn't my brothers, it was her. She did that to me... if it hadn't been for Richard, God knows where it would have ended. He mightn't know much, poor soul, but if there's one thing he does know, it's how to protect his old mum."

George was shaking his head. Without looking at Sharon, he said, "I still can't believe... What the fuck were you doing getting involved with someone like her, Shaz? Apart from the obvious fact that you were fucking me at the time and shouldn't have needed that fucking minge-muncher, the whole estate knew what she was like. She did everything but howl at the fucking moon—rumour even had it that she beat her mother up regularly, and, while I can certainly relate to wanting to do such a thing, well, it just isn't on, is it?"

"Since when have you listened to rumour?" she said.

"Since I learned it could save my life."

They had reached something of an impasse, and now seemed a good time for Tara and I to leave. With unspoken agreement, we walked to the door together as their argument picked up again— handing everything back to them, as we had promised each other we would. I risked one last glance over my shoulder as we left, and I think I knew in my heart of hearts, as I watched George roll his eyes and tell Sharon that she was "fucking clueless", that they would be gone by the time I returned here to work later that morning. George was capable, in his way, and he would know that if Tara and I were choosing to return home, it wouldn't really be safe for them to stay here any longer than was absolutely necessary. I briefly wondered if we were doing the right thing, but then Tara was pulling me outside and closing the door behind me, and I realised I had no other choice. It was all we could do.

"They'll be alright now," Tara said, and I nodded as she linked my arm.

On our way past Lovers' Leap, a fox crossed our path. It stopped and looked at us, its eyes taking in more than I ever would have wished—reaching down deep into my soul, it seemed, and sifting through the spiritual silt and slough. Finding us both somehow lacking, it sniffed the ground and continued on its way, back to a world of far fewer complications than ours, a world with rules far more basic and sensible.

"It's up to them, now," Tara said.

Chapter Thirteen

The following Saturday found the two of us walking through one of the thickest fogs I'd ever experienced, returning to my flat after an uneventful and perfectly ordinary shopping trip. Tara had wanted new shoes for the planned visit to my parents the following day and, while she had insisted that I would only be bored, I had nevertheless decided to go along with her. It had seemed to me that as a couple a boring shopping trip was just what we needed.

As it turned out, though, I found the whole experience thoroughly enjoyable, and once Tara saw that I wasn't going to be your typical whining bloke, she'd enjoyed it, too. She stuck out her leg and wiggled her foot at the ankle to show me the latest offering and I somehow managed to say all the right things. It had gone on for all of Saturday morning and most of the afternoon, and as we now walked along the road to my flat, Tara swinging her bags and looking about as cheerful as I'd ever seen her, I realised that I could have gone on all weekend. I didn't give a fuck how it made me sound, shoe-shopping was fun.

"Can we do it again next weekend?" I asked her, grinning.

"Nope," she said. "I'm afraid next week it's something entirely different. The real test."

"Sensible winter coats?"

"No."

"Woolly hats?"

"Absolutely not."

"Cardigans?"

Shaking her head, she smiled. "Underwear. If you can cope with the various temptations and pressures of underwear shopping, you're the man for me."

"Aren't you afraid of losing the mystique?" I said, already looking forward to our next shopping expedition.

"Not really." She linked my arm and leant into me as we walked. Her breath was warm against the side of my neck. I inhaled deeply, again wishing I could smell her but also remembering the way in which a number of people in town had moved away from us. It hadn't been as bad as I'd imagined it might be, but I'd still felt for her. "I think I'll always be a bit of a mystery to you. Right?"

I didn't see how I could argue with that. She had come into my life with a picked lock and a warning on pink notepaper—and while I understood the why, I still didn't quite get the how. There had been simpler ways of approaching me, but Tara had chosen to do it her way. And however odd, I knew I didn't need to question it. Her modus operandi had worked. That was all that mattered.

Back in the flat, I broached the subject I'd been meaning to bring up for a long time. Sitting Tara and her shoes down on the bed, I put the fire on and made us both a mug of tea. She eyed me suspiciously when I made myself comfortable on the bed beside her, Marc Almond singing Dusty Springfield's I Close My Eyes and Count to Ten on the stereo.

"What's going on?" she said.

"Who says anything's going on?"

"Me. You've got something on your mind. What is it?"

"Something and nothing."

"We're not having sex. We've just got in and my legs are killing me."

"I don't want sex."

"You don't?"

"Well, actually, yes I do—but that isn't what I wanted to talk to you about... hey, wait a minute. I said, 'Something and nothing', and you started talking about sex. What's that all about?"

Chewing the inside of her mouth and doing her best not to

smile, she said, "I'm sure I haven't got a clue what you're talking about."

"I'm not sure I should tell you, now."

"Why fight it? You know you'll tell me in the end anyway. Might as well get it over with."

Now that the time had come to actually say it, I wasn't all that sure that I could. The risk was too great, I told myself. It was too early and there was far too great a chance that it might put our relationship in a difficult place if she (as I had now convinced myself she must) didn't think it was as good an idea. I fidgeted and almost spilt my tea, finally seeing sense and putting it on the floor by the bed. Tara seemed amused, sipping from her mug to hide her smile, and this certainly didn't make it any easier.

"What is it?" Tara said, a little more sympathetically, seeing that I was struggling. "Just spit it out, love. You know you can say anything to me."

Nodding, I swallowed hard and took the first step. "I've been living here too long," I said, still unable to get straight to the point. "Much too long. For... all that time it was... it was a comfort, in some kind of perverse way. It was always here. I could come back, shut the door behind me, and that was that. It was my haven... but it was also my prison—a prison whose walls were all the stronger because I had built them myself.

"I think that's possibly why the note you left in here affected me so deeply," I told her. "I doubt very much that this was what you intended, but coming into my room and putting it in one of my books was perhaps the best thing you could have done. So much better that just slipping it under the door."

"I wanted you to know that you could let people in," she said, quite suddenly. "I wanted you to see that sometimes they could get in whether you wanted them to or not, but I also wanted you to understand that it could be your choice, too, and that... I don't know. I wanted you to open your mind to the possibilities, I suppose."

"It worked," I said. "You made me look out of the window –"

"I'm glad."

"—and this room, this poky little bedsit, it became something else. Something that doesn't really fit with the life I want anymore."

Tara squinted at me. I think she had an idea where this was going, but she didn't seem willing to take the chance – or that was how I read it, at least.

"Which means?" she said.

"I think we should get a place together." There. Finally it was said and I prepared myself for what I saw as the inevitable laughter. I picked up my mug of tea so that I didn't have to look at her and I clenched my teeth, but the laughter and derision never came.

"That's what you really want?" she said, quite calmly.

"That's what I really want."

Sitting quietly beside me, Tara was (I think deliberately) difficult to read. You can imagine just how difficult I found this, and the numerous ways in which, during those few, short moments, I berated myself for presuming that this was a dream, a life, that Tara would actually want to share with me in such a committed and real way. Granted, I hadn't asked her to marry me or anything, but this was still a huge step.

"I take it you've really thought about this?" she said, gravely. "This isn't just you being impulsive, is it?"

"I've thought about it," I assured her. "Long and hard. It's what I want but I'll... I'll understand if –"

She put a finger to my lips to silence me, smiling gently. She'd untied her hair when we'd returned to the flat and it now fell about her face and neck—softening her features and seemingly inviting me to hide in it with her. I thought about kissing her, but the time wasn't right, yet. She had something to say. Something important. Something I was suddenly quite sure I wanted to hear.

"I think that's a marvellous idea," she said.

And now I kissed her.

Tara had the hiccups, again. Lying in my arms, the lights out and the curtains open so that we could look out at the stars (or, rather, the light pollution), she jumped and made a little clicking sound in the back of her throat, and the bed juddered and creaked. I smiled. The cat that had not only got the cream but who had just discovered he'd inherited the whole fucking dairy—not to mention all the shops just down the road from it.

"Is it okay if I take off my new shoes, now?" Tara asked, and I nodded. "Good," she said, kicking them off the end of the bed. "Wouldn't want them scuffed for tomorrow... although I suppose my shoes should be the last of my worries, under the circumstances."

"I've told you," I said. "Everything will be just fine. They'll love you." If I were truthful, however, and while I would never have said as much to Tara, I did have misgivings. I knew what my parents were like, and I saw quite clearly that their meeting with Tara could go any number of ways—the vast majority of them bad. As I had already told Tara, though, ultimately, what they thought didn't matter. I wasn't answerable to them and nothing they said could ever change what we had together. Still, it would be nice to have them like her.

"I hope so," she said. "'Normal' seems such a reasonable thing to strive for, doesn't it?"

I was about to point out that we had made it a lot further along that particular road than a lot of people do, when my mobile beeped for a message. Reaching over and getting the old Nokia from the bedside cabinet on Tara's side, I hoped it wasn't Tony asking me to come in and do some emergency pruning or something equally ridiculous, and, thankfully, it wasn't.

"George," I told Tara, and she shuffled closer so that she could read it with me.

The message said: All fine n safe. Don't try to find us. Unnecessary. Will be in touch. GR.

"What makes him think we'd want to find him?" Tara asked. "Frankly, as long as Sharon and Richard are safe, which they apparently are, I couldn't give a flying fig. Like I said, normal isn't such an unreasonable thing to strive for."

She seemed rather annoyed by the interruption and, when I

asked why, she shrugged and explained as best she could. "I'm still a little scared that it isn't over for us," she said. "That we're going to get dragged back in, no matter how hard we try and however many promises we make to each other. I mean, we just seem to have got off too lightly. Sharon's brothers haven't been to see us and you haven't even seen that Renault that kept popping up."

"George explained that in his last text," I reminded her. "He and Sharon got in touch with them. Told them that they were somewhere they'd never be found and that it was no good asking anyone about them because nobody knew where they are."

"And they've just accepted that?"

"Well it would appear so, yes."

Tara thoughtfully rubbed the edge of her fingernail, staring into space with a frown and a slightly congested sniff. She didn't speak, but she didn't have to; I knew she didn't buy that—and, while I would never have said as much to her, neither did I. When I thought about it (which I conscientiously tried not to), it seemed that we were being deliberately left alone—lulled, almost, into a false sense of security. In town, I had felt safe enough, and even out on the street, with people around us, it hadn't been all that much of a concern. But now, here in this poky bedsit... had Tara not been there, I would have got up and gone to the window, surreptitiously looking down at the street below. I probably wouldn't have seen anything, but it would have made me feel better nonetheless. As it was, I merely set the phone on the floor by the bed and pulled the duvet up over our heads, hoping to find a suitable way of taking her mind off the issue of Tom, Dick and Harry and Donna Kesey.

It took a while, but we got there in the end.

We arrived early—a little after ten-thirty—my mother having insisted that we'd need plenty of time for drinks beforehand, and, of course, to get to know Tara. My instinct had been to turn up when we felt like it (a couple of weeks' time, for example), but Tara wasn't having any of that. She wanted to start off on the right foot by making a good impression—and whatever I said or did in an attempt to delay the inevitable was not only frowned upon, but greeted with the promise of punishment later that evening. "This is serious," she insisted. "It's not something I want to do, but I will if I have to. Today is too important for this kind of nonsense."

And so, much to my mother's delight, we arrived on time—a few minutes earlier than we'd promised, actually—shiny and well-scrubbed in new clothes, Tara triple-deodorised and antiperspiranted, beaming our best Sunday smiles and, speaking for myself, generally wishing that some impressive but non-fatal natural disaster would intervene and prevent further discomfort.

Mam showed us into the living room, taking our coats after my mumbled introductions and nattering on about how cold it was and how it was going to be a long winter. I could tell she was nervous—as nervous as Tara, almost—but I didn't feel particularly inclined to do anything to help alleviate her anxiety. This was what she'd wanted and I'd delivered. My role was fulfilled.

Dad wasn't anywhere to be seen and Mam—looking distressingly young in her bootleg jeans and hippy blouse—eventually got round to explaining his absence. Sitting us on the sofa in a manner that was oddly reminiscent of that first Sunday afternoon at Bernie's, she explained that he wouldn't be too long. He'd just had to pop down the road to check on an old neighbour. "He's in his nineties," Mam said. "You remember him, Price, surely. Old Mister McAllen. Lives at number forty-three. Over the road from the chip shop."

I nodded. "He was in his nineties when I was a kid," I said. "He used to shout out of his window at us every time we walked on his side of the road. Apparently he knew what we were up to and we should bugger off, if we knew what was good for us."

Mam was chortling. I didn't remember ever having seen anyone chortle before. I wondered if she'd learned it especially for the occasion.

"He still does that," she said. "He can't shout these days, of course, but the kids around here are quite considerate; they stand there nice and quiet while he whispers at them."

It took me a moment longer than it should have to realise that she was joking. Tara got there before me, chortling along with her, and I eventually followed suit, feeling a little left out.

I glanced at the dreaded computer in the corner of the room while Mam continued to tell Tara all about the neighbourhood 'characters', of which there were many. It now showed a screensaver featuring what looked like New Age symbols, though I couldn't have sworn to it, and I distantly wondered just what it was she was into this week—Reiki massage, crystal healing or something far more esoteric. I wasn't exactly unsympathetic to her all too numerous obsessions. I understood that they fulfilled a role for her and that she was, at heart, one of life's seekers. What annoyed me, however, was her overwhelming need to apply the resulting knowledge—use it to make the world around her a better place. It was quaint to a point, then it just became boring and, at times, offensive.

"Price's dad," Mam was telling Tara. "He isn't exactly the type for getting involved. He doesn't believe in meddling in other people's lives, as he puts it. But sometimes even he has to recognise that you just have to do your bit—for the sake of the individual and for the sake of community. Sometimes you've got to help, simple as that, even if those involved don't especially want your help."

That final sentence summed up Mam more accurately than I ever could. I recalled my last visit and her continued attempts to 'fix' my Anosmia, and sincerely hoped there wouldn't be any of that silliness today.

"My mother used to do a lot of voluntary work through the WI," Tara was telling Mam. "Until she got tired of the internal politics and the snobby atmosphere, and quit. She always said that the hardest part of helping people was convincing those who couldn't manage on their own to let someone lend a hand and convincing the able but bone-idle that they could and should manage on their own. She said they were always getting requests for help from those who, frankly, just didn't need it, while they had to practically hunt down the genuinely needy."

Mam was just about to tell us a story that, I was sure, would perfectly highlight Tara's point when, thankfully, we heard the front door go; Dad returning home. Mam bustled out in her super-animated way to tell him that we had arrived, leaving Tara and I on our own—for the moment, at least.

"Such energy and enthusiasm," Tara said. "She's lovely. You did her a disservice."

"I've had that energy and enthusiasm to deal with all my life," I pointed out. "You've had it for all of five minutes. Give it time."

Tara shook her head, smiling. She made me feel like a lost cause. I would never change my opinion where my parents were concerned and she wasn't about to waste her breath trying. Instead, she nodded at the computer and said, "That's where she finds all her information, is it? The fount of all human knowledge that is the internet."

"That's it," I said. "Looks deceptively innocuous, doesn't it?"

Tara rolled her eyes and was about to say something no doubt scathing and chastening when Dad came in—without Mam, who I suspected had zipped off to the kitchen to get on with the lunch preparations. He beamed at Tara, the anxiety over what he was going to find washing from his face like a watercolour in the rain. Tara was wearing a tight black skirt that finished just above the knee, a simple but fashionable white short-sleeved blouse and, of course, her new black shoes. Her hair tied back with a white ribbon and wearing only a little make-up, she managed to appear both understated and elegant. Dad took in the overall effect and clearly approved.

Introducing himself, he offered her his hand and then quickly withdrew it before Tara had a chance to touch it. "Needs a thorough washing," he explained. "After the morning I've had... well, trust me, you don't want to know."

"Old Mister McAllen," I said. "Mam was telling us that's where you were."

Dad nodded. "Poor old sod's in a right state," he said. "Shouldn't be left on his own, really, but that's the way he wants it and... well, people like that will only do what they want to do."

He seemed to realise that this wasn't perhaps the kind of conversation we were meant to be having—not upon meeting his son's new girlfriend, at least. He shook the grave look from his face, rubbing his hands together with the kind of enthusiasm I usually only expected from Mam, and said, smiling, "Right. A quick wash of the old hands and then I'll sort the drinks out."

He paused by the door, frowning, and then sniffed his hands and left.

Towards the end of what was both a traditional and a very pleasant Sunday lunch, it all started to get rather uncomfortable—for Tara, especially. The kitchen, where we ate, was hot from all the cooking and baking Mam had been doing that morning, and I could see that the couple of glasses of wine that Tara had consumed (a little too quickly, I thought) had already flushed her up considerably. On top of this, adding to Tara's evidently growing unease, Dad kept pulling faces and complaining that he couldn't get the smell of Old Mister McAllen's out of his nose. Mam repeatedly told him to be quiet. We didn't need to be thinking about things like that while we were eating, thank you very much. And I could tell that she knew the smell had nothing to do with Old Mister McAllen. In that moment I loved her for her attempts at shutting Dad up.

But he just wouldn't let it drop. He kept on and on about it and as lunch progressed I saw Tara grow more and more embarrassed. She squirmed in her chair and dabbed at her top lip with her napkin, her arms clamped tightly to her sides, and finally she cleared her throat, looked down at her plate and said, "I don't think it's Old Mister McAllen that you can smell. It may be me."

It was the bravest thing I'd ever seen. Mam and Dad stopped eating and stared at her, their puzzled faces each mirroring the other. I took hold of Tara's hand, just to let her know that I was there, that I was with her all the way. She glanced at me out of the corner of her eye. I smiled encouragingly and she looked down at her plate again, her voice low and faltering when she spoke.

"I have this condition," she explained. "Axillary Hyperhidrosis.

It causes my armpits to sweat excessively. Especially when I'm nervous. I think that's what you may be smelling."

Her explanation was greeted with silence, initially at least. Mam studied her sympathetically, her mind already working overtime, while Dad merely frowned heavily, his hands folded together on the table before him. It was a horrible moment for Tara, and I struggled to find something to say, something that would release the tension and make them see that this wasn't the big deal they so clearly thought it to be... that we were, in fact, meant for each other. I didn't want Mam pitying Tara (I knew where that could lead) and I most certainly didn't want Dad frowning at her in the way he was. What we had together was wonderful and real, and their superficial assessment based on smell could only ever be an affront to this.

It was Mam who spoke first, however, filling the gap in her characteristic way—with self-serving sympathy and good intentions.

"I think I've heard of that," she said. "I have a Canadian friend who, if memory serves me well, has a distant cousin who suffers with it. What treatments have you tried, sweetheart?"

And so the conversation for the rest of the afternoon was set. Mam asked questions and Tara answered as best she could, while Dad looked on—finally catching my eye and leading me out into the back garden (he started to say "for a breath of fresh air", but stopped himself.) This was what I'd been dreading most of all— even more than Mam's attempts at helping. It was going to be that day when he had introduced me to Tony all over again. I just knew it. He would be the dad and I would be the son, and if I didn't like it, I would just have to bloody well lump it.

"Now just hear me out," he said, leaning against the garden fence.

"When have I ever done anything else?" I asked.

"And don't start that, Price. This is serious. There are things I need to say and things you need to hear, and you being obstructive isn't going to help matters."

"Unless I decide that the things you need to say aren't the things

I need to hear, after all," I pointed out. Dad bristled noticeably and cursed under his breath. "You see, Dad," I added, my tone less adversarial, but only marginally so. "I have a fair idea just what it is you want to say to me. More or less. And while I know you mean well, you really need to understand that nothing you can say will change the way I feel about Tara. I'm going to stand by her no matter what, Dad. Axillary Hyperhidrosis or no Axillary Hyperhidrosis."

He clearly hadn't expected me to so successfully cut him off at the pass. Nodding thoughtfully and looking down at his feet, he folded his arms and said, "I respect that, Price. I respect it and I'm proud of you for thinking that way. But I'm your father and I happen to believe that I'd be failing in my responsibility if I didn't at least try to point out just how difficult and... well, socially limiting this could be for you."

"I don't care, Dad," I said. "Tara has... you know, I'm not even going to explain it. I don't need to. What we have, it just works for us, and that's all you really need to know."

"I understand that," Dad replied, putting a hand on my shoulder as if he were about to break the news of a death to me. "But you don't know how bad it is, son. Bless her, but she's stinking the place out."

I started to really have a go at him at this point, in a way that I never had before, calling him a narrow minded son of a bitch, among other things, but he calmly held up a hand and I stopped. This wasn't the man who wanted to keep me a boy forever. This was someone else entirely.

"I like her, Price," he told me. "She's clever, pretty and I like what she's done to you."

"What do you mean?"

He smiled. "You know what I mean. The way you hold yourself. The way you talk to me. Everything. It's all changed— and for the better, too. She's done that to you, whether you realise it or not. And I can't help but love her for that. But I need to know that you're fully aware of the facts, Price. If you're committing to her the way I hope you are—"

"We're getting a flat together."

"Good. But you must understand, for your sake and hers, that it's so bad that some people will refuse to be in the same room as her."

"Some people being you and Mam?"

He gave me his best tight-lipped, pissed off look. "Price," he said. "You know better than that. You and Tara are always welcome here."

We found Mam and Tara, as I had predicted to Dad, in the living room—sitting in front of the computer, chattering away as if they'd known each other for years. The novelty hadn't worn off for Tara, yet, and I hoped it never would, but Mam's persistent wish to 'fix', now transferred from me to her in some bizarre pseudo-Freudian game would wear on her in time. Seeing my mother, she would no longer smile the tolerant, slightly smitten smile she wore then; she would instead feel the all too familiar dread rising up from the pit of her stomach, peppering her present with feelings of failure and thoughts on how best to avoid the encounter. Guilty, knowing that my mother meant well, she would do her best not to let it show—simply keeping away from her for as long as possible, making up (very plausible) excuses not to see her. I knew these things. I knew them because I had travelled this path before her.

Tara looked up and smiled at Dad and me. She made an open-mouthed, compassionate face—a silent 'awww'—that suggested that she thought Mam was very sweet and loving. Dad winked at me, no longer merely my father but also a friend... it was a peculiar state of affairs, and one to which I wasn't entirely sure I would grow accustomed, but I thought I liked it. Dad was right. Tara had changed so much in me. Just by being who she was she had made me stronger in ways that I hadn't even realised. It affected me and it affected those with whom I interacted. And it was good.

Tara stood and came over to me—putting her arms around me and making it known that she was happy. Dad put a hand on Mam's shoulder and they both looked at us, smiling slight but sincere smiles. It made an almost perfect picture. Nineteen-fifties suburban America in all it's sponsor-ad glory. I couldn't help feeling that there was too much surface, though—too much show and not enough of the dyed-in-the-wool reality we were all still, minute by life-affirming minute, learning to live with. The talk with Dad had helped. It had made me see that we, when we got right down to it, were all on the same side. Their wish to help me (and, now, by default, Tara) was genuine and forged from some aspect of will that I'd previously underestimated. But I didn't see how it could last. It was too perfect. Too complete. Tara and I were going to get a place together. We were going to get a place together and my parents approved of her, in spite of her smelly armpits. Like I said, too perfect.

The night before, falling in and out of sleep, Tara had told me something. Her words had been rather jumbled and slurred, fighting their way through, I imagined, half-dreams of soft sands and tomorrows that were a lifetime away, but I got the gist of it easily enough. We were okay, now, she told me. Everything was as it should be. She knew, now, that I wasn't going to walk away from her. The sun would rise and the sun would set, and I would still be there. I would always be there.

As she held onto me in my parents' living room, happy and relieved, I felt all these things as certainly as she did—but I also felt something else. I felt fear. Fear that it would all end. Fear that I wouldn't be the equal of all that was expected of me. More than anything, though, I found myself fearing the unknown. I feared the things we couldn't yet see beneath the surface—and, however many times I told myself I was being ridiculous, I couldn't shake the sense of foreboding.

When it finally came time to leave, it was a relief, in spite of the remarkably pleasant afternoon we'd spent together. It was good to be back outside again with Tara, and I found that my mood lifted a little—managing to convince myself that it had merely been my parents' proximity that had had such a negative effect on me.

"Went better than we ever could have expected, didn't it?" she said softly, her tone rich with contentment and ease. "Your mam is such a love. She bent over backwards to make me feel comfortable. And your dad... I thought he was going to be a problem, at first, but he really seemed to... I don't know... he seemed to absorb it really quickly. What did he say to you outside?"

I shrugged. "This and that," I told her.

"That's not an answer."

"It was men talk."

"About me?"

"More about me, actually," I said. As I saw it, I could avoid the issue and let her imagination go into overdrive, or I could be straight with her. Naturally, I didn't want her torturing herself and, so, I gave her the full story of what Dad had said to me. "He wanted me to know that he thinks you're wonderful and that he could see the positive effect you're having on me—but for both our sakes, he wanted me to know how bad it was."

"I told you," she said.

"He was adamant, though. He thinks the world of you. He just didn't want my... he didn't want me to find I couldn't cope with other people's reactions and hurt you by walking away from you."

"He said that?"

"Yes. Slightly different words, perhaps, but that was the long and the short of it."

She thought about this for a while and then asked, "Did you tell him we were planning on getting a flat together?"

"Yes," I said. "That's what really made his mind up, I think. He better than anyone knows that I've never been this serious about anyone or anything in all my life."

"So I must be special," she said. "An angel with sweaty pits."

I smiled at this but didn't say anything. In truth, I suddenly didn't know what to say. It was beginning to grow dark—and while it was still relatively early, I felt it had been a long day. A long day that had taken its toll on me. That sense of foreboding returned, and I thought quite suddenly of Primo Levi's account of his time in Auschwitz, If This Is a Man—and especially his thoughts on happiness. If I remembered it correctly, he had maintained that happiness was never complete because, try as we might, when one sorrow, pain or worry was removed, there was always another waiting to take its place. Or maybe that had just been my interpretation. I don't know—but now I wondered if that was it with me. Was this just another manifestation in me of the human condition?

It seemed perverse and vile to apply the thoughts of a man who had known true suffering to my own life—but I suspected that that was, in part, at least, what Levi had wanted. To understand the big things in life, the Holocausts and other horrors, we have to understand human nature—and a big part of that has to be, I thought, the understanding of Self.

When Tara asked me if I was all right, I thought about sharing all this with her, but decided against it. She didn't need me bringing her down, not when she was so obviously happy. At another time I might have jealously resented her for this, but not today; today I understood that any joy in her life must also be shadowed and temporary, and so I embraced her and told her that I was fine, just fine. Everything was good and as it should be.

She gave me a squinty, suspicious look, but I think she bought it.

Monday afternoon saw me raking up dead leaves with Tony and doing my very best not to think about what I was planning on doing after work. I'd been fairly uncommunicative most of the day and it was becoming clear that Tony was growing... well, not exactly concerned, but intrigued. It wasn't like me to be so quiet around him, and it could only ever provoke mystified glances and too numerous scratches of that head of his.

I thought he might come right out and ask me what was wrong, although I prayed he wouldn't, but instead he took a completely different approach.

"I never told you, did I?" he said.

"Told me what?" It was the most I'd said to him all day. He did his best not to be taken aback.

"About the decision I reached."

"Regarding?"

"What I believe Claudia wants me to do for her."

I stopped raking the leaves and looked at him, feeling my heart start to pound a little more fiercely in my chest. "No," I said, not really wanting to have this conversation, but knowing that it was unavoidable. "I don't believe you did."

"Pretty thoughtless of me," he said. "Lumbering you with something of such weight and then not relieving you of it. For that, Price, I owe you an apology."

"You owe me nothing, Tony," I assured him, already feeling guilty.

"I do," he insisted. "You listened when others probably wouldn't have and you didn't judge. That's a lot, Price. A lot more than most of us can expect from life—and I should have brought you up to speed a long time ago, to put your mind at ease, if for no other reason."

"The longer it went on," I said, "the easier it was to assume that you weren't going to act on what you believed to be her wishes."

Tony nodded and made a few desultory attempts at raking together more leaves, before sighing and sitting down on a nearby bench.

When I accepted his invitation and joined him, he said, "You assumed correctly. It meant I had to reassess everything I have with her, Price—the very fabric of our relationship—but... well, the bottom line was, I just couldn't do something like that to her... for her, even. I wanted to, because certain things she's done since seriously suggest that that's what she wants, but I... how do you do something like that, Price? How do you just write everything out of the equation except for the wish of the individual to die?"

"I don't know," I said softly.

Tony continued to talk, but I wasn't really listening. I had a decision to make. After work it had been my intention to drop in on Messrs Banks and Jaudice, Claudia's former partners in law, but now I just couldn't see how I could in all good conscience do that. Claudia had trusted me, but so had Tony. I considered both of them to be my friends. Helping Claudia was important to me, but when it came at the cost of my having to betray Tony, a man who was now confirming with every word spoken that all my positive thoughts about him had indeed been true, I just wasn't sure that I could do it — or, for that matter, should.

"When she looks at me sometimes," Tony was saying. "I know she loves me. I know she loves me but I also know — don't ask me how — that she wants to be away from me. And I don't get that, Price. It just doesn't make any kind of sense to me."

The wind blew frostily through the denuded trees, bringing with it that old, all too familiar sense of trepidation and the sudden realisation that Christmas was but a matter of weeks away. I thought of all the time that had been lost — that had passed in the blinking of an eye while we had been busy elsewhere, and I understood that it could no longer go on like this. It had to be over for me. If I put it off and went, as planned, to see Claudia's former partners, it would only drag on. I would find some reason to prevaricate or something else would come up to divert my attention. Better to do the right thing and get it over and done with. Better to treat Tony with the respect he deserved.

"There's something I have to tell you, Tony," I said.

Chapter Fourteen

Christmas was upon us and as hectic as the two-week run up promised to be, Tara and I found ourselves to be in the best of all possible places—certainly the best we'd thus far experienced in our relationship. We bought presents together, shopping in town like we'd been made for it, Tara's condition apparently (judging by the reaction of fellow shoppers) not such a problem in the colder weather. And we felt a routine establish itself—one which we embraced enthusiastically, wanting only predictability and safety after all that we'd been through. A few days earlier, George had (we suspected at Sharon's insistence) phoned us to see if we were looking forward to Christmas and to let us know that all was well with them, and this somehow seemed conclusive—not an end, as such, but the closing of a particularly difficult chapter. This, together with Claudia's graceful acceptance of my sharing with Tony all that she had told me and, more to the point, how she had told me, provided the permission we felt we needed and, as I had snuffled about under the duvet with Tara after returning from talking with Claudia, Tara had said, "So that's that then. You did the right thing and Claudia's happy."

"I don't know about happy," I said. "She isn't angry with me, at least."

"Still more than we ever could have hoped for." Tara moved her leg for me and sighed. "Makes me feel as if we're doing the right thing."

"With regard what?"

"Looking at that flat on Thursday."

I had caressed her deeply and told her that I couldn't agree more, before saying, "What flat?"

She'd seen it advertised at the estate agents and, believing it to be just what we were looking for, had made an appointment to view. I'd been a little bit peeved that she hadn't discussed it with me first, but, as she had pointed out, it was just a viewing. It wasn't as if she had made a commitment to rent or anything.

And, so, the following Thursday found us looking at the flat on Garland Square—being shown round by a woman in her fifties who looked as if she was about to audition for the Beryl Reid role in The Killing of Sister George. She was a lovely lady (Tara especially, a little worryingly, seemed to warm to her), but I just wanted her to get the fuck out of my face for a bit.

"Positively reeks of happiness, doesn't it?" Miss Foster Hyphen Gill said (that was how she said her name; Miss Foster Hyphen Gill). "I always feel when I come into these delightful little residences that—call me silly—they already have 'home' stamped right through the middle of them. A rare quality, in my many years of experience. Very rare, indeed."

For all her rhetoric and hyperbole (or what I initially took for rhetoric and hyperbole), I had to agree with her. A spacious, two-bedroomed, first-floor flat—empty of furniture and, Tara would later tell me, smelling of fresh paint—it felt clean and inviting. Outside there was snow on the ground but the sun was now shining again, the low winter lustre lifting the place and giving it a feeling of transcendence, an otherworldliness that, as alien as it might be, wasn't in the least bit off-putting.

Tara's face was pink and shone with, I assumed, the happiness of which Miss Foster Hyphen Gill had spoken. She kept casting me secret glances to see if I liked it as much as she did, and, try as I might, I couldn't conceal my joy. I nodded and smiled and she glowed some more.

"One thing," Miss Foster Hyphen Gill announced, opening the door to the main bedroom. "One thing, depending on your nature and view of life, that you might find somewhat disconcerting..."

We entered the surprisingly large bedroom and, at first, I just couldn't see what she was referring to. There was nothing in the least bit disconcerting that I could see. The light through the ample, double-glazed window was as uplifting as it had been in the other rooms and I foresaw no problems fitting all of our things in there. It was everything we could have wished for and more, and...

... Tara was by the window, looking out and down at the world below. Miss Foster Hyphen Gill eyed her warily—knowing, in her "many years of experience", that this was the pivotal, shit or bust moment. I joined Tara at the window, putting my hand on her waist and thinking of that night when we had looked out of Sharon's bedroom window and seen Richard dancing on the moor in the moonlight.

Sooner or later, it all comes back, I thought, before quickly dismissing this, determined not to let the past bleed into our possibly quite perfect present.

"Saint Judith's," Miss Foster Hyphen Gill said behind us. "Quite beautiful at this time of year, in my opinion, but I can certainly see how some folk might not appreciate it quite the way I do."

"A cemetery," Tara said to herself.

"Victorian," Miss Foster Hyphen Gill said. "No one's been buried there in something like sixty years."

With the layer of fresh snow, Saint Judith's Cemetery did indeed look quite beautiful—a scene from bygone times, unsullied and quintessentially romantic. More snow was falling, but as cold as I imagined that place to be, it was nevertheless inviting. I didn't want to die. That's not what I'm saying. I merely found the peaceful beauty of the place attractive. It didn't matter that the ground there was packed with the skeletal remains of long dead, one time stuffy Victorians—I could still imagine myself sitting on one of those benches with Tara, reading a good book and possibly sharing a sandwich.

"I've shown a few couples round," Miss Foster Hyphen Gill said, walking over to us, her voice suddenly rich with compassion, no longer the estate agent but, rather, the woman hidden beneath the surface bluster. "And every time, they've loved the place. The space. The sense of light. Everything about it until they get to this room and then... well, they quite suddenly change their minds, which I can understand, in a way, but look at it. It's beautiful. So calm and picturesque. The most attractive of memento mori—something we all need in this silly, ultra-fast-paced world of ours."

I wanted to agree with her, but I didn't yet know what Tara's reaction was going to be. She knew death, I reminded myself. She had seen her beloved father taken from her in the most cruel of ways, and while I had seen old relatives die—all of my grandparents and my mother's sister — I hadn't yet had that closeness to a death quite so earth-shattering.

"I've always thought that cemeteries are important places," Tara said. "We've just forgotten how important because we've made the newer ones so regimented and... socialist in appearance. Places like this—" she nodded down at Saint Judith's, "—they're rich with history and information, a sense of what it was like to live and die in those times. You don't get that, now. You don't get the paupers' graves and you don't get the gothic monuments. Just a bland uniformity that echoes the lives we twenty-first century people live."

"Lives that are still better than the ones that many of the people down there experienced," Miss Foster Hyphen Gill said, and Tara nodded. "Which is why I find it so beautiful, I suppose. It's a reminder we all need every once in while. We are alive, living comparatively blessed lives, and they are not. Carpe diem, and all that."

Tara was smiling, and I wondered if, perhaps, Miss Foster Hyphen Gill was a little more crafty than I had given her credit for. Maybe this more human approach wasn't the woman beneath the surface bluster, after all, but, rather, merely another aspect of the estate agent.

"I think Price and I need to discuss this for a moment," Tara said—and Miss Foster Hyphen Gill dutifully retreated, telling us to take as much time as we needed.

Once she was out of earshot, I said to Tara, "It's just what we are looking for. I honestly don't think we could have wished for anything better."

"And the cemetery doesn't bother you?"

"Not at all. How about you?"

"I felt a twinge of... well, revulsion is too strong a word. When I first saw it I had this knee-jerk reaction of mild horror, like I'd been programmed to behave that way. But once I got beyond it... no. No, it doesn't bother me in the least. I can't think of anywhere else I'd rather live. Especially if you're going to be here with me."

"To protect you from the ghosts and ghouls?"

"Yes."

After a brief kiss in what was set to be our new bedroom, we found Miss Foster Hyphen Gill and told her the good news.

I suppose it was entirely predictable. Sitting here now, writing this with the distracting dull ache of tiredness behind my right eye, I can still see how easy it must be to guess what came next—and I make no apology for it. It was the way it happened. All I can do is share these events with you and hope that the form finds a sense of its own.

After saying goodbye to Miss Foster Hyphen Gill and watching her drive off in her BMW, we stood looking up at the front windows of what would be, in about seven days, if Miss Foster Hyphen Gill had anything to do with it, our new home. Dressed for the cold, we nevertheless held onto each other for added warmth and comfort—but there was also an excitement to our embrace, me squeezing repeatedly, Tara giggling and shuffling her feet. It occurred to me that this was the first time she had, properly, moved out of the family home, and her excitement suddenly seemed all the more profound and understandable.

"I predict we are going to be very happy here," Tara said. "I was that comfortable in there that I hardly perspired at all. Can you believe that? Miss Foster-Gill was standing right next to me and she didn't seem to smell a thing."

"That might just have been the result of good training," I said.

"It isn't," she said, laughing and slapping at me. "I hardly sweat at all in there. That has to be a good omen."

I wasn't all that sure that I believed in omens, good or bad, but I didn't disagree with her. It seemed to me pretty unlikely that she had actually perspired less in our soon to be new flat, and instead I put it down to a finely honed sense of propriety in Miss Foster Hyphen Gill that Tara's smell hadn't been mentioned—but what point would there have been in my saying this to her? The truth was, the future was so bright we had to wear shades, to paraphrase some shitty old song I barely remembered, and while I tried not to allow myself to get too carried away, I couldn't really help but get buoyed along by Tara's energy and enthusiasm.

Walking home through the cemetery—something we just had to do after seeing how beautiful it had looked from the bedroom window—Tara said to me, "When I was a little girl, I never wanted to be a princess like some of my friends."

"Me neither," I told her.

She drank deeply of the icy winter air, her breath billowing out in a thick, milky plume—making me think, our being in a Victorian cemetery, of ectoplasm and spiritualists and Arthur Conan Doyle—and then said, "You'll laugh, but I never really wanted anything all that special—"

"I'm not sure I like the sound of this," I said. "If you're about to tell me that you wanted only a bland, simple and uncomplicated existence with one of life's plodders, now might be a good time to think of revising the story a little."

"That's not what I was going to say," she laughed—and then stopped and added, "Actually, no. That's exactly what I was going to say. But you shouldn't be offended –"

"Too late," I mugged.

She smiled up at me, growing more serious as we passed an impressive monument featuring an angel holding up its arms to the sky. "You shouldn't be," she repeated, more quietly. "The point is, I knew I wouldn't find happiness in the big things. Even as a little girl, I knew that what I wanted resided in the finer detail—in the everyday and the uncomplicated. Holding hands, sharing your cup of tea, laying in bed without speaking, listening to the sounds outside our window. That's what I wanted all along, and now I've got it."

"So you're happy, then?"

"I'm happy."

"Even with Mam popping in every five minutes with a new 'cure' for your condition?" I asked.

She smiled, and held onto me more tightly, her head resting against my neck. "Even with that," she said.

"I was thinking of having a word with Dad," I said. "See if I can get him to get her to back off a bit."

"Don't do that. There's no need. Apart from anything else, I like it. I like that she's so intent on making things better for me... and, who knows, she might actually 'fix' me, after all."

"As far as I'm concerned, you're not broken."

"Smooth-talking son of a bitch."

"I'm serious," I insisted. "You're perfect just the way you are. You wouldn't be you without your Axillary Hyperhidrosis."

"I wouldn't?"

"No. You'd be someone else entirely."

"Who?"

"What?"

"Who would I be?"

It was intended as a silly, teasing question—but I couldn't help but take it seriously. Was it really possible that who we were hinged so completely on what some (though not Tara) might consider such a minor condition, I thought. Did these things really shape our personalities for good and bad, alter us in ways we never would have thought imaginable? Had I met a hypothetical Tara without Axillary Hyperhidrosis, would I still have fallen in love with her so completely?

"Well?" Tara said, waiting for an answer. "Who would I be?"

"I haven't got a clue," I finally admitted. "Someone regal and lippy, no doubt. Out of my league, that's for certain."

Apparently bored with the conversation, now, Tara allowed us to walk on among the gravestones in silence, stopping occasionally to read the odd inscription or take in the sheer grandeur of the two or three large family tombs. We took in names and dates, worked out ages and, with disturbingly very little effort, spotted epidemics, and, all the while, I felt more at peace and whole than I had in a long time. I could have stayed there all day.

Walking out of the gates in the east wall of the cemetery, I felt it before I saw it. Hanging in the air around me like some unshakable revenant, I almost tried to slap it away before I realised it was nothing physical but actually a sensation, an awareness that, a few moments before, I simply hadn't had. I looked. I listened. But still I couldn't make sense of it. Something had changed. Coming out through the gates, that sense of calm had suddenly dissipated and I was left instead with a kind of foreboding that threatened to overwhelm. I looked around, trying not to let Tara see my discomfort. And then I saw it.

Parked once again down a side street, the Renault hunkered down like a predator waiting to pounce. I couldn't be certain that it was the same car—the car that George and I had seen numerous times and which was most probably driven by Donna Kesey—but what with the way my life kept turning up unexpected surprises and the fact that we'd thought it strange that she hadn't shown herself in some way, it seemed likely that it was. I stiffened, and then quickly forced myself to continue walking and loosen up. Tara hadn't seen it yet, and a significant part of me bucked against all the decisions we had made together as a couple and insisted that I shouldn't tell her, that I should be the man and handle this myself. We walked, and I surreptitiously continued to eye the car. Someone behind the wheel. It was too far away for me to be sure if it was a man or a woman, but there was something quite feminine about the way in which they turned to look at the two figures on the back seat. I wanted to walk over to them. I could have just stepped away from Tara, taken my fate—our fate—in my own hands, walked over there, tapped on the driver's side window and asked just what the hell it was they thought they were doing. But that would have meant letting Tara in on it and, in spite of all the promises I had made her, I still wasn't entirely convinced that that was the right thing to do. The car would probably drive off the minute I started walking towards it, anyway.

Tara looked up at me and I smiled, my mind working ten to the dozen. If I said something to her now, she, like me, would want to confront them. She'd stand with me for a moment, glancing from me to the Renault, and then she'd insist that we couldn't go on like this—not when we were just beginning to get our life back, not when we were finally beginning to make a place for ourselves. It would have to end, she would insist. We would have to let this Donna Kesey (if that was, in fact, who it was) know that there was nothing we could do to help her—that we didn't know where Sharon and George were, only that, together with Richard, they were somewhere safe and didn't intend on being found. This, Tara would want known. She would put herself in danger. We were quite possibly dealing with a murderer, here; if it really was Donna Kesey, there was no telling how she might react if confronted.

And so I kept quiet—telling myself that it was in Tara's best interest and that I would tell her what I had seen the minute we got back to my flat. As it would turn out, I would tell her. I couldn't keep it from her. But I would later wonder, during those darkest hours, if perhaps it would have been better if we had confronted Donna Kesey when I had seen her then. I tended to believe that it would.

Mam was waiting for us on the doorstep when we got back to my flat. I was not happy to see her. The Renault was still playing on my mind and the last thing I needed was her well-meaning silliness.

She grinned at us as we approached, stamping her feet and blowing into her hands to keep warm, and Tara trotted over to her—disappointingly puppy-like and eager. If she continued to receive Mam like this, I thought, we'd never see the back of her. She'd end up living with us.

Maybe getting a two-bedroomed flat was a mistake.

Inside, Mam and Tara made themselves comfortable on the bed while I made three mugs of hot chocolate. It was the only place for them, but I must admit I found the idea of Mam sitting where Tara and I made love rather unsettling. Maybe I was being childish, but it struck me as intrusive and rude, and when I handed her her mug of hot chocolate, I did so silently, sulkily even.

"Now," Mam was saying, unfolding some printed sheets of A4 that she'd taken from her coat pocket. "I know this is probably an obvious one, but I thought that you might have overlooked it. Botox."

"I've heard that it can be used for my condition, yes," Tara said, "But I've heard that it can cause the body to compensate by sweating excessively in other places."

"Can it?" This seemed to take Mam by surprise. She riffled through her papers, but didn't seem to find what she was looking for. "Obviously something I need to research a little more." She laughed and patted Tara on the leg. "I must be getting sloppy in my old age."

I stood by the window, sipping my chocolate and looking down at the street below, trying not to listen to my mother waffling on. I couldn't see the car but I knew that Donna Kesey was out there somewhere — waiting, watching, planning something I was sure I wouldn't even want to begin to contemplate. She'd probably been following us ever since we returned from our trip with George. We just hadn't seen her. And if she had... what did that say about how determined she was?

She'll do whatever she has to do, I told myself. The Donna Keseys of this world are dangerous principally because, as they see it, they have nothing to lose. She's survived rejection and abuse and incarceration — what can society throw at her that's going to make a difference, have any kind of effect on who she is and what she believes?

She would take this to its inevitable conclusion, I realised, no matter what the possible consequences... and that was why I couldn't keep this from Tara. She had to know. She had to understand the dangers. If we were to protect ourselves, if we were to keep ourselves safe, we both had to know that the threat still existed, and understand its full extent.

"I hope you don't mind, Mam," I said, interrupting her mid-flow, "but Tara and I have a few things to discuss and finalise regarding this new flat we're getting together and... can this wait for another time?"

As soon as I'd started speaking, they'd both turned to look at me—Mam's face blank and uncomprehending, Tara's showing disquiet beneath a furrowed brow (she knew for a fact that we had nothing at all to discuss regarding the flat).

A little flustered, Mam started gathering her papers together. "Of course, love," she said. "You should have spoken up sooner. I really didn't mean to be a nuisance."

"You're not a nuisance, Mam," I said, not wanting her leaving upset.

"No, you're not," Tara agreed. "Far from it. I really appreciate what you're trying to do for me."

"That's nice, pet," Mam said, touching the side of Tara's face.

She came over and kissed me on the cheek, before saying quietly, "Moving forward. A nice feeling, isn't it, love?"

I nodded, forcing a smile and thinking, It was. For a short while it was the best feeling in the world.

Once Mam left, I made myself comfortable as possible, in the circumstances, on the bed beside Tara and took a deep breath.

"The flat?" Tara said.

I shook my head. "It was just the first thing I thought of. What I've got to say," I told her, "has nothing to do with that."

"Then what?"

"Donna Kesey."

I hated to see such a look of loss and disappointment on her face. It was so exaggerated and pained that it was redolent of grief—surely the most painful of emotions—and I thought I could understand this. Those spoken two words, that otherwise utterly innocuous name, took so much from us. Where moments before there had been only thoughts of our peaceful future life together in our new flat, now stood uncertainty and fear. I saw her face, no doubt so similar in expression to my own, and I didn't want to tell her anymore, wished I hadn't brought up the subject in the first place. But I had to go on. She had to know everything I knew.

"I saw the car again, today," I told her. "The Renault. I can't be certain that it was the same one but... I think it was."

"You only think it was?"

I considered this. Tara knew me better than anyone. Even George. "I know it was."

She nodded, satisfied. "So it isn't over, then?" she said. "We're still as involved as we ever were, and all our attempts at denial can't change that. We're in this until the end – whatever that may be."

I didn't like the sound of that. From where I was sitting, Tara was being too bloody accepting, and I told her so. "This has nothing to do with us," I said. "Not really. We can't help her and we need to make sure that Sharon or someone makes her understand that."

"From what they've said, they've already made that clear to her."

"Well they clearly haven't made it... they haven't made it clear enough."

"So what do you suggest we do?"

As far as I could see, there was only one thing we could do— short of going to the police, and we both agreed they wouldn't be interested and it would only cause trouble for George and Sharon. "We have to have another word with them," I said. "We have to make them understand that hiding away like this might be all right in the short term but they can't go on like this indefinitely... we can't go on like this indefinitely. We just don't know what she's planning on doing and... they need to confront this, Tara, for our sake as well as their own. We need to make them see that."

Nodding thoughtfully, she nevertheless said, "We'll have our work cut out. As I see it, George isn't going to do anything to endanger Sharon and Richard. And he won't involve the police, for obvious reasons."

"They could lie," I said. "Make out that they happened to mention what the Jag man had done to George and she decided to kill him off her own bat. They could make out she's deluded— which mightn't be that far from the truth."

"They could," Tara said. "But I can't see it. George won't want to go to the police. Whatever the circumstances."

"Then there's only one thing for it," I said, taking my mobile out of my pocket.

"What?"

"We make sure we talk to Sharon."

We tried for about twenty minutes, sitting in the growing dusk—becoming increasingly frustrated with the apparent lack of service at George's end. Wherever they were, it was remote, and, as the battery of my mobile gradually ran down with the repeated efforts, I realised that this was exactly how George would have wanted it. To be able to contact us when it suited him, without our being able to reciprocate.

"There's got to be another way of getting in touch with him," Tara said—but she knew as well as I that that was highly unlikely. George didn't want to be found, so George wouldn't be found. And fuck everyone else.

Finally, we gave up trying. Sitting in the dark, the flat silent around us, I tried not to imagine what Donna Kesey was doing now—what she was planning and how it might affect us. I wanted to go to the window, check and double-check that she wasn't out there still, watching us from the parking space in front of the doctors' surgery. But I couldn't do that. Not without risking further unnerving Tara. So far, she had been very pragmatic about it all. But she was, to my mind, growing more and more uneasy with each passing minute. She tried to get comfortable on the bed and couldn't. She rubbed her fingernail as she struggled in vain to find a solution to our problem. When I asked her if she wanted something to eat, she merely shook her head and looked to the window—her eyes unfocused and hooded.

As I stood putting a ready-meal tikka masala in the microwave, I heard Tara moving and turned to find her standing square in front of the window, arms determinedly folded across her chest, looking down at the sepia-washed street below with an attitude that belied the unease I knew she must be feeling. "I won't let it be like this," she said. "I won't let this carry over to our new flat, to our new life together. This has got to stop and we are the only ones who can make that happen, Price." She turned to look at me—the flecks of green in her hazel eyes seeming to spark in the strange winter half-light. "If we see the car again," she told me. "We go to the police. Tell them everything—whatever the consequences for George and Sharon." I started to object, but she held up her hand and walked the couple of paces between us. "They've left us in a predicament, Price," she told me. "They've run off in order to keep themselves safe, without any real thought of what the consequences of their actions might mean to us. They made the token gesture of letting Sharon's brothers and Donna know that we knew nothing of their whereabouts—but that's all it was, a token gesture. They must have known that Donna especially wouldn't be inclined to take them at their word. They're sitting pretty, with the luxury of being able to take their time working out what they're going to do next, while we are stuck here, not knowing what this Donna lass is going to do next. It's unacceptable, Price, and whatever I might have said in the past, however sympathetic I might have been, it has to end... and it's going to end."

Tara had warned me. That was how we had met. And however many times I might fool myself into believing the contrary, I don't think I ever fully understood the nature of that warning. It had many meanings, I was sure, some concrete and obvious, others more nebulous and difficult to grasp, but now I also saw that it was a lesson—a lesson that Tara had tried to teach me and, for all intents and purposes, failed for one very simple reason; it was a lesson she hadn't yet managed to learn herself.

"We need to be careful, Tara," I told her.

We both of us would rather have been back at our new flat, gradually getting everything in order and making it feel like home, but as we had been told on numerous occasions over the past few days, Christmas was a time for family, so it was only right that we should spend Christmas day with Bernie, and Boxing Day with my parents. As we had walked over to Bernie's, a little happier since neither of us had seen the Renault since our walk through the cemetery a little over a fortnight ago, it had felt like a mistake to me. We were letting others dictate the course of our lives again, and after recent events it was difficult for me to see that as a positive thing. Upon arriving at Bernie's, however, my misgivings evaporated and, while I still would have rather been hidden away in the relative security of our new, spacious flat, I thought that today might actually be enjoyable. I knew Bernie to be a good host and, of course, this withdrawal of control was very different to the one we had experienced with George.

The living room was a Santa's Grotto of fairylights, trimmings, fake snow, Christmas cards and, bang smack in the middle of the window, a six-foot Norwegian Spruce—the needles already starting to drop, in spite of the fact that, Bernie said, it had "allegedly" been treated...

She caught me staring, open-mouthed, at the fairy perched at the top. It was a decrepit, crapulent looking thing made from cotton wool, cardboard and crepe paper—with paper doily wings—and I expected it to hiccup at any moment. "Tara made that," she said, proudly. "When she was about seven. Ugly little thing but I can't bring myself to part with it."

I put my arm around Tara and said, "She has that effect on me." Tara did her best not to be amused, but I knew they highly approved of an appropriate level of leg-pulling.

After we'd exchanged presents in front of the blazing gas fire— a new watch for me from Tara, a shirt with country and western tassels I believed I would never wear from Bernie, a bracelet for Tara from me and a book of proverbs and some makeup from Bernie, Tara and I giving Bernie a knitted hat, gloves and scarf set that had 'last minute effort' stamped all over it—I sat enjoying a whisky in front of the television while Tara went through to help Bernie with our Christmas lunch.

It was good to be alone for a while, watching the dull Christmas morning fare (at times like these I really found myself missing Noel Edmonds... Deal or No Deal was a welcome return, but it certainly wasn't one of his Christmas morning specials) and listening to Tara and Bernie chattering and clattering away in the kitchen. I didn't need much, I realised. Just a little security and decent, caring people in my life. Very deliberately trying not to think of Donna Kelsey and the fact that we still hadn't managed to get in touch with George, I picked up the shirt that Bernie had given me and smiled. The shirt I would never wear. An unusual fawn and red plaid, I supposed that the tassels across the breast were the least of its problems. It was ghastly but it was unique — unique in the fact that it was the first present I had ever received from Bernie (other than the gift of her daughter) — and as I sipped my whisky and looked at it, a choir of tone-deaf children singing Once in Royal David's City on television, I knew what had to be done.

Standing, I started unbuttoning the shirt I was wearing and patted myself on the back for thinking of such an act of festive selflessness, and hummed along with the carols.

I walked into the kitchen, half-empty whisky glass in hand, as if everything was still the way it had been, doing my best to underplay the moment. The shirt felt stiff and starchy, itchy, but I made myself forget about it and act as if I were still wearing the shirt I had arrived in.

Bernie looked at me and my appearance seemed to take a moment to register. She stared. She smiled. And then she beamed — her delight turning to laughter as she finally admitted not only how ridiculous the shirt looked, but how much of a good sport I was. "Oh my Lord," she said. "What was I thinking of? You look like Burt Reynolds without the moustache and the wig!"

"People get arrested for wearing shirts like that," Tara added. "Or deported. It's practically an act of terrorism."

"I quite like it," I said, looking down at myself and jutting out my bottom lip. "I think it lends me an air of... well, something."

Tara turned away, chewing back a smile. "In the short time I've been wearing it I've grown quite attached to it. I think it's very me. What do you think, Tara?"

Without looking at me (it was almost as if she couldn't bear to see me in that shirt again), she said, "I think you should stop being an arsehole and go and change. Before you put us all off our food."

When I returned wearing the shirt I had arrived in (mission accomplished), Tara was in the process of topping up our drinks. I got the distinct impression that today was going to be pretty boozy, and I welcomed the prospect—believing that Tara and I deserved the opportunity to let our hair down, however improbable it was that such a mood was likely to last.

The image of the Renault flashed at the back of my mind again, and I pushed it away, swallowing against the peculiarly strong sour taste at the back of my throat.

"I nearly made a terrible mistake the other day," Bernie was saying to Tara. They'd both sat down at the kitchen table with me, enjoying their pre-prandial plonk. "Amazing how much shit good intentions can get you in when the Fates make up their mind to be unkind, isn't it?"

"What did you do?" Tara asked.

Bernie sat quietly for a moment, sipping her wine and listening to Slade sing Merry Christmas Everybody on the radio. She sighed and shook her head and then said, "I was feeling... I don't know—full of the Christmas spirit. And I don't mean this stuff," she added, holding up her glass. "You know how important family's always been to me, Tara. It means something, and yet I have so little of it."

"What did you do, Mam?" Tara repeated, her voice heavy with foreboding.

"I dropped in our Carla," she said. "I was worried about how she'd be coping without George there. Oh I know she makes a big show at times of being able to manage just fine, but I'm her sister. I know her. I know it's all show and, really, she struggles without him there to... well, I realise it sounds ironic, but to keep her on the straight and narrow."

I recalled that day I had found Carla drunk and naked, and thought I understood what she meant.

"So I dropped in," Bernie continued. "Just to see how she was doing. I'll be honest with you, I didn't know what to expect. I've seen her when she's been left to her own devices too many times before to be optimistic about such a visit, so I was thinking that it might be pretty bad."

"And she didn't disappoint?" I said.

"I'm afraid she did," Bernie said. "Well, no—actually, she didn't, if you see what I mean. I was very impressed by what I found. She was presentable and clean and sober as a judge, and I just couldn't get over the transformation. She was chatty and hospitable – saying how I'd just caught her because she'd been about to go out to buy herself a Christmas tree. It was remarkable, but it was also unnerving. I know my sister, you see, and I didn't like this image she was presenting. Her son was God alone knows where with that lass of his..."

Tara mouthed, "I told her" to me.

"... and she's skipping about merrily like everything's as it should be—like it's better than it's ever been. She wasn't missing him at all, and, naturally, I was suspicious."

Bernie took another good gulp of her wine and pushed a stray strand of hair back from her face—and in that moment, with that gesture, I thought I saw the woman Tara would be in twenty or thirty years time. Down to earth but elegant, beautiful, but a little careworn. Only ever wanting the best for those she loved. I had a future to look forward to with Tara. Even with the Donna Keseys of this world, lurking offstage and awaiting some unknowable cue, I knew that this was something that could not be taken away from me—and I gave thanks for that.

"I was suspicious," she was continuing, "but I couldn't help liking what I was seeing. This, in many ways, was a step in the right direction for her. Okay, so I didn't like the fact that she seemed to be totally unconcerned about George—but, at the same time, I was also pleased to see just how well she was coping without him. And so I asked her." She looked at Tara, eyes soft and apologetic.

"What?" Tara said, warily.

"I invited her for Christmas lunch."

Tara rolled her eyes and I felt my heart drop a couple of

inches—a couple of feet, actually, plummeting to the floor with, I imagined, a resounding thud.

"Oh Christ, Mam, you didn't?" Tara said. "What did you want to go and do a thing like that for?"

"It seemed like a good idea at the time," she said, shrugging. "But you needn't worry. She was very grateful. It was a lovely thought, she insisted, but she had prior commitments."

"She did?" Tara and I said this in unison.

Bernie pulled a face that suggested that she'd just swallowed something bitter and foul-tasting. "She did," Bernie told us. "Apparently, she's spending the day with her new boyfriend—or old boyfriend revisited. Victor Pynchon."

Tara and I looked at each other. "The Jag man," I said.

Bernie was nodding. "Got it in one," she said. "When I heard that... well, everything changed. Any sympathy I had for her just went out of the window. He was the worst thing that ever happened to her. Or one of them. And she's let him back into her life? I told her, she's a fool and if she wants to throw her life away on some twisted loser like him then she's welcome to it, but, as far as I'm concerned, she's no sister of mine. I want nothing to do with her while she's with that jerk. I've never been so ashamed of anyone in my life. How can a person be so desperate that they have to hook-up with a no-mark like that?"

"Beats me," Tara said, looking rather more relieved now that she knew that Carla wasn't going to be having lunch with us. "If they both remain true to type, though, I can't see it lasting that long. If the booze doesn't come between them, something else will."

"If George finds out..." I said.

"Unlikely, under the circumstances," Tara told me. "And maybe he's got more important things to worry about currently."

"Whatever," Bernie said, "it's their business, now. If she wants to live like that, it's up to her. I've washed my hands of her."

Bernie seemed sincere and determined enough, but I didn't for one moment believe her. I thought that I already knew her well enough to know that, whatever she might say to the contrary, she would bow under the first sign of trouble and be around her sister's to do whatever was needed of her. She wasn't foolish. She most certainly wasn't one of life's suckers. She merely cared and she had a strong sense of what was right. Bernie could no more leave Carla to deal with her troubles than she could her daughter. As she had already pointed out, family was important to her.

Lunch went well. It was a sumptuous affair, considering there were only the three of us (thank God!), with turkey and all the trimmings. I couldn't truthfully say that I enjoyed it all that much—to me the food was bland and merely booze-absorbing fuel, though I never would have said as much to Bernie. I yearned for some hot chilli sauce, something spicy that I would actually be able to taste, and made a mental note to bring some with me the next time we came to eat.

At two-thirty, just as we were sitting down with coffee to watch a family movie, there came a heavy knocking on the front door— a hammering, almost. I looked at Tara and she looked at her mother. We heard loud, 'merry' voices, laughter and a brief verse of a Christmas carol that I couldn't quite identify, and when Bernie got to her feet to answer it, Tara and I, thinking it advisable, joined her.

In the hallway, we waited patiently for Bernie to unlock the front door. Tara took hold of my hand and I wondered if she was feeling as apprehensive as I was. But it was Christmas Day and just someone a little the worse for wear was dropping in to pay Bernie a festive visit.

But all that was just wishful thinking on my part, denial, even, if you will. Even before Bernie opened the door, I think I had a fairly solid idea who it was. There was really only ever one person it could be.

Carla Ruiz stood on the doorstep with a big, unseemly grin on her face—tinsel in her hair and lipstick on her chin, her arm draped like a dead mink robbed of its fur around the neck of her companion. She could not have come here herself, I realised. Neither of them could have, for they needed literal mutual support. Of the four of them, Carla's artificial leg seemed to be functioning best.

I heard Bernie groan and Tara swore under her breath. Carla called out "Merry Christmas!" at the top of her voice, almost losing her balance, and her companion, a certain Mister Victor Pynchon, stared at me squarely—or as squarely as he could under the circumstances. Tara was gripping my hand more tightly and I realised that, like me, she was concerned that Pynchon was going to recognise us.

Shit like this isn't meant to happen on Christmas Day, I thought. It should be all Tonka toys and The Wizard of Oz on the telly, not piss artists and pederasts.

"What do you want?" Bernie said, surprisingly (not to mention impressively) cold.

"We've come to accept your offer of festive hospitality and to wish you all a merry very Christmas," Carla said. Gripping the door jamb for support, she added, "Aren't you going to invite us in, Bern? Aren't you? Hmm? Not going to keep us on the doorstep all day like a couple of strangers, are you?"

"Why shouldn't I?" Bernie said. She seemed to be making a concerted effort to keep her voice low and calm, which made her sound all the more imposing. "For all intents and purposes, you are strangers to me. Heaven knows I've tried to understand you, but this..." she waved her hand at Victor Pynchon, "... this defies explanation or understanding. Anyone who makes such a decision is, as far as I'm concerned, a different order of beast entirely."

"So you're better than me?" Carla spat, leaning in and wobbling. At other times, she had, at least in part, struck me as a sympathetic creature. On occasion she had even seemed halfway normal and intelligent. But today there was none of that. Today I looked at her and saw only drunken spitefulness.

"I didn't say that," Bernie said, still remaining remarkably calm. "But now that you mention it, yes, I think I am better than you. In fact, I'd even go so far as to say that I know I'm better than you."

"Doesn't surprise me." Carla sniffed and took a staggering step back. "You've always been a sup... a soupy... a supery... a superior bitch." She looked at Pynchon with one eye squinted half-shut, pointing at Bernie with her thumb. "Miss Fucking High and Mighty. Was just the same when we were kids. I used to think, if you say 'actually' one more time, I'm going to put your head down the bog and flush. Again."

"Oh don't get me wrong," Bernie said, almost breezily. "I haven't always been of this opinion. It's recently formed."

Carla stared at her, one eye still half-shut. "It is?" she said.

"It is." She paused for a moment, and I saw just how wrong I had been when I had thought earlier that she would not stick to her guns where Carla was concerned; Bernie was indeed wilful and strong. She wasn't about to give an inch and, I thought, there was a hell of a lot that Tara and I could learn from her. "You see," she continued, "up until fairly recently, I actually thought quite highly of you. You were my sister and I loved and even admired you. Oh, yes, you weren't perfect, but none of us are, are we? You had it worse than most, if I'm truthful. It might not have always been easy for me to admit that, but you had—and whatever your faults, you coped with your life better than I ever could have. But recently, the other day when I dropped in to see you to be exact, when you told me that you'd once again taken up with this piece of shit..." she pointed at Victor Pynchon, "... my opinion of you was altered permanently. It's your choice, Carla, and I'd never dream of denying you the right to choose, but the day you let him back over your doorstep was the day you stopped being my sister."

Victor Pynchon had smirked his way through all of this, not flinching in the least when Bernie had called him a piece of shit. He hadn't been looking at Bernie, however, and, truth be told, I wasn't sure he'd been paying her all that much attention. Instead, he seemed concerned with Tara and me—his eyes never leaving us, the frown slipping into the smirk and then, finally, a full-blown knowing smile.

Once Bernie had finished her little speech, Pynchon leant forward and pointed at Tara and me. "I know you," he said. "You're the two little fuckers that came knocking on my door and trying to rattle me, aren't you?" He shook Carla's arm off his shoulder, almost sending her sprawling to the ground, and asked her. "These two. Who are they?"

"What?"

"I said, who the fuck are they? Him and her?"

Carla still seemed somewhat dumbstruck after Bernie's admirable address and was struggling to get her head around his words, but I decided to help her out—simply to move things along. If this has to happen, I thought, I'd rather we got it out of the way as quickly as possible.

"I'm Price Waters," I said. "George's friend. And this is Tara, his cousin. We found out that you were trying to get your feet under Carla's table again and... we thought George might know about you. We came round to make sure he hadn't done anything stupid."

"Like tell more of his lies and try to have me killed again, you mean?" he said. Surprise must have shown on my face for he then added, "What? You thought I didn't know about that?" He laughed, suddenly more sober than I ever would have thought possible. "Over the years, the little prick's spoken about it so often around town that it had to get back to me sooner or later. Dumb little fuck never did know when to keep his trap shut."

Carla was looking increasingly bewildered. She glanced from Bernie to Pynchon, apparently trying to decide who to talk to first, before saying, to no one in particular, "George. What did he do?"

"Tried to have me killed," Pynchon said absently. "Wouldn't be surprised if that was the real reason these two came round, now that you mention it. He's probably fed them the same bunch of lies and expects them to be suckered into doing the dirty deed for him. That's it, isn't it?" he said to me. "He fed you all that rubbish about what I'm supposed to have done to him and you came round to balance the books. Came round to kill me but you bottled it. Right?"

Bernie had apparently heard enough. Taking the matter into her own hands, she stepped back and slammed the door in their faces—locking it and telling Tara and I that she'd heard quite enough silliness for one day. She struck me as determined and removed from the whole situation but, nonetheless, I thought I saw her hand shaking as she drank her coffee silently in front of the telly.

We none of us spoke for a good while. Carla hammered on the door for a few minutes, shouting obscenities through the letterbox, and then left—my mind spinning through all that Pynchon had said, almost believing that George might have lied and that he, Pynchon, was the victim in all this. After all, George had lied before. If it was required for him to get his own way, I knew from bitter experience that he would stop at nothing...

... but that smirk. Victor Pynchon's smirk. I thought about it and it seemed to speak volumes. The man was a snake. George was bad, but I was suddenly quite sure that Victor Pynchon was worse.

Later that evening, back at home in our still sparsely furnished but comfortable and welcoming flat, I stood alone in the bedroom, while Tara took a shower, and looked down at the cemetery. The snow of our first viewing had long since vanished and tonight it didn't look quite so picturesque. Shadowed and sullen, it reflected my mood since returning from Bernie's. I watched the trees bow in the building wind, dappling the headstones with moonlight, and I exhaled, long and slow—feeling the weight in my chest lighten, but only slightly. I couldn't, even now, stop thinking about Victor Pynchon and what he had said. I no longer doubted George, but what still disturbed me about Pynchon was his self-possession and assuredness. That he could do the things he had done and, in effect, return to the scene of the crime suggested to me that he had done many similar things before—done them and, more to the point, got away with them. It was a sickening thought, and one I would rather not have had to think about. This was our new home. Fresh and clean. Wholly us. And I didn't want to taint it with such thoughts. Nevertheless, it pushed in on me, demanding my attention, and only when Tara returned from her shower did I succeed in stepping away from the window and thinking about more pleasant things.

Wrapped in a fluffy, white bath towel, hair still wet, Tara turned on the portable television and made herself comfortable on the bed, gesturing for me to join her. I dutifully obliged, kicking off my slippers (a Christmas come new-home present from Mam) and plonking down beside her.

"What we watching?" I said, taking the remote off her and flicking through more channels than I'd ever thought possible. Dad, in a rare, insightful moment, had decided that the best gift he could give us for our first Christmas in our new home was, much to my mother's disgust, a Freeview box. No washing machine (though Tony was fixing us up with a knock-off one, anyway), no cooker, no vacuum cleaner, no fridge-freezer—but, instead, a shiny new Freeview box. I could have watched BBC Parliament alone for hours on end, it was that much of a novelty.

"As Good As It Gets is on in half-an-hour," she said. "Jack Nicholson. You like him, don't you?"

"Like him?" I said. "He's up there with Pacino and De Niro as far as I'm concerned. One Flew Over the Cuckoo's Nest? A classic work of literature and a perfect cinematic interpretation. The guy's a fucking genius."

Tara regarded me with one eyebrow cocked. "That's alright then." She rearranged her towel, providing me with a brief but pleasant flash of bare breast, and then added, "About Schmidt's on Film Four tomorrow night, so we should get a nice Nicholson fix over Christmas. Just what we need, if you ask me."

I thought I knew what she meant, but I didn't say anything; I didn't want to get drawn into yet another 'serious' conversation about other people. Instead, I moved closer to her and we watched the news together, myself finding it oddly uplifting to discover people dealing with more complex life conundrums than we. Watching a piece on the radicalisation of Bradford's Muslim youth, I breathed a sigh that I didn't have to contend with such complex problems. Likewise the child abduction story that followed and the report on Blair's latest nonsense that followed that. The world was in a right bloody mess, the BBC informed us (interactively, if we so wished), and in comparison we were doing just fine and dandy.

When the film finally came on, Tara and I fell into it—laughing out loud so often that we had to watch we didn't choke on the chocolate brazil nuts we were eating. It was indeed, as Tara had predicted, just what we had needed; respite from the events that—although we didn't yet know it—were about to get much, much worse.

Chapter Fifteen

It would be easy for me to dismiss it, now, as imagination or the retrospective urge to romanticise the relatively mundane, but the truth is I knew on some instinctive level that something was wrong the minute I woke up on Boxing Day morning. We had fallen asleep with the television on and, while the volume was down very low, I jolted awake with the overwhelming impression that someone was in the room with us. I sat up quickly—the still relatively unfamiliar surroundings throwing me slightly—looking around, still half-asleep, rubbing my hands over my face as my heart rate slowed and I gradually began to realise that everything was as it should be. We were alone in our new flat and, I told myself, foolishly, no one could touch us.

Tara made a snorting noise and rolled towards me, her eyes opening and a smile spreading across her face like butter on warm toast. "Morning," she said, stretching and yawning. "How's my fella this fine Boxing Day morn?"

"Never better," I told her. It was something of a lie, since I was still experiencing a peculiar sense of foreboding, but she thankfully seemed too sleepy to see through it. "And how's my number one girl?"

"Busting for a pee, but otherwise fine." She glanced at the television, which was showing the breakfast news. "Anything interesting?"

"Not really. They say we might get some more snow later."

"Spiffing." She yawned again and said, "Well, I suppose I better go have that pee."

"I can't do it for you. As much as I'd like to."

"Such a kind, thoughtful soul," she said, patting my leg as she passed by on her way to the bathroom.

Alone again, I relished the relative silence. Compared to the old flat—the bedsit, I corrected, for, now more than ever, it was obvious that it had never been a flat at all—it was a haven of peace and tranquillity. Although we had neighbours above, below and on either side of us, the flats were so well sound-proofed, their occupants so respectable and well-behaved, that it was almost as if we were living alone out on the moors.

I sat back on the bed and waited for Tara to finish in the bathroom. The local news came on the television—and, while I wasn't really all that interested, something familiar caught my eye, something I couldn't immediately acknowledge, and which later, when realisation struck and information was acquired, I didn't want to.

It was an outside broadcast, to-camera piece featuring Sophia Marn, the local 'roving reporter' usually reserved for such delights as summer fetes and the opening of new shopping malls. Now, she stood talking to the camera as a light snow started to fall—the same light snow that was also starting to fall outside our bedroom window. Behind her was a semi-detached house, its shabby, loose curtains closed as best they could be, its environs sealed off with police tape. In the background, I saw a couple of SOCOs, dressed in their familiar white, hooded overalls, entering. I quickly grabbed the remote and turned up the volume, finally recognising the house as thirty-one Mount Drive... the home of Victor Pynchon.

"The body of Mister Pynchon was found at two-thirty this morning by a close friend," Ms Marn was saying, clearly chuffed to finally have something meaty into which she could sink her perfectly whitened teeth. "Police are, as yet, releasing few details but have made it known that they are conducting a murder enquiry and will be making a further, more detailed statement later this morning." A question then came from the studio anchor, something concerning Pynchon, the kind of man he had been, and

Ms Marn dutifully held an expert finger to her earpiece, replying, "It is believed that Mister Pynchon was a quiet, unassuming gentleman that kept himself to himself. Neighbours have expressed shock and sadness at these events and the overwhelming impression I get from the immediate community is one of a man who will be greatly missed."

Back in the studio, they started talking about the day's football fixtures and I turned off the set—trying to take it all in, work out what, if anything, I should be doing. Victor Pynchon, a man I had spoken to only the day before, was dead. Finally, after all these years, he had been murdered and I couldn't help thinking, even as the implications disturbed me, that this was really how it was meant to be. The imbalance had been corrected and it should all just be left alone. He was dead because he deserved to be dead. It was long overdue and it didn't matter who'd done it.

Tara, dressed in an old pair of joggers and a 'Grumpy but Beautiful' t-shirt, stood in the doorway staring at me. She looked pale and shaken and I realised that I didn't have to tell her the news.

"I was making some coffee," she said. "I had the radio on..."

"You heard?"

"She's killed him," Tara said. "Jesus, Price, she's finally fucking killed him."

It didn't have to be Donna Kesey. That had been one of the first things that had occurred to me as I had watched the news report. If Victor Pynchon had indeed been the man we had believed him to be, it was perfectly possible that there had been a queue of people lining up to kill him. In spite of what the esteemed Ms Marn had said about him, there was no doubt he had been a nasty piece of work and would have had numerous enemies.

"Still seems like a massive coincidence," Tara said, once I'd explained this to her.

"They do happen. She wouldn't be so foolish as to go after him so soon after getting out of prison, surely."

"Why not? There's nothing to connect her to him. As far as the police know, she killed the man she set out to kill all those years ago. If what Sharon said is to be believed, Victor Pynchon was never mentioned."

"That's as maybe," I said, "but it's common knowledge that she has a thing against paedophiles. She's the first person they'll take in for questioning."

"Only if Pynchon's known to them as a paedophile."

She had me there. Only the day before I had considered Pynchon's attitude to be that of a man who had seen his sins and crimes go unobserved and unpunished. I was quite certain that the police knew nothing of his twisted little predilections.

We followed these arguments around for the rest of the morning (or they followed us around—it was difficult to say which) as we prepared ourselves for lunch with my parents. I made up my mind around ten-thirty that some time during the afternoon I would take my father to one side and discuss everything that had been happening to us of late, in as much detail as possible, and see if perhaps he could suggest anything we hadn't yet thought of. As it would turn out, however, I wouldn't get the chance for, at a little after eleven, just as we were thinking of setting off to my parent's, we had a couple of unexpected visitors.

The intercom buzzed and both Tara and I jumped—neither of us accustomed to the noise, yet. I looked at her, wondering if she was expecting anyone, and she shrugged, pushing the talk button and asking who it was.

"Ms Pearson?" and authoritative voice asked. "This is Detective Inspector Daniel Murrey. I have a D.C. Karen McCarthy with me. We'd like to come up and speak to you regarding the murder of a Mister Victor Pynchon."

I suppose it shouldn't have come as any great surprise, but it did. The colour drained from Tara's face and when she reached up to press the button to let the detectives in, her hand shook perceptibly. "We have to tell them everything we know," she said, as we waited for them by the door. "We can't lie to them. Not to the police. There's too much at stake, now. This has all gone too far."

I nodded. Of course, she was right. As it was, we had done

nothing wrong. Not really. And we had to make sure that it stayed that way. However this played out for George and Sharon, we had to be straight up with the police. I had a bad feeling, though. I didn't share it with Tara but it couldn't be a good sign that they were visiting us so early in their investigation.

When they arrived and we'd all made ourselves comfortable in the living room, I was pleased to see that they didn't seem to be the hardened copper type. D.I. Daniel Murrey had an almost apologetic air about him, his long winter coat hanging on a frame so thin for a man apparently in his late-thirties that I deduced he had to be a smoker, while D.C. Karen McCarthy wore a delicate smile that seemed to communicate that she didn't believe we were suspects in the murder of Victor Pynchon. The only thing that really worked against them in my mind (and, I was sure, Tara's) was the way in which they wrinkled their noses and exchanged a glance when they thought we weren't looking. Tara was nervous – she couldn't help it.

"I assume you've seen the news reports," D.I. Murrey said, sitting on the edge of the settee with his forearms resting on his knees.

"We saw them first thing this morning," I told him, keeping my voice flat and neutral.

"And your reaction was?"

"Shock," Tara said. "We only spoke to him yesterday."

D.I. Murrey nodded, as if this confirmed more than just the fact of our conversation with Pynchon the day before. "This was at your mother's, yes?" he asked.

"Yes. We were spending the day with her. She's a widow. Pynchon came round with my aunt, and... well, there was a bit of a scene. It wasn't very pleasant."

"Your aunt. That would be Carla Ruiz, right?" he said, taking out a notebook from the inside pocket of his coat and referring to it. "Mother of George Ruiz?"

"That's right."

D.I. Murrey chewed the inside of his mouth thoughtfully. D.C. McCarthy studied him patiently, happy, it seemed, to take her cue from him. "Hmm," he said. "So... you were telling us about this doorstep scene you had with your aunt and Mister Pynchon. I believe Mister Pynchon levelled some accusations at you? According to your aunt, he seemed to think that you were trying to kill him? That you'd been round there once and lost your nerve?"

Carla. God bless you, I thought. That's the last time I clean up your piss and vomit.

"Do we need a solicitor?" I said.

Murrey shook his head. "Neither of you are under caution. This is informal and all we are doing, as they say, is following up certain lines of enquiry. It was brought to our attention, although with a great deal of malice, that Mister Pynchon suspected you of trying to kill him and we, naturally, felt we had to follow that up. Given that there are far more likely candidates, however, you can safely assume it's something of a formality."

"Far more likely candidates?" Tara said.

D.I. Murrey nodded and Tara looked at me questioningly. Murrey had been studying his notebook and missed this, but D.C. McCarthy was on the ball. "Is there something you'd like to share with us?" she asked.

Murrey's eyes snapped up to regard us, his detecting faculties suddenly firing on all cylinders. The formality was unexpectedly showing rather more promise.

Expelling more air than I remembered inhaling, I took another breath and said, "One of these far more likely candidates wouldn't happen to go by the name of Donna Kesey by any chance, would they?"

"I'm not at liberty to share that information with you," D.I. Murrey said. "But... just supposing... what would you want to tell us."

"She killed a man over twenty years ago," I said, Tara nodding encouragingly. "She was convicted and sentenced and recently got out after serving her sentence. But what few people know is that the man she'd been meant to kill was Victor Pynchon."

I told them the whole story from beginning to end—leaving

nothing out and dressing nothing up. I covered our involvement, how we had tried to help George and found ourselves being increasingly drawn in to something we weren't sure we fully understood. Emphasising that we believed George had genuinely been abused by Victor Pynchon, we explained that, in our opinion, George's and Sharon's attempts at getting Pynchon murdered had been a childish, ill-considered reaction to a very traumatic experience. "It's not something either of them would consider today," I told D.I. Murrey. "They've got too much at stake, now— a son and... well, that's about it, but it's still far more than George has ever had before."

"Quite a couple of months you've had," Murrey said, once I'd stopped talking. "George must be a very good friend to you—to inspire that kind of loyalty."

"Not really," I said. Tara was smiling and shaking her head. "To be frank, he's a complete pain in the arse, but I've known him a long time and... and before I met Tara I didn't exactly have friends coming out of my ears, you know? Letting go of George hasn't been easy, but I'm getting there." I smiled, a little anxiously, feeling that what I'd just said was somehow crucial to how this conversation would proceed, but not quite knowing why.

"It certainly seems that our George has had it tougher than any of us realised," Murrey said. "I'll be honest with you, Mister Waters, before you told us about Donna Kesey, George was top of our list of people we wanted to talk to. And, of course, he still is."

"Of course," Tara said.

"But, now, we clearly need to find Donna Kesey as quickly as possible. You say you have no idea where George and Sharon are?"

"Haven't got a clue," I said. "We've been trying to get in touch with them to tell them about the Renault and get them to do something about it, but we haven't been able to get through."

"This is a mobile phone, yes?"

"That's right."

"Can you give us the number? If he's still got the phone and he isn't somewhere too remote we might be able to triangulate the signal and track them down that way."

I duly obliged, though adding, "In my opinion, I'm afraid the phone's either lost of turned off."

"If it's a new-ish phone, being turned off won't matter," D.I. Murrey told us, enjoying himself it seemed.

After a few more questions concerning the involvement of Tom, Dick and Harry, Sharon's well-known brothers, D.I. Murrey concluded that they had kept us long enough. He gave me his card in case we thought of anything more and told us that they would be in touch if they needed to know anything else.

Closing the door behind them, I felt an overwhelming sense of relief. Everything that had happened over the last couple of months had now, in the most irrefutable way possible, been handed over to someone else. As a literal door closed, so did the figurative one—and as Tara and I stood in the hallway looking at each other, smiling, I think we both understood that for the first time in our relationship we were actually free of George and his problems. Or that was how it seemed, at least.

"That went better than I expected," Tara said. "I thought for a minute that they were going to slap the cuffs on us and haul our sorry asses down to the station."

"Thankfully real cops aren't as dumb as those we see on television."

She checked her watch and said with a raised eyebrow, "You do realise we're late, don't you?"

I nodded. "I don't feel like going, actually. My head's still spinning."

Whenever I suggested that we not go round to visit my parents, Tara habitually put up some argument to counter it. Today, however, was different. She was as overwhelmed by the events as me, and when I said that I thought they would understand if we phoned and explained what had happened, she was quick to agree with me.

"I just don't feel like talking," she said. "I feel as if... I don't know. I feel as if I might be able to relax, just forget about everything that's happened and sit quietly. But not quite yet. It's almost as if... it's almost as if I need to spend a little time learning to relax again. Does that make sense?"

I told her that it did, got her settled on the settee and then made the phone call to my parents.

I spent most of the afternoon on the settee with Tara, the two of us eating Pringles and talking. On a bit of an emotional low, Tara asked me to tell her about my childhood Christmases and I was more than happy to oblige.

"When I was really young," I said, my arm around her, "they were pretty uncomplicated. It was something most people we knew saved up for all year long, putting a little money away each week in the mutual aid, but Christmases still weren't the decadently excessive messes they can be today. There were presents and food and alcohol, but there was more to it than that. We weren't especially religious, but it wasn't just about being self-indulgent.

"There was this one Christmas I especially remember. I must have been about seven or eight and Mam had decided that she wanted to do something worthwhile this particular year. It wasn't enough to sit at home in front of the telly thinking nice thoughts. She wanted to take Christmas to the people. That's how she put it. 'Take Christmas to the people.'"

Tara was smiling. I could tell she was still rather shaken after the morning's events, the realisation that people could be murdered so close to us, people we knew and had spoken to, slowly sinking in and oppressing her. But the story of my mother at Christmas, so typical of her need to be involved and help, amused and reassured Tara.

"She cared about people's feelings," I told her. "But not enough to worry about denting their pride with unexpected acts of charity. As far as she was concerned, people had to be helped, and if that made them feel like charity cases, then so be it. Their foolishness, she always insisted, wasn't her problem.

"Anyway, this particular Christmas, it hit her right after Christmas lunch. She stopped in the middle of washing up the pots, staring out of the kitchen window with this bizarrely quixotic look on her face. Like she was experiencing an epiphany or something.

"So you can imagine how me and Dad must have felt. There goes my afternoon playing with my new toys and Dad probably pissed off because he was going to miss The Great Escape or something on telly. I made a break for the hallway, Dad about to follow me, but it was too late. Mam held up her hand and told us to stop. She sat us down at the kitchen table and explained. Apparently all the old people around about where we lived had company for Christmas lunch. She'd checked and those that weren't spending it with friends and family were, apparently, having lunch and a festive game of bingo at the community centre. So what was the problem, Dad had wanted to know."

"I bet I can guess," Tara said. "Your mam was worried about what would happen to them once lunch was out of the way," she said. "Those poor old souls sitting there in front of their televisions in the certain knowledge that obligations had been fulfilled and they were now utterly and completely forgotten again. It would have broken her heart."

"Broke her heart that she'd missed the opportunity to play the do-gooder," I said, rather uncharitably, I must admit.

"That isn't fair," Tara chided. "Your mother has nothing but the best of intentions in mind when she sets out to help someone. She's the most altruistic person I've ever met."

"Rubbish," I said, laughing. "Oh come on, Tara—you can't really believe that. I'm not saying she isn't a good person. But she does what she does, at least in part, because it makes her feel good. It gives her a sense of accomplishment and saves her from the boredom of spending every hour of every day with Dad."

"And what's wrong with that?"

"Nothing," I said. "Just don't confuse it with altruism."

"You don't think she'd help people if she didn't get something out of it?" she asked.

"I think she'd certainly be less inclined, yes."

"Well I don't agree," she told me. "I think, in fact, that that's a pretty shitty and cynical opinion to have of someone who'd gladly do anything to help anyone. Especially when she's your mother."

I got the feeling that I wasn't going to get this story finished today—though I couldn't say I was all that bothered. Tara pushed away from me and folded her arms protectively in the corner of the settee, and I knew that if I didn't do something to remedy this right away it would make for an uncomfortable and wasted afternoon.

"She hasn't always made it easy for me, love," I told her, quietly. "I know I'm wrong about her a lot of the time. I know it's just my cock-eyed, biased perception of her. But when I was growing up, her need to 'fix' my Anosmia was overpowering, at times. My condition wasn't inititially an issue to me, but she inadvertently made it one because I felt... I don't know, I just felt like I'd let her down, somehow."

"She made you feel that way?" There was still a slight chill when she spoke to me, but I could tell I was making headway. "Or was that just a manifestation of your need to find something to resent her for so that you could comfortably spend the rest of your life playing the victim?"

Ouch. In one, fairly straightforward sentence she had succeeded in hitting on an analysis of my behaviour that was, if I was to be truthful, both accurate and cruel. While I had changed dramatically since meeting Tara, it wasn't painless for me to hear her say this.

"Now who's being shitty and cynical?" I said.

I supposed it was a result of the tension that we had been under for the past couple of months, but Tara, where she wouldn't have normally risen to such provocation, curled her lip and said, "You really think it's that simple, don't you? Avoid it. Throw it back. That's how you've always lived and that's how you'll always live. Taking the path of least resistance—except where George is concerned. Oh yes, you'll jump through fucking hoops for him, but when it comes to a simple thing like keeping your mother happy, you get all resentful and childish. It's about time you grew up, Price Waters. It's long overdue."

"I thought I had," I said, now backing away from the argument as best I could, not wanting this to get silly.

"When?"

"When I met you." She rolled her eyes and I tried to take hold of her hand. She wouldn't let me, however, so I instead sat with my hands folded neatly in my lap... just like my mother had taught me. "I've changed, Tara. Even my dad recognises that. I've changed because of the influence you've had on me but also because I had to. I was playing the victim. You were right when you said that. But it's something I'm working on and... and I really don't need you using it in an argument against me. That's just unfair and beneath you."

I was rather proud of this little speech. I'd managed to say everything I'd wanted to say without shouting or becoming irrational—and, under the circumstances, that struck me as quite an accomplishment. Tara studied me, but before I truly had chance to expand and relish it, however, we were interrupted by the intercom buzzing.

I had a bad feeling. Speak of the Devil and he shall appear.

Standing beside Tara in front of the wall where the intercom was mounted, I listened as my mother explained that she was only going to stop a moment. She understood that we needed some time alone and she was just dropping by to bring us some sandwiches. "I know you probably haven't got much in," she said. "What with being round your mum's yesterday, Tara, and having been meant to come round ours today, so we've got turkey, turkey and ham, ham—and some turkey with hot chilli sauce for our Price."

Tara pressed the button to let her in.

I thought that maybe her presence, as brief as she'd promised it would be, might help to defuse the situation but the minute I saw the effusive mood Mam was in and, more to the point, the way in which Tara went out of her way to encourage her (just to spite me, I was sure), I felt my heart drop. I needed this like a needed liver cancer.

"So you knew this man that was murdered?" she said, making herself comfortable on the settee—sipping the sherry Tara had poured for her, the Tupperware containers of sandwiches safely deposited in the kitchen.

"Yes," Tara said. "We were speaking to him only yesterday. He's my aunt's boyfriend. Or he was."

"Oh, dear. That's such a shame. How awful for her."

"It's good riddance as far as most folk are concerned," Tara said, and my mother frowned.

"He was a bad one, Mam," I clarified. "Whoever killed him did the world a favour. I get the impression even the police think that."

"I see," she said, though I doubted she actually did. "And do they have any idea who did it?"

"We think so," Tara said. "They're following up a few leads, at least."

Mam looked rather anxious. I could appreciate how she was feeling. If I knew her as well as I thought I did, she would already be working through all the possibilities, trying to figure out if Tara and I were safe. I would have liked to have been able to reassure her, but I couldn't; the truth was, the more I thought about it, the more anxious I became.

"Your dad knew a man who was murdered once," Mam told me, gravely. "Back before you were born, this was. Used to work with him down the docks. Right nice chap he was. Never did or said anything to upset a soul but, still, one night he was walking home from the pub and he got jumped. Was in a coma for three weeks and then that was it. No one ever found out who did it or why but... your dad and his mates did their best to find out. They got pretty close, too. Someone warned them off. This bloke called Francis. One of the big boys. Got hold of your dad one day and told him they should leave it alone. It was being taken care of... Your dad still regrets that he didn't take it further, but I don't." She pointedly met my gaze. "Sometimes you've just got to know when to walk away," she said.

"Your point being?" I said. It's difficult for me to see how I managed to arrive at such a conclusion, now. I can only assume that it was because Pynchon had been going out with Tara's aunt and Mam had made a reference to walking away. But whatever the reasoning behind it, the only conclusion I saw at that time was that she was telling me that I should walk away from Tara.

She looked at me quizzically. "My point being," she said, a little uncertainly as she sensed my hostility. "That we all at one time in our lives or another have to be careful we don't get involved in something we can't handle."

"Like a relationship with a woman with smelly armpits?" I knew the minute I said it just how stupid I was being, but it was too late now.

"Oh for fuck's sake, Price," Tara said. "That's not what she's saying at all."

And, of course, it wasn't. I sat there, looking at my mother and wondering how I really could ever have thought such a thing. All the years I had known her, a lifetime, had not, in spite of what I had said earlier to Tara, given me any valid reason for thinking of her in such a negative way. She most certainly had never done anything to deserve this.

I saw nothing I could do or say to put this right. Mam was already on her feet, making her way to the door with Tara close behind her—making excuses for me more in an attempt to make Mam feel better than to get me off the hook. I'd been under a lot of stress recently. The murder had shaken me up more than I was willing to admit. I was overprotective of her and hadn't yet managed to find a way of judging and reacting appropriately.

"Come back," Tara told her. "Come back and I'm sure he'll apologise."

"Better to leave it for another day," Mam told her at the door, patting her on the arm. "He's like his dad that way. Once he gets something in his head, no matter how ridiculous, he has a heck of a time shaking it."

"He didn't mean it." Tara's voice was low. She didn't sound all that convinced.

"Of course he didn't."

And with that, Mam was gone—Tara closing the door quietly behind her and returning to the living room. Standing behind the settee, she studied me for a minute or two before saying, "I'm going out for a while. Right now I don't want to talk to you. I'm a little afraid of what I might say."

"I don't know why I said it," I replied, desperately.

"I don't want to hear it, Price." She paused and then started to tell me just how awful I had been, how unforgivable what I had said was, before stopping herself and shaking her head. "I'm not going to do this," she insisted. "If you want to talk to anyone about this, talk to your mother. And don't even think of talking to me until you have."

I stood and watched her put her coat on, willing her not to go but knowing in my heart of hearts that nothing I could say would change her mind. I understood the conditions: I first had to "fix" things with my mother.

Once she'd left, I returned to the living room and watched her from the window walking in the direction of her mother's. She looked reluctant, her pace slow and hesitant—and I prayed that she'd change her mind and come back. Behind me, the flat seemed so silent and empty that I believed even a blazing row would have been preferable to having to endure this alone. I'd spent too many years by myself already and the prospect of living here—of living anywhere—without Tara made me feel physically sick. I had my books. I had a bed. There were sandwiches in the kitchen and the heating in this place was far more reliable than my old gas fire. And yet, however much of a cliché it might have been, I had nothing if Tara wasn't there with me to share it.

She was two-thirds of the way down the street now, and as I thought about putting on my coat and going after her—catching her up and telling her that I was going around my mother's immediately, that I was going to make this right—something caught my eye and I stiffened. Tara had walked right past it, so caught up with our disagreement that she had completely failed to see it.

It was unmistakably the same Renault and, even if it wasn't, I couldn't afford to take any chances.

Without bothering to grab a coat, I ran out of the flat and down the stairs, bursting onto the street below and almost knocking over a young couple who I believed were neighbours of ours. Throwing an apology over my shoulder at them, I turned, running in Tara's direction... just in time to see her bundled into the back of the Renault by two of Sharon's brothers. I yelled Tara's name, running faster, and, struggling, she turned to look at me.

All I could see were her eyes, or that was how it seemed. Large and beseeching, filled with love and horror. She said something I didn't hear, and then repeated it ("Find them. Be careful. I love you.") and then they were in the back of the car, being driven off at speed even as the doors were being slammed shut behind them.

The young couple I'd almost knocked over (they later introduced themselves as Len and Lucy) had seen it all. They rushed up to me, Len saying that he'd got the reg number and offering me the use of his mobile.

"That was your girlfriend, right?" Lucy said. "We've seen you around."

I took the phone off Len, nodding, my mind suddenly a blank. What was I supposed to do now? Tara. Phone. Kidnapped. It was all there, but I just couldn't...

"Nine, nine, nine," Len whispered to me. Again I nodded and started to thumb in the number, only stopping when I remembered the card in my trouser pocket.

Len and Lucy watched me, intrigued, as I dialled the number on the card, raising their eyebrows at one another when I got through and said, "D.I. Murrey? It's Price Waters. Something's happened."

Once D.I. Murrey and D.C. McCarthy had left, having taking all the necessary details and assuring me that everything was being done that could possibly be done, I curled up in the corner of the settee with one of Tara's pullovers around my shoulders and tried to think what I should do next. Murrey, who hadn't liked the fact anymore than I that Sharon's brothers appeared to be involved with Donna Kesey, had told me to stay where I was—believing that I would be contacted, sooner or later, and that it would all then become clear.

I had agreed, in the midst of my haze of fear and unknowing. But now I wasn't so sure. Had I agreed merely because this was the path of least resistance, because it meant I didn't have to do anything, or did I truly believe that it was the right thing to do? Tara had told me to find them—Sharon and George, I could only assume—but when I had told Murrey and McCarthy, McCarthy had shook her head and told me to leave it alone. They were taking care of it and the last thing they needed was me running around taking unnecessary risks. But who was I going to take notice of, I asked myself. Some cop fresh out of police school or the woman I loved—the woman I had pissed off but who had still told me that she loved me, the woman who had told me, yet again, to be careful and find them?

My mind made up, I put on the warmest coat I had and picked up my phone. It was all very clear, now. I knew exactly what I had to do, and in what order.

Speed-dialling Tony's number, I waited for him to pick up. With George and Tara gone, he was pretty much the only friend I had— and once I'd acknowledged that this wasn't something that I could do on my own it seemed only natural that I should call him.

"Shit, Price," he said, once I'd explained what was going on. "I'm so sorry. That's awful."

"I need your help, Tone. Is there someone who can take care of Claudia for you for a while?"

He thought for a moment and then said yes. "She's actually been going into the office now and then. Since you told me everything," he said. "I could drop her round at one of the partners. What do you want me to do, mate?"

I explained that I principally required a chauffeur—there were a few places I needed to visit as quickly as possible—but I might also need a little muscle, someone who could look threatening if the situation called for it. He seemed reluctant, at first, and then he remembered that this was for Tara, and that she had quite possibly been kidnapped by a double murderer.

"Whatever you need from me," he said, "you've got it."

I gave him the address for Tara's mam's house and told him to meet me there as soon as he could. He responded with a hearty "aye, aye, captain" and then added, more quietly and with feeling,

"I know it was difficult for you—the whole thing with Claudia, Price. You were a good friend to both of us, and we appreciate it. We'll find Tara. I promise you."

He hung up before I had the chance to say anything more, and I took that as my cue to head round to Bernie's. I wasn't looking forward to it, but it had to be done.

Bernie's anguish took an unexpected form. Where I had envisaged tears and lots of hair-pulling, boxes of man-size Kleenex and an effort to understand, I was instead confronted with the kind of precise, concentrated laser-beam anger from which I could only take strength. Her daughter had been kidnapped by some arsehole who thought that she could get to George and Sharon this way and, by Christ she wasn't about to just sit back and let it all go on around her. "If that bloody sister of mine had never got hooked up with that sodding Victor Pynchon, may he rot, this would never have happened," she said.

I tried to explain that it was a little more complicated than that, sitting on the settee and putting my hand on hers. "There's a lot more going on here than meets the eye."

"Is there?" she said, a little sharply. "You see, I don't think there is. From where I'm sitting, it's all very clear; two lovely people have got dragged into something silly and pathetic—and if Carla had never met Victor Pynchon, or if that bloody George had never been born, this would never have happened."

Before I had chance to respond, Bernie was up on her feet and into the hallway. I followed, panicking a little when I saw her taking her coat off the peg by the door. I didn't want her coming with me. This was risking it turning into an episode of Hetty Wainthrop Investigates and, under the circumstances, that was rather more than I could bear. As it turned out, however, she had something else entirely in mind.

"I'm going round there," she told me. "Our Carla's." She must have noticed a look of horror on my face, because she then added, "Oh don't worry. I'm not going to do anything silly. I'm just going to give her a bloody good talking to and see if I can find out anything useful. I'm assuming you've got plans?"

I nodded. "A friend's picking me up," I told her. "I need to see my parents—I owe my mam an apology and Dad might be able to help—and then I'm going to hunt down a few of George's... friends."

"Good," she said, patting my arm. "I've got your number if I find out anything useful."

I didn't want to stop and think about what might be happening to Tara—but it was a good ten minutes before Tony arrived to pick me up, and, as I stood outside Bernie's waiting for him, I couldn't help but go over everything I knew about our particular predicament. As I figured it, Donna Kesey was trying to ingratiate herself with Sharon. Since her release from prison, her prime objective had been to get back with Sharon, re-establish the relationship they had shared, however fleeting. That had been what Pynchon's murder must have been all about. To prove that she always kept a promise, however long it took. So why kidnap Tara?

When I had spoken on the phone to D.I. Murrey, he had talked about "leverage"—about Donna Kesey looking for a way to get Sharon to do what she wanted. As he saw it, that was what Tara was. Nothing more than a device in Donna Kesey's mind, a means to an end and one, he assured me, where the threat of harm was more effective than harm itself. I wasn't entirely sure that I agreed with that. The added complication of Sharon's brothers being with Kesey—the woman they had supposedly been trying to keep away from their sister—didn't bode well. It changed things. I didn't know how... but the more I thought about it, the more urgent I felt it was to find Tara.

I didn't recognise Tony's car when he pulled up at the kerb. Apparently he'd changed his old one for a bright and shiny new MPV. It seemed a cruel quirk of fate that it was a Grand Scenic— a Renault Grand Scenic—and only when he beeped his horn did I manage to shake my sudden revulsion and get in.

"Nice car," I said.

"Better for Claudia," he told me. "Easier for getting her in and out."

I nodded and he studied me, patient, his presence oddly calming.

"So where's it gonna be?" he said after a short wait.

I looked at him, the question hanging over me—for a moment utterly unanswerable. Suddenly heavy and exhausted, I wasn't sure I could do this. I knew I had to, for Tara's sake, but what use could I really be? D.C. McCarthy had been right. I should have stayed at home and waited for Kesey to contact me, taken it from there. All this running around wasn't going to achieve a single bloody thing... except, maybe, to make matters far worse than they already were.

Tony, apparently sensing my doubt, leaned over and put a hand on my shoulder, squeezing. "You can do this, mate," he said. "You're stronger and more able than you give yourself credit for. You've just got to continue the way you're going. Don't let anyone stand in your way."

I looked at him and smiled, eyebrows raised. "Let me guess," I said. "You got that out of a Christmas cracker, right?"

"That bad?"

"A little nauseating, but the thought is appreciated."

He slapped me on the back of the head and then sat back in his seat. "So," he said, "I say again, where's it going to be?"

Tony waited in the car while I went in. I was looking forward to this even less than I'd been looking forward to telling Bernie what had happened to Tara, but I had no choice—for a couple of reasons; one, Tara had wanted me to apologise to my mother as soon as possible and, two, I wanted Dad on side. As annoying as he could at times be, he knew this town and the people in it far better than I ever would and I certainly wasn't going to let my pride get in the way of asking him for help. Tara was too important to me.

The reception I got was frosty, to say the least. I found both of them in the kitchen, Dad leaning against the sink unit, Mam sat at the table with her hands wrapped around a mug of coffee. They looked up when I walked in, but neither of them said a word.

"I have a few things to say," I told them, without preamble. "I have a few things to say and I need you both to hear me out without interrupting." Neither looked as if they'd ever have anything to say to me ever again, but I hoped that that would change once they'd heard what I had to say.

I started with my apology to Mam, explaining how Tara had always feared that I'd walk away from her and how, when she had used that phrase herself, it had created a very negative and wholly inaccurate association for me. "I was wrong," I said. "And I apologise... and I wish I could be more long-winded about it, but there's something of even greater importance that I need to discuss with you."

Finally, Dad spoke. "Right now," he said, "I don't think there's anything more important than you making it right with your mother."

"Tara's been kidnapped," I said, tears bubbling up.

Mam was out of her chair and sitting me down at the table before I had chance to so much as blub. She sat down beside me, holding my hand, and Dad went down on his haunches, arms folded on the tabletop. "From the beginning," he said. "Take your time."

Once I'd finished, Dad got to his feet, knees popping, and ran his hands through his hair. "Tony's outside?" he said, and I nodded in reply. "Good call, son. Something like this, the Tonys of this world can be very useful. Now, where do you intend we start? You do have a few ideas, right, Price?"

I nodded. "I'm not sure that they'll amount to much but, yes, I have a few ideas."

"Good," he said. "We'd better get going."

It had been a long time since I had last been in Gilhooney's. Long enough for me to wonder if we had the wrong place and, yet, once we stepped inside, not so long that I didn't kind of wish we had. It wasn't so much that it was a seedy little dive. That much I could cope with. It was more the sheer hopelessness I couldn't contend with—the sense that all the lives in that poky little room, ours included, had somehow reached the end of the line.

It was early, so there were only a handful of pathetic individuals in. An old girl in the corner coughed noisily into a handkerchief and sipped at her pint of stout, smiling toothlessly at us as we passed her table. She seemed friendly enough, but I wouldn't want to see her at the end of the evening.

Eying us suspiciously from beneath thick, tenebrific eyebrows, the barman asked what he could get us in a tone that suggested he'd rather not serve us at all. Dad ordered a couple of whiskeys and an orange juice for Tony, leaning against the bar between Tony and me and saying, quietly, "The less time we spend in here the better. George really used to come to this shithole?"

"Yes," I said, looking over my shoulder at the two old men at the far end of the room and wondering if either of them was Old Ray. "Brought me here, once. Possibly one of the worst nights of my life."

Dad briefly chuckled to himself. "So who is this bloke we're looking for, again?" Tony asked, once the barman had brought our drinks and taken payment.

"Old Ray," I said. "The local drunk."

"There's only one?"

"He's the one the drunks call a drunk," I explained. "Puts it away impressively, by all accounts, but if anything's going down he still somehow manages to know about it. Or that's how George always tells it. He wouldn't have found Sharon without Old Ray's help."

Dad sipped his drink and beckoned the barman over. Reluctantly, the barman joined us, leaning proprietarily on the other side of the bar and breathing through his mouth. Judging by the way in which Dad pulled back a couple of inches, I guessed our friend the barman could have done with sucking a Polo mint.

"You might be able to help us," Dad said.

"That's what I like to see," the barman told us. "An optimist. We don't see many of your kind in this neck of the woods."

"As I see it," Dad replied, "an optimist is just someone who knows enough to know that he can make things go the way he wants, if he has to."

The barman turned down the corner of his mouth thoughtfully. "Interesting worldview," he said. "Why not try applying it? See what happens?"

"Sounds good to me." Dad sat forward again, risking the barman's breath. "George Ruiz. You know him?"

"Maybe I do, maybe I—"

"We're looking for drinking buddies of his," Dad went on. "Specifically some bloke called Old Ray. Think you can point us in his direction?"

I noticed that our barman friend had clusters of acne scars on both cheeks. This, together with an inch-long scar by the outer edge of his left eye and his close-cropped hair, made him look tougher than he possibly was. On the other hand, I thought, willing Dad to take it easy, maybe he's twice as tough as he looks.

"Old Ray's easy enough to find," he told us. "You don't need my help. He comes in six-thirty on the dot. He always has a carnation in his lapel and piss stains on his pants. Can't miss him."

He started walking away but Dad grabbed his arm. The barman stared menacingly at Dad's hand but Dad didn't remove it.

"Maybe you could point us in the direction of a few more people who might have spoken to George over recent months?" he said, smiling. "This really is very important."

I'd never seen this side of Dad before. There was an ease and certainty to the way he was handling this that I could never have achieved—something youthful and, yet, age-old and wise. I worried that he wouldn't know when to back off but his manner told me that he had dealt with plenty of situations like this in his time. I wondered how I could have lived so long without knowing about it.

The barman looked back at us with the kind of contempt you usually only see in old black and white movies—something with Bogart, perhaps, grainy and almost forgotten. His lip curled and he pulled his arm from Dad's grasp, smoothing the creases out of his sleeve and saying, with deliberate menace, "Anyone comes in, I'll point them out to you. That's the best I can do."

This seemed agreeable enough to Dad, and we retired to a table, well away from the toothless old harpy in the corner of the room, to await Old Ray's arrival.

At this point, the day truly caught up with me. I sat back in the chair while Dad and Tony discussed in an undertone the advantages of the direct approach with people like our barman friend and felt suddenly quite small and powerless. The lights in Gilhooney's suitably dim, I was sure I could easily have lost myself in there—melted into the woodwork like one of the regulars, never to be seen again, never to be missed. It was a hopeless place and, after the day I'd had, I could see the attraction of that.

It wasn't a wholly new sensation to me. It was highly reminiscent of all those nights I had spent alone in my old flat—curled up on my bed, reading Tolstoy and wallowing in that ineffable sense of being separate, of being blameless simply because my interaction with the world was so minimal. I'd hated that flat and I'd hated that way of 'living', but it had also had its attractions. The attraction of a retreat. The attraction of the convent to the nun—the hole in the ground to the pursued fox. I'd discarded that life, looked up one evening, discovered that there was more and went after it never believing that it would end here, in Gilhooney's, drinking with my father and Tony, worried about Tara and, yet, wishing I'd never started this.

George had been right. At heart, I was a coward. I was a coward and I was out of my depth, and if Tara had had only me to depend on in all of this, then she was most assuredly condemned, doomed, written off, left to whatever devices cruel Fate held in store for her. Even with the best of intentions, with the bravest of hearts, there would be nothing I alone could do for her, because the best of me was still back there in my old flat, hiding under the duvet and telling myself that this was how it needed to be, how I was worth nothing more because anything more was simply an unreasonable expectation. Murders and kidnappings were for others. I was equipped only for loneliness and solitude, the long, dark night of the soul and microwave chicken tikka masala.

"And there's no one else who might be able to help?" Tony was saying, looking around at the still almost empty room.

"Not that I can think of," I said. I sounded far away, even to myself, and Dad looked over at me, clearly concerned.

"You alright, lad?" he said. I nodded and smiled, but not very convincingly, it seemed. "You don't look it. You had anything to eat today?"

"We had a big breakfast," I lied. "I don't think I could stomach anything right now." I pushed my whiskey away. "This, especially."

"Probably just as well," he said, taking the glass from me and pouring its contents into his own. "I have a feeling you're going to need all of your faculties in the coming hours."

I didn't want to think about that. What the coming hours had in store for me was something shadowed and distant, and, the more I considered my own incompetence, the more I thought it best that it remain that way. The police would do whatever they did best, and I would curl in a corner doing what I did best. And whatever the outcome, and however much I didn't want to think about it, it would be the same.

"I'm not sure I have any faculties to give," I muttered under my breath, and Tony looked at me sharply. "Well, I'm not," I told him. "What have I ever done to make anyone think that I can be of any help to Tara in all of this?"

Dad was about to get on his high-horse and tell me not to be such a defeatist—I could tell by the way in which he pulled himself up, sitting a good couple of inches taller in his chair, it seemed. Thankfully, however, Tony beat him to it.

"What have you ever done?" he repeated. "I'll tell you what you've done, mate—you've made a commitment to that lass. The kind of commitment that, if what you tell me is true, no one else ever has. Now, whatever you might think of yourself, that's a pretty big thing as far as I'm concerned. You've already helped her. Just like you helped me and Claudia. And if you've done it for her once, I'm sure you can do it for her again. Mark my words."

"Any help I've given in the past," I said, "has been... a residual effect. This time it's different."

Tony gave me a tight-lipped smile and nodded exaggeratedly. "Damn right it is," he said. "This time it's a choice. You either give it your best shot or –"

"Walk away from her," Dad said.

A man entered and staggered up to the bar—all piss stains, carnation and rheumy eyes. We looked at him and then, determined never to walk away from Tara, I downed the remaining whiskey in Dad's glass and said, "It must be six-thirty."

Old Ray had a noxious look about him. Dad and Tony recoiled noticeably, but I only stood there staring at him, oblivious to whatever stench he might be generating, waiting for him to look up from his pint of best bitter and struggling to assure myself that this sorry excuse for humanity before me really could help us in our search for George, Sharon and Richard. Old Ray was well aware of our presence. Already well into his cups, he was nevertheless not so far gone that he couldn't register the three of us looming over him. Still he did not rush to look up. Well practiced in this malarkey, he knew how to use the little power he had.

Dad moved to one side a little more, leaning on the bar so that he was almost directly in Old Ray's face. I didn't envy Dad; even with the benefit of my Anosmia, I still wouldn't have much fancied being that close to Old Ray. He looked like he might have half a dozen highly communicable diseases.

"You Old Ray?" Dad said.

"Depends what you mean by 'old'," he replied. "I prefer to think of myself as internally youthful. The Peter Pan of Pubs." He chuckled at this while I was still struggling with 'internally youthful'. His hands wrapped around his pint as if he were warming them on a mug of tea, he grew more serious, staring Dad square in the eye (remarkably impressive given his condition) and saying, "Why? What's it got to do with you?"

"You know George Ruiz," I said, forcing him to twist unsteadily on his barstool to look at me.

"I do?"

"You do."

"So what of it?"

"I need to speak to him. Urgently."

Old Ray nodded thoughtfully and took a sip of his pint. "You and about a dozen others," he said. "Seems our George has suddenly become quite popular. Who would have thunk it?"

"Others have been asking about him?"

"Just a few."

"The police?"

"And the Brothers Grim. I tell you, it's coming to something when a retired gentleman such as myself can't have a quiet drink in peace without being pestered by hordes of George-hunters." He looked up at the barman, who'd been taking this all in—wiping out a glass and wearing a wry smile. "What do you say, Buzz?"

"I'd say that to be retired you have to have had a fucking job to retire from in the first place," he told Old Ray. "And what with you being internally youthful and everything... well, the image don't quite fit."

"Since when have I given a fuck about image?"

"Since you started wearing that plastic carnation in your button hole."

"Plastic, is it?"

I tapped Old Ray on the shoulder, hoping to get him back on track. "You were telling us about these hordes of George-hunters," I reminded him. "They ask a lot of questions?"

"Some."

"And you told them what?"

"Everything I knew."

Dad and Tony exchanged a glance. "Such as?" I asked.

"Such as how he made a right fucking mess of my car for starters," Old Ray said, turning back to his pint. "The Brothers Fucking Grim seemed to find that a bit annoying, actually."

"I was with him," I said. "He sideswiped the Brothers Grim's

Porsche and managed to lose them. That car of yours made their racy little heap of fascist junk blush with shame. It didn't know what hit it. Just like Hitler in his bunker."

Just as I had imagined, this had the desired result. Old Ray chuckled and patted the stool immediately to his right. "He really did that?" he asked me as Dad and Tony sat down on Old Ray's left. "He actually took on a Porsche in my old Austin Allegro?"

"He did. Not to mention a train."

"Fuck off."

"Seriously."

"He sideswiped a train?"

"Ah, well, no," I said. "Not quite. We were almost hit by a train. At a level crossing. That's how we got away from the Brothers Grim. We made it over the crossing before the train got there; they didn't."

Old Ray shook his head at this, utterly in awe of George, it seemed. "You know," he said. "Normally, I don't have a lot of time for Ruiz. I knew his father and he was, still is, actually, just the same." A strangely appealing glow lit up Old Ray's face and he chuckled to himself again. "George would piss himself if he knew," he said. "Life just seems like one big bad fucking joke at times." He put his arm around me. "Have you noticed that?"

Nodding, I said, "Knew what?"

"Eh?"

"George would piss himself if he knew what?"

"Oh that." He took his arm from around my shoulder and let it flop on the bar beside his beer. "Best left for another day. The point I was making was that I haven't ever really had all that much time for George. He's a user, which is fine if there's free beer in it. Just got to be sure to get the beer in advance. But... anyone who takes on a Porsche in a borrowed Allegro... you've got to admire that just a little, haven't you?"

"I didn't much admire it at the time," I said.

"Praying to the The Great God of Shit Stains and Skid Marks?"

"Oh, yes. He was in there somewhere."

We laughed like the best buddies we weren't, Dad looking

vaguely amused, Tony merely as if he could have done with something stronger than an orange juice, and finally we calmed down—Old Ray shaking his head and smiling, as if at an old, familiar memory. "So what is it I can tell you?" he asked me. "I'll warn you, there's not much—but what I do know, I'll gladly share."

"He took off with this Sharon lass that you helped him find," I explained. "They're trying to keep out of the way of Sharon's brothers and this other lass called Donna Kesey and now... they've kidnapped my girlfriend for leverage. To try, I assume, to get Sharon to come to them. We think that it was Donna Kesey that killed Victor Pynchon. You might have seen the news story?"

Old Ray was nodding thoughtfully. "Messy," he said. "If I'd've known, I never would have helped him find Sharon. I should have realised it would all end in tears—for some other poor fucker." He sighed and emptied his glass. I signalled to Buzz to pour him another. "The problem is," he continued, "I don't reckon there's all that much I can tell you. There's a lotta rumours going round about this Kesey lass at the moment—made some interesting connections while she was inside—but they don't amount to a whole lot, and I'm inclined to take even the most plausible of them with a pinch of salt. As for where George might be, your guess is as good as mine. Nobody's talking about him, so my guess is he's pretty well hidden. Either that or people are too scared to talk."

"Which would mean?" I said.

He shrugged. "If you're forcing me to draw conclusions," he said. "I'd have to say that I believe boyo has had some help. George isn't good enough to scare people into silence, and he certainly isn't good enough to disappear so bloody effectively. No. He's definitely had some help."

"From whom?"

He studied me—his rheumy eyes squinted and red around the rims. "What's your name, again?" he said, and I told him. "George mentioned you. Never forget a name like that. He said you were the best friend he ever had. The only friend he ever had, I wouldn't mind betting."

"Very probably," I said. "Though what that says about me, God only knows."

He smiled and then sucked his top lip, deep in thought. Finally, he spoke. "I'll tell you something, Price," he said. "Nobody's going to talk to you about George. Something's definitely going on, he's being helped, and it's more than anyone's life's worth to voice suspicions. But there's one man who might be able to tell you something. His great uncle. You might have heard of him. Francis Ruiz?"

Chapter Sixteen

Dad sat in the back of the Scenic in silence. He hadn't spoken since we'd stepped out of Gilhooney's and I was worried enough about him to keep glancing over my shoulder to see if he was alright. Tony gave a little twitch of his eyebrows and shook his head. "Best leave it," he said, ever so quietly. "If I'm right, he's lost in memory. I recognise the look. He'll find his way out soon enough."

We were driving through quiet, nighttime countryside, heading in the direction of the address Old Ray had given us for Francis Ruiz—the old-time gangster that I hadn't taken seriously. The drive reminded me of the ride back from Everburn, and as I sat there worrying about my father's sudden silence and just how many of Great Uncle Francis's stories had been true, I saw—or, rather, felt—all of the connections that had led me to this point. They were, it seemed, infinite and impossible to separate, but the two that had the greatest effect on me, the two that mattered most, both involved Tara. I had found her. I had lost her. That was what this was now about. That was what it had become. Everything else was incidental. George, Sharon, Richard—I didn't care about them, not in any real way. All I cared about was finding Tara.

Such a small word, and yet so rich in meaning—so suggestive of its component parts. It was not a place, it was a state of mind... a state of being. But without Tara there was no home. Without her, our new flat was just that; flat. Empty. Heartless and without soul. Without her (and, yes, I know I'm stumbling into the realm of cliché again, but fuck it—this is just the way it was)... without her, my life lacked meaning.

"He's fair," Dad suddenly said from his place on the back seat. I shuffled round in my own seat so that I could see him more easily—but it was too dark to effectively read his features. "He's fair, but he's hard. Talks like he's ninety-nine per cent horseshit, but he isn't. That was what made him so dangerous. People underestimated him." I thought he smiled, but it was difficult to be sure. "For all the stories they tell about him, you know what I remember most? His keen sense of justice. He wasn't just in it for the money. He cared for his community. Cared enough to kill for it."

I recalled what Mam had said earlier that day. I hadn't seen the connection at the time, but now it was obvious. "Francis?" I said.

"The worst thing they ever did was disempower blokes like him," he said, nodding. "Oh, there's plenty that wouldn't agree, but the likes of Francis, they kept the nutters in line. Today, all you've got is nutters. Francis was to the professional criminal what the bobby on the beat was to the law-abiding citizen. A visible deterrent."

It was disconcerting, sitting there in that dark car, listening to Dad talk about such things, and so I turned back to look at the road ahead, hoping that he wouldn't say anything else, that we would soon arrive at the home of Francis Ruiz and that he would help us find George and Sharon.

Blessedly, Dad did remain silent, and as we drove it occurred to me that maybe, as Dad himself might have put it, we had got this arse first. Tara had told me to find them, of that I was certain—just as I was equally sure that she had meant George and Sharon. I felt compelled to follow her plea but what if this wasn't what we should be doing? What if, instead of dashing around like blue-arsed flies looking for George, Sharon and Richard, we should have actually been focusing our efforts on finding Tara? In many respects, it was the obvious route to take, and while it would most probably lead us to nowhere, I still couldn't help feeling that we were approaching this from the wrong direction... and that, bizarrely, we were, in fact, being disloyal.

Tony, more quiet tonight than I'd ever known him, nevertheless seemed to be very attuned to my mood. Maybe it was working together that did it, I don't know, or possibly the whole thing with Claudia, but it was almost as if he knew what I was thinking.

He changed down a gear as the winding country lane we were following, high, shadowed hedgerows on either side, became a steep incline, and glanced at me. He said, softly, "I was thinking, back there in that shithole Gilhooney's, if there was a more direct way of doing this, but if there is, mate, I sure as hell can't see it."

"I feel like I should be looking for Tara," I said.

"I know. And you are. You're looking for her in the only way you can."

Dad chose this moment to speak up from the back seat. I'd briefly entertained the notion that he'd fallen asleep—a Christmas with Mam could do that to you—but apparently he was as wide-awake as Tony and me. "Why do you think she said that to you?" he said. "Why do you think she told you to find them?"

"Because... I don't know. I suppose because she knew it was the best way of seeing to it that Donna Kesey got what she wanted."

Dad was nodding. I didn't have to look round at him to know this, I just knew. "That too," he said. "Tara's a bright lass. But I'm betting that as well as that, she was also told to say it. As she was being pushed into the car, they told her what they wanted. That's the main reason she said it."

"How do you figure that one?" Tony said.

"Simple." There was satisfaction in his voice. I found it reassuring. "Like I said. Tara's a bright lass. She would never risk sending our Price off on a wild goose chase. If she said something like that, she did it fully knowing that it was exactly what they wanted. Or that's my belief, anyway."

He had a point. Tara would have known better than anyone the seriousness of her predicament, and she most assuredly would not have taken any chances—of any kind. I was not as reassured by this as I had hoped, however. I nodded thoughtfully and agreed that that was a good point, that I'd never thought of it quite like that, but in my heart of hearts, I still had my doubts—and I supposed they would remain until Tara was sitting safely by my side again.

After a few more twists and turns, Tony drove us along a narrow, winding road, overarched with trees. Without any kind of lighting other than the Scenic's headlights, the darkness seemed to bear down on us on both sides—the threat of illness and suffering with nothing to redeem it or us. It shushed past us as we drove, solid and weighty and yet fleetingly breath-like, and I flashed on an image of the crushed can experiment we had done when I'd been a lad at school. That was what would happen to the car if we didn't arrive at our destination soon, I was sure. The night would bear down on us and it would be crushed—we would be crushed.

And then we broke free—free into the garishly lit realm of the suburban. Streetlights at their most orange, houses bleeding from even the slightest of orifices, traffic lights synchronising with the flashing of car indicators—overwhelming for a nanosecond, my brain screeching with the effort to assimilate it, and then dropping once more into the background, its rightful, heartening place.

On a very respectable, well-maintained private housing estate, Tony parked the car outside of a relatively modern bungalow (uPVC double glazing and moss-free key-block paving) and turned off the engine. "Well," he said. "Here we are." He checked the piece of paper that Old Ray had given us with the address written on and then added, "Yup. This is definitely it."

Dad removed his seatbelt and leant between the two front seats. "I have to admit," he told us. "It's not quite what I was expecting."

"What were you expecting?" Tony said.

"I don't know—but that isn't it. Anyone'd think he was a retired insurance salesman, not an ex-gangster."

"And they're not one and the same?"

Dad conceded the point with a chuckle and we got out of the car.

He looked younger than I remembered—a seemingly healthy seventy-five-year-old rather than the eighty-plus wannabe spiv who had once bored me rigid. Looking down at us from the doorway, his hair still slicked back but tonight far more casual, in slacks and a crisp white shirt with a heavily starched collar, I got a sense of the man he had once been. Whatever he was now, he had formerly been imposing—and a trace of that lingered in the way in which he held himself, the confidence with which he made eye-contact, the authoritative tilt of his chin. He was not a man who lived in the past, I concluded (contrary to what I had once believed.) He was a man who had brought some of the past with him—who carried it in his marrow and, when necessary, traded with it quite successfully.

Seeing my dad, Francis nodded and smiled, holding out a hand to be shaken. "Waters," he said, impressively. "Good to see you again. It's been a while."

"About thirty-five years," Dad said, taking the proffered hand. "Maybe longer."

Francis rolled his eyes and sucked air through his teeth. "Where do they go, hey?" he said. "Only seems like yesterday since I finished off that little fuck for you boys. Doesn't bear thinking about." Straightening himself, he looked at us and smiled. "Anyway," he said. "You better come in. Old Ray called to tell me you were coming. Price, isn't it?"

Surprisingly minimal in its decoration, without so much as a single bauble in sight, the living room into which we were shown was spacious and clean—all bright lights and uncluttered lines. There was no TV, but I did spot a laptop computer and more books than you could shake a stick at, arranged in precise alphabetical order in a bookcase at the far end of the room. Francis made himself comfortable in a black leather armchair (it looked as old as him, and just as welcoming) and gestured for us to make ourselves at home on the matching settee. We all made synchronised farting sounds as we settled ourselves.

"You should have come sooner," Francis said to me. "I told you, didn't I? I said, if that little shit George gives you any trouble, you come and see me, did I not?"

"You did," I conceded.

"So why didn't you?" he asked.

It was like being back at school, only worse. Francis was more imposing than the strictest of headmasters. I therefore reminded myself to chose my words very carefully.

"I like to take care of things myself," I said. "Whenever possible. And, also, I didn't like to disturb you."

Francis drummed out a little tattoo on his thighs and laughed. I didn't know what that meant. I vaguely recalled him doing something similar that night at George's Aunt Martha's, but that was no guarantee that we were safe.

"And I suppose," he said, "it had absolutely nothing to do with the fact that you thought I was all wind and piss, correct?"

I didn't want to lie to him. But I didn't want to tell him the truth, either. I stared at him gormlessly, mouth open as I struggled for the right thing to say. Looking at Dad, desperately, in need of his assistance, I saw that both him and Tony were grinning at my obvious discomfort.

"Shit," I said, looking back at a positively jubilant Francis and laughing my first real laugh since Tara had been taken. "I really need this, don't I? My girlfriend gets kidnapped and then I have to contend with three old farts ripping the piss out of me. Simply wonder-fucking-ful."

Francis reached across and gave my knee a hearty smack, still laughing. "Just my little ice-breaker," he said. "Forgive me. Always a good idea to start a serious discussion with a bit of a laugh, I find. Might be the last chance you get," he added, with a wink that I thought was meant to appear friendly.

Francis chose this moment to reach down and pick something up from the floor beside his chair. I tried not to flinch, but it was difficult. What if this was all part of it? I thought. What if Old Ray had been paid to send us to Francis because Francis was, in fact, in on it—whatever 'it' was? Christ, I told myself, we've been way too fucking trusting. For all we know, this old fuck's probably the ring-leader.

As Francis took a cigarette from the packet and lit up, after first offering us all one (the three of us politely declining), my phone started ringing. Tony, Dad and Francis stared at me expectantly, but only when Dad elbowed me did I take it out and check the caller.

"It's from Tara's phone," I said—knowing that this was the moment I had been waiting for, hoping for even, but nevertheless dreading having to answer it.

Naturally, it wasn't Tara. I think I would have been surprised if it had been.

"Don't talk, just listen," a gruff, female voice that I assumed belonged to Donna Kesey said. "This is how it's going to be. You're going to cooperate fully and Tara is going to remain safe. Simple, isn't it? We will take good care of her and you will do what I'm sure you've already started doing; you will find Sharon and arrange for her to meet me alone. Once this is done, Tara will go free and the two of you will live happily ever after.

"With one little caveat," she continued; at the same time I could hear Dad filling Francis in on the background to what was happening. "I know you involved the police. Understandable. But no more, okay? I'm keeping this phone so you can contact me easily. Don't give them the number. I'm trusting you not to. I know what they can do and... well, let's just say Tara's health should be at the forefront of your mind and leave it at that."

"I want to speak to her."

After what I took to be a moment's consideration, a lengthy and profound silence, I heard a rustling, crackling sound and what I thought was whispering. I held my breath, my three companions regarding me gravely—even Francis quite literally sitting on the edge of his seat.

And then I heard her voice. My Tara's. Strong and proud and determined. "Do as she says, Price," she told me, and then the line went dead.

Still with the silent phone to my ear, I thought of the first day I saw her—standing in the rain in her green wellies and raincoat, stroking one of Carla's cats as if she were a reformed Bond villain. How far we had come since then. How very different she was to the woman I had initially imagined her to be. I saw now that that was in part due to me; as she had had a positive effect on me, so had I helped to provide the foundation she'd needed all along. It was more than just love. It was something unspoken and difficult to define, something that centred around the respect and understanding we had for one another, the connection that it was, I suspected, best not to examine too closely. We had been brought together for a reason. That was how it seemed. When we had most needed each other, there we had been—my Anosmia and her Axillary Hyperhidrosis merely signs that our compatibility was beyond doubt, that, as I was sure Tara believed, it was somehow God-given. I'd never bought all that 'there's someone out there for everyone' nonsense—but now I had to wonder if anything was as random as it seemed. There was a reason to who we were together. An undeniable logic. And when the line went dead on me, I think I understood that more completely than I ever had.

When Dad touched me on the arm, I carefully put the phone in my pocket and sat back—telling them in a tired voice all that Donna Kesey had told me. Francis took a pull on his cigarette and inhaled deeply, squinting at me through the smoke as he said, "She's trusting you. That's good. She doesn't have to do that but she wants you to see that she understands that you and Tara are innocent bystanders in all of this. She won't take any chances, though. If you give her the impression at any time that you aren't playing ball then everything will change, you mark my words. She's a killer, Price. Don't forget that. Do it exactly as she says and you'll be fine. Don't so much as think of deviating."

"What if I try my best and fail?" I said. "What if I find them but can't get Sharon to meet her."

Francis cleared his throat and sat back in his chair, blowing smoke rings and following them with his eyes—as if those nebulous, transitory forms held all the answers. "I can only tell you how I'd handle it," he said. "I wouldn't want to kill Tara—and the more I think about it, neither will she. She's only killed people who some would say deserved it so far, yes?" I nodded. "Good, good, good. I like that. I like it because it's what I believe in, but also because it makes things simpler for you. Betray her, and she won't hesitate. She'll kill Tara. Do everything you can to help her and, even if you fail, she'll let her go. Or that's how I see it, anyways. No guarantee, mind."

The evening was rolling on and it felt as if we had nothing to so far show for our efforts. I didn't want to rush Francis, but at the same time I realised that we had to get to the point as soon as possible.

"Can you help me?" I asked him, quietly.

Francis sighed and stubbed out the cigarette in an ashtray on the floor by his chair. "In nineteen-seventy-two," he said, "things were bad. Everything was changing fast. The space race was over. The moon had been abandoned. And everything seemed to be turning to shit. I was having to work harder at keeping it all together, which meant more people were getting hurt. They tried it on, I snapped them back into line—but, by Christ, I knew I couldn't keep doing it forever without there being a significant comeback at some point. So I made preparations. I set up a number of safe houses around the country. Ran by my most trusted. Only a handful knew about them. Best thing I ever did, I tell you. There were times when I needed those houses like you wouldn't believe. And when I was through with all that, I made myself a pretty penny hiding other people. Invisibility is a valuable commodity in our game.

"Anyway," he went on, "I can see that you're getting a wee bit twitchy, Price, my friend, so, to cut a long story short, I still keep a few of them. And that little shit George knows it. He came to see me a few weeks back and... well, I loath the bloke, but he's family."

"He's at one of your safe houses?" Dad said.

"Yes." Francis seemed to be weighing something up and I realised that he still hadn't actually decided whether he was going to help us or not. I'd taken it for granted that he'd tell us all that he could, but now I saw that it was more complicated than that. "I'll be compromising the security of others, too, if I share this information with you," he said "You do realise that, don't you? There are people out there—people I care for and respect—who depend on me. If I tell you where George is, I have to have your word that the nature of the place where you find him will go no further. And I need you to know, also, that there will be consequences if it does."

I caught myself before I asked him "what kind of consequences?", but only just. The more I thought about the situation in which I found myself, the more absurd it seemed to be—increasingly removed from the plodding but dependable life I had known before. I didn't fit. Not really. And the very notion that we were sitting there talking to someone who, if he chose, could see us off with no more than a nod in the right direction, if I examined it too closely, seemed bloody preposterous. But I knew it to be true. If Dad was to be believed, Francis had done it before and, however ridiculous a part of me thought it was, I had no real doubt that he would do it again.

"We understand that, Francis," Dad said. "And you have absolutely nothing to worry about. We won't tell a soul. You have my word."

Getting to his feet, his old knees popping, Francis said, "Give me ten minutes and I'll tell you which one he's at."

He left the room and I sat back, closing my eyes and breathing out the tension that (I had barely realised) had been building up inside me since our arrival. I felt Dad and Tony breathing with me, just as relieved as I that this wasn't going to be a (no pun intended) dead end—but right then I couldn't think about them, right then all I could think about was Tara. She'd sounded so strong on the phone—not so much as a tremor in her voice—but I knew just how scared she must be, and that thought filled me with the kind of pain and sorrow that I'd at one time thought myself incapable of feeling. I didn't want her to be scared. I didn't want her thinking the thoughts I knew she must be thinking. Call it romantic, call it the chivalric ramblings of a deluded fool, but she was my girl and, as I now saw it, it was my job to protect her from such a twisted reality. So far I had failed her, but no more. With the help of Francis, we would find George, Sharon and Richard and arrange a meeting between Donna and Sharon. They would meet and discuss whatever it was they were meant to discuss and then Tara would be released, we would be reunited and—I swear to fucking God—we'd then only ever set foot out of our flat when we really had to. I'd even get a computer like Mam. We'd do all our shopping at Asda dot fucking com and if someone (George) we didn't want to talk to came to the door, we'd ignore them—leave them standing there until they got fed up and fucked off home. It would be even better than it had been before because we would know where to draw the line. Experience. We would value it and learn from it. We'd see Bernie and my folks, but beyond that we wouldn't let anyone interfere with the smooth running of our life together. I thought about our bedroom overlooking the Victorian cemetery. I wouldn't be able to sleep in there without Tara. We would be back together, I told myself. We would be because we had to be.

"Is it really that simple?" I said, not realising I'd spoken the words out loud.

"If Francis says so, yes," Dad said. "We'll have George in the time it takes to travel from here to wherever he and that Sharon lass is."

"Nothing ever goes the way you hope where George is concerned," I said.

Before we had left, the address for the west coast bed and breakfast, where we were assured George, Sharon and Richard could be found, safely zipped away in my coat pocket, Francis had shaken my hand and wished me luck. "If there's ever anything else I can do for you," he had said, "don't hesitate. Oh," he'd then added, "and when you see that little shit, give him a message from me, okay? Tell him I'm still counting. He'll know what I mean."

And so a few hours later we found ourselves parking outside a three-storey terraced house on Dean Street—not that far away from the beach and, at this time of the morning (a few minutes after two), the only house to still have any lights burning. It had been a long journey, only made easier by Tony's sat-nav and the flask of strong coffee that Francis had insisted we let him make for us. As I looked out of the car window at the 'no vacancy' sign, I wondered how true that was. Would they perhaps have a bed for a weary traveller—if I begged real nicely and told them I was a close friend of Francis?

I put the thought out of my head (there was no time for sleeping) and got out of the car with Dad and Tony.

Checking the address with the slip of paper Francis had given me, I said "This looks like the place."

This was going to achieve nothing—I was already convinced of that. We would knock on the front door, ring the bell, only to be informed, politely but firmly, that George, Sharon and Richard had gone, done a runner, as they say, without leaving a forwarding address. He left the minute Francis had informed them that we were on the way, they would tell us, and no one had any way of finding him. And that would be that. A good three hours wasted. More. An entire night and most of the following morning spent trying to find a way of helping Tara and we would still be no further on.

However, sporting a patchy and rather amusing new beard, George was waiting for us. Standing on the doorstep and watching as we walked up the steps towards him, hands in his trouser pockets, illuminated by a light overhead, he looked tired and somewhat dispirited. I wondered if being a lover and father on the run was beginning to wear him down. Was he perhaps finally regretting going looking for Sharon? Did he wish he'd listened to me and just left well alone? Were I in his shoes, and assuming I felt as strongly about Sharon as I did about Tara, there was no way I would ever regret doing what George had done—not really. It was only what any half-decent human being would do. The question was, however, was George a half-decent human being? For all he had seemed to change, was this a relationship—were these relationships—he could, and would want to, maintain? These were questions I couldn't answer. Not yet, at least. But as I looked at him and our eyes met beneath that stark exterior light, I thought I got a sense of everything he was going through, the hope and fear and regret, a mass of contradiction that I believed George could never be equipped to deal with.

In that moment, I pitied him. But not as much as I pitied Sharon and Richard.

Without saying a word, George beckoned us in and led the way through to a grotto-like lounge—after first pausing to securely lock the front door. "House rules," he said, quietly. "You unlock it, you make sure you lock it up again afterwards. Makes sense, I suppose, but a part of me still wants to leave it open—just to see what'll happen."

The four of us were sitting down on a tatty old three-piece suite, Dad sneezing and Tony looking like he wished that, as well as being the woman he loved, he'd remembered that Claudia was also a wonderfully convenient excuse for not getting involved in shit like this. George sighed and said, "Francis told them what's happened but he wouldn't speak to me. Surly old fuck still thinks he's Mister Fucking Big but... never mind. It's something to do with our Tara, right?"

"Donna Kesey took her," I told him. "Her and Sharon's three brothers."

George's brow knotted. "Kesey took Tom, Dick and Harry, too?"

I shook my head, wishing I wasn't quite so tired. "No. Kesey and Sharon's brothers took Tara. They seem to be working together, now."

George sat back and gazed up at the ceiling. He looked as though he wanted to smile at the ridiculousness of it all but didn't quite have the strength. "Kesey and Sharon's brothers," he said. "Working together. Fuck me."

"There's more going on here than meets the eye, isn't there, lad?" Dad said to him. "Has been from the beginning, right?"

George nodded, reluctantly.

"So why don't you explain," Dad insisted. "Just so we all know what it is, exactly, we're dealing with here?"

"I can't do that," George said.

"I think you'll find you can," Tony told him. "I didn't drive all this way to have a jumped up little twat like you fob us off."

George tried to stare Tony out, for all of five seconds, and then gave it up as a bad job. He sighed and sat forward, forearms on his knees, head slumped as he studied the pattern on the manky carpet. "I didn't just find Sharon because I wanted to pick up where I left off," he told us. "I needed her help."

I can't say I was all that surprised. Since when had George ever told me the truth when a half-truth would do, a half-truth when he deemed an outright lie more appropriate? I laughed bitterly and shook my head.

"I needed her help," he repeated. "I'd... her brothers... let's just say that our paths had crossed again, they weren't best pleased and leave it at that."

"Let's not," Dad said. "What was it? Drugs?"

George tried that staring-out thing again. He seemed to have lost the knack. I thought it might have had something to do with the beard. It made him look oddly adolescent, and I think he knew it.

"Yes, it was drugs," he finally said. "I've never exactly dealt all that much. Just a little here and there to keep my head above water. But this day... well, it wasn't so much what I was doing, it was where I was doing it."

"Their patch?" Dad said. The lingo seemed a bit dated, a bit too Kray twins, but he carried it off with far more authority than I would ever have imagined.

"Apparently." George itched his beard and gave Dad an honest, appraising glance. "I made a small fortune. It was good stuff. Pure as fuck. But by the time they caught up with me, I'd blown it all playing poker. They gave me a fortnight to hand over the money I'd made or... well, you've seen the movies. You know how these things work."

"A fortnight," Tony said. "That's pretty generous."

With a half-hearted shrug, George told him, "They said it was because I knew their sister. Normally they'd have given me a few days, tops. That's what made me think about finding her. I sure as fuck couldn't find five grand in two weeks, so it seemed the only plausible course of action."

"But nothing worked out the way you hoped," I said.

"Does it ever? We went there that first time. You remember that. We went there and disturbed Richard and... I just bottled it. I'd heard rumours, you see. About her having a kid all those years ago. But up until then, they'd been just that. Nothing more. But when I saw that poor fuck it became real. I did the sums and I just... well, I didn't know, exactly, but the thought was certainly niggling away at the back of my mind. And I bottled it. Seeing Richard and the way that Sharon looked at me... my head was all over the place and I just bottled it. I knew I'd have to go back. I needed the matter with her brothers sorting out, but there was more to it than just that, now. I had to see her. I had to know."

"But still you walked away." I kept my voice low and mesmeric, a psychologist trying to tease memories from a reluctant patient. "You couldn't face her that day."

"I had to think," he said. "My head was spinning, but once I'd settled myself I went back. You know all about that. You were with me then, too. And our Tara. That bitch Kesey had hurt her, although we thought it was her brothers, at the time, and I... I felt like a fucked up kid, again, Price. She knew her brothers were after me. It was obvious to me immediately. Well, maybe not immediately, but I certainly had an inkling—and when I went back later, without you, she confirmed it. They'd told her that if I got in touch with her and didn't let them know, there'd be hell to pay. She told me not to worry, though, Price. She told me not to worry and that was when I realised that things had changed in a way that I hadn't thought possible. She wasn't going to tell them and, yeah, okay, we weren't exactly back where we'd been when we were kids, but we were friends again—and, yes, I knew what some people would think of Richard, but he was mine. Mine and Sharon's, and I liked that. I loved him for it, though I probably wouldn't have admitted it at the time.

"Sharon explained that there was nothing she could really do to stop her brothers coming after me. She could try, but she knew it would do no good. They didn't especially like her and as for Richard... well, he was nothing more than a blot on the family tree. That bit she told us about them wanting her to have him put away somewhere? That was true. Them and her parents had wanted her to do that. Wouldn't help her with him or anything. Poor cow had to rely on friends. Without them she'd have been well and truly stuffed."

His breath hitched and I realised that, while he may not have been close to tears, the emotion of all they'd been through, together with the evident fatigue, was beginning to take its toll. Again, I could empathise. I wouldn't ease up on him, however. And, even if I'd wanted to, I don't think Dad and Tony would have let me.

"So where does Donna Kesey fit into all of this?" I said.

A shuddering sigh. A quick glance up from the carpet and then back down again. "All that about killing Victor Pynchon," he said. "About what he did to me and how Sharon tried to help me. It's all true. But... from the little that Kesey told Sharon after she got out, she had some stuff on Tom, Dick and Harry that could prove very useful. That's why the bastards took Sharon and Richard. They found out about it and wanted to use Sharon as a bargaining tool. We kind of fucked that up for them, though—turning up in Old Ray's Allegro like that."

He almost smiled.

"So how do you explain Kesey and Sharon's brothers working together now?" Tony asked.

"I can only assume that she's told them that if they help her find Sharon, she'll forget everything she knows," he said. "And possibly let them have me."

Now that he'd explained everything, it seemed a lot more simple than I had thought it would. Donna Kesey wanted Sharon. Sharon's brothers wanted Sharon as a bargaining tool. George wanted Sharon and Richard. Sharon wanted George (I assumed) and Richard. Richard wanted his toy cars. Sharon's brothers also wanted George or the money he owed them. I wanted Tara. Tara wanted me. And, on top of all that, Kesey wanted my full cooperation. What could be more straightforward than that?

"We need Sharon's help," I finally told him, once I was certain he had no more to say. "Kesey wants to talk to her. Alone. She won't let Tara go until she talks to Sharon. She's threatening to hurt Tara if I don't do exactly as she says, George. We really need Sharon's help on this."

George was on his feet before I'd even finished speaking, shaking his head and laughing—as if this was the most outlandish thing he'd ever heard. "You've got to be fucking joking," he said. "Let that nut anywhere near Sharon? I don't bloody think so. It just isn't going to happen, Price. You know she killed him, don't you? Kesey. She finally killed Pynchon after all these years. The girl's tapped. One wrong word from Sharon and fuck knows what'll happen. No. Sorry, mate. I want to help our Tara as much as anyone but there's no way I'm letting Sharon talk to Kesey."

"I don't think it's your decision to make, mate," Tony said. "Surely what she does or doesn't do is up to Sharon. She doesn't need you to speak for her."

He looked at each of us in turn, working out what his chances were, I assumed, or maybe wondering how he could back down without losing face. George liked control, I reminded myself. In a world where, in real terms, there was very little over which he had any say, he liked to at least create the delusion of omnipotence. And so I prepared myself as best I could for the two options— hoping it was the latter rather than the former.

"She isn't here," he told us, and I knew right off that he wasn't lying. "I thought something like this might happen—that under the right circumstances Francis might tell you or someone else where I was—so I made other arrangements. I stay here, most of the time, to make sure no one is sniffing around, and Sharon and Richard... well, let's just say they're safe where no one can find them."

"Then you won't mind us taking a look around," Tony said, standing.

I looked at him and shook my head. "There won't be any need for that," I told him. "He's telling the truth."

Tony appeared uncertain, about to argue with me, but then he seemed to grasp the fact that I knew George and he sat back down. Turning my attention back to George, I massaged my neck despondently, knowing where this now had to go and not liking it one little bit. It looked set to be every frustrating conversation I'd ever had with George all rolled into one—and before the next hour was over I suspected that, one way or another, our relationship would be forever changed.

"I need you tell us where Sharon is, George," I said, very quietly. "I need you to stop being such a fucking arsehole and help me—help Tara, your cousin, for Christ's sake."

"Which is directly at odds with what I need," he told me, equally calm.

"Which is?"

"For you to fuck off back home and leave me to look after my girlfriend and son."

At one time I would have had admired George for making a stand of this kind—and I suppose that even under these circumstances a small part of me acknowledged that this had been what my friend had needed for a very long time; something to believe in, someone to care for... responsibility. And now that he had found it? He wasn't about to give it up without a fight.

"That isn't going to happen," I said, and then sighed deeply before adding, "For fuck's sake, we're on the same side, here. I don't want anything happening to Sharon or Richard and I'm sure you don't want anything happening to Tara."

"That's true. But if I have to choose between ensuring Sharon and Richard's safety and Tara's, I'll choose Sharon and Richard every time."

"Who says there has to be a choice?"

"You."

"I'm not saying that at all."

"You're asking me to let Sharon meet Kesey on her own," he said. "That sounds like a choice to me. A choice between risking Sharon's life to save Tara or not. No. I'm sorry, Price. I wish I could help, but I can't. I won't. I know what Kesey's like. She beat Sharon up, remember? If it hadn't been for Richard, fuck knows what would have happened. She won't take no for an answer, mate, and I'm just not prepared to put Sharon in that position.

She's been through enough."

"And Tara hasn't?" We both rose to our feet—me placing myself directly in front of George, him trying to avoid making eye-contact. "Tara's had it easy, right? Even though she's probably had years of shit from you about her condition, she came along with us to help find Sharon and now she's been kidnapped—but that's all right, because Sharon's had it tougher. Jesus, George, you make me sick."

"You're looking out for Tara," he said, matter-of-factly, "I'm looking out for Sharon and Richard. Deal with it."

It wasn't like the time in my old flat. As angry as I was and even though it was once more an attempt at protecting Tara, it bore no resemblance to that shambolic episode.

My first punch landed squarely on George's jaw—but I refused to be surprised by my luck and instead swung again, catching him on the nose this time and bloodying it good and proper. I stepped back, keeping my guard up and my eyes open for any of his funny tricks.

George wasn't going to fight back. I knew that before my second punch landed. I could have stood there swinging at him all morning and he wouldn't have lifted a finger to defend himself. All he had to do to achieve what he wanted was remain silent— and the more I hit him, the more likely it became that I would win that particular battle for him. And so I took another step back and sat down on the edge of the settee, deflated.

Dad looked at Tony. Tony looked at Dad. One shrugged, then the other, and all the while I tried to fathom just what it was I was supposed to do next. I'd tried reasoning with him. I'd tried arguing with him. I'd even tried knocking seven shades of shite out of him. But he wouldn't budge. The more pressure I applied, the more entrenched he became.

... and then it came to me. It mightn't work, but it was certainly worth a try.

"I have a message for you," I told him. "Francis said to tell you that he's still counting."

Deceptively picturesque, the cottage by the lake made me think of Tara again. She would love a place like this. Just the two of us, alone and remote under a crescent moon. It was all we could ever wish for and, as we stood outside, George explaining that he was renting it cheap off a bloke he'd met in a local pub, I felt suddenly quite certain that Tara would never have the things she wished for. Her dreams, whatever they might be, would remain unfulfilled— and it would all be my fault.

Before we went into the cottage, George took me to one side. In among a cluster of out-of-place conifers, blood—black in the moonlight—crusted around his nostrils, George looked me in the eye, touching me on the arm. "I'm sorry," he said. "For what happened back there. I should have told you where Sharon was right away, it's what she would want, but... I'm scared, Price. I'm scared of where this is going to end. It's... it's taken me so bloody long, you know? So long to find something that, someone who, makes everything make sense—someone I didn't even know I was looking for, not in that way, at least. And now I'm just scared that it's all going to end, that she'll talk to Kesey and one way or another it'll all be over. She'll either walk away from me, arm in arm with that fucking dykey psychopathic cunt, or Kesey'll kill her when she refuses to go with her. And I'm not even sure which scenario's the worst. That's the most awful thing about it—I almost think I'd rather have her die than choose to walk away from me."

"You don't mean that."

Shrugging, he said, "You're probably right. Death is final. All other scenarios at least offer the possibility of my getting her back." He took a deep breath through his nose—taking in the night air in a way that I never could, savouring its scent, taking it apart and storing its component parts. "I just don't want either of those things to happen," he continued. "That's what it comes down to. I want her with me, Price. I want the two of them. I don't want it to be the way it used to be."

"I know," I told him. "It's the same with me and Tara. If it's any help, mate, if Sharon decides to help us –"

"There's no 'if' about it. You know she will."

"If she tries to help us I'll do everything in my power to make sure that Sharon's safe."

"That's good of you. Donna Kesey plus Tom, Dick and Harry and you're going to do everything in your power to keep Sharon safe. Excuse me if I'm not reassured by that."

In spite of my recurring urge to hit him on the nose again, I smiled. He had a point, I supposed.

"I'm sure if we all apply ourselves to the problem, we'll work something out."

"She wants to meet her alone, Price. How are you planning on getting around that one? We can hardly keep her safe if we aren't there, now, can we?"

We were getting ahead of ourselves, I told him. Sharon hadn't even agreed to help, yet, so maybe the best course of action was for us to simply go in and see what she had to say. "Then we can take it from there," I told him.

He started to say more, but I knew he was stalling. Taking him by the arm—firm but friendly—I led him out from among the conifers and along the garden path towards the front door of the cottage.

"I'm glad you came," Sharon said. "I hadn't realised things had got this bad." Sitting on a straight-backed chair at the kitchen table, the nightie she wore showing the shape of her breasts in the most unflattering way imaginable, she looked so much older than George—older and more careworn—and I promised myself that, one day, when all this was over, I would sit down with her and listen to the story she had to tell—the story of those years coping alone with Richard, the no doubt cruel behaviour that had forced her to live out in the middle of nowhere, alone with her deformed son and a handful of might-have-beens. Today, however, we had no time for that.

"We need to get back as soon as possible," she said to George (I thought there might have been an accusation in this, but I could have been mistaken). "We need to nip this in the bud before it gets even more out of hand."

"And how do you propose to do that?" he asked.

She got to her feet and glanced down at herself. "By getting dressed, for starters," she told him.

It's difficult to remember what it was like when we all returned to mine and Tara's new flat later that morning. I think we got back at about six-thirty, but I was so exhausted that I was starting to come awake again in that glaring, adrenaline-tinted way that sharpened edges while blunting perception and the whole concept of time was already well beyond me.

I remember at one point, I decided we all needed coffee. I went into the bathroom and stood looking at my face in the mirror, trying to remember what I was meant to be doing. I think someone else eventually made the coffee, but I couldn't say who or when.

Dad suggested that I rest for a while. I remember that clearly enough. After phoning Mam to let her know we were alright, he cornered me in the living room and told me that I would be no good to Tara in this state. "You're exhausted, son," he told me. "You need to lie down for a while—an hour would help, trust me on this one."

"I'm fine, Dad."

"You don't look fine."

I'd seen myself in the bathroom mirror and I hadn't thought I'd looked that bad. No worse than anyone else, at least. And that aside, there was only one bed—and he and Sharon had already made an especially cranky Richard comfortable in it.

"I won't be able to sleep until this is over, Dad," I told him. "If I tried, I'd just lay awake tormenting myself."

He accepted this, putting a hand on my shoulder and briefly massaging. "Just don't push it too far, okay?" he said. "The last thing we need is you cracking up on us."

Richard settled in mine and Tara's bedroom, the rest of us made ourselves comfortable with coffee in the living room. Dad handed round the sandwiches Mam had brought the day before and they seemed to hit the spot.

"She wants to meet Sharon alone," I said—breaking a quiet interlude during which we all drank and ate. "That's the main problem we have to solve. If Kesey gets wind of the fact that just one of us is watching her, there's no telling what she might do to Tara—but we can't leave Sharon to deal with Kesey on her own. Not after what happened before."

"A balancing act," Dad ruminated, chewing on a sandwich. "Break the rule just enough to keep Sharon safe without jeopardising Tara's safety. Won't be easy."

"I don't know," Tony said. "If all we have to do is make Kesey think Sharon's alone... well, it should be a piece of piss."

"A piece of piss?" George said, incredulously.

"Okay—maybe not a piece of piss, but certainly doable."

"You think?" Dad said.

"I'm certain."

This was just what I wanted to hear—someone being sure about themselves, being positive—and I quickly latched onto it, before George or Dad could spoil it.

"You have an idea?" I asked him.

He leant forward, eagerly, forearms on his knees, coffee mug in his hands. Smiling, he said, "Tell Kesey Sharon will meet her at... I don't know, name anywhere you want to begin with. I'm guessing she'll object and suggest somewhere else. Which is just what we want. We say no. That's no good and so on. At this point, Sharon takes the phone off you. Sharon, you tell her that if she wants you to meet her, she's gotta promise that your brothers won't be there. She'll agree to this, I'm sure, and return to the problem of where the meeting should take place. Bat it around a bit and then suggest Lovers' Leap in the Italian Gardens at Redburn. Make it sound as if it's just occurred to you. We can get there within quarter of an hour and, as long as there's only a couple of us, I think I know a place where we'll be able to watch unseen."

In spite of my initial enthusiasm at Tony's positive attitude, it was now my turn to express doubts. "I don't know," I said. "It sounds a bit too risky, to me. And we can't be certain she'll even go for it."

Sharon was smiling. Not a good sign.

"Oh she'll go for it," she said. "Lovers' Leap? Image like that, she won't be able to resist."

It worked like a dream. We made the phone call and, against all the odds, it played out exactly as Tony had said—and before hanging up, Sharon handed the phone back to me, saying that Kesey wanted a word.

"You've done better than I ever would have thought," she told me. "It can't have been easy and I want you to know I appreciate it. If everything goes the way it should and you don't balls it up in the end game, you'll have your girlfriend back before the day is out." I held my tongue and listened as the line went dead.

Chapter Seventeen

We'd agreed that Dad would stay back at the flat with Richard. Mam was coming round to provide back-up if required, but Sharon had assured him that as long as he had toast, orange juice and his cars when he woke up, everything would be just fine. Dad hadn't looked too sure as he'd seen us to the door, but he'd nevertheless managed to slap me on the shoulder and tell me to be careful (a recurring theme in my life, it seemed.) "No heroics, okay?" he whispered. "Do what can safely be done and no more. Top of the list, and as hard as it might sound, this is about you helping Tara. Everything else takes second place."

I wondered if anything could ever be that simple, and then realised that it had to be. I nodded and then gave Dad a hug. We didn't do enough of that; it felt right.

The drive to Redburn was a relatively silent affair, none of us especially in the mood for chit-chat—locked in our own little worlds of expectation and, I imagined, regret. Day was starting to break, but I got the feeling that it was going to be one of those winter days that never managed to get fully light. Dull and overcast, cold and brittle – just how it should be, I felt.

Pulling into the kerb by the promenade up on the cliff, once-grand, foreboding Victorian buildings over the road from us on our right, the slate-grey inevitability of the sea on our far left—time started to move again. It was as if we had been in suspended animation for the fifteen or so minutes it had taken us to get here, and now the stillness and silence of the car was overwhelming. I noticed, glancing over my shoulder, that George and Sharon were holding hands—each strapped safely into their respective seats, George in the middle, Sharon on the right behind Tony. It was yet another reminder, one I really didn't need, and I quickly looked away—fixing my eyes on the low, heavy sky ahead, trying not to think about Tara even as I recalled her hiccups and that thing she did with her finger when she was deep in thought. Only by being willing to embrace the whole package would I ever stand a chance of getting her back, I told myself—making a dozen pacts with a god I didn't in all honesty believe in (and I was sure He knew it— though I convinced myself that if He was as good as they said He was, He probably wouldn't hold that against me). I would take all she was and whatever she brought with her (and believe in the Bloke Upstairs... for a week or two, at least).

"I think the best way of doing this is if you stay with the car while we go down and get ourselves nicely concealed, Sharon," Tony said, looking at her through the rearview mirror. "We can make sure everything's as it should be and then you can follow at the designated time. How does that sound?"

"I'd rather stay with Sharon," George said.

"You can't." Tony spoke with real authority, turning in his seat to meet George's slightly belligerent stare. "The longer you're with her—the longer we're with her—the more chance there is of us being spotted. We simply can't allow that to happen."

"Sounds fine by me," Sharon said, effectively silencing any further objection George might have. "You better get going."

Tara's safety was, as my father had pointed out, my prime concern—but leaving Sharon alone in the car like that was nevertheless extremely difficult. During our journey here, I'd kept a careful eye out for Renaults and Porsches (and, for that matter, any other cars that I thought might be following us) and spotted nothing. That didn't stop me having a right good look around once I got out of the car, though. Sharon's brothers and Kesey had been doing this kind of thing longer than me. I had to assume they were better at it.

"See something?" George said, standing close to my shoulder.

"No. Nothing."

"That doesn't mean that they aren't out there," he told me.

"I know."

"There has to be a better way of doing this, Price." This wasn't the George I'd grown up with. I heard fear in his voice. A plea. The breaking of a restless wave, relentless and needy.

"If there is," I told him, "I can't think what it might be."

Touching my elbow, Tony said, "We need to get a move on."

I'd seen Lovers' Leap in the dark before, so glimpsing it in this wintry dawn held no real surprises for me. Snow still on the ground in places, it seemed oddly welcoming in its austerity. Tony scouted ahead a bit, just to make sure the coast was clear, while George hung back a few yards. This left me somewhere between the two, checking the undergrowth and generally wishing that I could sit down among the sparse winter bushes and doze for a while.

"It's up here," Tony told me, George following. "It's going to be a bit of a squeeze for the three of us, but I think we'll be okay."

He led us up the steep, grassy incline on the opposite side of the path to the Leap, the three of us grabbing at roots and branches, our shoes struggling to find purchase. In the lousy light, it was difficult to see where he was taking us but, once we were in front of it, it seemed perfect.

A recess in the face of the hill, obstructed by bushes and the branches of a leaning tree, we could only just manage to squeeze in. We grunted and struggled, George grumbling that this had to be the most ridiculous idea anyone had ever had (I gently reminded him of that first time we had gone in search of Sharon)—but once we were in place, it was comfortable enough and offered us a bird's eye view of the Leap and the path immediately in front of it. It gave me the impression of being further away than we actually were, but I soon got used to this and relaxed (as much as I could, under the circumstances).

There was something I hadn't done. I couldn't shake the feeling that I'd forgotten something. I went back over all the preparations for our trip out here... everything seemed as it should be and, yet, that feeling persisted... That was it. Dad had phoned Mam and, very briefly, I had remembered something I'd been meaning to do since getting back with George, Sharon and Richard.

"Tara's Mam," I said, quite suddenly. George told me to keep my fucking voice down and Tony asked me what about her. "I meant to phone her. When we got back to the flat." I took my phone out of my pocket and started looking through my contacts for her number. "She'll be worried. I really should –"

Tony took the phone from me and turned it off before handing it back. "You can phone her when all this is over," he said. "The last thing we need is that going off while Sharon's talking to Kesey."

I stared at the shitty little Nokia in the palm of my hand and thought how easy it was to overlook the obvious.

"You all right?" Tony asked me and I nodded my reply. "Strange being here when we aren't working, don't you think?"

"Like school on an open day," I agreed.

He laughed quietly. "That about covers it," he said. "Not that I ever spent that much time at school. I was a bit of a skiver." His voice dropped an octave. "Not like Claudia. By all accounts—not to mention the arm-long list of qualifications—she was a bit of a swot."

"How is Claudia?" I said, sensing that something wasn't quite how it should be—or, at least, wasn't quite how he wanted it to be.

"Hmm," he said, smiling down at his boots sadly and shrugging.

"Not good?"

"I'm not sure. It isn't bad, exactly, just... Different. She's... she's left me, Price. Temporarily. She's got these carers and this nice little flat and it's as if she's got this whole new lease of life. It's really good to see—"

"She's left you?"

"Temporarily. The way she tells it, it wasn't healthy. The way we were living. She'd truly believed that her death was my only possible salvation—which is pretty ridiculous, but I can understand how she must have felt." He made a big (and utterly unnecessary) fuss of making sure that he could see the path clearly from where he was sitting and then said, "She wants it to be more like it was before the accident. Can you believe that?" Again, the quiet laughter. "She's even making me court her again. Roses, chocolates—I'm having to do the whole Milk Tray man thing, just about. I am kind of enjoying it, though."

It didn't take a genius to see that Tony wasn't enjoying it in the least. His life, the image he'd had of it and the way in which he'd believed it had been meant to be, was being tested. Just as mine and George's were, I supposed. And while he was determined to struggle on and make the best of it, he didn't want to have to. The three of us had had any control we might have possessed wrested from us and now it was up to other people to decide where and how this would end. Yes, we sat among the undergrowth pretending that we could make a difference if it was required of us, but ultimately we weren't even pawns in this so-called end-game.

Sharon arrived bang on time—standing a good few feet from Lovers' Leap and hugging herself to keep warm. She was wearing a knitted bobble hat of Tara's I'd managed to find for her and in the poor light there was a vague resemblance that made this whole process even more difficult for me. Tara was there with me, and, yet, she wasn't.

Tony nudged me. "Someone's coming," he said.

I'd never really thought about what Donna Kesey might look like before actually seeing her up close—but if I had, I expect I would have envisaged an overweight bull-dyke with borstal tattoos (all coppers are bastards) and a crazed look in her frenzied eyes. The reality seemed to be quite different, however. From the admittedly little that I could see of her, she appeared delicate and even slightly elegant in the way in which she approached Sharon—short and trim, her clothes (though the poor light made it difficult to be sure about this) refined and understated. She walked slowly towards Sharon, completely focused on her—not once looking around her to ensure that they were alone and unobserved—and I got a very clear impression of just how much Kesey thought of Sharon.

There was a hesitation to her step. A halting moment that betrayed her wish to get this right... to ensure that she didn't lose Sharon again. She stepped. She stopped. I imagined her smiling tentatively—quickly dropping it when it wasn't returned and she realised just how inappropriate it actually was.

Beside Tony, George stiffened and I noted that Tony seemed prepared... prepared to make a grab for him should he decide to make an attempt at intervening. And Kesey spoke—her words distant and vague, carried away from us, it seemed, on a light breeze of her own making. I caught the word "hello", to which Sharon made no reply, and then something that might have been a comment on how beautiful the gardens were or a compliment on how Sharon was looking, it was difficult to be sure. George sniffed indignantly, and Tony stiffened further in readiness.

I moved my focus away from the two of them, however, looking down through the trees at the path further along from where they were standing in the hope that Tara might be there, that Kesey might already have given her her freedom and that she might simply be waiting to walk away from all of this with Sharon once she and Kesey had finished talking. But, perhaps predictably, she was nowhere to be seen. Tara was still confined, still held against her will, and, now—seeing Kesey standing before me looking so natural and normal, even—this single fact struck me harder than ever. Did they have her tied up and gagged somewhere? Or were they more humane—keeping her in a location far from populated areas and allowing her a certain amount of movement within her confines? The thought of Tara being ill-treated was one that I just couldn't afford to entertain. Not if I didn't want Tony having to hold back both George and me.

Tony nudged me and pointed at Sharon. Something, it seemed, had caught her attention. She stiffened and looked beyond Kesey—pushing past her urgently and then spinning round to confront her, slapping Kesey hard on the face and saying, "You promised. You said they wouldn't fucking be here."

I thought Kesey would react violently—especially after having seen the way in which she had left Sharon out on the moor—but she didn't. She merely stood there looking cowed and uncharacteristically afraid. She was fighting for someone she loved, too, I suddenly realised. Just like the rest of us.

It was difficult to hear what Kesey was saying but she seemed to be making an effort to calm Sharon down and reassure her. She touched Sharon's arm and Sharon pulled away from her—telling Kesey to keep her hands off her and to "get them the fuck away from me".

The three of us in our little hidey-hole on the hill craned our necks to see who she was referring to, even though I think we'd all pretty much worked it out for ourselves. I looked towards the gap in the trees where I'd last looked for Tara and once again saw nothing—no one. I leant forward, careful not to slip and rustle the undergrowth, and then Tony touched me on the arm and pointed.

A little further along from where I'd been looking stood an oak tree that had seen better days (Tony and I had discussed felling it a couple of times, but we just couldn't bring ourselves to do it). It leant at a ridiculous angle and the arthritic twist of its branches seemed to cry out in complaint, and within the shadows beneath it I thought I counted three, possibly four forms. The Brothers Grim, and—my heart skipped a beat—Tara? I couldn't be certain, but it certainly looked like her, and it took the greatest of efforts for me to stop myself from jumping up there and then and running to her.

Kesey seemed to be working hard to get things back under control. She waved to the figures beneath the tree, telling them that everything was okay and that they should move back. Now. Immediately. "What the fuck are you waiting for, you fucking imbeciles?" Her voice cracked on this and I couldn't quite work out if this was a mark of weakness or strength. It certainly seemed to do the trick, though; the figures (there were definitely four of them) retreated out of sight and Kesey, satisfied, turned back to Sharon.

Sharon wasn't so easily appeased, however. "You really think that's all there is to it?" I heard her say. "Wave them away and it's as if they were never there in the first place?"

Looking, from what I could see, extremely unhappy and

uncomfortable—one hand repeatedly going to her forehead, as if to brush away the fringe she didn't have, pacing back and forth as she tried to figure out what she should best do next—Sharon turned from Kesey and looked out over the gardens. Kesey said nothing in reply, perhaps understanding that there was nothing she could say, possibly simply at a loss, and eventually Sharon spoke again.

"I should never have agreed to this," she said, her voice very clear in the dawn stillness. "If it wasn't for your having Tara, I never would have—you do realise that, don't you? After what you did back at the Lodge I never wanted to see you again. I would have been happy to hear that you were dead. I hated you that much. I hate you that much."

"You don't mean that," Kesey said.

Sharon looked over her shoulder. I thought I saw a bitter smile. "Oh, I think you'll find I do," she said. "I've never meant anything more in my entire life. I hate you, Donna Kesey, and nothing you can say will ever change that."

"I can look after Richard," Kesey said. "I can help with him, now. I have... I have enough money to make sure that he has everything he needs."

"He already has everything he needs."

Kesey approached Sharon eagerly and then stopped when Sharon threw her what I imagined to be a withering look. "He could be so much better, though, love," Kesey told her. "With those expensive therapies they have these days, he could... well, he could be so much better. You wouldn't have to do half of the stuff you have to do for him now."

This wasn't the woman I'd spoken to on the phone, I thought— even though the orders she had shouted to Sharon's brothers told me that it most emphatically was. Sharon was the one who was in control, and I felt a sudden and unrelenting surge of optimism lift me. This could work out the way we wanted, after all. If Sharon only continued the way she was going and didn't let Kesey gain any ground, everything just might go our way.

"What therapies?" Sharon said, and I heard George groan.

Tony told him that it was alright. Sharon was just playing her, showing her a little line, but George wasn't in the least bit convinced. "Kesey knows," he whispered. "Anyone who's spent even a little time around Sharon and Richard can see it. He's the way in. If you can convince her that you give a shit about Richard, you're her friend and ally and that's it. It doesn't matter who you are or what you've done, if you can help Richard in some way you are, as far as she's concerned, on Team Sharon."

This seemed something of an exaggeration to me. I'd seen Sharon and Richard together—and while she did tend to look favourably on anyone who was kind to him, she was, in my opinion, a shrewd assessor of character. She certainly wouldn't, as I thought, allow Richard to be used in such a crass and predictable way.

"I was reading this piece in the Lancet about a year back," I heard Kesey say. "I had a lot of time for reading, as I'm sure you can imagine, and it was time I put to good use. I even did a couple of Open University courses –"

"This article," Sharon interrupted. "What was it about?"

"A new therapy they've developed in Sweden or Switzerland, somewhere like that," she said. "A behavioural therapy. They focus on task repetition. Effectively rewire the brain by doing the same sequence of tasks over and over again. They know that kids like Richard can't be taught. Not in the commonly held definition of the word. But that doesn't mean that they can't learn. That's how they put it. They had this one kid. Couldn't do a thing. Within a month they had him dressing himself."

Sharon said something I almost missed, though I managed to work out that it was something along the lines of "Richard can dress himself already."

"And how did he learn?" Kesey said, already starting to sound rather too smug.

"I taught him."

"Through task repetition?"

"It was cold in the Lodge," Sharon told her. "It didn't take much in the way of repetition to convince him that putting on a thick pullover was a good idea."

George chuckled with evident relief. Nevertheless, Kesey wasn't about to give up, launching into another example of just how effective this new therapy could be.

Sharon cut her short. "What do you want, Donna?" she said, turning to face her, again. "I mean. What do you really want?"

"I want you back," Kesey told her, without a moment's hesitation. "I want you back and I want everything to be the way it used to be. I don't want anything complicated, Sharon. I don't want excitement or glamour, I just want you." I was fairly sure that this last line was intended as a compliment, though if I'd been rooting for Kesey to succeed I would have groaned at her choice of words. "I appreciate things more, now. I know what it's like to truly be alone and I just don't want that anymore. I can't live like that anymore."

"And you felt you had to kill again to prove this?" Sharon said. "Kill and then kidnap Tara?"

"Pynchon was unfinished business. A loose end. And as for Tara, that was just my way of getting to you. You know I would never have hurt her."

"I don't know anything of the sort," Sharon said. She then added something more quietly—something I didn't catch and I still would have probably missed even if she'd shouted it at the top of her voice. I was too busy thinking about Tara. How close she was and what it would have meant to me if Kesey had done something to hurt her. While she was no longer within sight, I was in no doubt that she wasn't too far away. Just around the corner, watched over by Tara's sweaty, ugly brothers. She was there and I was here—and what was I doing? I was sitting in a hole in the side of a hill, listening to a conversation I really didn't give a flying fuck about.

I touched Tony on the arm in order to get his attention. He turned a little to look at me, nevertheless still engrossed with what was happening down below. "I'm going to find her," I told him, not allowing myself time to change my mind. "Tara. I'm going down there to find her."

Nodding, Tony returned his attention to Sharon and Kesey, before snapping his head back around towards me and hissing, "What?"

"I can't just sit here," I said. "Not when she's so close. I need to get to her and get her away from all this—in case things don't work out the way we want them to."

"You can't do that," he said. "Sharon's brothers are with her. You try to get her away from them and all hell'll break lose. Christ knows what they'll do to you."

"I'm not going to just leave her fate in the hands of Kesey and Tom, Dick and Harry. If they hurt me, they hurt me—that's something I'll just have to live with."

"If you're lucky," George said, barely taking his attention off Sharon and Kesey. "Remember the Heckler and Koch. That wasn't a fairytale. When they had their little chat with me I even got to see it. Up close. Ugly little fucking thing it was, too—though I expect it would have looked a lot prettier had I been the one holding it."

I'd forgotten about the gun. How in hell was I supposed to contend with something like that? But Tara was why I was here and, even if they were armed, I would have to find a way to right the imbalance.

"I'll deal with that if and when I have to," I said, starting to move carefully around them on my hands and knees, meaning to head down the side of the hill just to George's right, knowing that I would be safe from view this way, a stand of dense shrubbery between Kesey and me.

Tony grabbed my arm and pulled me back down beside him. My instinct was to hit out at him—I had to get to Tara—but I didn't. He deserved better than that.

"Think about this, Price," he whispered. "Think about yourself and think about how much help you're going to be to Tara if those sons of bitches get hold of you and give you a bloody good working over."

He was talking sense, of course, I saw that right away, but that didn't really alter anything. As I saw it, I had a job to do, one that meant everything in the world to me, and I was going to do it, whatever the consequences. My fatigue fell away as the adrenaline started pumping and I saw it all so clearly. This was why Tara and I had met. This is why we had been brought together.

"I'm not going to let that happen," I told Tony, very quietly. "They're not going to lay a finger on me. I'm going to be careful."

"I can't let you do this," he said.

"You can't stop me."

"If anything happens to you your dad'll never forgive me, Price."

"Nothing's going to happen to me," I assured him. "And apart from that, you're not my keeper, mate. This isn't something you've got any say in."

He nodded thoughtfully and then said, "Okay. But I'm coming with you. George. You'll be all right here on your own, won't you?"

Shrugging, he said, "I think I can take care of Kesey by myself, if I have to." He looked at us and winked. "I'll be seeing you, then. Or not, as the case may be."

I remembered how good it had felt to hit him back at the bed and breakfast. If only I hadn't had other things on my mind I might have tried it again.

Tony and I worked our way down the hill, being careful to stay out of sight and remain as quiet as we could. Now that we were on the move, I felt somewhat better. Maybe this wasn't one of the smartest ideas—I couldn't then say—but we were at least doing something, at least snatching back a little of the control that had been so cruelly taken from me. Progress was slow, both Tony and I making absolutely certain that we had secure footing ahead before we made our next move, but within the space of about five minutes we were down by the side of the path, concealed behind some shrubs and ferns—Tony glancing about anxiously, me wondering why on earth we hadn't concealed ourselves here in the first place. I could hear Sharon and Kesey more clearly from here, and it was tempting to stick around and listen to whatever it was they had left to say to each other. Kesey was telling Sharon a little of what it had been like for her in prison all those years, how she'd grown really afraid when she'd realised that it was fast becoming an environment she relished. "I knew that if I didn't set my sights on getting out of there and making my way in the world again I'd just turn into on of those vegetating, institutional dykes." Sharon made a vaguely sympathetic sound and then told her, in no uncertain terms, that that was all well and good, but it still didn't change anything. "I don't want you in my life anymore," she said, as Tony grabbed hold of my jacket and pulled me away.

Tony was a remarkable man, I realised. Whatever differences currently existed between him and Claudia, the truth was he had always pretty much known how to read her. When he had put thoughts in her head and words in her mouth, it seemed to me that they had largely been accurate. And now it appeared he was applying that skill to me. He was one of the newest (and, yet, closest) friends I had, and he could read me like a book.

We walked steadily along the edge of the path—staying among the shadows and undergrowth where possible, ever conscious that Sharon's brothers might be just around the next corner, waiting with Tara for some signal that would mark the beginning of God only knew what. I still didn't know what we were going to do when we found them (always assuming we would), but one thing I did know was that I wasn't going to walk away from Tara.

We heard voices up ahead—low and sonorous, jocular in tone, but also tinged with something reminiscent of fear, concern at the very least. Tony put out a hand to stop me, just in case I hadn't heard them, and we moved more deeply into the trees, being careful not to step on any twigs or rustle too loudly. Moving round the corner by the shortest possible route, we finally found ourselves within a few metres of Tom, Dick and Harry. From our place behind the trunk of an ash, I could see the three of them very clearly—huddled together smoking, sharing brave-talk on what they planned on doing to Kesey when all this was over. However, at first I couldn't see any sign of Tara. The Brothers Grim stood in their little huddle and only when the biggest of the three looked over his shoulder and said, "Don't come any nearer, you smelly fuck, but don't even think of trying to run away, either," did I look along the path and see her, sitting alone on a bench.

She was such a forlorn figure, sitting there, hugging her coat around her with her chin pulled into the collar, that I thought my heart was going to break just looking at her. Her appearance hit me with as much force as it had on the first day I had seen her, and it was all I could do to stop myself breaking cover and approaching her. The reference to her condition was enough to tell me a little of what it must have been like for her through the recent hours, and all I wanted to do was hold her in my arms and tell her that it was over, that it was behind us, and nothing like this was ever going to happen to us again. But three things stood in our way, and I couldn't for the life of me think how I was going to get to her without their seeing me.

As it now seemed to be his brief, Tony took charge (they were his gardens, I suppose, so maybe he felt somehow obligated... or maybe it was merely an act of friendship). He leant in close to me, keeping one eye on Sharon's brothers, and said, "They don't know me from Adam. Maybe I can distract them while you get her away from here. What do you think?"

I thought it was possibly one of the most dangerous suggestions I'd ever heard. It was true, as far as we knew, that Sharon's brothers had no idea that Tony was helping us in all of this—but it was equally true that they weren't as stupid as they could sometimes appear. They'd had a fairly chequered criminal career, but by and large they'd succeeded in avoiding any serious prosecution. Given the gravity of some of their crimes, this was no mean accomplishment, and so they were no doubt more than capable of reading a situation. If I said yes to Tony's suggestion, there was no question in my mind that I would be placing the two of us in quite possibly grave danger.

"Sounds like a plan to me," I said to him, hoping I wouldn't regret it. "How are you going to approach them? You can't just come bursting out of the bushes."

"I'm going to make it look as if I've come along the path past Sharon and Kesey," he said, very quietly, after a moment's consideration. "That way they won't think me anyone to be all that suspicious about."

There was a certain logic to that, I supposed, but the more I thought about it, the more weighty my initial thoughts regarding his plan became. Could I really let him do this? Knowing just how violent Tom, Dick and Harry could be, could I let him walk out there and distract them for me—risking the possibility of having the barrel of a Heckler and Koch pistol shoved with little ceremony up his left nostril? This was about Tara, it was true, but to put Tony in danger was something that, I realised, was beyond even me.

"I don't think you should do this," I told him. "I really appreciate it, but I can't let you. It's just too dangerous."

"I'm doing it, Price," he said. "After everything you did for Claudia and me, it's the very least I can do."

"I didn't risk my life for you and Claudia," I told him. "I just... helped the two of you communicate. This is very different."

"Not from where I'm standing it isn't," he insisted. "Look, Price, you and I both know that this is the best chance we have of getting Tara away from them. We could sit around trying to think of a better idea, but by then it might be too late—the opportunity might have passed. I say we do it. My choice. We do it and we do it now."

I could see he was intent on carrying this, and so we prepared ourselves—Tony walking a little way back through the trees so that he could come onto the path somewhere between Kesey and Sharon's brothers while I waited patiently for him to approach. We'd agreed that I would make my move to get to Tara as soon as he had Tom, Dick and Harry suitably distracted, getting her away from them as quickly and as quietly as I could. The ideal scenario was for Tony to get away, too, before they realised that Tara was gone—but that seemed a pretty unlikely proposition to me.

The light was rather better, now. I wasn't sure if this was a good thing or not, but it at least meant that I could see Tara more clearly. She looked well if rather unkempt. Tired but with the kind of resolve that made her sit a little straighter than was her normal inclination. She looked like she might make a run for it at any moment, and I found myself silently begging her not to—not yet, not until Tony had at least had a chance to distract her guards.

I then heard Tony approaching—his footsteps purposeful and confident. When he came in sight of Tom, Dick and Harry, he stopped, looking surprised, and then approached them, smiling, hands in the pockets of his jacket. He spoke to them, but did so quietly – so quietly that not only could I not hear what he was saying, but the three hulking forms before him had to lean in close to him to catch it. Whatever he said seemed to do the trick. The four of them chuckled together and Tony said something else, edging round so that Sharon's brothers had their backs to me.

I had to move now. Tara had spotted Tony and had already put two and two together, getting to her feet and looking about anxiously. I stepped out onto the path, crossing quickly to her, grabbing her hand and holding the index finger of my free hand to my lips. To say that her face lit up when she saw me is an understatement. Whether we got away or not, I was quite sure she didn't care. I was there with her. I had proved (as if proof were needed) that I wouldn't walk away from her the minute things got difficult and, it has to be said, in that moment I could have almost been grateful to Donna Kesey.

"I knew you'd come," she whispered as I started to lead her away.

"No, you didn't," I said, smiling.

"No, you're right. After the argument and everything I wasn't sure. I thought you might leave it to the police."

"Like I could do that." I kissed her and then glanced back over my shoulder. Tony still had his audience thoroughly engrossed and it seemed that this was actually going to work. I started herding Tara away more quickly while luck was still on our side.

And then it happened.

We heard the screams.

At first I thought it was coming from Tony, as ridiculous as that may seem. I turned with Tara and, as foolish as I knew it to be, looked back at him and Sharon's brothers—ready to run to him should he need my help while telling Tara to run like hell in the opposite direction. But Tony and the Brothers Grim kept their backs to us, staring down the path in Sharon and Kesey's direction.

"Sharon," Tara said, and I nodded—the two of us following when Tony and his new bosom buddies started running towards the Leap. I was quite sure I knew what had happened, in one form or another, and when Tara took hold of my hand, I held onto it as tightly as possible, determined that I wouldn't let go of it until all of this was over.

It seemed that some kind of truce, albeit temporary, had been called. Tom, Dick and Harry saw me with Tara, closing in behind them as we approached the Leap, and they seemed to shrug off the development. We were inconsequential. We didn't matter. And as the scene began to unfold before us, it seemed that we were out of danger.

Much to our relief, Sharon was standing in the middle of the path, with George, having what appeared to be the biggest disagreement I'd ever seen them have. "Why the fuck did you have to do that?" I heard Sharon say. "For fuck's sake, George, it was totally unnecessary. We were all going to walk away and everything was going to be okay. Jesus." She pulled off Tara's hat and ran a hand through her hair, walking to the edge of the Leap and looking over, before turning away—pale, shaken and appalled.

Kesey wasn't there with them, but it didn't take genius to work out where she was. Taking control of the situation with Tony—no longer afraid, feeling unusually safe now, on my home turf—I went over to the edge of the Leap, the barrier broken, and looked over the edge while Tara went to see if there was anything she could do for Sharon. Sure enough, far below, Tony and I could see the crumpled form of Donna Kesey. She didn't look like a broken doll, in the best tradition of literary cliché. She looked like a woman who'd fallen from a great height. A woman who'd started falling a long time ago and was now merely grateful of the chance of a rest.

"Someone should go down to her," Tony said. "Make sure that

she is actually... you know."

"Dead," one of Sharon's brothers said from behind us. I later found out it was Dick. The most sensible of the three and clearly the ring-leader. "I don't think there's much chance of her being anything else, do you? A fall like that, if she isn't dead, she'll want to be."

Tony and I had immediately moved away from the edge the moment Dick had joined us—not comfortable with the idea of being so close to such a long drop with him there. Now Tony stood back from him and said, "Nevertheless, I think it's the right thing to do."

"And I think it isn't," Dick insisted. "I think we should all leave her a little while longer just, you know, to make sure, and have a little chat. What do you say?"

Tony glanced at me and I fired him a warning look. I heard George say something to Sharon about Kesey threatening her and then Sharon laughed bitterly, telling him that he saw exactly what he wanted to see, and then Tony was shaking his head and telling Dick, in no uncertain terms, "I say I can't just leave her like that. If she isn't dead, it's partly my job to see to it that she gets the help that she needs. Surely you understand that."

"I understand that you are a conscientious and highly moral man," Dick said. "Unfortunately for her, I'm not. You're staying here with us. For the time being, at least."

Sharon now turned her attention to Dick, coming in on Tony's side of the argument. "Don't you think this has gone far enough?" she said. "The chances are she's dead—or most certainly will be before anyone who can help her can get here. Let him go down there. What harm is it going to do? You don't even have to stay. You can go and we can take care of it. No one need ever know you were here."

"Generous offer, Sis," he said, his brothers looking at each other as if was the best proposal they'd heard all year. "And I'd gladly take you up on it. Except there's the little matter of your boyfriend and the money he owes us. The deal with Kesey was that we get Georgie Porgie to do with what we will once this was all sorted."

"I've told you," George said, rather impotently, "you'll get your money—I just –"

"Kesey?" Sharon cut in. "Ah, yes. The bitch who's had the Sword of Fucking Damocles hanging over your head for the past few weeks. The bitch that this prick..." she pointed at George with her thumb "... has just pushed over that fucking edge over there and most probably killed for you. From where I'm standing, and as pissed off as I am with him, that about makes you even."

"She's got a point," Harry said, and Dick glowered at him.

Nevertheless, he considered what she had said, before replying. "I can't just leave it like this," he told her. "He tried to fuck us over and he needs to pay."

"The way you made me and Richard pay for not doing what you wanted?" she snapped. "Jesus, Dick, you are so full of shit.... Here's the deal. We'll go away. Once this is all tidied up, me, Richard and George will get the fuck out of town and never come back. How does that strike you?"

It sounded good to me, but I thought it best not to say anything.

Dick thought about this long and hard. His brothers, even though they didn't actually say anything, clearly liked this idea as well, but I didn't want to get my hopes up. Dick was a man who liked to call the shots and was unwilling to lose face, whatever the degree. I briefly considered trying to rush the proceedings along a little, maybe point out that this was a public place and that in a very short time it would be packed (not quite) with post-Christmas early-morning joggers. Whatever we were going to do, we needed to decide quickly and do it now.

Before I could say anything, however, Dick reached his decision.

"The three of you'll go and never come back?" he asked, and Sharon gave him her word. "I see him again," Dick said, nodding at a blessedly silent George, "I'll have to kill him. You do know that, don't you? Even if it is only a short visit."

Sharon sighed and put Tara's hat back on. "That sounds fair enough to me," she said.

George sniffed. "Thanks a fucking lot."

It had to fall apart sooner or later. Everything was going too much our way. I glanced over the edge of the Leap as Tom, Dick and Harry started to walk away and Tony joined me. "I'll go down there," he said. "As I see it, there's no need for you and Tara to get caught up in all of this." He spoke loud enough for Sharon and George to hear. "We can sort out a convincing story, I'm sure. I can be the independent witness on my way in to work. I'll gladly confirm whatever George and Sharon decide to tell the police."

"We could just leave her here for someone else to find," George said.

"You could do that?" Tony asked him.

"Easily," George answered. He was fooling no one, though. Maybe a few months ago. Maybe the boy-man I had grown up with. But not now, not the George I currently saw before me. He was a lot of things (a murderer for one, it seemed) but he was not the man this false comment suggested.

Before Tara and I left, Tony heading down to check that Kesey really was dead, Sharon said to us, "She jumped because I told her no. George didn't really kill her. That was for my brothers' benefit. She jumped. After all those years she couldn't take me saying no. Can you believe that?"

Holding on tightly to Tara, I thought that I could. All too easily.

Epilogue

New Year's Eve.

Over a year has passed since the events of that morning by the Leap, and only now am I finally beginning to believe that it's behind us. I recall it, still more often than I would like, and I find it difficult to believe that we allowed ourselves to become so consumed by George and his convoluted reality, but that's the way it happened and I suppose all we can do is hope that we've learned something from it. I think we have. Tara thinks we have. Tony and Claudia, newly married and busy setting up their own adaptive computer communications firm, think we have. Even my parents, my mother still flabbergasted by the whole Donna Kesey story, think we have. But sometimes I wonder. Sometimes it all still seems so fresh, and I think that tonight—our first meeting with Sharon and George since they left town nine months ago—will be the ultimate test.

Earlier, I caught Tara, fresh from her shower and wearing a soft, fluffy pink bath towel, standing by the bedroom window, looking down at the cemetery. I went over and hugged her from behind, reassured by familiarity, by the sure-fire knowledge of how we fit together.

"Penny for them," I said, and I felt her soften and smile.

"I was just thinking what it must have been like for her," she said. "Donna Kesey. She used to talk to me, you know. When... you know. And she was a nice enough person. She just wanted what we've got, that's all, and when she found out for certain that it was never going to happen... can you imagine what that must have been like for her."

I told her that, yes, I could, but I'd rather not have to.

"I'm glad you came to get me," she said, a few minutes later.

"Me, too."

"It was an ideal opportunity, you know."

"For what?"

"For you to walk away from me." She breathed out softly and I imagined I smelt the sweetness of her breath. Essentially her. Essentially real. "But you didn't."

"No," I said, "I didn't."

"Don't imagine that that means you can relax, though," she told me. "I need continual reassurance."

"And you'll get it."

Turning to face me, she said, smiling, "Will I?"

Legend Press
Independent Book Publisher

This book has been published by vibrant publishing company Legend Press. If you enjoyed reading it then you can help make it a major hit. Just follow these three easy steps:

1. Recommend it
Pass it onto a friend to spread word-of-mouth or, if now you've got your hands on this copy you don't want to let it go, just tell your friend to buy their own or maybe get it for them as a gift. Copies are available with special deals and discounts from our own website and from all good bookshops and online outlets.

2. Review it
It's never been easier to write an online review of a book you love and can be done on Amazon, Waterstones.com, WHSmith.co.uk and many more. You could also talk about it or link to it on your own blog or social networking site.

3. Read another of our great titles
We've got a wide range of diverse modern fiction and it's all waiting to be read by fresh-thinking readers like you! Come to us direct at www.legendpress.co.uk to take advantage of our superb discounts. (Plus, if you email info@legend-paperbooks.co.uk just after placing your order and quote 'WORD OF MOUTH', we will send another book with your order absolutely free!)

Thank you for being part of our word of mouth campaign.

info@legend-paperbooks.co.uk
www.legendpress.co.uk